LIVE TO *Tell*

INSPIRED BY TRUE EVENTS

ROWAN NOIR

Content Warnings

This novel contains material that some readers may find distressing. It is intended only for mature audiences. Please be advised that the following subjects are depicted or discussed in *Live to Tell*:

Drug Overdose/Drug use

Emotional Abuse/Manipulation/Gaslighting

Explicit sexual content

Gun Violence

Realistic Portrayals of Physical Injury

Physical Assault by a Physician

Sexual Assault/Stalking

Mental Health Issues/Exploitation

Reader discretion is advised. If you are sensitive to any of these topics, please take care when deciding whether to proceed.

To my *Jackson,* those with the courage to change, and survivors everywhere.

Contents

CHAPTER ONE

The Town

ACT 1

T he air hung heavy with the scent of spices and the tang of sweat, a typical symphony of aromas in southeast Georgia's balmy mid-afternoons. The chatter and clinking glasses momentarily paused as the door to *Luis's Creole Bar and Grill* swung open with a protesting creak. All eyes turned to the disheveled figure that stepped across the threshold. She was a mosaic of contradictions: her petite frame clothed in wrinkled designer labels, her tired eyes flashing with insolence despite her exhaustion. The woman clumsily approached the bar, her steps echoing an unspoken desire for solace and a strong drink after a seemingly endless journey. The locals watched as she settled at the corner end of the bar, her presence stirring an undercurrent of curiosity and speculation in the otherwise routine ambiance of their little watering hole.

"Long day?" the bartender, Lavonte, a tall, athletic man with a soothingly pleasant, warm southern voice cheerfully asked her with a light smile.

"Something like that," Willa said, pushing her deep chocolate-colored wavy hair back from her face, revealing her equally dark, exotic eyes. "More like a long year."

Willa's response was weary yet laced with an intriguing hint of defiance. A New England accent in Georgia was as out of place as snow in July.

From that moment, it was clear—this wasn't just another humid day in southeastern Georgia. It was the day that Willa Sullivan, a woman lost in transition, found herself seeking solace in the comforting unfamiliarity of an old southern bar.

"You stopping by for a visit, or are you a transplant?" he asked, noting her luggage.

"I don't even know," she said hopelessly. "All I remember is going to the airport, asking for the first flight out of DC to...well ... anywhere. When I landed, a guy said to take a cab over the bridge, that this town was where I could find a cheap place to crash, so here I am." She tossed her hands up, signaling her frustration. "No plan, no purpose, completely lost," she said, cradling her head as her elbows rested on the bar. "Scotch, neat, unless you have something stronger..."

"Well, Princess, you're in Magnolia Shores...Georgia," Lavonte said, his voice comforting as he fixed her drink. "Now you know where you are. You're no longer lost," he said with a chuckle, his warmth attempting to ease the tension in the air with a little joke.

But Willa was in no mood for small-town pleasantries. "Eh... Are you completely insensitive?" she snapped at him. "I'm kinda of hurting here," she said, swirling a cocktail straw in her glass.

"Aww, all right, I'm sorry, you just look like you could use a laugh." Lavonte moved down the bar closer to Willa.

"Wanna talk about it?"

"Are you a therapist, some other qualified health professional, or...just a nosy bartender?" Willa bristled.

"I'm actually a nosy bar...owner." Without missing a beat, he added, "This is my place."

"Oh," Willa paused, "sorry...I don't mean...to be a bitch." Willa said remorsefully, "It's just been a lot."

"Goooo...ooooon," Lavonte prodded, laughing while wiping down the bar.

"I don't think I like you...ugh...okay...okay...fine." She raised her hand. "Hi, I'm Willa. I'm a 27-year-old train-wreck. I'm a power-obsessed workaholic who is oblivious to anything happening around her, not related to money or building an empire, resulting in a string of terrible interpersonal relationship choices and other bad decisions. I'm fairly certain I'm color-blind, given the number of red and green flags I confuse."

"Ah, so boy trouble, huh? Sounds like boy trouble," Lavonte said while drying a rack of glasses. "I see it all the time." He smiled compassionately.

"Ha, yeah, that's it. Bingo." Willa rolled her eyes. "Because that's what it always is, right? Anytime a woman is upset...simple boy trouble. That's it, silly boys. That's what made me flee my apartment in the middle of the night, taking only what I could pack in these bags, destroy my career, my reputation... myself; 'boy trouble.'"

A striking woman, early 40s, about five-eight with lush, naturally coiled hair, stepped out through the kitchen's swinging doors.

"Lavonte, are you harassing the patrons?" she said with a smile. "Ya know they don't like that."

"Oh, Cass," Lavonte said. "I'm just talking to my new friend Willa here about her 'not so simple as boy trouble' boy trouble."

"Yeah...I definitely don't like you..." Willa glared at Lavonte.

Cassandra Mitchell, a.k.a. Cassy, a.k.a. Cass, walked over to the part of the bar where Willa was sitting.

"I'm sorry," Cassy said with a genuine sweetness that instantly put Willa on guard.

"Lavonte doesn't mean any harm; he's just...well... He just doesn't know when his humor don't quite land." Her sincerity was palpable, and it started to reassure Willa.

"She didn't say I was wrong." Lavonte laughed, leaning over to Cassy.

"That's because I'm ignoring you now," Willa said snarkily, tapping her glass in Lavonte's direction before turning to Cassy. "Do you work here, too?"

"No, no, not really," Cassy said. "This is Lavonte's place, well...was his father's, but now it's his. I'm his wife, Cassy." Cassy smiled gently, sitting down at the bar next to Willa. "I'm actually a real estate agent in town; I have a small office across the square." Cassy pointed across the square to a light blue Victorian-style multi-unit historic house.

"Is it for sale?" Willa asked, noticing a real estate sign in the yard.

"Oh no," she said. "That's for the first-floor apartment. I own the building. The office is on the lower level, too. After Lavonte and I married, we renovated the top two units, joined them, and I started renting the downstairs apartment."

"So...you're looking for a tenant? Is it cheap? Because I'm realizing I'm going to need a place to sleep...tonight... I really didn't think any of this through..." Her voice softly trailed off as she settled into the consequences of her impulsive Washington, DC, departure.

"Actually, she is looking for a tenant," Lavonte chimed in, trying to regain his southern charm from his earlier comments, "and you sound perfect."

"Perfect? And why is that? Because I'm that pathetic or because this creepy-ass town is itching for another undisclosed traveler to go missing so their organs can be sold on the dark web?" Willa said as she looked over at Lavonte cynically.

"New York?" Lavonte raised an eyebrow.

"DC." Willa scowled.

"Damn, girl...you city folk are...dark," Lavonte said with an uncomfortable laugh. "Cass just tends to take in strays from time to time and...well..." He pointed at Willa. "You look like her type," he said with a deep guttural chuckle.

"I know I should be offended by that...but...I'm desperate," she said, turning toward Cassy.

"How long are you planning to be in town, Willa?" Cassy said, interrupting the awkward tension. Her hazel eyes were almost maternal.

"Open-ended," Willa stated.

"Well, there's no better time than the present. Come on, I'll show you around, and we'll get you set up for the night, and then see what we can do." Cassy gently placed her hand on Willa's arm, encouraging her to follow.

* * *

The square was picturesque—like something in one of those cheesy stock photos that come preset in store frames. The town was lined with lush, overgrown oak trees covered in Spanish moss, casting a spell of enchantment. A farmers' market in the center square added to the charm. People milled around from place to place at a snail's pace, unlike what Willa was used to in DC, but it only added to the surreal feeling of the town.

"Well, Willa, we're not in DC anymore," she said out loud to herself.

After a few minutes' walk, they approached the house. They ascended the few steps to the wrap-around porch, which led to two identical doors. "The stairs to the upper level are around the back." She guided Willa past the first door, which had a gold sign on the outside: "Magnolia Shores Realty—Cassandra Mitchell, Luxury Realtor," to the second door, opening it.

"What type of work did you do back in Washington? Self-made or old money?" Cassy nudged Willa's shoulder as they entered the front door of the first-level apartment. "I can tell by those shoes you're likely *someone* special there."

"Oh, umm, marketing executive," Willa spurted out, surprised at the words that came out of her mouth. She wasn't exactly lying, but her bachelor's degree in marketing had taken a back seat to other career ambitions as soon as she had been accepted into medical school. Dr. Willow Aria Burke, psychiatrist, no longer existed, and Willa Sullivan, apparent marketing executive, was born.

"I did all right for myself, ya know, big city, lots of people and things to...market," Willa said, rubbing her temples with her fingers. What the hell was she even talking about, she wondered. Twenty minutes into a new town, the lies were already flowing.

"I'm sorry," Willa continued, "it's just been a really long day."

"Completely understandable. Let's get you settled in, get some rest, and we can talk tomorrow."

Cassy walked Willa into the fully furnished Magnolia Shores apartment before giving her a key and saying goodnight. Willa wandered around the space. It was larger than the apartment she had in DC. But that wasn't surprising. The cost of living had to be much more reasonable in Magnolia Shores, and with what savings Willa was able to scrape together before she fled, she would be able to survive for a while. Exhausted, she curled up on the bed, fully clothed, pulled the throw blanket over herself, and fell asleep. She laughed to herself as she thought, *Maybe moving up in the world meant moving south.*

***

The next morning, sunlight creeping through the window, birds chirping, and chatter on the streets woke Willa. Not having a clock in the room, she reached for her phone, which she had forgotten to charge, and found it was dead. "What the hell time is it?"

Willa climbed out of bed, changed her clothes, brushed her teeth, wandered down the porch stairs, and crossed the square to *Luis's*, where she had met Cassy and Lavonte the day before.

"Good morning, Princess. How are we feeling today?" Lavonte said.

"Coffee, no talk, coffee," Willa barked. "What time is it?"

Willa glanced at the clock on the wall.

"06:45."

"What the actual fuck, 6:45 on a Saturday? Why are all you people awake?!" She spun around on her bar stool, looking at the other customers.

"Here ya go, Princess. Strong and black." Lavonte handed Willa a mug of coffee.

"Strong, black, and handsome, just like you," Cassy said while giving Lavonte a sideways hug.

"How can coffee be handsome?" Willa, still drunk with sleep, laughed sarcastically.

"Today is the first day of Magnolia Shores's homecoming weekend," Cassy said. "The whole town gets involved bright and early, and it's such a wonderful time. People from all over who have a connection to the town come back."

"Yippee," Willa said, folding her arms on the bar and laying her head on them.

"This is good for you, Willa," Cassy said. "It will give you a chance to get to know your new town family."

"What?" Willa said.

"Oh, last night when you said your visit was open-ended, I assumed you were planning on staying for a while before heading back to DC."

"I can't go back to DC. DC is nonnegotiable; DC is over. He is in DC; he is fucking DC." Willa snorted. "And even if he isn't, he still is... Whatever, it made sense in my head."

Cassy gave Lavonte a heartbroken glance.

"See, boy trouble," Lavonte silently mouthed at Cassy.

"Refill, Princess?" Lavonte offered.

"Sure," Willa said, "but make it Irish."

Chapter Two

The Ghost

It'd been three years since Willow Aria Burke, now Willa Sullivan, arrived in Magnolia Shores, which meant it was once again homecoming weekend. Sitting on her porch with a cup of coffee, she reminisced about her first arrival in the sleepy southeastern Georgia town.

She refilled her coffee from her kitchen and made the one-minute commute along the porch to the office, passing the Magnolia Shores Realty sign and, just below that, a smaller sign reading *Sullivan Marketing & Management Services.*

"Three years." Willa smiled as she patted the sign. What had started as a random idea for a cover job had blossomed into a nice little business for Willa. She had set up her business in one of the empty former bedrooms, now turned office suites in Cassy's realty practice. For the past three years, she had been helping the local small businesses grow and expand their reach into the larger Savannah area.

***

Today would be fun, Willa mused to herself while walking across the town square. The town was busy preparing for its annual homecoming traditions. Because of Willa's involvement, this year's event was destined to be larger and more financially successful than the previous years.

Willa walked into *Magnolia Books & Brews,* the cutest little café and metaphysical bookshop in Magnolia Shores' Square. Willa was still proud of the logo she had created for them, which was a cauldron overflowing with books and coffee beans. The shop was owned by Sydney Harper and managed by Sydney's brother's girlfriend, Emma.

"I have the provisions!" Willa announced as she walked inside, placing the random assortment of items Sydney had begged Willa to pick up for her—flowers, rope, zip-ties, duct tape, bleach—on the counter. "Just want to let you know the guy at the hardware store gave me a weird look as I bought all this." She laughed, her dark humor never leaving her.

"Why do you think I didn't want to go?" Sydney laughed. "People think I'm weird enough."

Sydney was a realist and had an edge to herself that Willa connected with instantly. Sydney was tall, about 5'9" with blondish hair, light skin, and hazel eyes. She was the second oldest of twelve children, most of whom she became responsible for. She grew up in a very strict religious family out west but moved to the Savannah area to open her shop. Savannah was much more accepting of those "hippy witchy types," Sydney would say. Willa loved how Sydney was the family's black sheep, leaving the faith and parents behind to find her path, and in the process, she had become content and happy as well.

Sydney still kept in touch with many of her siblings, especially Eric, one of her younger brothers. Eric went off to NYC to study finance and became very wealthy. He ended up purchasing a home in Savannah to have a place to visit Sydney when he wanted to escape the chaos of Wall Street. The visits became more and more frequent when Sydney hired the young, starry-eyed Emma to work in her shop.

"Thank you!" squealed Emma, collecting the supplies to hang the banners outside and put the bleach in the bathroom. "Wait...what's wrong with the stuff?"

Emma was the type of person Willa envied. Emma was the living embodiment of "ignorance is bliss." Innocently naïve about most things but by no means stupid. Just an eternal little optimist always looking for the best in people and situations as if she had been untouched by the harsh realities of the world. Sometimes, she would say things that would make jaded Willa and Sydney exchange knowing glances of "poor little thing has no clue."

Emma was a local, Magnolia-born and raised. She was about five-six with naturally red-orange hair and giant green eyes. She was thin and had the pale, freckled skin you would expect in someone with such apparent Irish ancestry. She grew up in a typical southern, white, upper-class family; cotillions, debutante balls, elegant dinner parties, and demure presentations were all things Emma excelled in, but deep down, Emma longed to be more of a rebel like Sydney or be a big-city runaway like Willa. But in Eric, Emma found a perfect mix. He was traditional enough to make Emma comfortable, but with just enough big-city edge, spontaneity, and left-leaning tendencies to have the excitement Emma always hoped for.

***

The hot Georgia heat dragged on through the day's homecoming parades and events. At the end of the evening, Willa, Cassy, Sydney, and Emma looked to unwind and have dinner along the river in downtown Savannah. Despite only being twenty minutes away, Willa never spent much time in the "big city," preferring to remain in the peaceful seclusion of Magnolia. So, every trip into Savannah made Willa a little bit homesick for DC—the good parts anyway.

The clink of porcelain and glass and the murmur of conversations enveloped Willa as she settled into the high-backed chair of a corner table. Her friends, animated with laughter and the sporadic rise of their voices over one another's stories, created a warm cocoon amid the hum of the busy establishment. Aromas of fried foods and whiskey mingled in the air, adding to the familiarity that Willa had grown to love.

"Willow?" A faint voice from across the room was overheard.

"Willow, is that really you?" The voice grew louder as it got closer.

Willa nervously turned away from the voice to try to avoid the inevitable.

"Hello, Burke! Dr. Willow Burke!" A hand grabbed Willa's shoulder and turned her swiveling chair around to face the voice. "Holy shit, it *is* you!" the voice said, choking back tears. Quickly, familiar arms wrapped around Willa.

It had been three years since Willa last saw her childhood best friend, Lillian "Lilly" Harrington. Lilly had been there through all the drama and pain Willa experienced in Washington.

The soft, friendly tone in Lilly's voice quickly shifted. "You're ALIVE? You left me! How could you just up and leave me there?"

"What is happening right now?" Sydney spoke up, looking over toward Willa with narrowed eyes. "Who is Dr. Burke?"

"I... I can explain... Just not right now," Willa stuttered as she stood up and grabbed Lilly by the arm. "Come with me," she said as she rushed Lilly out the door into the alley next to the restaurant.

"Willow ... what is going on?' Lilly interrogated.

"Please, Lilly, don't call me that. It's just Willa now, Willa Sullivan. Not Willow Burke, not Dr. Burke."

"You changed your name," Lilly softly said under her breath, raising one eyebrow, putting the puzzle pieces together. "I've been looking everywhere for you. I've been searching for you nonstop! I thought you died. But no, you're alive and well?! It never occurred to you to tell me that!? Your best friend since you were sixteen years old.... You just... disappeared."

"I had to, Lilly." Willa confessed, "I couldn't stay; things were getting so bad."

"You could have told me; you could have trusted me!" Lilly pleaded.

"How?! Are you still in DC? Do you still see him?" Willa continued.

"I never would have told him where you were. How could you even think that?" Lilly's eyes shifted toward the ground.

"Because I know him, Lil. If he knew that you knew, which he would, somehow, he would, I couldn't bear to think what he would have done to get that information from you. I couldn't be responsible for anyone else getting hurt because of me." Willa's voice was cold, and there was a glaze over her dark, nearly black eyes.

"They had a funeral for you, Will. Your parents did. About a year ago. They stopped looking. We all did, so did he…"

Willa looked hard at the ground in front of her. She knew it was coming.

"You have to come home, Will."

"I can't go back."

"You have to. We need you back, I need you. Things are different now," Lilly begged. "Remember when you were working with Dr. Randanowitz?" Lilly continued, "That residential domestic violence recovery unit thing you wanted to create?"

"Yes, of course, I do."

"Well, they did it…or are doing it. They broke ground a couple of months ago, and they will be having a huge fundraising event when they officially cut the ribbon." Lilly paused. "I've been helping to organize it. They named it in memory of you or after you—*Willowbrook Women's Residential Center.*"

It had been Willa's dream since she decided to specialize in women's mental health after her residency. She had done the research, applied for grants, been accepted into the best fellowships, and then disappeared in the middle of the night.

"Is *he* still there?" Willa asked.

"Will, it's over. He's over it," Lilly said, knowing it was a lie. Of course, he wasn't over Willa, and if he knew she was alive and well, he would absolutely start looking for her again. "Yeah," Lilly succumbed. "He's still there."

Killian Helmar was still on staff as an attending psychiatrist at Saint Asclepius or simply St. Al's. The same hospital that was opening Willa's dream program.

"But that doesn't matter, Will," Lilly continued.

"This is all too much, Lilly."

"Too much? You're telling me… I thought you were dead. It's the only thing that made any sense as to why you never contacted me."

"There you are," Cassy said, stepping out of the restaurant with Sydney and Emma in tow. "Are you okay?"

"Yeah, umm, everyone, this is Lilly, an old friend from DC," Willa introduced. "Lilly, this is Cassy, Sydney, and Emma."

"Nice to meet you, Lilly. We haven't met anyone from Willa's DC life," Emma chimed in with a smile.

"Could you give me a few minutes?" Willa asked. "I'll catch up."

"Sure, we'll be right across the street by the car. Take your time," Sydney said.

Willa turned back toward Lilly, who had taken a seat at one of the outdoor tables.

***

Lilly and Willa met as roommates during their first year of college and had been for the most part inseparable ever since. Lilly was tall, and her model-like features always made her stand out in a crowd. She had short black hair that she wore in a sleek pixie cut and was the undisputed top socialite and event planner of Washington. The Harringtons were an impressive family of Senators and high-profile political strategists had made Lilly one of the undisputed top socialites in Washington. If there was an important party, political campaign event, or philanthropic Gala, Lilly was involved somehow.

The two sat in silence for a few minutes.

"What are you doing here, Lilly?"

"Meeting with members of the Savannah Orchestra for a thing back in DC. The Georgia governor may run for president, but that's not important. Why are YOU here, Will? Why Georgia, of all places? No note, no call, nothing; you were just...gone."

Willa released a deep sigh of remorse and glanced down at the table before them.

Lilly continued, "You remember our neighbors...they said there was a fight at the apartment. Tall, drunk, angry blond man causing a scene. They said they threatened to call the police, but he left. I knew it had to be Killian, but when I asked him, he said he hadn't been there."

Willa rolled her eyes. "Liar, he's just a liar," she began. "It was him. And he was screaming about my leaving him, demanding I come back. The neighbors came out of the apartment and threatened him. He said we would 'finish' the argument 'tomorrow' and that I 'knew what he meant'…and I just…couldn't take it anymore, Lil. It was never going to end."

Willa paused, turning her head so Lilly couldn't see her eyes starting to well up.

"I threw whatever I could in a carry-on bag, hit up a couple of ATMs to get as much cash as I could get, ran to Reagan International, and asked for a ticket for the first flight leaving to anywhere…anywhere I could go using cash. The first flight out was to Savannah…" Willa continued to explain. "Willow Burke died that night in DC, and Willa Sullivan was born."

After a moment, Lilly spoke, "I wish you would have trusted me. It's not fair how you left things…"

A pang of guilt overwhelmed Willa. She had not considered how her leaving would have impacted others.

"I'm sorry, Lil."

Willa missed her friend. She had never wanted to cut Lilly out, but with Killian being so unstable and Lilly being the easiest person for him to target for information, Willa thought disappearing would protect those like Lilly that she cared about.

While writing her number down on a cocktail napkin, Willa said, "This is me. I can't make up for how I left, but …"

"I miss you too," Lilly said, forcing a slight smile.

"Please, I know I may be paranoid, but please don't tell him where I am," Willa begged while handing over the napkin.

***

"Sooooo, your name isn't Sullivan, and you aren't a fancy marketing director from DC?" Sydney asked with a raised eyebrow, reflecting in the review mirror as they drove back to Magnolia.

"Syd, don't pressure her," Cassy pushed back. "Willa, you don't owe us any explanation."

"But we are here if you do want to talk," Emma voiced. "Honestly, Syd and I thought you were in some kind of witness protection thing or something anyway, so I guess we weren't that far off."

"It's not a total lie...back before I came here..." Willa chose her words carefully. She wanted her chosen family to understand but was concerned about how they would respond if they really knew the truth. That Willa had been, in essence, lying to them for the past three years.

"I had been working...with...the marketing department of a large hospital with the plan to create a residential facility where women could come and feel safe and work through their traumatic experiences. Sort of part domestic violence shelter meets upscale luxury mental health facility located right on the coast near the water. Everything would be provided, and the women and their kids could heal. It was a different path than I had thought I would have followed, but there was a huge need, and helping these women was something I was really becoming passionate about. Yes, my real name is Willow...Willow Aria Burke, I was...a psychiatrist there."

"Impressive," Sydney said.

"Wow," said Emma, "that is amazing, and they are actually building that Center now?"

"Yeah, I guess so, that's what Lilly said. Lilly wants me to come back for the grand opening, like some huge reveal that I'm back and nothing has changed."

"Go!" Emma yelled.

"I don't think it's that simple," Cassy said, looking toward Willa with a soft glance.

"It's not. My ex is still there…and I just don't think it's a good idea to go back given the way we left things," Willa said.

Cassy gave Willa's arm a quick but loving squeeze.

Her friends nodded, their expressions shifting to ones of understanding and empathy. Willa had never gone into detail about her life in DC or why she left. It was a part of her mystery that Cassy, Sydney and Emma respectfully never pried into. All her friends knew was that Willa was from DC and had left a bad relationship with the plan to start over.

Willa's heart swelled with appreciation for these women who had so lovingly accepted her into their lives, but she felt anxious because she knew she had only given them half the story. They had helped her through those dark, confusing days when she first arrived. But how would they feel if they knew the whole story? Would she lose them? It was a risk she was not willing to take. Right now, she decided discretion was her best friend.

"But that is okay, it's an achievement nonetheless, and you should be proud, Will. Even if you aren't there, those women will have a safe place to go," Cassy said.

Stepping out of Sydney's car, the group said good night, and Cassy and Willa walked toward Willa's apartment.

"You know it's okay for you to talk about it," Cassy said.

"I have," Willa deflected.

"No, I mean, really talk about it," Cassy said. "Will, I have known you for three years now, almost to the day. You and I know how to read people. I know there is something you're not telling me, and I just want to let you know…I'm here. No judgment. You don't need to carry whatever this is alone… I know he's not just a *typical* ex."

Maybe it was seeing Lilly, the drinks they had, the anniversary of Willa's arrival, or Cassy's offer so straightforward with genuine sincerity, but tears flooded Willa's eyes, streaming down her face. No one in Magnolia Shores had ever seen Willa cry.

"Let's get you inside," Cassy whispered, wrapping her arm around Willa's shoulders.

Back in the apartment, Cassy started making tea, and Willa cuddled up on the couch under a blanket, drying her eyes. Cassy placed the cups of tea on the coffee table and put her hand on Willa's knee. Again, the tears began to flow.

"You don't understand, Cass. It was…it…it was me. It was all my fault. I brought this on myself. I knew what he was capable of, I didn't care, I pushed him…I—"

Cassy cut Willa off. "First off, there are two people in a relationship. It's never all one person's fault. I know I don't really know because you haven't shared but I can imagine given the state you were in the day we met… It's never your fault… It's never okay for a man or anyone to hurt you."

Killian was a monster, a wolf in sheep's clothing. But, Willa, back then, she was just a wolf. How would Cassy react if Willa were completely honest and vulnerable right now? The arrival of Lilly had already cracked the glass, and bits of Willa's past were seeping out.

Chapter Three

The Backstory

Willow Burke was eight years old when she realized no one was coming to save her.

Her mother, crying, was standing at the kitchen counter, wrists thin and trembling under the weight of the phone held to her ear. She had just received word that her mother, Willow's grandmother, had died.

"I can't handle this, I can't do it," her mother, Whitney, cried, clutching the gold cross around her neck. "I could die too, God will understand, it will be over then…finally peace."

"Die? What about me?" Willow's soft voice was barely audible. Her mother didn't notice.

Emotional neglect is often quiet. It doesn't leave bruises. It leaves absences—empty seats at piano recitals, unreturned glances, silence in response to pain. Her mother lived in a slow-motion collapse, her days blurring together in depression-soaked inertia that even her faith in Jesus could not relieve.

It would be another twenty years before Willow would understand the depths of her mother's fragile mental state at the hands of her father, Walter.

Walter Burke was a prominent surgeon at the world-renowned St. Al's.

That sentence alone used to be enough to shut people up. There's something about that word—*surgeon*—that makes people assume excellence. Precision. Authority. And Walter Burke was all of those things...on paper.

In real life, he was a master of the long game. He didn't scream or hit. That would've been too obvious. He dismantled people quietly, through logic, suggestion; the way he'd glance at them like they'd just missed something obvious. Like, your existence was vaguely disappointing.

He had a belief system he'd never express outright in public, but behind closed doors, he made it very clear: men were meant to lead, and women were meant to follow—preferably barefoot and smiling.

He thought women were *decorative.* Useful, in a limited sense. But the real business of the world—the important decisions, the legacy, the authority—belonged to men.

Once, when Willow was around twelve years old or so, she corrected something he said at dinner, and he barely looked up from his plate. He said, *"No man will ever love a girl who can't keep her mouth shut."*

"Yeah, Willow, shut the fuck up. No one cares what you think," her older brother, Warren, had chimed in.

Warren was Walter's pride and joy, the golden child destined for greatness.

She watched over the years as Warren molded himself after their father, which led to more adoration and praise.

When Willow had just started high school, she had asked her father for advice. Willow didn't want to be like the girls her father and brother looked down on. She was witness to how terribly Warren would treat the women in his life, from belittling his mother, cheating on girlfriends, to being physically abusive to Willow when he didn't get his way.

"How can I be better than them?" she once asked her father. "I want to be more than just some dumb bitch who doesn't even know she's being cheated on."

He told Willow that if she wanted to be taken seriously in life by him, she needed to be desirable first. *"If a man wouldn't sleep with you, he'll never care what you have to say. Make yourself worthy of their attention and you'll do fine."*

That was Walter's version of parenting. Not guidance—*indoctrination.*

And God help her, Willow believed him.

She learned to keep her body polished, her humor crass, and tone flirtatious. She knew how to make herself desirable enough to hold a man's attention, because once she had that, she could manipulate her way in with the actual substance. Charm first. Strategy later.

And she became damn good at it. Willow became a force of nature. Brilliant and determined, once Willow set her sights on something, nothing could deter her. She was always the youngest in her class, a prodigy who stood out and thus carried the weight of heightened expectations. Starting college at sixteen and earning a doctorate by twenty-three, Willow's life was a relentless pursuit of excellence. By the time Willow graduated from medical school, something her brother had not been able to achieve, she had crafted a reputation for being wildly desired but unattainable.

She became obsessed with excelling by any means necessary, pushing herself to the brink of destruction to achieve the unachievable. Every accolade, every achievement, and a brief moment of recognition were quickly overshadowed by the next goal, the next mountain to climb.

The pressure was immense, but Willow thrived on it, or so she told herself. She buried her insecurities beneath layers of perfectionism, her outward confidence masking the fragile child within who just wanted to be seen, to be protected, to feel safe, finally.

***

"This is all bullshit!" Willow Burke slammed her hand down on the conference table, making the papers jump. "You keep bringing in these trainwrecks who quit after two weeks, and now you're shocked we're hanging by a thread? What exactly do you think happens if V and I both walk? You'd have to shut the entire psych service down."

"Dr. Burke—now listen—"

"No, *you* listen, Pam. Safe staffing for a program this size calls for seven attendings. We have two. Two, Pam. Do you know what it's like to run this hospital with two actual psychiatrists and a skeleton crew of residents? I've been on-call 27 days straight. And now V's on deck for his month of Hell. You're lucky no one's made a serious error yet. One missed diagnosis and you're liable. *You.* Not your consultants. You want a malpractice suit in your inbox? Because this is how you get one."

"You don't get to speak to me like this."

"What are you going to do? Fire me? Go ahead. I'll hand you my badge and watch you explain to the board why the psych department collapsed under your tenure."

Pam's jaw flexed. She reached into her briefcase and shoved a stack of papers across the table toward Willow. "Here. Residency transfer files. The consultants say we need cheaper labor, so we're padding the residency program. You think you can do better? You pick the next hires."

"Gladly." Willow scooped up the pile and walked out without another word.

Back in her office, Willow dropped the stack of transfer applications onto her desk and sank into her chair. Her head throbbed. She could leave—she had offers, connections, degrees, and more glowing letters of recommendation than she knew what to do with.

But St. Al's wasn't just a hospital. It was her legacy. The place where both the Sullivans and the Burkes had once held top titles—Chief of Surgery, Chief of Human Resources, VP of Clinical Affairs. She got her first job there washing dishes in the cafeteria. She wore her family name like armor.

Now, it felt more like a bullseye.

When Walter retired and her mother's side faded out of leadership, the place had started bleeding from the inside—mismanaged budgets, unpaid vendor contracts, no-shows at HR meetings. The administration was scrambling to avoid being absorbed by the massive global conglomerate snapping up failing hospitals like Monopoly properties.

In a last-ditch effort to "cut costs," they'd hired a consulting firm to tear down and rebuild psych from the inside out. The result? A department so understaffed and overworked that even desperate hires didn't last long. New attendings quit within weeks. The atmosphere was toxic. No one wanted to stay.

The psych residency program was now their band-aid strategy: fill every available slot, even if it meant taking borderline candidates. Cheap labor. Warm bodies.

Willow sifted through the files. Most were trash. A few had red flags—board actions, professionalism warnings, unexplained gaps. *"Cheaper" came with a cost.*

"Rumor has it the hospital's future is in your hands."

Willow looked up to see Molly, the charge nurse on behavioral health, dropping into the chair across from her desk.

"Oh hey," Willow said, rubbing her temples. "Yeah…this stack is bleak. Honestly, only two are even worth calling."

"So call them."

"One's relocating from Oregon—actually grew up here. Impressive record, but he can't start for at least a month. The other just got out of the Army. Not as experienced, but solid credentials. Clinical research background. Could help us salvage our reputation, maybe even get some grant funding."

She paused, flipping to the bottom of the stack.

"And this pile?" Molly asked.

Willow frowned. "Full of people with redacted records, disciplinary flags, weird program exits. People who'll work for less because they have no other options."

She pulled one file halfway out. No red flags on the surface. Strong test scores. Graduated top third of his class. Former med school classmate listed in his references. But there was something…curated about it. Like someone had scrubbed the file too clean.

Helmar, Killian. Transfer request. Prior program: confidential release terms.

"And that one?" Molly asked, catching the shift in Willow's expression.

"Says he wants to be closer to family. Transferring from a more competitive program. Strong rec letters. Almost...too strong." Willow stared at the neatly typed summary. "I don't know. Could be a game-changer. Could be a disaster."

"So what's your gut say?"

Willow hesitated, flipping through his application again. There was something compelling in the way he wrote about patient advocacy. Something that reminded her—if she was being honest—of *herself*.

"Let's meet him."

***

Three Months Later

"So the new guy starts today, huh?" Andre Percy leaned in Willow's doorway, arms crossed with practiced ease, grinning like he was in on some joke Willow hadn't heard yet.

"I remember when I was the new guy," he went on, casting a dramatic glance toward the ceiling. "Fresh off the boat from Oregon..."

"You're still the new guy," Willow said without looking up from her laptop. "This one's just the *newer* new guy."

Andre smirked. "Guess I'll have to share your attention now."

"Oh, sweetie," she said dryly, "you'll survive. You're a big boy."

He clucked his tongue and walked off. Willow didn't turn to watch him go.

These men. Always circling every conversation back to sex—some crude innuendo wrapped in a joke, like the punchline would fall flat without her being the target.

Willow had been trained to tolerate it. To laugh along. To be "cool." To play the game. Growing up in Walter Burke's house, there wasn't another option.

She'd once asked her father how to get boys to like her—not just use her—and he'd barely paused before answering: *"You have to prove you're worth their time."*

And when she asked how, he laid it out like a formula: *Sexy enough to get their attention. Funny enough to hold it. Smart enough to make your own money. Chill enough to never take offense. One of the guys.*"

Unicorns, he'd called women like that. "They don't really exist," he added. "If they did, I'd have married one instead of your mother, and my life would've been a hell of a lot easier."

So Willow became the unicorn.

She kept her body small, her humor sharp, her mouth clever. She earned her degrees. Smiled through harassment. Carried the weight of the psych department without flinching.

She had become the female version of her father—ruthless, strategic, impossible to rattle. And yet, despite all of it, he still looked at her like she'd come in second to a ghost version of Warren who never even made it to med school.

A knock on the door snapped her out of it.

"Yes?" she called, eyes still on her screen.

"Burke?"

"What?" she sighed.

She glanced up—and froze.

He stood in the doorway like he already owned the place. Six-foot-four, broad shoulders under a navy suit that fit too well to be off the rack. Blond hair. Cool blue-grey eyes. A smile that walked the line between boyish and devastating.

"Killian Helmar," he said, stepping in. "I was told this is where I'd find my new babysitter."

"Helmar?" Willow blinked. "Huh. Not what I was expecting."

He raised a brow. "Thought I'd be taller?"

She didn't answer that. "Have a seat."

Killian lowered himself into the chair across from her desk like he had all the time in the world.

Willow straightened, re-centering herself. "I don't know what Pam or the consultants told you about this place but let me be honest with you: it's chaos. We're barely holding this program together. You're the fourth psych resident we've had to transfer in the last year, and the first three didn't make it past six weeks."

Killian gave a slow, practiced smile. "And yet here you are. Still standing."

"Not for lack of trying to quit," she muttered. "We're supposed to have seven full-time docs. With you, we now have four: me, you, Andre, and V. I'm doing everything I can to make this survivable for us—but I need you to do your part. Give me one month. Just one. Please don't burn out on day five."

"I'm sure I've lived through worse," Killian said, smoothing his tie. "This place should be less likely to get me shot than Kabul. That's already a win."

Willow snorted despite herself. "Dark sense of humor. Good, you're going to need that."

He grinned. "You'll learn I'm full of surprises."

Willow studied him for a second too long, then looked down at her screen. Her cheeks felt warm. *What is happening to me,* she thought to herself. *Do I have a crush on the new guy? That's never happened before...that won't make things more complicated*, she though wryly.

***

They'd just wrapped afternoon rounds when Willow found him alone in the call room—feet up on the cot, chart open in his lap, but eyes unfocused. The late sun poured through the cracked blinds, painting half his face in amber. He didn't flinch when she knocked.

"You busy?" she asked.

Killian glanced up, slow and deliberate. "Not really. Just pretending to be productive."

She leaned against the doorframe, arms crossed. "I wanted to talk to you about call."

His brow lifted slightly. "What about it?"

"I'm pushing your overnight call start date back a few weeks."

He sat up straighter. "Wait, what?"

"We've had too many residents burn out fast," she said, tone firm but not unkind. "I want you stable and settled before we throw you to the wolves."

Killian tilted his head, studying her. "You really think I can't handle it?"

"No," Willow said. "I think you're smart, talented, and hiding the fact that you're one bad week away from crashing." She took a breath. "And I've seen too many people—good people—get ground down by this place."

He smiled softly. His eyes held a kind energy that seemed to be thankful for Willow's protective instinct.

"You're not wrong," he said, rubbing the back of his neck. "I haven't exactly had an easy time getting here."

Willow arched her brow. "What do you mean?"

He paused for just a moment, then released a deep sigh.

"I didn't transfer because I wanted to be closer to family," he said. "That was the official line, yeah. But the truth is..." He shook his head. "I'm going through a brutal divorce. It came out of nowhere. Now she's making everything hell. Custody filings, emergency hearings, random court orders. It became impossible to focus on anything else."

Willow stayed quiet.

"She started telling people I was unstable," he added, voice quieter now. "I wasn't. I was just...heartbroken. She wanted to 'try again' so we moved here. We both grew up around here...but it didn't change anything. Now she just has a new audience to perform for."

His hands flexed around his knees. "Anyway. I didn't mean to dump that on you. I just—being home right now? It's worse than being on call. I'd rather be here."

He looked up and met her gaze. "So if there's a call to take...I'll take it. I *want* to."

She didn't say anything at first. Her gut twisted with something protective she was too afraid to admit.

Willow turned her face slightly to avoid looking directly at him—his eyes were like early winter: a beautiful coolness one could easily get lost in.

"I appreciate the honesty," she said finally. "But I'm not putting you on call until I say you're ready."

"I won't fall apart," he said softly.

"No," Willow said. "But someone else might, and we don't need more collateral damage around here."

That made him smile.

Her pulse ticked upward. She hated it. Hated how aware she was of the space between them. Of the subtle flex in his forearms, the relaxed confidence in the way he leaned back, how his gaze occasionally dropped to her lips like it wasn't even intentional.

He was attracted to her. That was clear. But she didn't flinch. She couldn't let him know that with each passing day she was becoming more addicted to his presence. That could shift the power dynamic and Willow couldn't let anyone else have control.

"I'll let you know when you're cleared for call," she said, turning toward the door. "Until then, try not to look too bored."

"Willow?" he called after her, just as she reached the threshold.

She stopped.

"Thanks," he said. Quiet. Almost sincere. "For treating me like I'm more than just a file."

She didn't respond right away.

Then, without turning back, "Don't make me regret it."

She shut the door behind her.

***

The ICU was quiet, the kind of eerie stillness that settled in after midnight. Machines beeped in soft syncopation. Dim overheads cast long shadows along the polished floor.

Willow stood outside room 822, flipping through a psych consult on a post-op delirium case. She rubbed the tension from the back of her neck as she skimmed the chart, eyes gritty from too many hours awake.

Killian trailed a few feet behind, clipboard in hand, sleeves rolled up. "You sure you want to handle this one?" he asked. "I can take it."

Willow shook her head. "It's mine. I got the page."

But something on the census board caught her eye. One name, in sharp block letters, stood out like a punch to the chest:

SULLIVAN, THOMAS M. Room: 823

Her feet froze.

She looked again. Same name. Same birthdate. Her grandfather.

Killian noticed the shift in her posture before she said anything. "What is it?"

Willow turned, pale and blinking. "That's...that's my grandfather."

Killian glanced at the board. "He's here?"

She nodded slowly, like she was putting it together in real time. "Room 823. He's been here four days."

"Four?" Killian echoed. "You didn't know?"

"No," Willow said, voice brittle. "I had no idea."

She turned on her heel and strode into the dictation room next door. Killian hesitated, then followed.

Inside, she leaned against the counter, gripping the edge like it could tether her to reality. The consult paperwork dangled from her fingertips.

"They didn't tell me," she said. "My own family. They didn't even bother."

Killian said nothing.

"He's my mom's dad," she continued, eyes shining now. "The one good one. The only one who used to ask me how I was doing, what was going on in my life. And they just...kept it from me."

Killian stepped closer but didn't touch her yet.

"They know I work here," she said. "They had to know I'd find out eventually. That's the part that gets me. It's like they wanted me to feel excluded. Like they wanted to prove I wasn't one of them."

She choked back a tear. She refused to show weakness.

Killian reached out slowly, placing a warm hand on her shoulder. She didn't pull away.

"You don't have to keep it together right now," he said, voice low. "Let yourself feel it."

She exhaled, a bitter laugh at the edge of a sob. "If I start, I won't stop."

"Then don't stop."

She turned toward him, and for a second, the strength slipped. Her eyes were glassy, jaw trembling. She looked ten years younger and twice as wounded.

"I'm tired of pretending it doesn't hurt," she whispered. "All of it. The family dinners I'm never invited to. The passive-aggressive texts. Reaching out only when they need something from me."

Killian stepped closer. His hand slid from her shoulder to her upper back, anchoring her gently. She didn't fight it.

"You deserve better than that," he said. "You give everything to everyone around you. I'm sure you did the same for them and what do you get back? Silence. Resentment. That's not love, Willow. That's control disguised as a punishment."

She closed her eyes as he pulled her into him, her forehead pressed against his chest.

"You're the only part of this place that doesn't feel like work," he added. "Honestly...you're the only part of my day I look forward to."

She opened her eyes slowly as she gazed up at him.

"I don't want to make this more complicated," he said, eyes holding hers. "Never mind."

"What?"

"It kills me to see you hurt... Willow, I think I'm starting to fall for you."

Killian reached up and gently tucked a loose strand of hair behind her ear.

"You don't have to say anything, in fact, please don't say anything," he added. "I just needed you to know." His hand lingered at the back of her neck, thumb brushing the tense spot just beneath her hairline. His breath was warm. His voice had softened into something intimate, confessional. It wasn't the voice he used on rounds or in team meetings. It was the version meant for her alone.

She couldn't respond, her thoughts a chaotic blend of duty, anger, and desire. Her heart pounded. His closeness was intoxicating but part of her craved it. Needed it, especially after the emotional gut punch she'd just taken.

Willow swallowed hard. Her heart thudded in her chest, not just from what he said but from what it meant—that someone saw her, wanted her, needed her.

"But you're still married," she whispered, not moving.

Killian didn't flinch. "It's over," he said, low and easy. "The paperwork just hasn't caught up yet."

Willow pulled back slightly—not enough to escape his embrace, just enough to breathe.

Her eyes narrowed. "Has that line worked before?"

Killian's expression shifted, barely. A flicker of something unreadable passed behind his eyes, then vanished. He leaned back, giving her space.

"It's not a line," he said. "I just stayed too long in a marriage that was killing both of us. Now she is just out for revenge. She's turning me into some villain to justify her actions. Trashing my reputation."

Willow looked at him, searching for any crack in the story. There wasn't one.

"She told people I was controlling," he added, softer now. "A drug addict of all things. Anything that would give her a leg up in getting custody of the girls. Those are my girls, Willow, she'll take them from me. I can't let her win."

He looked down at her, eyes steady. "I'm tired of being punished for trying to move on."

Willow exhaled, slow and deliberate. Her chest ached with a pressure she couldn't name.

Killian was saying all the right things. He wasn't pushing. He wasn't leering. He was...vulnerable. A father desperate to protect his young girls from the harm the world could cause, to protect them from the damage their *mother* could cause. The kind of man who noticed when a loved one was hurting and didn't pretend not to see it.

She wanted to be held. To be chosen. To matter. So she did what she'd done her whole life. Ignore her feelings and stay on course. "You should get some sleep," she said, pulling away from him. "We've got consults piling up in the morning."

Killian studied her face. "Willow..."

"Don't." She tried to smile. "I can't do this right now. Just—thank you...for being with me tonight."

He nodded, stepping back fully now. The space between them stretched like something unspoken.

She turned to leave.

"Hey," he called softly, just before she reached the door. She looked over her shoulder.

"I meant what I said," he said. "You deserve more than the scraps these people give you. And when you're ready to believe that...I'll be here."

***

Willow was in the resident lounge, finishing chart notes and trying to ignore the lingering stares in the hallways all morning. Ever since Killian arrived, Andre had started showing his resentment towards Willow and making it known to the staff he believed Killian was getting "special treatment." Willow felt the shift—colleagues whispering, looks held just a beat too long, polite smiles with razor edges.

The door slammed shut behind her.

She didn't need to look up. She already knew the sound of Andre's anger.

"You have *got* to be kidding me," he said.

Willow exhaled sharply, setting her pen down. "What now?"

"You're pushing for Killian to be Chief Resident?"

She turned slowly. "Who told you that?"

Andre crossed the room in two strides. "It's not exactly a secret. I overheard you talking to Radz outside the lecture hall. You're lobbying the attendings to back him. *Him*, Willow."

"Keep your voice down," she snapped.

"You're the most qualified!" Andre's voice cracked—half fury, half disbelief. "You've carried this department for *years*. You wrote the new med-student curriculum. You handled three call schedules solo last year. And now, after *everything*, you're just handing it over to Killian?"

Willow's expression didn't move, but heat rose in her face.

"And if not you," Andre added, "then it should be *me*. I've worked my ass off too. But instead, you're throwing your credibility out the window to make sure *he* gets another notch on his belt."

"I think he's the best choice—"

"Bullshit," he snapped. "You're handing over a leadership role to the guy who's been here five minutes, and why? Because he makes you feel wanted? Because he knows how to talk to you when you're tired and vulnerable? Or is he just that good of a fuck?"

"Don't do this," Willow warned.

"You're sabotaging yourself," Andre said. "You think this is just about a title, but the board knows your name. You and Radz just secured a quarter-million dollar grant for the Women's Mental Health Residential Center. Do you understand how rare that is for a resident? You're on track to become the face of psychiatric reform in this state."

Willow's breath caught—but just for a second.

"And yet," Andre continued, "instead of stepping into the role *you earned*, you're propping up a guy who couldn't even handle the pressure of his last position. And you still don't see it."

Willow stood now, slow and deliberate. "You have *no idea* what's happening behind the scenes."

"I know Killian is playing you," Andre said. "I know he's making you feel like you need him. Like he's some big protector. But he's not the savior he's pretending to be, Willow."

Willow stared at him. "Is this really about Killian? Or is it just that it wasn't *you* I chose to spend effort on?"

Andre shook his head. "This isn't about jealousy—"

"Of course it is!" she snapped. "You don't care about the Chief spot. You care that I didn't fall into your arms when you hovered in doorways and made jokes like I was supposed to be flattered."

"I care that you're not seeing what's happening," Andre said, quieter now. "You're being brainwashed, Willow. And your *daddy issues* are making it real easy for him."

The words landed like a slap.

Her voice dropped to a razor's edge. "You don't get to bring my father into this."

"He's *already in it*," Andre said. "You've been trying to impress that man your whole life. And now Killian shows up looking like a shinier version of Walter Burke, and you're throwing your future at his feet so he can call you a '*good girl.*'"

She stared at him—furious, flushed, but silent.

Andre stepped back, shaking his head. "You're the smartest person in this building, and you're letting a guy who lies with each breath walk around here like he's already been forgiven for hijacking *your* legacy."

Willow laughed coldly. "Don't you mean *your* legacy."

Andre's eyes narrowed. "What's that supposed to mean?"

"It means maybe you should stop obsessing over *my* legacy and *my* sex life and start worrying about your own," she said, voice shaking now, not from fear—but from rage. "By the way, how's your wife, Andre? Is she also fully invested thinking your career isn't moving forward because we haven't fucked?"

The silence hit like a gunshot.

Andre flinched, a quiet rage brewing in his eyes. There it was.

Willow pressed forward, her voice low. "You don't care that I'm making a mistake. You care that I didn't make it with *you.*"

Andre said nothing for a long beat. Then:

"You've changed," he said. "And not in the way you think."

He turned and walked out without another word, the door slamming shut behind him.

***

Willow sat in Dr. Radz's office, blueprints and budget spreadsheets spread out across the table. The Women's Mental Health Residential Center project was finally real—the grant money had cleared, the planning committee was scheduled to meet next week, and Willow could almost taste the impact they were about to make.

"You did good, Burke," Radz said, sipping his coffee. "It's rare to see a resident get this far on a project like this."

Willow allowed herself a small smile. "It feels surreal."

"You'll be leading rounds in your own facility one day soon," he said. "Hell, you'll probably be running this department within five years if you want it."

"I'd rather not run anything," she said. "Just fix what I can."

Radz gave a knowing chuckle. "That's how it starts."

As they flipped through space allocations, Radz paused.

"Listen," he said, closing the folder. "I wanted to ask about something—not as your supervisor. Just…mentor to mentee."

Willow looked up, alert.

"You've been working closely with Dr. Helmar," he said. "Endorsing him for Chief?"

Her shoulders tightened. "It's not official. I just think he's the best candidate we have right now."

He nodded slowly. "He's got presence. I'll give him that. But he's a bit…slippery. Charming, polished, but always seems one step away from saying something he doesn't quite mean."

Willow bristled. "Not you too…you think I'm being manipulated or did Andre put you up to this?"

"I think you're under a lot of pressure," Radz said gently. "And when people are stretched too thin, they can make some errors in judgment."

Willow looked away.

"I'm not telling you what to do," he added. "I know your personal life is none of my business…just…maybe don't get too close to him right now."

"I know what I'm doing," Willow said, more forcefully than she meant. "There is nothing inappropriate going on between he and I."

Radz raised a hand in surrender. "I believe you. I just want you to remember—you are so close to the top. You're an inspiration to so many. People recognize *your* work. You're no longer just Walter Burke's daughter."

***

It was after midnight, and the psych wing was running on the low hum of computers and fluorescent lights. Willow stood alone in the empty unit conference room, staring at the whiteboard she'd just wiped clean. Her body ached from the over twelve-hour shift, but her mind was still spinning—Andre's accusations, Radz's concern, Killian's unwavering devoted gaze all looping on repeat.

She didn't hear him enter.

"You okay?" Killian asked softly from the doorway.

She didn't turn. "Define okay."

He stepped inside, letting the door click shut behind him. "You've been off all day. I got worried."

"I needed quiet," she said.

He moved closer, slow and careful. "I figured you'd be in here. You always retreat to this room when you're unraveling."

She finally turned to face him. "And what makes you think I'm unraveling?"

"Because I know you," he said, voice low. "I see the way you hold everything together when no one else can. This place just dumps more and more on you. I know what it costs you."

Willow exhaled sharply. "You don't know anything about me, Killian."

"I know enough to see when you're about to break."

She laughed once—bitter and tired. "You think this is breaking? This is me on a good day."

He took another step toward her, closing the distance. "You don't always have to be strong."

"I do," she said.

His eyes locked with hers. "Don't do that...not with me. Don't shut me out like I'm one of them."

The words hung between them, electric.

"You have no idea what I've been through," she whispered.

"I don't need to," he replied. "I just need to know you're still here."

His hand brushed a strand of hair behind her ear, then lingered against her jaw. She didn't move.

"Willow...I'm tired of pretending I don't feel this," he said. "And I know you feel it too."

Still, she hesitated—just enough for the doubt to flicker.

Killian leaned in, closer now, his breath warm against her neck. "Everyone in this hospital already thinks we're sleeping together. We're already being punished for it."

Willow's breath caught. His presence, his words sent a warm chill down her spine.

He held her gaze. "So what's really stopping us now? We could just...give in."

That was it. The last domino.

Her fingers tangled in his shirt, yanking him down to her. Their lips crashed together—hungry, angry, starved.

His arms wrapped around her like instinct, pulling her into him, anchoring her as if claiming her would make it real.

Her back hit the wall, and he lifted her easily, her legs wrapping around his waist. She didn't care. About the rumors. About Andre. About the voice in her head warning her this was all happening too fast, and she was falling too deep. But the way he touched her felt like she was already his.

"This is a mistake," she breathed, even as her fingers slid beneath his scrub top feeling every delicious muscular ridge of his abs and chest.

"Then let it be the last one we make alone," he murmured, lips trailing down her neck.

She didn't stop him. She wanted to let go. She'd never craved the touch of a man as deeply as she did in this moment. Everything else faded away—it felt good to be wanted. To be seen. To be chosen even if just for tonight.

***

The on-call room felt like a secret cathedral, its only light a single desk lamp dumping molten gold across the tangled sheets of the cot where Willow lay curled beneath a scratchy hospital blanket. Killian, half dressed, hovered beside her, one arm slung possessively across her hip as if he belonged there. Since their first night together, their hunger had become a ravenous force—unstoppable, unapologetic. They stole every moment, no longer caring who might catch them.

Outside, the hospital slept. No urgent pages shredded the quiet, no wails of pain pierced the walls—just the low mechanical hum of ventilation and the throttle of 3:00 a.m. secrets.

Willow rolled onto her back, her dark hair fanned across the pillow. She studied the ceiling's water stains like constellations.

"I have to tell you something," she murmured, voice husky with intent.

Killian stiffened but didn't pull away. "Okay."

Her eyes met his in the dim glow—razor-sharp, burning. "St. Al's is bleeding cash. The merger whispers? They're more than whispers. Consultants are here to carve us up, to prep us for sale—or full liquidation. We've got maybe eighteen months, if we're lucky."

He held her gaze, silent.

"I've been planning," she continued, fingers trailing through her hair. "We need an exit strategy . We build something massive: security, power."

A slow, knowing smile curved Killian's lips. "You want to leave?"

"Eventually," she said, sitting up, eyes aflame. "But first we need something substantial. Not a lateral move. I know I can get grant funding."

"And what would you build?"

"I don't know yet, but, probably some kind of women's facility. Always vulnerable and underserved it would be a great reputation boost."

"And me?" His heartbeat thudded in his throat.

"You'll be the face," she replied, leaning in so close he felt her breath. "The next Dr. Oz—or Dr. Phil—but real. I'll leverage the hospital media folks to film your educational series. Social media blitz. Panels, conferences, sponsored tie-ins—therapy apps, wellness supplements, the next breakthrough in sleep tech—your name on all of it." She batted her eyelashes and chuckled, "The dashing doctor looking out for us poor vulnerable little women."

He whistled low. "You've plotted this."

"I've dreamed it," she said, leaning in until her lips brushed his ear. "But I never had the right man."

He shifted, ignited. "Why me?"

"Because you're smart—charismatic—irresistibly disarming," she whispered. "You look like trust: handsome, white coat, edge-of-rebellion sexy. Just enough danger to intrigue, but safe enough to comfort our demographic."

He laughed, soft and dark. "And you?"

Her fingers gripped the blanket's edge. "I stay in shadow. People loathe women like me: bold, beautiful, unblinking in ambition. If I walk onstage with these words, I'm vilified. You say them, I'm a genius."

He watched her, captivated.

"I don't crave applause," she breathed. "I crave control. I want an empire built on my blueprint—my fingerprints everywhere, unseen."

He swallowed. "You get the power. I get the glory."

She grinned. "That's the pact."

Killian studied her for a long moment, then exhaled. "That's...the sexiest goddamn thing I've ever heard."

She slid onto his lap, blanket slipping free, every inch of her against him. He groaned as she straddled him, her thighs slick with heat.

"I need you as Chief Resident," she said, voice silk and steel.

He paused, hips responding. "I thought you didn't give a damn about titles."

"I don't," she replied, rocking her hips, drawing him closer. "Institutions do."

Her body pressed against him, the wet friction electric. "If the sale goes through, they'll axe costs, consolidate power, cut anyone not in their inner circle. A Chief Resident? They see leadership—they keep you. Transition you to attending. Auto-safety cloak. Especially if they want a male physician's face in their PR campaign."

Killian's gaze raked her skin. "So I become their golden boy."

"Exactly," she purred. "Then we spend that year building your brand—keynotes, podcasts, soft media drops. Maybe a co-authored book. By board-certification, you'll have every option in the world."

She ground harder, urgency spiking between them.

"Fuck, Willow…" he moaned, arching his back.

Her lips brushed his ear. "While I'm untouchable—running the Women's Center with locked-in funding, state support, national headlines. They'll need me alive to keep the donors sweet."

He nodded, cocky confidence building. "So we become…fireproof."

She captured his eyes. "Together, we outlast this place."

He lifted her hips, clearing the way for her to guide him in. His voice dropped to a rough whisper. "You've thought of everything."

"I always do," she smiled.

He thrust up, breath ragged. "One question—what if they want you in the spotlight too? Offer you that attending role?"

She ground down on him, nails grazing his shoulders. "Then we make them think it was their idea." She arched her back, her own breath catching. "But I'll stay unseen. The darkness is where true power lives."

Killian leaned back, seeing her as though for the first time: strategist, lover, force of nature.

Willow wasn't just turned on by power—she was power incarnate, and he was hers.

"Why be in the spotlight," she whispered against his chest, "when you can control it?"

***

Their love story was a perfect blend of passion and deception, but as they climbed the ranks, the actual cost of their ambition began to reveal itself.

The relentless pursuit of success and the weight of Killian's lies threatened to unravel everything they had built, setting the stage for a dramatic and tumultuous journey ahead.

CHAPTER FOUR

The Other Other-Woman

Over time, Killian's obsession with Willow intensified. He couldn't stand the thought of losing her or the empire she was building for them. She was the mastermind behind their success, and without her, everything would crumble. This obsession fed a growing jealousy. Every time someone praised Willow for her brilliance, beauty, or humor, Killian's anger simmered beneath the surface. His pride couldn't handle that she was outshining him in their world.

The alcohol and drugs he had been using only exacerbated his insecurities. His once-charming demeanor became increasingly volatile, and Willow noticed. She tried to brush off his outbursts at first, attributing them to the stress of managing an understaffed program. But it was becoming too frequent to ignore.

One evening, after a particularly grueling shift, Willow returned to their apartment to find Killian sprawled on the couch, a half-empty bottle of whiskey in his hand and disturbed lines of white powder on the coffee table. He wasn't even trying to hide it anymore. The evidence of his spiraling behavior was easy to see.

"Really, Killian? Seriously?" Willow snapped, her patience wearing thin. "You're on fucking call tonight. I'm exhausted. We have a plan. We're so close. You can't keep doing this to me."

Killian's eyes, bloodshot and unfocused, flicked toward her. "What's your problem, Willow? You think you're better than me or something? Queen Willow pissed again because her puppet won't play nice?"

Her temper flared.

"Yes! Now get your shit together. You're going to blow this for us," she yelled, her voice echoing through the apartment. "I haven't come this far for you to fuck it up."

Killian stood up unsteadily, his towering frame casting a shadow over her. "You think I need you? I'm the one who got us here," he slurred, the words dripping with misplaced bravado.

Willow took a deep breath, trying to steady herself. "No, Killian. You filled out an application for a program. *You* needed *me* to get *here*. You need me now more than ever. Just look at yourself! If you keep this up, you'll lose everything because I'll be damned if I let you take me down with you."

The tension in the room was palpable. Killian's face twisted with rage and desperation. He knew she was right but admitting it was a blow to his fragile ego.

For a moment, they stood in silence, the gravity of their situation sinking in. Willow's heart pounded in her chest, but she refused to back down. She had sacrificed too much to let it all go to waste now.

"You're fucking replaceable Killian, remember that," Willow raged, grabbing her coat and heading back to the hospital to cover once more for Killian. She couldn't handle the possibility that she had picked the wrong man on whom to build her empire.

***

As the candlelight flickered on the restaurant table, a sad attempt at an apology, Killian's third glass of bourbon was nearly empty. His speech was slurred already, and his eyes had a drunken gleam. Willow sat across from him, dressed impeccably as always, her eyes cold and wary despite putting on the practiced show of the doting girlfriend.

Killian leaned in with a smug grin. "You know she wants me."

Killian was on another tangent to try to make Willow jealous. This time, he was talking about one of the nurses at the hospital. It was starting to grate on Willow's last nerve.

"Sure, like you could get her to go slumming with your obnoxiously drunk whiskey dick for a night." Willow laughed to herself.

"How do you know I haven't had her already?"

Willow froze; there was something different in his tone this time.

"No, you haven't," she said, forcing a laugh. "She's too good for you."

"Just ask her," Killian retorted, his grin widening.

"Fine, I will." Willow, determined to call his bluff, smirked and sent a quick text to Molly, the nurse Killian had been talking about: *"We need to talk."*

The reply came swiftly.

"Oh My God. He told you? I'm so sorry. I never meant to hurt you."

Willow's face drained of color.

"Are you fucking serious?" she hissed, slamming her phone on the table. She stood up abruptly, grabbing her bag to leave.

"I told you she wanted it." Killian laughed. "It's not like it's a big deal, Will. It's just sex, calm down."

Flames raged in Willow's eyes; Killian didn't notice, lost in his own story. He had just admitted he had been cheating on her, at the hospital no less. The polished untouchable power couple she had created was hardly believable if he was fucking around and openly bragging about it. This was something she would not be able to cover without looking downright foolish. Killian's actions were about to destroy everything Willow had built, not just their future goals, but her carefully cultivated reputation of someone to be idolized as much as feared, which was far worse.

***

Willow and Molly met for drinks at a quiet bar, far from the prying eyes of colleagues and friends. Molly's eyes were red-rimmed, her hands shaking slightly as she sipped her drink.

"I'm so sorry," Molly cried.

"I'm not mad at you," Willow said, her voice composed despite the storm brewing inside her. "I'm mad at him. I want to know everything... I *need* to know."

Molly took a deep breath, recounting the events with evident remorse.

"It happened when I was too drunk to drive after that work thing. Remember, Killian offered to take me home."

Willow listened, her expression hardening with each word. She remembered that night, she had been there.

"I was so lonely," Molly explained, her voice trembling. "My marriage was falling apart, and I wanted to feel loved. And he's so, you know...persuasive."

"Yeah, I know," Willow replied bitterly.

Molly's eyes filled with fresh tears.

"It gets so much worse, Will. He's married."

Willow shook her head in disbelief. "No, he's not. He's divorced or separated or whatever; custody of the kids, the co-parenting plan is holding it up or something, but...no, they aren't *together* anymore."

"No...Will. He told me. I asked how someone like him could ever have landed someone like you given his fucked-up history...and...how that...I said it just didn't seem like something you would do...like...be his mistress...and he said he lied to you. That you thought he was working through this terrible divorce, you'd be engaged when the court paperwork was finalized, but...Will...he never even filed."

Willow's heart pounded in her chest. "What the fuck are you talking about?"

"He said he didn't think there was any other way he could get you into bed or ride your coattails unless you saw him as your future."

"Molly...that was...years ago. He's been telling me about the divorce, complications of custody, meetings with lawyers, how much it's all costing him...all the fucking time."

"He told you every weekend he goes over to Arlington to relieve his sister from being caregiver to their parents, right?"

"Yeah."

"His parents and sister live in Michigan, Willow... His wife and kids are in Arlington. He stays in the city with you during the week and goes back to them."

Willow's world spun. "That's impossible... She...moved back to her parents in Nebraska...she has the kids there...it's...why...it's taking so long."

Molly reached out, her voice barely above a whisper.

"He threatened me, Will. He said if I told you...he'd tell my husband about us. I panicked. He said he knew you didn't know. That he had lied to you since you first met. I don't know why he told me all of this. I think he thought he was impressing me or something. I just asked how he could land someone as brilliant as you, you were too smart to fall for all his shit." Molly sobbed. "And he just said it all. He said there were others too. I'm so sorry. I know he'll tell my husband now, and that's on me."

"No, he won't," Willow said, her voice icy. "Killian won't risk his reputation. If he tells your husband, call me. I'll tell him Killian never slept with you. I'll say you found out about his marriage, the lies, and warned me and this is just his sick retaliation."

"Why...why would you do that?" Molly asked, eyes wide with disbelief.

"You could have lied, said it never happened or that it was just some one-night stand. You didn't have to tell me the real truth, but you did. I won't forget that. I protect those loyal to me."

***

Willow's key rattled in the lock before the door gave way to a wave of rot—burnt alcohol and pungent weed. Killian was sprawled on the sagging couch, eyes heavy-lidded, a smirk half-buried in the haze.

"You bastard," she hissed, fury crackling in her veins.

He blinked slowly, that lazy grin curling his lips. "What?"

"I talked to Molly."

"That little bitch. It's all a lie," he said, sitting up.

"Is it, really? I didn't even tell you what she said," Willow replied, her eyes cold as ice. "What is it that the 'little bitch' would have lied about?"

Killian's face flushed red, his anger rising to match Willow's intensity. He knew she knew. Outside of money and power, the only thing that mattered to Willow was loyalty.

"After everything I've done for you!" Willow screamed, her voice breaking. "I fucking made you! You're nothing without me! And this is how you repay me?"

In a rage, Killian sprang up, eyes blazing. He caught her by the shoulders and slammed her against the wall. His lips crashed onto hers with brutal force—hungry, demanding. Their fights always ended in their passionate, entangled flesh, but tonight the old rhythm broke.

Willow pushed, palms digging into his chest.

"Are you fucking serious right now? I don't want you! What the hell is wrong with you?"

Killian's eyes darkened, rage eclipsing reason. He was losing control of the moment, and that infuriated him. This argument wasn't going to end the way Willow wanted it. He stepped closer, his presence menacing.

"You're mine, Willow. Don't you forget that."

Willow's pulse thundered in her ears. She had seen this predatory look of his before but never directed at her. She had to get out. For the first time, she realized there was a reason to be truly afraid of him.

Without warning, he yanked her down. The world spun in a brutal tumble as his weight pinned her, every breath a battle. One hand ripped at her jeans, the other snaked around her throat. The carpet's coarse fibers scraped her skin as he dragged her down, the rough threads biting.

Willow gasped for air, the room a suffocating blur of heat and fear. His cologne, once a comforting presence, now choked her with its cloying intensity. She could feel the coarse fibers of the carpet biting into her skin, the oppressive weight of his body crushing her lungs.

She pleaded, "Stop," her voice a thin, reedy whine, but he didn't relent.

His eyes were ice—starless, devoid of mercy. He invaded her with a savage cruelty, flesh against flesh, tearing through her plea for mercy. Her screams died in a choked sob as she felt him inside her, relentless and cruel.

"Killian...stop." Her voice was like her pulse, weak and thready.

The edges of her vision fuzzed and darkened as his grip tightened, her life receding like the tide.

Everything went dark.

She woke on the cold, hard floor, her entire body ached with a deep, bruising pain. The room was a dim cavern, shadows flickering along the walls like restless spirits. Her throat burned, a raw, searing agony where Killian's hands had crushed her windpipe. Each shallow breath was a rasping reminder of his violence. She could feel a sharp, pulsing wet throb between her legs; she was bleeding. The coarse carpet beneath her was an abrasive kiss against her tender skin, and she curled into a fragile, broken doll.

Memories crashed over her like a violent surf, each one more crushing than the last. Killian's cold, dispassionate eyes. The suffocating weight of his body. The cruel, unfeeling hands that had once caressed her with tenderness. Tears streamed down her face, hot rivers carving paths through the desolation of her features. She tasted their salt, mingling with the metallic tang of blood in her mouth.

The room was thick with silence, an oppressive, suffocating thing that bore down on her with the weight of a thousand unspoken words. In the stillness, she heard the soft jingle of his belt buckle being fastened, a sound that sliced through her like a blade. The apartment door opened and then closed. He had left her there, discarded like so much refuse.

The scent of his cologne lingered in the air, a ghostly presence that haunted her with memories of better times. It mixed with the acrid odor of sweat and fear, creating a noxious cocktail that turned her stomach. She tried to sit up, but her body rebelled, collapsing back to the floor in a heap of shattered will.

Her mind was a maelstrom, swirling with thoughts she couldn't grasp, emotions she couldn't name.

How had it come to this? How had she been so blind? She had known Killian's darkness but never had she imagined he was capable of such...not to *her*.

The edges of her vision wavered, a surreal haze creeping in as if the world were dissolving around her. She was alone, utterly and terrifyingly alone, and the realization struck her with the force of a physical blow. Alone with her pain, her fear, her memories.

Willow picked herself up, went to the shower, and cried on the floor as the water rushed over her.

Wait, showers remove evidence. Her domestic violence training popped into her mind. "Evidence," she said to herself. "What fucking evidence? No one will believe me."

It wasn't a secret that Willow and Killian had a history of giving into each other's needs. Loud, aggressive sex, in parking lots, on-call rooms, deserted stairwells, anywhere. There were few places where they hadn't ravaged each other, but there was never anything like this. He never continued if Willow told him to stop.

As she dried herself off, the apartment door opened.

"You're on-call," Killian coldly said, throwing the on-call phone towards her, it hitting the floor at her feet. "You're taking my shift. Get yourself together and go to work."

Willow was speechless; who the fuck was this man?

"How could you?" she whispered in her hoarse voice. "You want me to show up to the hospital like this?" She pointed to the bruising on her neck.

"Use makeup or whatever sluts like you do," Killian said coldly.

No, this was not how this would go, Willow thought. She was in charge. Maybe he lied, cheated, but everything they had was because of her, and she wouldn't let him ruin it.

"Fine," she hoarsely said. "Maybe I will swing by the police station first and then head in," she threatened.

"Try me, Willow. Do you think this was bad? You have no idea what will happen next time." He grabbed the phone, stalked past her, and slammed the door so hard the walls shook.

In shock, Willow sat and stared at the wall. She had no plan for this. Who could she turn to? Who would believe her? The amount of lying, cheating, and ruthless pursuit of success with complete disregard for anyone but her and Killian... Who would come to HER rescue?

Her fingers trembled as she dialed the only number she dared. "Lil...please..." No answer. She pressed her forehead to the cool phone. "I need help," she whispered into the void.

CHAPTER FIVE

The Guilt

The next morning, she emerged with a mask of makeup and a chic designer scarf wrapped tightly around her throat, concealing the brutal bruises left by Killian's violent grasp.

She went to Dr. Abraham Randanowitz, her mentor's office, knocked on the door, and entered when she heard his voice beckon. As expected, he wasn't surprised to see her.

"Killian said you might show up," he remarked, gesturing for her to sit.

"He was here?" Willow asked, feeling a pang of disappointment.

"Last night. He was pretty upset."

"Of course, he was."

Her hand instinctively went to her neck, pulling off the scarf and revealing the dark marks left by Killian's fingers.

"He did this..." she said, her voice trembling. "I was hoping to switch services for a while."

Her mentor sighed, shaking his head. "He said you two got into a fight and that you had been drinking, which is why you missed your shift last night, and he had to cover. Said you basically attacked him, he couldn't get you off him, so he accidentally grabbed your neck. He feels awful."

Willow felt tears welling up in her eyes as she struggled to find the right words. "That's not what happened... He...he..."

"Dr. Burke, I don't want to be involved in this. You're both adults, figure it out." Her mentor pointed to the door, dismissing her with silent finality. Feeling defeated, Willow went down the hall to one of the unused offices and closed the door behind her. She collapsed onto the floor, gasping for breath as tears streamed down her face. Everything was slipping away.

Willow's heart thundered against her ribs as she heard the door creak open behind her. She spun around, eyes blazing, to find Killian stumbling in, his face a mess of tears and anguish, a pitiful sight, but her fury was relentless. Every muscle in her body tightened, ready to snap, as the brutal memories of his betrayal came rushing back, igniting an inferno within her.

"Stay the hell away from me, Killian," she hissed, her voice laced with venom, trembling with a mix of rage and pain.

He dared to step closer, arms extended in a pathetic plea for absolution. "I'm so sorry," he choked out, his words nothing but empty air. "I was drunk, high, I wasn't myself. I would never hurt you, Willow. I couldn't bear the thought of losing you. I panicked."

Willow's mind screamed in disbelief. Not long ago, he had raped her. And now he expected her to forgive him? Willow's voice rose with each word until it cracked with raw emotion.

"You would 'never hurt' me? You cheated on me with a friend, and when I confronted you...you...*raped me*...and..." Her voice choked, "You're still married!"

"You knew I was married," Killian retorted, a spark of defensiveness in his eyes.

"Don't you dare try to spin this on me!" Willow's anger boiled over at his audacity. "From the moment I met you, you claimed you were going through a messy divorce, custody battle, crooked lawyers... Oh My God! You lied to me for years, about everything. You never even *filed* for divorce from her?!"

"You don't understand," Killian begged, his voice a desperate, clawing thing. "The second I first saw you, I knew. I'd never felt anything like it. You make me lose control; I can't bear the thought of losing you. This isn't who I am. I promise it will never happen again. Please, Willow, forgive me."

Torn between love and fury, Willow faltered as he pulled her into his embrace. She yearned to shove him away, to scream until her lungs gave out, but a traitorous part of her still craved his touch, for the familiar lie of comfort he offered. She didn't want to be wrong.

Killian lifted her chin, forcing her to meet his gaze, and crushed his lips against hers. Memories of their past surged through her like a tsunami, threatening to drown her. This was HER man, her champion, her livelihood. They had weathered storms together and built a life together. Could she cast it all aside? Could they survive even this? Did she want them to survive this?

Before she could react, Killian lifted her onto a nearby desk, wrapping her legs around him. She felt his length, hard and insistent, pressed against her, but the echo of the previous day's agony held her back.

"Wait, don't...it's going to hurt," she whispered, instinctively pulling back.

"I'll take care of that," Killian murmured, shifting her hips forward, pushing her skirt up her hips, and sliding her panties off in one fluid motion. He tucked them into his pocket as he slowly lowered himself to his knees.

Willow felt guilty for succumbing to his touch, but she couldn't deny the heat that spread through her body as he rhythmically kissed, licked, and sucked at her intimately between her thighs.

Why am I letting him do this, she thought, torn apart by conflicting emotions. *Because I love him*, she reminded herself, even as a voice inside her screamed, *Make him stop!* But the ghost of his past rage, the monster that had taken her by force, kept her compliant. *Just give in, don't fight,* she told herself, praying he'd be gentler.

"I still hate you..." she moaned as Killian continued his penance.

"I hate me too," he panted, rising up to kiss her neck, distracting her from the discomfort as he penetrated her.

Willow gasped, the mix of pain and pleasure, lust and rage, consumed her as he thrust faster, deeper, bringing her closer to climax despite all the chaos and turmoil rushing through her mind.

"Killian..." she moaned, "wait...we can't...we can't do this...stop..." she panted, arching her back in a mix of desire, guilt, and confusion.

"Willow, please...fuck, Willow, please," he begged her to let him finish, his voice desperate and pleading.

He was begging her. He needed her. A wave of intoxicating power passed over her. She had regained a sense of control amid the chaos.

She leaned in, her lips brushing Killian's ear, and commanded, her voice a sultry purr. "Cum for me...Killian. Cum for me like a good boy."

Feeling him release inside her pushed Willow over the edge.

Then it was over, and Willow was consumed by self-loathing and shame. *You just let him get away with it? Nothing has changed. He's still married, he cheated on you, and he raped you last night...and you just got off as he came inside you,* she screamed internally, her mind a jumbled mess of emotions and confusion.

***

Cassy held Willa in her arms.

"You don't understand, Cass," Willa cried. "I deserved this. The things I did, the people I hurt, the careers I ruined...I didn't even care..."

Cassy wrapped Willa in her arms tightly, like a mother holding her child after a nightmare.

"I stayed, Cass, for a fucking year I stayed...He'd get pissed or fucked up, I'd get hurt, he'd get off, he'd apologize... I'd try to forget. I just kept pretending it wasn't happening. Or maybe I liked it. How fucked-up is that!? How do I make it right?"

"Hush, you stop that right now," Cassy said. "You did leave. Maybe not when you first wanted to, but sweetheart, you did leave. And that takes a lot of courage..."

"He just kept getting worse. I couldn't fight anymore... I knew exactly the number of pills I would need for the perfect, peaceful final cocktail. I could have just drifted away...but Cass, I never..." Willa paused to reclaim her breath. "I saw a photo of me and Lilly. White Coat Ceremony, end of my first year of medical school... It's kind of a big deal...and it was before Killian even existed to me... That girl never would have put up with this shit. She was destined for greatness but turned into a monster."

"I don't know *that* Willa. And yeah, maybe if I had met her, I wouldn't have liked her. Honestly, I would have probably hated her, but Willa... Willa, listen to me... That is not who you are. For the past three years, I have watched you. I've watched you care about your friends, about me, about Lavonte, and the people in this town. You have put other people's needs before your own. Would your 'Old Willow' be like that?"

"No, I don't think so," Willa sighed.

"I'd say I've never seen you do anything truly selfish. You hid the truth from us when you got here to protect yourself, and I don't think that's selfish." Cassy continued, "The trauma will fade in time, sweetheart. It will get better if you embrace it and not run from it. You will heal, but first, Willa, it sounds like you more than paid for your sins. It's time to forgive yourself."

CHAPTER SIX

The Opening

The next afternoon, the door of *Luis's* swung open, ushering in a gust of city air, which caused Sydney, Emma, Cassy, and Willa to all jump.

"Rude!" Emma yelled toward the door. The group all laughed.

"Speaking of deep, intensive healing," Sydney said, "Em and I thought it might be good for us all to take a real break. Get away for a bit."

"Absolutely," agreed Cassy enthusiastically. "A change of scenery can do wonders."

"And we can celebrate!" Emma squealed and raised her left hand to show off her new sparkly engagement ring, which she had, of course, received from Sydney's baby brother, Eric.

"Sisters!" Emma and Sydney cheered.

"Escape reality for a little while," Emma said, her eyes alight with the idea. "You have to come; you all have to come."

Willa rolled her eyes. "I don't know, guys. Maybe I've had too much excitement for one lifetime."

"Just imagine, Willa, waking up to the sound of waves, salty-sweet air. It could be a fresh start of sorts," Emma pleaded, her eyes wide and smiling.

Willa felt the gazes of her friends settle on her, each pair of eyes conveying a cocktail of concern and excitement. She took a deep breath, the notion of escape weaving its allure through her thoughts.

"It does sound intriguing," Willa admitted, the words floating like a tentative leaf on a breeze. The table erupted with animated chatter, plans to form like constellations in the night sky.

"Think about it, Willa," Cassy said gently. "No expectations, no pressure. Just...freedom."

Freedom. The word echoed in Willa's heart, a resonance that hummed with the promise of new horizons. As the conversation around her blossomed with the details of potential departure dates and lavish adventures, Willa allowed herself to consider the idea that it was time to step out from under the protective umbrella of Magnolia with this new little family of hers.

Since arriving in Magnolia Shores, Willa had been torn between her desire to remain hidden and safe and the natural instincts of success and power that once defined her. Those instincts, though, had led to harm in the past, making her wary of trusting others—and herself. Her past haunted her, leaving Willa feeling trapped, both from her history and her current self-imposed limitations. She longed to transform into someone new yet feared reverting to the heartless person she once was. Still, she couldn't continue as the timid, fearful version of herself that Magnolia had seen.

Magnolia had shown her a path to kindness and compassion, but it felt like a cage rather than liberation. She was stuck, not healing but hiding. And now, as these girls offered a glimpse of freedom by accepting her despite the truth, she wavered. Could she risk letting her guard down just enough to grow, or would it only lead her back into familiar traps?

Like another gust of wind, Lilly Harrington, still in town, extending her trip after finding Willa, swept into the bar. Her presence as pronounced as her sharp stilettos clicking against the hardwood floor. The sunlight streaming through the large windows caught the glint of her oversized sunglasses, which she perched atop her head like a crown upon entering.

"Sorry I'm late, darlings. I know, I know it's been far too long!" Lilly chucked using a fake British accent. Her voice was smooth yet edged with something unplaceable as she approached their table. Willa watched her, noting the precision of Lilly's movements, an elegance that felt rehearsed, a performance meant to captivate an audience.

"Hi, Lilly, we didn't realize you would be popping over," Sydney said.

"But I see you've all started without me." Lilly teased, leaning back in her chair, a manicured hand tracing the rim of her coffee cup with calculated nonchalance. "What are we gossiping about, ladies?"

"We're going on a trip!" Emma burst with excitement. "To celebrate my engagement!"

"Charming," Lilly commented while looking at Emma's ring. "A little getaway. Where to?"

"We haven't decided yet, but somewhere exciting, New York, LA, or Vegas," Emma said. "I've never really been anywhere outside of Georgia."

"So, does that mean you've never been to Miami?" Lilly asked.

"No, but that could be fun!" Emma chirped.

"Well, as it turns out," Lilly continued, "I am actually going to be heading to Miami next weekend to go to the opening of a brand-new club. I know the club promoter. It's going to be a big deal, lots of rich, famous, and powerful people should be in attendance. So, of course, I have to be there," Lilly said playfully in Willa's direction.

Lilly hoped deep down that "Willa in Magnolia Shores" was nothing more than a phase Willa had yet to outgrow. Lilly knew Willa was a city girl through and through. The slow pace and lack of excitement in Magnolia Shores had to be torture to Willa, but with enough proper persuasion, she would be able to get her best friend back to DC in no time. Lilly hoped the trip to Miami would spark Willa's interest in going back to her old life.

"It will be VIP all the way," Lilly continued.

"That sounds amazing, Lilly," Sydney exclaimed.

Willa felt the muscles in her jaw tense. Outside of the rare trip twenty minutes west to Downtown Savannah, she had not been outside Magnolia's protective cover.

She pictured herself in Miami, surrounded by strangers who thought she was charming, bright, and beautiful. And with Lilly's loose acquaintances and their carefree laughter mixed with low inhibitions chatting up Willa like the lost member of their proper flock, the type of attention that Willa missed, but that was a stark contrast to the shadows she currently felt clinging to her soul.

Cassy reached across the table, her fingers brushing against Willa's hand in a gesture that spoke volumes. The clinking of glasses and the murmur of conversations around them faded into the background as Willa felt the weight of her friend's gaze.

"Listen to me, Willa." Cassy's firm voice was laced with an undercurrent of tenderness. "Miami, it's just another city with beaches and restaurants, just like here, just like Downtown Savannah. It doesn't have to be anything more than that. No need to feel any unnecessary pressure to make this trip anything more than it is...a week away with friends."

Willa hesitated, her expressive eyes reflecting the tangle of emotions within. She admired Cassy's unwavering belief in her, the way she seemed to see a strength in Willa that felt so distant at times.

"You've been holding onto the reins so tightly, trying to control every outcome because of what happened in your past," Cassy continued.

"Maybe you're right," Willa finally admitted, her voice a mere whisper, yet it resonated with a pivotal moment. The idea of true freedom, something she had not fully tasted in a long time, was alluring, but terrifying.

"Of course, I'm right," Cassy said with a wink, her hazel eyes dancing excitedly. "Besides, I'll be with you every step of the way. We all will."

CHAPTER SEVEN

The Stranger

Under the pulsing neon lights of Miami's latest hot spot, Willa, Sydney, Emma, and Cassy sashayed through the crowd of partygoers to locate Lilly, who had used her socialite connections to reserve a VIP table for the group.

"Here's to our baby girl Emma and her exciting next phase of life," Sydney proclaimed, raising her glass to toast their little circle of sisterhood. Her voice was barely audible over the rhythm of the music.

"Absolutely," Willa shouted, leaning over to clink her drink against the others, her laughter infectious.

"Make good choices tonight, ladies." Cassy, the mother hen of the group, laughed.

"And if not good choices, then at least ones that will make a hell of story!" Lilly chimed in as she joined the group.

Sydney grabbed Emma's arm and dragged Emma onto the dance floor.

"I'll grab another round," Cassy said, leaving Lilly and Willa alone.

Willa continued to scan the crowd as she and Lilly made their way to their booth.

"Girl, stop. You have got to stop. It's been three years, I get that you went through some shit, I'm not minimizing that, but what? Do you really think you will...what, like run into *him* here?" Lilly said.

"It's just second nature now, Lil. I don't even realize I'm doing it," Willa responded.

"Here we are in this beautiful club, with this amazing VIP table, you're welcome by the way." She winked at Willa. "And you look exceptional, except for the massive resting bitch face."

Willa smirked. "It's become my trademark."

"Trademark man repellent," Lilly laughed.

Lilly let out a deep sigh. "You have barely left the borders of that Podunk little town in years. I get it, it's comfy there, you made some nice townie friends, but Will, that's not you, and you know it... Come home. This is ridiculous. They are building your Center; don't you get that? *YOUR* Center, and you aren't willing to even stop by, wish it luck, cut a ribbon, and take some credit?"

"I thought you said everyone thinks I'm dead, remember?"

"I mean, they do, but they don't. Your parents had this memorial sort of thing as a signal that the official search was ending. You know how your folks are. The local headlines were a bit too much bad press for them."

"Yeah, they would rather I be dead than bring the shame and disappointment of running out on the Center project because my crazy, married, drug-addicted boyfriend beat the shit out of me one too many times. So proud, I'm sure."

"Can you imagine the impact if you show up and tell your story? You're basically the type of person the Center was created for!"

"What if he's there...at the opening? I know he's still on staff, Lil," Willa said despondently.

"Ugh...Will...ok...you remember Randanowitz, right?" Lilly questioned.

"Oh, you mean my former *mentor*? You mean the man who was so focused on women's mental health, women's trauma recovery? You mean the man who left me high and dry when I was desperate to get away from Killian? You mean that Randanowitz?" Willa paused. "A man so dedicated to helping abused women, to just abandon one when she needed it most—"

Lilly cut Willa off. "He talks about you a lot. Things really changed after you left. I think Radz didn't realize how serious it was with Killian until you were just gone. For a long time, people assumed Killian had something to do with you disappearing, but nothing ever came of it... He played the grieving lover role perfectly."

Willa sighed, looking down at her glass, stirring the ice with a cocktail straw.

"Leaving the Center project was a slap upside the head for basically everyone who realized they had it all wrong." Lilly continued, "I don't think anyone really believes you're dead. It was just easier to say you were than to acknowledge those fuckers were partially responsible. While you were screaming for help, they did nothing."

"They didn't care, Lil. 'Good riddance,' I'm sure they thought. Manipulative, home-wrecking bitch got what was coming to her."

"That's not true!"

"Too little, too late," Willa huffed.

"Killian fell apart after you left—"

Willa, eyes ablaze, cut Lilly off. "Don't you dare try to make me feel sorry for him."

"Oh, God, no, no," Lilly quickly confirmed. "What I mean is that he started breaking...badly. You weren't there to keep him in line, cover for him, or fix his mistakes. Willa, Killian never left St. Al's because no one else would hire him after he finished the rehab program the medical board forced him into, which...didn't stick, by the way. He's as delusional as ever, but people see it now. They understand what happened to you and would understand why you disappeared."

"How do you know all this, Lilly?"

"Radz's daughter." Lilly shrugged. "What? We're in a book club together."

"I don't know what part of that statement is more ridiculous, that Radz actually cares after all these years, or that...you are in a book club." Willa chuckled.

"Umm, hello. Book clubs are about gossiping and drinking champagne at inappropriate hours, but it's socially acceptable because you have a book on your lap." Lilly smiled.

Willa laughed. "God, I've missed you."

With that, Cassy returned with more drinks for the girls. She had temporarily gotten pulled into dancing with Emma and Sydney.

"What have I missed?" Cassy chirped.

"Is that Taylor? Taylor! It's Lil. Look!" She screamed from their private table. "Dave hooked us up!" Lilly announced, "BRB, I have to rub this table in her face."

Lilly grabbed a cocktail from the table and went off after one of her many neo-socialite connections.

"She is a handful, that girl," Cassy chuckled, shaking her head slightly.

"I think she means well; her delivery, however, can definitely miss the mark," Willa said.

Amid the revelry and chaos, Willa's gaze drifted across the sea of bobbing heads and gyrating bodies. That's when she saw him: a man stationed at the far end of the bar as if he had emerged straight from the pages of a glossy magazine. His posture was relaxed, yet a deliberate intensity to his stare set him apart from the rest.

His eyes locked onto hers, and something inside Willa fluttered, a sensation she hadn't felt in a long time. She tried to look away, but his magnetic pull was insistent, drawing her gaze back like the tide to the shore. He raised his glass in a silent salute, a corner of his mouth lifting in a knowing smirk that suggested something playfully devilish.

"Who's THAT?" Sydney squinted, shielding the bright strobing lights from her eyes as she plopped down in the booth, having caught the exchange.

"He looks kinda familiar, do we know him?" Emma said.

"Em, you're drunk." Sydney laughed.

"Nobody I know," Willa murmured back, feeling the weight of his stare as a tangible touch against her skin.

"From what I can see, it seems like you've got an admirer," Sydney noted, her tone playful yet protective. "And there are a lot of good-looking men here."

"Or it's just the lighting and alcohol in here making everyone look twice as good," Emma chimed in with a slightly tipsy giggle, though she followed Willa's gaze with interest.

"He's hard to ignore," Willa whispered to herself, her heart skipping. Her past held chapters she didn't want to revisit, yet the stranger's attention stirred a curiosity she couldn't quite quell.

But even as she turned her attention back to her friends' laughter and chatter, part of her remained tethered to the mysterious stranger at the bar. His presence, a question mark in the night that beckoned an answer.

The pulsating beat of the club's music synced with Willa's heartbeat, each throb echoing the intensity of the evening. Her eyes, however, couldn't help but wander back toward the bar where the mysterious man remained stationed, his gaze fixed on her as though she were the only one in the room.

"Are you two still eye-fuckin' each other from across the room?" Cassy said, a mischievous glint lighting up her hazel eyes as she leaned closer to Willa. "Looks like someone has made quite the impression tonight."

Willa felt her cheeks warm at Cassy's words. "It's probably just the way I'm sitting. A trick of the light or something, or maybe he's just as hammered as Em." She tried to dismiss it playfully, but the slight quirk of Cassy's lips told her she wasn't fooling anyone.

"Uh-huh, sure, like you don't know how amazing you look in that dress," Cassy teased, nudging Willa's arm with a playful elbow. "Come on, Willa, do something. When was the last time you let yourself flirt?"

Before Willa could respond, Lilly's voice cut through the commotion, carrying an edge that didn't go unnoticed.

"Please. Will, back in the day was 100 percent heartbreaker. Guys falling over her all the time thinking they had a chance. I don't think, Will, have you ever actually had to hit on a man? Or make the first move?" Lilly inquired. "I mean once you locked down Killian it was over but... Oh...shit...sorry Will, I didn't mean to say his name."

"Go for it, Willa," Cassy urged, her voice a mix of support and daring. "What do you have to lose?"

"Just her dignity," Sydney mumbled, but her eyes twinkled with humor.

"Thanks for the vote of confidence, Syd," Willa replied dryly, though a part of her wondered what it might be like to step out of the shadows of her past, even if just for a moment.

"But seriously, you haven't even really looked at a guy since I've met you," Sydney continued.

"Waaaaait a minute." Lilly's eyes widened. "Are you saying our little Will is not running the streets of your little town? Will...how long has it been since you've had sex?"

"With a person?" Willa glanced over at Lilly. It wasn't that Willa hadn't thought about it. It wasn't that she didn't want to, in fact, she really did want to. It was just the idea of letting someone get close to her, to make her feel vulnerable, out of control, or worse to make her emotionally fall for them was scarier than the actual act.

"I don't know...probably about three-ish years." Willa shrugged.

"So more like four years since you actually enjoyed it?" Lilly somberly.

Lilly leaned over and whispered into Willa's ear, "Honestly, I think you need to do this. It doesn't have to mean anything. You just need to move past what he did to you. Let some hot man show you some passion and then...Killian won't be the last one to...you know."

Lilly faced the rest of the group. "Okay, this just got way too serious. Willa needs our support. Commence Operation 'Get Willa Laid.'"

"Ha, I love this," Sydney said. "We each have to head to the floor and find at least two possible suitors for Willa and whoever's man she picks, that girl pays for the morning mimosas!"

"Agreed," Cassy chimed in, "but only if Willa makes a move on tall, dark, and sexy over there, first." Cassy squinted over by the bar.

"Seriously, go talk to him, it could be fun! And if nothing else, you can see close up if he's as hot as we think he is. Plus, we're all here to rescue you with plans B, C, D, E..." Cassy trailed off, rolling her eyes and laughing.

"Or we can just watch you crash and burn from a safe distance. Either way we win," Lilly added with a laugh. Her cynical, dark humor was something Willa found comforting.

"Just what best frenemies are for, huh, Lil?" Willa countered with playful annoyance.

"Whatever, you love me," Lilly said, giving Willa a quick peck on the cheek as she bounced out of the booth to go schmooze some other club patrons Lilly felt needed to know who she was.

"Oh, fine, I'll talk to him." Willa grabbed her clutch with her phone. "If this goes poorly, its all of your faults and you WILL be making it up to me," she said pointing a finger at each one of them. With a steadying breath, she straightened her posture, readying herself to take a step forward that felt more significant than merely crossing a dance floor.

Willa's heart thrummed a fierce rhythm, urging her feet forward through the pulsating energy of the nightclub. Her eyes, usually so expressive and clear, were clouded tonight with a mix of hope and trepidation. She wove through the crowd, each step an act of will against the gravity of her past; years chained to memories she yearned to eclipse.

Ahead, he was the epicenter of attention, his laughter, a melody that soared above the bass. The light caught on his raven hair, and the depth of his dark brown eyes sparkled like shards of glass in a darkened world. Willa felt the pull, an inexplicable connection tugging at her soul's frayed edges.

"Excuse me," she murmured as she brushed past a couple lost in their embrace. Her gaze locked onto his like a lighthouse guiding her from stormy seas. But then, the shore seemed to crumble beneath her feet. The entourage surrounding him, a wall of suave and polished figures, cast shadows that felt like barriers. They laughed, their voices a discord that drowned out her courage. Her resolve trembled, faltering under the weight of her insecurities.

What am I doing? This is absurd. Willa's stride broke. She faltered between the desire to advance and the instinct to flee. She glanced at this mysterious stranger, his eyes finding hers again. Her pulse quickened, not with excitement now, but with panic, and she turned, retreating into the shadows of the hall leading to one of the exits.

The chilled night air embraced her as she stepped into the alley beside the club, a welcome contrast to the oppressive heat she left behind. She pressed her back against the cool brick wall and closed her eyes, seeking refuge in solitude. The clamor of the club dulled to a distant thrum, allowing her thoughts to surface—one by one, they came like stars piercing the night.

"Deep breaths, Will," she whispered to herself, the gentle firmness of her tone a lifeline amid the turmoil. "You don't need to push yourself. You have nothing to prove." She inhaled the crisp air, tasted the freedom it promised, and exhaled the bitter remnants of doubt. Her shoulders relaxed as she leaned her head back, the tension seeping out of her body and dissipating into the quiet darkness around her.

"Let go," she urged herself, the words almost a prayer for the courage to seek happiness beyond yesterday's confines. Her heart began to steady, finding its rhythm again, in harmony with the new-found strength rising within her.

As the cool night air began to soothe Willa's frayed nerves, a sudden warmth enveloped her arm. Her pulse quickened, and she spun around, coming face to face with *him*. He stood alone, his entourage nowhere in sight, the dim light from the club's back entrance casting shadows across his chiseled features.

"It's you..." Her voice was barely above a whisper. The words felt foreign yet familiar on her lips.

His intense, dark eyes held hers, an unspoken conversation passing between them. His grip on her arm wasn't forceful but firm, filled with intent. Willa's heart hammered against her rib cage; each beat echoed the vulnerability that this man's proximity stirred within her.

Before words could bridge the gap of silence, he stepped closer, closing the space between them. With a tenderness that contradicted his strong exterior, he cradled Willa's face and drew her toward him. His lips met hers in an unexpected and electrifying kiss, igniting a spark that had been dormant for far too long.

Willa's mind reeled with the surprise of his touch, yet her body responded with an instinctive longing she hadn't realized she harbored. The world contracted until there was nothing but the warmth of his mouth on hers, the gentle pressure of his fingers weaving through her hair.

As quickly as it began, the kiss ended, leaving Willa breathless and leaning into him. He pulled back slightly, his gaze searching hers, a silent question hanging in the air.

"I'm sorry," he murmured, the calm cadence of an English accent laced with genuine concern. "I shouldn't have…"

His apology flowed with heartfelt sincerity, resonating with the part of Willa that yearned for connection, for honest and raw passion. She searched his face, the apology in his eyes reflecting the same intensity she felt pulsing through her veins.

"It's okay," Willa managed to say, her voice a mix of confusion and wonder. At that moment, as the night held its breath around them, Willa saw beyond the allure of the mysterious stranger, he was simply a man reaching out to her, a man who had acted on a shared impulse that neither of them fully understood.

Willa's heart throbbed. His concern etched lines of exposure across his rugged features, and she found herself moved by the raw honesty in his eyes. The cool night air did little to quench the heat that lingered on her lips from his kiss.

"Thanks," she began, her voice steadier than she felt. "Thank you for doing what I knew I couldn't." She took a deep breath, feeling the weight of her past retreat into the shadows for just a moment. "I'm not used to…this," she gestured vaguely between them. "It's been a long time."

The alleyway was quiet, except for the distant bass throbbing from inside the club. Willa could sense his unwavering and intense gaze upon her. It was the look of a man who wasn't afraid of baring his soul, even if it meant making mistakes.

In the depths of her mind, Lilly's voice echoed, a playful taunt wrapped in encouragement, *Life's too short, Willa. Go for it.* Her words sparked a daring flame within Willa's chest. This was a chance to step outside the confines of her reservations to embrace the unknown with a man who had unexpectedly ignited something within her.

"Do it again," she whispered.

He was clearly surprised by her words. His eyes widened slightly. The corners of his mouth curved into a gentle smile, revealing dimples on his cheeks. He traced her lips lightly with his thumb, the touch sending tingles down her spine. He leaned in slowly, brushing his lips against hers once more, and this time, she welcomed it with open arms. Their kiss deepened as their tongues met in a dance that sent shivers through her whole body. Her breathing quickened, and she felt a warmth spread through her chest, filling every inch of her soul. His hand found its way to the small of her back, pulling her closer to him like magnets attracting each other in the night. The sound of their passionate kiss filled the alleyway as they stood there leaning against the brick wall. The taste of his tongue was sweet with whiskey and reminded her of the cocktails she had earlier. She breathed him in; he smelled like leather and something—a scent she couldn't quite place but found herself longing for more of. Their kiss broke apart again, leaving them both panting for air as they stared deeply into each other's eyes.

"Take me," she said, her decision firming with each word. "Take me home with you."

Her declaration hung between them; a delicate offer extended without expectation. Willa saw something shift in his expression—a flicker of surprise followed by a softening around his eyes as if he understood the gravity of her choice.

"Are you sure?" he asked, his voice low and intense, making her shiver.

"I'm sure," she replied, nodding, her resolve mirrored in her steady gaze. The night air seemed to hold its breath, anticipating what might unfold between these two souls, drawn together under the most unlikely circumstances.

CHAPTER EIGHT

The Surrender

His hand was warm in Willa's as he guided her through the labyrinthine corridors of the upscale hotel. The plush carpet muffled their footsteps, and peaceful tranquility enveloped them, isolating them from the rest of the world. Willa's heart drummed a frantic rhythm, each beat reminding her of the step she was about to take, a step toward the unknown with this nameless man.

They arrived at a door marked with elegant numerals that gleamed softly under the muted lighting. The mysterious man retrieved a key card from his pocket, the motion fluid, and practiced. With a soft beep, the lock disengaged, and he pushed the door open, ushering Willa into a space that felt worlds apart from the raucous club they had left behind.

The room was bathed in the glow of strategically placed lamps, casting gentle shadows across the walls. A subtle scent of sandalwood floated through the air. Velvet drapes framed the large window, adding to the room's ambiance of quiet luxury.

Willa stepped inside; her senses heightened. She could feel the shift in the atmosphere, thick with anticipation, charged with an electric current that made each breath catch slightly in her throat. The intimacy of the setting wrapped around her like a silken shawl, simultaneously comforting and exhilarating.

As the door clicked shut, sealing their privacy, he turned to face her. The gold in his deep brown eyes shimmered with layers of emotion, a fierce flame reflecting both the heat of his desire and the depth of his vulnerability. At that moment, Willa saw the elusive club playboy and the man...raw, earnest, standing before her as though she held the key to his very soul.

Their gazes locked, speaking silent volumes that words could never capture. It was a conversation of glances, breaths, shared uncertainty, and mutual yearning. Time seemed to be suspended, leaving only the two of them entwined in an intangible web spun from threads of connection, neither fully understood.

A ring came from Willa's clutch. "Friends, probably looking for me," she whispered, her voice heaving. She retrieved her phone swiftly, dropped a pin in response to Lilly's text before tossing her bag and phone on the entryway table.

With a magnetism neither could resist, they moved closer. His hands found Willa's waist with a tenderness that contrasted his firm grip, pulling her gently toward him. Willa's heart fluttered like a bird caught in the exhilarating swirl of a breeze as their lips met once more.

The kiss ignited with a spark that quickly became a blazing fire, consuming all thought and hesitation. It was passionate yet somehow reverent, a tribute to the brutal honesty that had marked their encounter from the start. Willa's fingers threaded through his dark black hair, anchoring herself to the moment, the man, and the burgeoning promise of release the night might hold.

Willa's breath caught in her throat as his lips trailed from her mouth down the elegant curve of her neck, lighting a trail of sensations that raced through her body. His hands, skilled and confident, explored her form with practiced expertise, leaving a trail of heat in their wake. Her fingers skimmed over his strong shoulders, feeling the defined muscles beneath his shirt and the tension in his pants as he pressed against her, a silent confirmation of her allure. In this moment, she reveled in her own sensuality, embracing the power she held over him without reservation.

This encounter awakened the dormant part of herself that relished being wanted and lusted after.

Willa leaned into him, her senses aflame, each touch eroding the walls built by years of guarded living. His scent enveloped her. She could feel the heat radiating from his body, the firmness of his chest against hers, and something more; an intensity that both scared and excited her.

He suddenly stilled. Willa opened her eyes to see him gazing at her, his eyes reflecting a storm of emotion.

"From…" he whispered, his thumb caressing her jawline, "from the moment I saw you, something inside me…knew…I just knew I'd regret it if I let you walk away."

His words hung between them, a confession laid bare in the vulnerability of the dimly lit room.

She nodded, not trusting herself to speak, her reply, a silent acceptance of his unspoken offer. They were two souls, momentarily escaping from the past, daring to reach out for a shared future, even if it lasted no longer than this single, electric night.

Willa traced his jawline with a shaking fingertip, her touch light as if she feared he might vanish like a dream at daybreak. His admission hung in the air, a fragile truth that connected them beyond the realm of physical desire.

"This isn't like me…anymore," she confessed, her voice a whisper that carried the pressure of years. "But…" She paused, searching for the courage to continue.

He drew her back into his arms, and their lips met. Willa lost herself in the sensation of his hands mapping the contours of her body, memorizing the places that made her sigh, places that made her moan.

It had been years since she'd allowed anyone this close to her. Her mind began to swirl. Instinctively, she felt the need to pull away. To run. The last man to touch her intimately had been Killian, and whether it would be intensely passionate or a violent struggle would depend on Killian's mood and his levels of sobriety.

Willa tried to remind herself this was a different man. This man didn't know her history, didn't know what she'd been through, and as far as Willa knew, he didn't care.

The stranger slid his hands from her waist to her hips, slowly raising the hem of her dress. Willa gasped as he slid his knee between her thighs, easing her legs apart.

"Wait," she gasped.

The mysterious man immediately stopped. He placed both palms on the wall, one on either side of her.

"Have you changed your mind?" he whispered into her neck. "It's okay if you have."

"I need a second," she panted.

He removed one hand from the wall, gently pushed Willa's hair away from her face, and looked deep into her eyes.

"We don't have to do this..." he said with sincerity in his voice. "I don't want to do anything you don't want to."

"I want to," Willa interrupted, "it's just...I..."

She really did want it. She wanted to feel someone else, anyone else. She wanted every last remaining cell aching to be desired, carnally craved, satiated. She wanted every last essence of Killian stripped from her body and her memory. Willa shook the hesitation from her thoughts.

"I want to."

"Are you certain?"

"Yes, just...start slow."

Her eyes locked with his as he slowly slipped the straps of her dress off her shoulders. The dress gathered momentarily around her hips before sliding to the floor.

Time became irrelevant, a trail of discarded clothing lining the floor from the door leading up to the bed. Willa let out a desperate sigh as the man laid her back on the bed, the weight of his body on top of her, the way his hands, his lips, his tongue, knew exactly where to touch her. She felt him slowly working his way down her body, licking, sucking, teasing her as he moved lower. Her hands ran her fingers through his hair, then gripped his scalp as she felt him spread her legs, the warmth of his breath caressing her skin.

"Should I stop?" she heard him ask rhetorically.

"Don't stop," she cried out as he slid his finger inside her, stroking her internally as his tongue moved expertly over her clit. By now, she could barely contain herself. She felt herself gently moving her hips to the rhythm he'd started. She hadn't felt this way in years; she had never allowed herself to release control... She never allowed herself that.

She felt him slide another finger in. Willa moaned, creating a desperate sound she had never heard herself make before. Her heart started beating faster, her breath matched the pace, and she was getting close.

"Not yet," she heard him whisper. "I want to feel it," he said commandingly.

He positioned himself on his knees, pulling her hips toward him. Her legs wrapped around his waist, close enough to feel him but not close enough for him to penetrate her. He worked his way back up her body, licking each breast, continuing up until he reached her lips. He kissed her, and she pushed his face to the side.

"Do it, do it, please," she begged.

With that, he pulled her hips to his and thrust himself deep inside her. She came almost instantly; she could feel her walls pulsing, pulling him in deeper. Waves of pleasure rolled over her as he kept going. Effortlessly, he turned her over, gripping her hips tighter as he entered her from behind; the heat from his body, the feeling of his breath on her neck, the sweat from his body dripping onto her, she felt him harden even more inside her.

Now, he was gasping for air, furiously trying to memorize every inch of her; the wet warmth of her around him, her scent, and her whimpers of pleasure intoxicated him. He could feel every tremble, pulsating, tightening inside her.

"Oh, God," she cried out again as she came.

The room was a hidden sanctuary where only their intertwined passions existed. They moved together, a fluid expression of the yearning that had blossomed between them.

"My turn," he said, his voice a low, intense groan before his release, then collapsing down beside her and cradling her in his arms.

And so, they continued throughout the night, passion and tenderness entwined, two people discovering a momentary connection that neither time nor circumstance could diminish. For those hours, they belonged solely to each other, and that belonging was a balm to every wound, a light in every shadowed corner of Willa's soul.

Chapter Nine

The Escape

ACT 2

The first light of dawn had yet to creep through the curtains, but Willa was already wide awake. Her dark eyes, usually so full of resolve, flickered with an unfamiliar uncertainty as she carefully disentangled herself from the crisp hotel sheets. She paused, watching the steady rise and fall of the man she met last night's chest as he slept, unaware of her internal turmoil.

With a silent grace that disguised her racing heart, Willa slid from the bed, her feet touching the plush carpet without a sound. She retrieved her clothes, strewn carelessly across the floor in the passion of the night before, a night that now felt like a fragile dream, poised to shatter at the slightest disturbance.

Willa's hands were steady as she collected the last remnants of her presence in the room: a stray earring here, a phone there, and her purse by the door. She dressed quickly, her movements delicate and efficient, a stark contrast to the chaotic whirl of her thoughts. The long, wavy hair that framed her face was hastily tied into a loose bun, a few strands escaping to brush against her cheeks. She glanced at the man in the bed again, his features softened by sleep and shadow, then turned away. She hesitated for a fraction of a second before slipping on her shoes, the soft heels clicking, muffled by the carpet.

In this quiet safeguard of the hotel room, nestled in the historic heart of Miami's South Beach, where the morning fog hung like ancient watchers, Willa felt a pull between her desire to flee and desperation to stay. But there was no place here for a woman who had learned that vulnerability often came with a price; one she would not pay again.

With her hand on the door handle, Willa exhaled a breath she hadn't realized she'd been holding. Just as the door began to open, a voice sliced through the silence, low and tinged with a rough edge of sleep.

"Jackson," he murmured, and she froze. His voice seemed to unfurl in the dimly lit space, reaching out to her retreating form. "My name is Jackson," he said softly and smirked.

"I'm...only here for a week," she said.

"Okay, Only-Here-For-A-Week, nice to meet you."

"Ugh...Willa," she said, pointing to herself, her back still facing him, blushing while looking at the floor with a touch of embarrassment that comes with being caught.

The words hung between them, heavy with implications and unspoken truths. Willa's grip on the door handle tightened. At that moment, the room felt simultaneously too vast and suffocatingly small as if it contained the entire breadth of her past mistakes and the slender hope of redemption.

"Regardless of what you might have heard," he continued, a note of earnestness threading through his groggy English voice. "I'm not someone who makes a habit of this."

Willa turned, her deep eyes meeting his in the half-light, acknowledging his confession.

"Suuure," Willa said, over-dramatically rolling her eyes and trying to deflect the touch of hopeful sincerity in her voice.

The silence stretched between them, laden with a vulnerability that Willa hadn't anticipated when she made the impulsive decision to leave. Her hand hovered over the knob, her resolve wavering as she turned back to face him, the early morning light spilling across the floor and casting long shadows.

"Look," she began, her voice barely above a whisper, "this isn't me either. I don't do this..." She trailed off, searching for the right words. "I've been trying to...figure some things out, trying to leave behind some...stuff weighing me down. That's...that's all this was." Her admission, which she immediately regretted sharing, hung in the air, a confession of her trouble.

He propped himself up on one elbow, the sheets slipping slightly to reveal a chest sculpted from a life of discipline, a complete contrast to the chaos that seemed to follow her lately. The warmth in his intense dark brown eyes seemed to reach out, offering solace in a world where Willa had become accustomed to finding none.

"Escape can be necessary sometimes," he said softly, his English accent wrapping around each word like silk. He swung his legs over the side of the bed, the movement fluid and sure. "But maybe instead of running away, you could walk...slowly...slow enough to be caught," he said with a harmless smirk on his face.

Willa's pulse raced at the implication. She wanted to scoff, to remind herself that connections made in the depths of dark alleys were as fleeting as the fog that clung to Miami's drunken streets come dawn. But something about his demeanor suggested he wasn't just weaving pretty words.

"I would very much like to see you again, Willa."

"Jackson," she said, letting his name roll off her tongue, tasting the possibility of it. Skepticism clawed at her, a familiar defense mechanism against potential heartache. Yet, a sincerity in Jackson's gaze chipped away at her reservations.

"I don't think so..." She paused. "See, my friend, were celebrating her engagement and there are so many commitments...that we...have...and not going to be here very long...and..."

His gaze never wavered. He quietly laughed at her list of excuses when it was clear Willa wanted to say yes.

"Fuck...okay, Jackson," Willa said, her voice steadier than she felt. She reached into her purse, pulling out one of her simple business cards. Her personal cell phone number was on the back of the card, as Willa frequently gave her cards away for networking purposes. She hesitated for a fraction of a second before handing it to him. The digits on the card felt like a lifeline thrown into the uncertain waters between them.

"Here's my number. Though, don't take it personally if I don't hold my breath waiting for a call." Her attempt at nonchalance couldn't quite mask the flicker of hope that betrayed her words.

"Trust me," he replied with a small, confident smile, "you'll be hearing from me."

As she stepped through the doorway, Willa felt the weight of her past begin to lift ever so slightly. Whether or not Jackson contacted her didn't matter. *Good choices or at least a good story,* she paraphrased Cassy and Lilly in her head. She was comfortable with a one-night stand, blaming lust at first sight. She hadn't allowed herself this type of indulgence in years. At that moment, giving her number was a small declaration of her willingness to open the door to new beginnings, regardless of how skeptical she might be.

***

Returning to her hotel, she reached the door to her room, fishing the key card from her bag. Sliding it into the slot, she felt a pang of guilt; Willa knew Cassy would be worried about her not coming home last night. Willa pushed open the door and was met by the disarray of their shared space; clothes strewn about, two beds in different states of being slept in, and travel brochures scattered across the dresser.

"Morning, sunshine," Cassy's voice greeted her from the half-light, tinged with humor but undercut with concern. "Seven a.m. You're up early."

"Nope, up late," Willa murmured, avoiding Cassy's probing gaze. "Need sleep." Willa collapsed onto her bed.

"Beachside brunch with the girls at 11:00, don't forget," Cassy teased.

"Shhhhhhhh," Willa noised while throwing an extra pillow mindlessly toward Cassy. "I just needed to get some air last night."

"Talk-dark-and-handsome air?" Cassy said, knowing her dear friend was lying. She gently tossed the pillow back on the bed. "You know you can talk to me, right?"

But her offer wasn't heard; Willa was fast asleep.

***

A sharp, piercing noise filled the room. Willa shot up out of bed. "What the hell?" she screamed. It was the alarm on the hotel clock next to Willa's bed. She smashed the button to make the infernal noise hush. 10:30 the clock read. Beside the clock, a note:

Beach bunch at 11. Love you! - Cass

PS Don't hate me for the alarm

The note made Willa smile. That was Cassy, the big sister Willa never had, always looking out for her.

"I don't deserve her," Willa mumbled to herself. She climbed out of bed, quickly washed up, and dressed for the day. Grabbing her phone as she walked toward the door, she noticed a missed text.

"Let's not make this a one-time thing. Meet me tonight? - Jax"

Willa blushed with disbelief. *"K,"* she responded. "K? Who the hell says 'K'...oh, whatever." She laughed, blaming her lack of sleep.

From the hotel room, Willa emerged refreshed, and pulled on a pair of oversized sunglasses, leaving the sanctuary of the room for the warmth and early Saturday morning chaos that awaited her on the palm-tree-lined streets of South Beach.

Chapter Ten

The Brunch

Willa's fingers traced the rim of her glass, the clink of ice, a subtle soundtrack to the noise of thoughts clamoring in her head. She glanced out over the beachfront, where the ocean met the sky in a seamless blend of blue, as if it were easy for two worlds to merge without destruction. Her gaze shifted back to her untouched mimosa, the bubbles rising and popping like the doubts surfacing within her.

"Earth to Willa." Sydney's voice, soft yet insistent, pulled her from her reverie.

"Cassy said you never came back to the hotel last night?" Emma's voice held a lilt of excitement as she leaned forward, elbows on the table, her green eyes sparkling with curiosity.

"Come on, you can't leave us hanging!" Sydney prodded gently, her warm brown eyes searching Willa's face for clues. "We need to know whose man you chose! I know it wasn't one of mine because I never introduced you."

"Neither did I," Cassy and Emma said in unison.

"Lilly?" Sydney questioned.

"Nope...what? Oh, yeah...I got distracted." Lilly laughed.

"Oh my God, was it him? Like HIM?" Sydney inquired. "We noticed he was gone too when you didn't come back to the table. Oh, I think it was him."

"Was he good?" Emma asked in a loud whisper, her hand almost covering her mouth as she asked, as if to make it unclear who asked such a provocative question at that early hour. Her bright green, innocent eyes sparkled.

The corner of Willa's mouth twitched into a shy smile, and she reflected on the previous night, an involuntary response betraying her. She knew her friends meant well, but the playful scrutiny was a reminder of just how much she had on the line. Her past, a shadowy specter, loomed behind every potential joy, tempering her smiles with caution.

"Sorry, girls, no one won," Willa responded, the words slipping out more subdued than intended. Her eyes flickered away, focusing on a seagull swooping down to snatch up a forgotten piece of bread on the sand. "I just needed to walk around and get some air. I'm sorry I bailed on you all."

"Completely understandable, and how was the air over at The M Hotel? Pretty classy place," Lilly chimed in.

"Refreshing," Willa responded with a scowl, almost like a toddler getting caught lying.

Sydney, Cassy, and Emma glanced at Lilly quizzically.

"Find a friend, anyone?" Lilly said, wiggling her phone back and forth in her hand. "Seriously? There are a million different apps that track your friends. Will and I have been dropping pins for each other for years when one of us...umm...'needs air.'" Lilly's eyes darted toward Willa.

A blush crept up Willa's neck, spreading across her cheeks as if painted by the softest brush. She tucked a loose strand of hair behind her ear, a small gesture of composure as she wrestled with the thrill of the unknown and the weight of history. Her heart fluttered at the thought of Jackson, his text message a promise of possibilities, but her mind caged her heart in ribs of steel, urging restraint.

"All right, maybe there was a guy," Willa managed to say, her tone light but her grip on the glass tightening imperceptibly.

"Ooh, she admits it!" Emma exclaimed, her laughter ringing clear and bright.

"Easy there," Sydney cautioned with a smile. "Let's not scare her off."

"Scare me off?" Willa quirked an eyebrow, the hint of a genuine smile playing on her lips despite her reservations.

Willa's fingers paused around her glass, the condensation cool against her skin. She watched Lilly's expression oscillate from incredulity to amusement, feeling a cocktail of emotions stir within her. It had been a long time since her romantic life was the subject of such speculation, and she wasn't sure if she relished the scrutiny or preferred to deflect it entirely.

"Really, though?" Lilly pressed, leaning forward with elbows on the table, disbelief ingrained in her features. "I mean...tell me about him and—"

"And what?" Willa sternly interjected.

"And is it a one-time thing, a little vacation fling, or are you head over heels already?" Lilly scoffed.

Willa straightened her posture slightly.

"He texted me this morning," she continued, holding Lilly's gaze. "We might see each other again tonight."

A ripple of disappointment washed over Lilly's face, her eyebrows arching high. The group fell into a brief silence, the crashing waves in the distance filling the void as they digested Willa's words.

"Hit it and quit it, girl!" Lilly finally said, her tone shifting from intrigue to annoyance. "You're setting yourself up for inevitable heartbreak. You do remember we don't actually live here, right? Will, what is your plan for when we leave in six days? Don't. Get. Attached." She laughed.

"I don't know, Lil, can't you just let me enjoy this for a moment?" Willa said, tossing her head back with an overly exaggerated whine.

She didn't want to reveal too much, especially when trying not to get too ahead of herself. She didn't know where this would lead and Lilly was right, sort of. The last time Willa felt an intense attraction to a man who seemed larger than life was Killian. And Willa had been spending the past three years, a shell of her former self, with the type of hypervigilant, overprotective, paranoia that comes with having your entire world shattered by the person you believed you could trust no matter what.

But the warmth in her chest at the thought of seeing Jackson again was undeniable, a spark that she cautiously wished to nurture.

"Let's not get ahead of ourselves," Willa replied, her pragmatic side surfacing. "As of right now, it was one…very enjoyable night. I'm glad I did it, and that's all I'm going to say about it." She made a motion to lock her lips and seal them. Yet inside, for the first time in a while, she felt the flicker of something more than just hope—a dangerous belief that maybe this time, things could be different.

The light banter of new topics and stories retold filled the air as the sharp buzz of her phone cut through the laughter. Willa's hand instinctively reached for the device, her fingers brushing against the screen as if they could sense the significance of the message awaiting her. It was Jackson.

"See you tonight - Jax" the text read, each word igniting a spark within her.

Willa couldn't help but smile, a genuine expression that lifted the corners of her mouth and brightened her expressive eyes. The flutter in her chest transformed into a surge of excitement, a current of anticipation that charged through her veins. For a moment, she allowed herself to bask in the warmth of the possibility that lay in those simple words.

"Is that him?" Sydney asked, leaning in closer, her instincts homed in on the shift in Willa's demeanor.

"The secret lover returns," Emma chimed in, her green eyes alight and curious.

Willa nodded, holding up her phone, her smile lingering like the shy afterglow of a beautiful sunset.

"He's looking forward to tonight," she shared, her voice carrying a note of complicated confidence, as if she were still piecing together the reality of it all.

Emma grabbed the phone from Willa's hand to see the text closer and read aloud, "Oh 'see you tonight – Jax.' So mysterious," Emma squeaked then exaggerating his name as it rolled off her lips.

"What kind of a name is Jax?" Sydney scoffed.

"Sounds like a frat boy," Cassy continued with a laugh.

"His name is Jackson," Willa laughed, covering her face with her hands in embarrassment.

"Actually, 'Jax' is a pretty common nickname. Hollywood's new little 'IT' boy is a 'Jax,' so expect the name to spread like wildfire," Lilly said while aimlessly scrolling through her phone, tagging herself in social media posts. "Will's man's ahead of the trend."

And there, amid the gentle teasing and shared smiles, the sun had begun its afternoon descent, casting a golden hue over the horizon as the brunch drew to a close. Willa rose from her seat. She was going to need to get some rest before tonight, having barely slept the night before.

CHAPTER ELEVEN

The Second Night

Willa perched on the edge of a plush velvet armchair in the lobby of her Miami hotel, her mind adrift in the sensual haze of last night's memories. The air was heavy with the scent of antique wood polish, and outside, the earlier day's heat began to retreat to evening coolness that promised to swaddle the city in a humid embrace.

She caught herself tracing the outline of her lips with her fingertips, each touch reigniting the tingling sensation of Jackson's kiss. Her heart danced to a nervous rhythm, eager for the sequel. Willa's eyes, those deep pools reflecting years of pain and new-found hope, betraying her anticipation as they flickered toward the entrance every few seconds.

A sudden roar shattered the serene atmosphere of the lobby. Heads turned toward the roar; a throaty growl of an engine announcing its dominion over the startled guests in the hotel lobby.

Through the grand arches of the entrance, a flash of yellow burst into view, as out of place among the genteel backdrop as a peacock in a flock of doves. Unimpressed, Willa let out a heavy sigh, and she stood abruptly, smoothing the fabric of her dress in an unconscious effort to calm her nerves.

The car, an audacious sculpture of metal and speed, pulled up to the hotel entry doors with unabashed confidence. The driver's door swung open, and out stepped Jackson, his athletic frame at ease even as he emerged from the beastly machine that seemed to snarl quietly behind him.

Jackson flashed a boyish grin enhanced by the five o'clock shadow dusting his jaw; his chiseled features softened by the gesture as he sauntered toward the hotel. "Back in a minute," he announced to the hotel valet, a kind way to tell them not to touch the car.

His dark brown eyes found Willa's immediately, locking onto her with a gaze that seemed to peel back layers of her very soul. He moved with the grace of someone utterly aware of the space he occupied, yet he seemed oblivious to the spectacle he'd caused with his arrival.

"There she is," he called to her, his English accent wrapping around the words like velvet. "I hope you're ready for a little adventure."

Willa felt a rush of exhilaration that matched the bold statement of his vehicle. She took a step forward, the pull between them undeniable, as the rest of the world faded to a mere backdrop for the story they were beginning to write together.

The lobby had transformed into a stage, the evening light casting long shadows that seemed to spotlight Willa as she took in the murmurs and sideways glances from the gathered crowd. Her heart fluttered with a mix of excitement and unease, a familiar anxiety creeping up her spine like ivy. She could almost hear the whispers weaving through the air, stitching her name into stories she hadn't lived.

"Is that..." a hushed voice trailed off near the entrance.

"Can't be...here," another muttered, barely audible above the hum of idle chatter.

Willa's eyes darted about, seeking the source of the murmurs. The heavy scent of whiskey mingled with the mahogany of the lobby bar, giving the air an extra charge as if an electric current was pulsing through the grand space, connecting each onlooker in a web of shared intrigue.

She pressed her lips together, bracing herself for the weight of judgment, when it dawned on her—the collective gaze wasn't fixed on her but rather slid past, locking onto the man who'd just stepped out of that screaming yellow spectacle. Jackson. Of course. It wasn't her they were dissecting with their curious stares, it was him.

A wash of relief tinged with embarrassment colored her cheeks. She should have known. In this town, she was unknown; no one knew her history or her story. But what about Jackson? It was Miami, well-dressed men with smoldering good looks, showing their wealth through toys that cost more than a typical house was the norm here. But people seemed to care an unsettling amount about him, and Willa was utterly unaware of why.

She stepped forward, her resolve firming with each stride toward Jackson. *Adventure indeed*, she thought, a slight smirk playing on her lips. This city, so diverse with experiences, now held the promise of new memories, ones not marred by shadows but illuminated by the unexpected brilliance of a mysterious stranger.

"Shall we?" Jackson's voice, his intoxicating accent she couldn't get enough of, binding around each word. His gaze held hers, and in the depths of those dark brown eyes flecked with gold, there was an unspoken promise; a journey away from the familiar cobbled streets and whispering palms, toward something unknown and thrilling.

Willa nodded, feeling the last tendrils of anxiety slip away with the warmth of his smile. He released her hand only to open the passenger door of the ostentatious yellow convertible top sports car. She slid into the seat, the leather cool and smooth beneath her, and watched as he closed the door with a soft click that signaled the beginning of their departure.

The engine purred to life, a resonant thrum that vibrated through the chassis and into Willa's core. As Jackson navigated the vehicle south, away from the hotel, the historic cityscape gave way to lush greenery, the change so gradual it felt like passing through a living threshold between two worlds. Willa let her gaze wander over the landscape as the wind flowed through her hair. She watched as the Spanish moss on the old Florida oaks danced lightly in the breeze, an ethereal ballet set to the evening light.

They drove in companionable silence, the tension that had wound itself tightly around Willa's thoughts unraveling with every mile they put between themselves and the city. There was a sense of liberation in the speed, in the freedom of moving forward without a clear destination, and she found herself leaning into the sensation, letting it wash over her like the fresh, crisp air that promised a reprieve from the humidity.

Before long, the road began snaking its way through a dense thicket of woods where the sunlight dappled the ground in patches of gold. The longer they drove, the more picturesque the view became, until finally, Jackson eased the car to a stop at the edge of a secluded beach just off an indiscriminate gravel and dirt road.

Stepping out, Willa took in the expanse before her, a breathtaking vista overlooking a part of the Atlantic that looked untouched by human hands. Here, on this precipice between earth and ether, surrounded by the untamed beauty of nature, she felt small yet infinite, tethered to the moment by the man who stood beside her.

Jackson turned to her, a soft seriousness in his expression. "I like to come down here when life gets a bit...unruly," he said, looking up at the overgrown oaks. "It reminds me of home, well, except for the heat." He smiled.

Willa could only nod, knowing words would fall short in describing the quiet majesty of their secret, completely secluded point. Here, with him, just for a moment, she could breathe, truly breathe, for what felt like the first time in years.

"Where is home?" Willa said almost to herself while sliding gracefully away from the car, her movements fluid as though she were part of the breeze that swept along the seaside. Delicately stepping through the rocky pseudo-road in her high-heeled strappy sandals, she found balance on the hood of the car, its surface still warm from their drive. The air here was different, crisper, tinged with the scent of pine and earth. The scent brought her back to her childhood along the Potomac to the Chesapeake Bay, long before life had corroded her innocence. With a sigh, she leaned back on her palms, tilting her face toward the sun, allowing the serenity of the secluded spot to envelop her.

"Quite an entrance you made back there. People seemed pretty interested," she said, her voice casual but her eyes flickering with amusement as she glanced at Jackson.

Jackson's lips quirked into a half-smile, his shoulders shrugging off the statement like it was nothing more than a leaf caught in the wind. "Ah, I suppose some people might know me from work," he said, his tone effortlessly light, yet Willa detected a hint of something guarded behind those intense dark brown eyes.

"Work?" Willa prodded gently; her curiosity piqued by the way he deflected attention from himself.

"London," he sidestepped smoothly, moving back to her previous question. The warmth of his smile didn't quite reach his gaze. Changing the subject, he leaned against the car beside her, his posture relaxed. "But enough about me. Tell me, Willa—what brings you from Georgia to Miami?"

"I never told you where I was from," Willa tensed, a slight panic in her voice.

"You didn't have to, Madame Sullivan," he said with a wink. "It was right on your business card." Jackson laughed, tapping his pocket where her business card from last night resided. Willa dropped her head down in embarrassment. She completely forgot the card had not only her cell phone number but also her name, office location, and company.

"Miami, this trip," she began, choosing her words carefully and deliberately, "it represents a turning point of sorts. When I leave here, I want to remember the past doesn't have to define the present." Her gaze found his, holding it. "Just...moving forward, you know?"

"Moving forward," he echoed softly. There was a depth of understanding in his response, a quiet acknowledgment of a life Willa didn't know yet.

Willa ran her fingers through the tendrils of her dark wavy hair, lifted by a gentle breeze that carried the earthy scent of the woods. She inhaled deeply, feeling the weight of the past beginning to dissolve in the fresh, wooded air.

"Four years ago, my world turned upside down," she confessed, her voice low but steady.

"I was...entangled...with someone who didn't really exist, who took more from me than I thought I had to give." She hesitated, her eyes reflecting the struggle of memory against the desire to move beyond it.

"Coming here was impulsive. My friend's engagement was a convenient excuse for me to have an attempt to replace some of those torturous memories with something lighthearted and fun."

Jackson's gaze lingered on her face, reading the lines of sorrow etched there and the resilience shining through. "Celebrating survival then?" he asked, his tone encouraging her to continue peeling back the layers of her story.

"Exactly," Willa affirmed, a small smile curving her lips. "I will never be who I once was, but I don't have to stay like this, anxious, constantly looking over my shoulder. I want to live for myself again...and not hiding in the shadows of regret...of what I used to be."

His eyes hardened, and she noticed the subtle shift in his demeanor—a momentary cloud shadowing his features as if her words resonated with echoes of his own history. To his surprise, Jackson found himself silently enraged by her words, oddly protective over the woman he barely knew. To him, her vulnerability was a flame of strength that no one should have tried to quench.

His gaze softened. "Sounds like a rebirth then," he mused, leaning back on his palms as he sat beside her on the hood.

"Letting go isn't easy," he continued. "I've had my share of moments I wish I could erase...choices that seemed right...but left scars too deep to ignore."

Her heart skipped a beat at the rare glimpse into his vulnerability.

"We all have our battles, I guess," Willa replied, finding courage in their shared confidences.

"Indeed," he said, a quiet strength returning to his voice. "But we also have now...this moment, always this moment...every day a new chance to be who we want to be."

The trees whispered above them, leaves rustling in agreement, as the last rays of sunlight spilled up from the horizon, bathing them in a golden glow.

Willa's breath caught as she watched the changing hues of deep browns and golds in Jackson's eyes, the waning sunlight revealing a sea of emotion across his gaze. In that suspended moment, the world seemed to shrink until there was nothing but the space between them, charged with a silent understanding.

She rose from the hood, drawn by an invisible thread woven through their shared confessions, and closed the distance with deliberate steps. Her heart drummed a frenzied rhythm against her ribs, each beat anchoring her deeper into the now.

"Jackson," she whispered, her voice barely audible over the rustle of leaves and the cascading waves.

He turned to face her fully, and the intensity in his eyes was like gravity, pulling her into his orbit. Willa reached out, her fingertips grazing the stubble along his jawline, tracing the contours of strength shown there.

"Yes," he replied, the word a soft caress that sent shivers dancing down her spine.

Their faces were inches apart, the air ripe with anticipation. The last sliver of sun dipped below the horizon, and in the twilight, Willa felt as if they were the only two souls in existence. She tilted her head, her lips parting slightly as she surrendered to the magnetic pull.

Jackson met her halfway, his hands finding her waist, guiding her closer. Their kiss was gentle at first, a tentative exploration that soon ignited into something more, a blaze of need and desire that consumed all thoughts of past pains and future uncertainties.

Willa wrapped her arms around his neck, pulling him nearer, lost in the sensation of his lips moving against hers. They kissed with a fervor that spoke of new beginnings and healed wounds, a promise of what could be woven into the very fabric of their embrace.

Around them, the natural amphitheater of the seaside echoed the whispers of leaves and the subtle shifts of the earth. But within the confines of Jackson's arms, Willa found a peace that had eluded her for years. Here, on this secluded little stretch of land overlooking the tapestry of colors in the south Florida sunset, she rediscovered a piece of herself long buried under the rubble of her former life.

The kiss deepened, and Willa pressed herself against him, feeling the solid warmth of his body now mixed with the chilled metal hood of the car behind him, grounding her to the present. This was not the desperate clutching of past encounters but the melding of two souls seeking solace and understanding in each other's touch.

They broke apart only when the need for air became undeniable, foreheads resting together as they shared the same breath, the same heartbeat. Words were unnecessary; the truth of their connection was written in the stars above and the earth beneath, in the entwining of fingers and the lingering taste of passion on their lips.

Something came over Willa, something deep and primal. She slowly started unbuttoning his shirt while lightly pushing his chest back, causing him to lean back bracing himself on his forearms on the hood of the car. She slowly guided her hands down his chest, her lips delicately following her hands, lips barely brushing against him and teasing him. Her hands made their way to his belt. She could feel him stiffen under her arms as she desperately worked at unbuttoning and unzipping his pants while she feverishly licked and kissed his lower abdomen.

He leaned back further and placed his hands on her temples in an attempt to gently guide her mouth lower to where he craved to feel her most. He lifted his hips as she worked to free him from his jeans, sliding them down just enough to release him. The cooled night air mixed with the heat of her breath on him caused him to gasp. She slowly began to lick around the base of him before wrapping her hand around where she had been so focused. She continued to lick her way up the full length of him while using her hand sliding up and down him rhythmically, with firm pressure that sent an eclectic shock through his system. She flicked her tongue rapidly back and forth over the head of his cock teasing him.

He moaned with a deep growl, "Oh, Will..." He started to call out her name but, in that moment, she took him full into her mouth. "Fuck," he purred, gripping the hood of the car tighter to remain balanced.

She continued to work him, her heart racing, confidence in her abilities returning. She knew him; instinctively, she knew what he would like. She slipped her free hand under him, caressing his balls.

"Willa, don't stop, fuck, don't stop."

She felt him harden more in her mouth; she could feel the pulse in his groin quicken, and she knew he was close. She didn't understand why he was important, but she knew after the hotel he was "someone," and now, bent over him, she had complete control over him. It was a type of power she hadn't felt in years; a piece of Old Willow was returning. The thought of her command over him, his vulnerability in this moment, intimidated and excited her.

Focus, she said to her mind. She memorized every inch of his cock with her tongue.

"Willa, I'm coming," he cried, but she didn't pull away.

She wanted to take him in, all of him. She felt the thick salted heat flood into her mouth.

I want to keep him inside me, her thoughts screamed as she swallowed. She straightened her posture, wiping the remnants of him off her mouth with the back of her hand.

"Holy fuck," he whispered trying to regain control over his breath. He sat up, adjusting himself, pulling himself back together. "I wasn't expecting that," he said, his delicious accent emphasizing each slowly released word.

"Who are you?" Willa demanded. "Why do people know you? Why are you here from London?"

Willa wanted to take advantage of his unguarded, post-orgasmic high when she knew his defenses were lower.

"Tricky girl," he deeply sighed, realizing her plan. "Actor," he said.

"Probably know me from work," she replied, mimicking his accent and his comment from earlier in the evening. "I guess I should apologize for not recognizing you from what I can only assume is a catalog of very important works," she said, adding a wink.

"Cute," he said with a huff, his mouth forming into that same smile that made Willa weak at the club. "Let's get out of here, and I'll tell you everything."

He took her hand and guided her back to the passenger side of the car, the devilish, sly smirk never leaving his face.

They drove not far to a small, quiet restaurant. They were seated in a small private booth near the back, away from prying eyes.

She knew she needed to eat something, but all she could think about was getting back to his hotel. She wasn't finished with him tonight.

***

Dinner seemed like a typical first date. They were obviously good at the *other* important parts of a relationship, but they still didn't know each other. They talked about the usually superficial things people talk about on first dates, but something inside Jackson told him to go deeper.

"This morning, you mentioned there were some things you were trying to escape. Is one of those things a man?"

"Are you intuitive, or psychic, or do I have 'my ex is an asshole' written somewhere on my face?"

"I like to think intuitive. I like to think I know how to read people. But I could be wrong." He paused. "Last night, there was just something...different... I felt it. You were clearly just using me at first, but then something changed. Tell me I'm wrong. It's been a long time since you were touched like that...and the last man who tried...didn't deserve you."

Willa's eyes glossed with tears that she instinctively forced away.

"How... did you know that?" Willa continued, "Three years ago, I finally realized there was no other option but to run. Run from my abusive ex, start over, become someone new, or at least change for the better... I didn't like who I saw myself becoming when I was with him," Willa stated. "He brought out the worst in me...and me in him. It scared me how similar we were. One time it was so bad...I didn't think I would survive." Willa caught her breath, scared by her vulnerability. "I'm sorry, I don't know why I'm telling you all this. I don't even know you."

"It's all right… I was once a very different person, too." He paused and stared off as if unsure if he wanted to continue. He felt the only way to ease her discomfort would be to be vulnerable and transparent himself.

"Back when things started to take off for me, I was young and stupid. I had this girlfriend since oh…I don't know…birth, I guess," he said with a slight, uneasy laugh. "She had supported my dream, my vision. She supported me through drama school and came to every stage performance. Truly devoted and I…I had just landed a supporting role in my first internationally released film. And just before I left to film, I broke up with her. I thought I was too good for her, and she wasn't enough to be seen on my arm anymore… What a prick I was to her. Day one of shooting, I started hooking up with a co-star, someone I thought was a better look for me. It didn't last, of course. She, my co-star, surpassed me, by leaps and bounds; she truly was an amazing actor, she still is. But I wasn't good enough, wasn't a big enough star…to be with her…"

"Tables turned," Willa said snarkily.

"I went through an angry phase, too arrogant to admit what an…" He shook the memory from his head. "I started shagging anything in a skirt, co-stars, bar maids, fangirls, drinking, drugs, I was out of control. My family was worried; my sister and my mates tried to ground me. Nothing worked. Obviously, I knew better than anyone, right?" He paused. "And then I saw her again a few years later. We made eye contact; she still hated me. She turned around and," he motioned with his hand, "gone straight away. And it hit…what the fuck was I doing, who the fuck had I become? A little bit of attention and I'd lost my fucking mind. These women around me, the "mates" and fans…none of it was real. She had been real…and genuinely cared about me, and I threw it away. Later, I tried to contact her. I just wanted to apologize, but she wouldn't have it…rightly so."

"Wow…you're an asshole," Willa chimed in with a smirk.

"Was. I was an arsehole." He smiled. "About a week later, she sold the story to a tabloid, made a nice lil mint, told them I had come crawling back."

He laughed nervously. "Such a backlash; no one wanted to put up with me...and I deserved all of it. I made myself a promise after seeing that story, the things I did in print for anyone who wanted to see...embarrassing... I was ashamed of that man. I vowed to stay grounded, keep around the people who would call me out on my shit. I would stay focused and work toward success but never make it more than it was...a job. True connection. Real relationships with real people, that's what matters. I don't ever want to see that arrogant little prick in the mirror. And thanks to some tough love and support, I think I've done all right since then."

"And here I thought when all my dirty little secrets came out, it was bad," she said, trying to lighten the mood.

"When I met you that first night, when I saw you, I couldn't stop looking at you. I know it sounds like a line, but I noticed you notice me and..." Jackson waved his fingers in front of his face, "no recognition. Like, truly no idea... I felt like you actually saw me. I know I'm not huge here in the States...yet... But in the UK, it's very different. If I'm being honest, it's been a very long time since I've felt genuinely anonymous."

Willa was intrigued, fascinated by this creature before her but all she could do was stare at his lips as he talked. She remembered last night when those lips consumed her. A flush came over her chest, and her pulse quickened. She gently shook her head and adjusted her posture to come back to the current moment with him.

He slid closer to her in the booth. "Are you even listening?"

"Actor, London, angry, asshole," she repeated in an attempt to prove she wasn't simply distracted by his looks.

He slid closer, put his arm around her shoulders and whispered into her ear. "I want you." He slid his hand up her thigh under her dress, resting his hand between her thighs; she was already wet. With a finger, he slid her panties to the side, simultaneously slipping another finger inside her. She inhaled deeply.

"Make a sound...and I'll stop," he whispered in her ear.

She bit her lip and slowly closed her eyes.

"Look at me," he commanded.

She turned her hips to the side, facing him, staring intently into his deep, dark eyes.

"Good girl," he whispered.

The way he was looking at her, his head tipped slightly down, but looking up into her eyes, the type of deep, penetrating, smoldering look she could only assume had graced numerous films and magazine spreads. He licked his lips lightly as if she were his prey and he was impatiently waiting to devour her.

"Check, please," Willa breathed.

***

The drive back to the hotel was excruciating. Willa was impatient. *Drive faster*, begged her mind. With every shift of the manual transmission Jackson would touch her thigh, an attempt to keep the fire he ignited in the restaurant ablaze until they got back to the room where he could privately finish what he started.

"Thanks, mate," Jackson said, tossing his keys to the valet. His urgency was palpable; he needed to get Willa upstairs. The elevator door opened, empty and inviting. Jackson quickly tapped the button for his floor, his eyes never leaving Willa's.

As the doors closed, Jackson pinned Willa against the elevator wall, his lips finding her neck with an almost desperate hunger. His hands firmly held her waist, pulling her closer, his body pressed forcefully against hers. Willa's breath caught in her throat as she felt the heat of his body through their clothes. She tossed her head back, surrendering to the moment, and noticed a small security camera in the corner of the elevator ceiling.

The thought of someone watching them sent a thrill through her. The excitement of being seen brought out an adventurous side of her she hadn't felt in a long time, a side she thought she had buried with her past. But then, a wave of terror washed over her. The vulnerability and the exposure—what if this got out? What if her past caught up with her through a lens?

The elevator dinged, the doors sliding open. Jackson grabbed her hand, leading her swiftly down the hallway to his room. Willa's heart raced, not just from their elevator encounter but from the conflicting emotions warring within her. She glanced at Jackson's determined face, feeling a mix of fear and exhilaration.

Finally, they were inside his suite. The door clicked shut behind them, sealing out the world.

Finally, we're alone, Willa thought, a sense of relief flooding over her. Jackson's demeanor shifted; the urgency of the elevator ride gave way to a deeper, more deliberate passion.

He led her to the center of the room, his touch now gentle, almost reverent. He looked into her eyes, searching for any hesitation, any sign of doubt. Finding none, he brushed a strand of hair from her face, his fingers lingering on her cheek.

"Are you okay?" he asked softly, his voice a tender contrast to the heated moments in the elevator.

Willa nodded, her anxiety ebbing away.

"Yes," she whispered. "More than okay."

Jackson smiled, his eyes darkening with desire. He pulled her into a slow, searing kiss, his hands tracing the curve of her back. The excitement of their public encounter transformed into a slow-building burn, a fire that promised to consume them both, but at a pace that allowed them to savor every moment.

Willa felt a calmness settle over her, the fears of the elevator slipping away. Here, in this private refuge, she felt safe, cherished. Jackson's touch was sure and steady, his kisses a promise of more to come. As their clothes began to fall away, piece by piece, Willa let herself be fully present, fully open to the possibilities of this new chapter in her life.

Jackson's hands roamed her body with a blend of familiarity and exploration, as if he wanted to memorize every inch of her. He guided her to the bed, laying her down gently, his eyes never leaving hers. Willa reached up, pulling him down to her, their bodies aligning perfectly.

The room was filled with the soft sounds of their shared breaths, the rustle of sheets, and the occasional murmur of a name whispered in the dark. The world outside ceased to exist, leaving only the two of them, lost in each other.

CHAPTER TWELVE
The Introduction

P ing. Willa's phone chimed.

"What time are we meeting at his hotel's pool?" Lilly texted to their Miami group chat.

"1 p.m. but I probably should tell you noon so you will show up on time =P," Willa responded snarkily at Lilly's constant insistence on showing up "fashionably late for fashionably late."

"Well, I do like to make an entrance," Lilly added.

"Welcome to the Lilly Show," Sydney wrote. *"Don't be mad when we are three drinks deep by the time you show up."*

"SQEEEE," a noise shrieked from the other room. Willa and Sydney dropped their phones to run to the adjoining room where Emma was waving her hands at the TV and jumping up and down.

"WILLLLA," she continued while running to Willa, grabbing her by the arm and dragging her over to the TV.

"Is THAT him???" Emma continued, but on the screen was a grey-haired news anchorman clearly in his 60s.

"Um...who?"

"Your Jackson! I KNEW he looked familiar!"

"Emma, that's an old man."

"No, no before, it was a commercial, ugh... Where is my phone?!" Emma scurried around the room, looking under the discarded clothing from her suitcase and looking for her phone. Once secured in her hand, she yelled, "Got it!" She started furiously typing on her screen.

"Em? Are you ok?" Sydney laughed. "What is happening right now? Are you having a stroke?"

"LOOOK!" Emma pulled up images on her phone and rapidly scrolled through them for the group. The images were of a man who was clearly "Willa's Jackson."

"Is your Jax, THE JAX, Jackson? As in JCD? As in Jackson Cole Donovan? THIS man?"

"Umm... Well, that definitely looks a lot like the man I've been sleeping with so...yes!" Willa laughed with a touch of embarrassment.

"How did you not tell us the man from the club was HIM?"

"I honestly didn't find out anything about him being an actor till last night, and even then, we didn't talk that much about it."

Emma reached over and gently popped Sydney in the shoulder. "I TOLD YOU HE LOOKED FAMILIAR. You said I was just drunk." She scowled.

"Okay, okay, yes, Em, you were clearly right."

"Willa, Syd and I binge-watched that show's first season over a weekend last summer. He's really good!" Emma's eyes gleamed, partly proud she had been kind of right about the mystery man and also filled with joy for Willa. "Willa's going to marry a celebrity."

"Whoa, easy there, kiddo. It's been two days, and we leave here in a few more. I don't know if we will even speak to each other again after this week." Willa laughed nervously.

"What is all the commotion?" Cassy entered the room with a tray of iced coffees for the group.

"Willa's dating a celebrity!" Emma jumped at the chance to share the fun news. She proceeded to catch Cassy up on the morning's gossip.

"Okay, yes, I guess he is kind of a big deal, but please, PLEASE, try not to focus on that today. Calm, simple, normal people today...especially around Lilly. I don't want her getting all...ya know."

"Lillified?" Sydney laughed.

The group knew precisely what Willa was talking about. Lilly had a desperate love of attention and having always dreamed of being on stage herself, being in proximity to anyone of note brought out a more dramatic starlet-wannabe side to Lilly that could be too much to take.

"Maybe she won't recognize him?" Emma said.

"Wishful thinking, Em," Willa retorted. "That girl knows everything about everyone."

***

The soft chimes of the grand clock in the hotel lobby marked a new hour, and as if on cue, Jackson emerged from the gilded elevator. The atmosphere seemed to shift upon his entrance, a current of electricity charged the air with anticipation. His dark hair was a stark contrast against his crisp pale blue shirt, the sleeves carelessly rolled up to his elbows, revealing tanned forearms. Willa held her breath quietly as she observed the confident manner in which he navigated through the sea of people, his gaze finding theirs across the room.

"Good afternoon, ladies," Jackson greeted them, his English accent adding an extra layer of charm to his words. "I hope you're finding everything to your liking."

Sydney was the first to respond, her voice betraying a hint of awe. "It's absolutely beautiful here. Thank you for inviting us."

Jackson's focus shifted seamlessly from one friend to another, his intense brown eyes locking onto Sydney's with genuine interest. "I'm glad to hear it," he said.

As the conversation flowed, Willa remained quietly observant, noting how each of her friends seemed to light up under Jackson's regard. It wasn't simply his looks or his fame that captivated them; it was the way he made each person feel seen, heard, and respected. The group stood together in the opulent terraced lobby, yet for those moments, they might as well have been in a world of their own making, crafted by shared laughter and the easy rapport that Jackson fostered among them.

"Ladies!" A familiar voice cut through the air. Lilly walked forward, a mischievous glint in her eye as she walked up to Emma by the bar. "See this is where we should have stayed. You will never guess who I passed walking in here."

"Who?" Emma asked.

"Jackson...Cole...Donovan, the actor. I swear to God he is even better looking in person," Lilly said.

"Oh yeah," Emma said calmly.

Lilly tipped her head to the side, confused by Emma's lack of excitement. "Oh, little Em, do you not know who he is? He's only Hollywood's new golden boy; everyone is trying to get a piece of him. Do you know what being tagged in a photo with him could do for me?"

"Sure...I don't think Willa would mind." Emma politely shrugged.

"What? Why would Willa care about any of this?" Lilly said, eyes squinting as if she could burn a hole through Emma.

"He's Willa's Jackson!" Emma said, pointing over to Willa and the rest of their little group, including Jackson. "See, look over there."

"What...Will's Jackson, the guy from the club the other night, and her mysterious disappearing act? Well, isn't this a fun little development?" Lilly said with a tinge of jealousy.

"Yep. They met at the club that night, Lil."

"Yeah, I put that together, Em," Lilly said shortly as she walked closer to the rest of the group through the crowds of inquisitive eyes.

"Hello, everyone," Lilly announced to bring attention to herself. "Looks like we are in the presence of Hollywood royalty, 'Jax,'" she purred, while using air quotes playfully trying to impress anyone in earshot of her knowledge and proximity to him.

As if compelled by some unspoken challenge, Lilly sauntered closer to Jackson, her hips swaying with confidence.

Willa felt an uneasy knot forming in her stomach.

Lilly's fingers grazed Jackson's forearm, a seemingly casual touch that lingered a fraction too long, the licking of her lower lip hinting at intentions far from innocent.

"Must be thrilling," Lilly continued, tilting her head to lock eyes with him, "having everyone know your name, hanging onto your every word."

Willa held her breath, watching the exchange. The tension in the air was palpable, the charged silence before a thunderstorm. She couldn't help but wonder if Jackson would be swayed by Lilly's overt display.

Shit, Willa thought, *here we go.*

Jackson met Lilly's gaze, his expression unreadable for a moment. Then, with a graceful ease that seemed inherent to his nature, he stepped back, breaking the contact between them. He offered Lilly a smile, warm yet distant, like how you would approach something fragile you didn't want to get too close to.

"Flattering as that may seem," he said, his tone even and calm, "I find genuine relationships far more rewarding than mere recognition." His eyes flickered briefly to Willa, a silent, calming message of reassurance shared between them.

"Besides," Jackson added, turning his attention back to the group, a playful note in his voice, "it's the stories and history of people and places that truly capture my interest. Fame is so temporary, nothing more than an illusion that far too many of us get wrapped up in."

"Damn," Sydney whispered to Cassy. "He's deep."

"I know." Cassy nodded with a pleasantly surprised look.

The others nodded in agreement, the atmosphere relaxing once more as Jackson effortlessly steered the conversation away from himself and back toward the collective experience. Lilly, though momentarily taken aback by his deflection, recovered her poise with a tight-lipped smile and retreated to her seat.

Willa exhaled quietly, her thoughts racing, she suddenly felt the pain of competition. Jackson was someone that was globally desired. She felt foolish for not recognizing him instantly as Lilly had, but one glance from Jackson and her heart slowed its frantic pace. Willa felt an unexpected kinship with him. Even amid the luxury and grandeur of the hotel, it was the simple, honest moments like these that resonated the deepest.

Lilly leaned against the intricately carved mahogany bar, her fingers trailing along the polished surface as she watched Jackson mingle with the others. The clink of ice against the crystal echoed faintly, mirroring the chill that had settled in her chest. Lilly was jealous of Jackson. He had the life she wanted. Loved by random people, casual acquaintances, and close friends alike. She wanted people to follow her, take her picture, and be influenced by every detail of her life. It was the type of jealousy she had felt toward Willa since college, but worse. Jackson was a real celebrity, and now, if this all worked out, Willa would be the one who skyrocketed to fame on the arm of Hollywood's elite.

Not fair, Lilly thought, *she doesn't even want that type of attention. It should be me with him.*

***

As Willa leaned against the marble high-top bar table, a trio of laughter caught her ear, drawing her gaze across the room. Three men, unmistakably part of Jackson's entourage from the night they met, approached with an easy confidence that matched their host's magnetic charm. One was tall with sandy blond hair, another sported a beanie despite the Miami heat, and the third, whose arm was slung over the shoulders of his companions, had an infectious grin that crinkled the corners of his hazel eyes.

"Meet the crew," Jackson announced as he guided Willa toward them. "This is Dean, Tyler, and the one with the smile that you'd be foolish to trust is Miles."

"Hey," Willa greeted, her voice steady despite the flutter in her chest. Each handshake felt warm and firm, their grins genuine—a testament to the company Jackson kept.

"Jax tells us you're the heart of this group," Miles said, his tone light but eyes assessing, as though trying to unravel the mystery of this "Willa" his mate was infatuated by.

"Only because they keep me around to bail them out of trouble," Willa quipped, and her friends erupted in laughter, a sound that threaded warmth through the cool elegance of the hotel.

"Sounds like my kind of crew," Tyler chimed in, tipping an imaginary hat in her direction.

The group migrated toward a cluster of plush canvas sofas under a private canopy near the rooftop pool's artificial oasis, arranging themselves in a semicircle that felt both inclusive and intimate. Like the drinks, conversations ebbed and flowed from the scenic beauty of Miami's historic skyline to shared anecdotes that had everyone chuckling.

As the evening unfolded, Jackson remained close to Willa, his attentiveness never faltering even as he engaged with each of her friends. He listened more than he spoke, but when he did share a story, it was told with such vivid detail that they all found themselves hanging on his every word.

"Remember the time we got lost on that backroad in Ireland outside Roundstone?" Dean nudged Jackson, prompting a round of laughter from the entourage.

"Lost is overly simplifying it," Jackson countered, his eyes twinkling with the memory.

"Yeah, ended with us sleeping in that tiny car and Miles sleeping on the roof because someone," Dean glanced at Miles, "claimed he was a human compass."

"Then it rained." Miles snorted with laughter. "You wankers wouldn't let me back in the car. I was soaked to the bone."

"You were too shitfaced to even know what was happening." Tyler laughed.

"Was a hell of a sunrise over those hills though," Jackson defended, his laugh echoing around them. "Totally worth it."

"See what I mean?" Willa said, her smile playfully softening as she looked at Jackson. "You find a silver lining in everything... Freak."

"Life's too short for anything else," he replied, his gaze lingering on hers for a moment longer than necessary.

As the night progressed, Willa observed the camaraderie between Jackson and his friends, a group that had known each other since their school and theater days having attended the same performing arts school. They had each taken a different path after school.

Tyler and Jackson pursued acting. Jackson eventually progressing into film while Tyler preferred to remain on stage and jokingly referred to Jackson as a "sellout" for leaving the "true art" of performance.

"There are no second takes on stage," Tyler prodded.

"You didn't care too much about my selling out when I was paying your rent," Jackson retorted.

"Willa, if you're not a starving artist, are you even an artist at all?" Tyler laughed.

Dean had transitioned to music production, and Miles was a stand-up comedian and comedy writer. Each was now at varying degrees of fame and recognition, but all were successful in their own right. Together, they seemed as if they were still as young as the days they had met, their jokes and easy banter revealing layers beyond the enigmatic personas that the world so often saw.

It was in the way Jackson threw his head back when he laughed, or how he made sure everyone felt included, that Willa recognized the traits of a man who was more than just a mysterious stranger.

"Hey, Willa, you up for a swim?" Emma's voice cut through the tranquility, her eyes sparkling with the suggestion.

"Yeah, get over here, Will! We want to talk about the boys without them around," Sydney smirked over in Miles's direction.

The Miami sun was blazing as Willa and her friends floated lazily in the rooftop pool, drinks in hand. The sparkling water provided a cool respite from the heat, and the ocean's view stretched beyond them, breathtaking and serene. The group laughed and chatted, enjoying the carefree atmosphere of their luxurious day at Jackson's hotel.

As they sipped their cocktails, the conversation naturally drifted toward the group of men lounging under a private cabana nearby. Jackson sat with his best friends: Miles, Tyler, and Dean. The women eyed the men with playful curiosity, their laughter occasionally carrying over the pool's shimmering surface.

Lilly, ever the skeptic, raised an eyebrow. "But don't you think it's a bit fast? You only met him...what...three days ago, and now we're all here like some weird family reunion."

Willa shrugged, trying to play it cool. "I don't know. It is fast. But I can't... I don't know. There's just something about him."

"Well, of course, there is, honey," Lilly added, the sun catching the highlights in her hair as she adjusted her sunglasses. "And I'm not complaining about the eye candy he brought with him. I mean, have you seen Dean's abs? They're unreal!"

"Girl, please," Sydney laughed, tipping her head back to catch the rays, "Miles has got that intense brooding vibe going on. I swear, if he looks at me with those deep-set eyes one more time, I'll—ugh."

"Are you two calling 'dibs'? Is that what is happening right now?" Emma joked.

"Eh, maybe, at least we found out where all the hot men live...England," Lilly snorted.

"Yeah, how is that fair?" Sydney laughed in Lilly's direction.

Unbeknownst to the women, the men were having their own conversation under the shaded cabana. Jackson leaned back in his chair, sunglasses masking his eyes, but his posture showed a relaxed confidence. Sitting beside him, Miles glanced over at the pool, then turned back to Jackson with a serious expression.

"So, Jax, what's really going on with you and this girl?" Miles asked, his tone carefully neutral. "We barely know anything about her. You two just met, and now...well, it feels a bit serious."

Jackson removed his sunglasses, his eyes narrowing slightly. "She's...different somehow."

Tyler chimed in, his voice filled with concern. "Different how? I mean, we don't even know where she came from. I tried to look her up, and there's nothing older than three years. It's like she appeared out of nowhere."

"What do you mean?" Jackson responded, raising an eyebrow.

"Well, we know she is from Georgia."

"I knew that already."

"We know she runs an ad agency or something in some little town no one has ever heard of." Miles laughed, trying to ease the tension.

"I also knew that."

"But that is where the trail ends," Miles continued.

Jackson leaned back in his chair. He recalled Willa mentioning that she had left a bad relationship and was in the process of starting over, so to speak, but with the lack of any additional information, her sudden appearance in his life now seemed a bit more sinister. Jackson quickly shook the idea from his head. It wouldn't make sense, when he met Willa, she had no idea who he was, and he truly believed that. If she had been able to fake that, well, she would be a much better actor than he was.

Dean, always cautious, leaned forward, breaking Jackson's concentration. "And you're not exactly being discreet, Jax. You know how the media loves a good scandal. They'll catch on to this if you're not careful."

Jackson's jaw tightened. "What are you saying, Dean? That she's some kind of gold digger? That she's using me?"

Dean hesitated, not wanting to escalate the situation but needing to voice his concerns. "Look, mate, we're just worried. You've been all over her, and given your increasing name here, it's risky. What if she's not who she says she is?"

"Just be careful; wrap it twice, ya know, mate," Miles said with a wink.

Jackson stood abruptly, fists clenched. "You think I'm just blinded by a pretty face and a great fuck? That I can't see what's real?"

Miles quickly stood up, placing a calming hand on Jackson's shoulder. "Whoa, mate, calm down. We're just looking out for you. You've been swept off your feet, and it's understandable. But you asked us here to meet her because you trust us, right?"

Jackson took a deep breath, running a hand through his hair. "Yeah, I did. And I appreciate it. It's just...with Willa, it's different. I can't explain it, but I feel something real... I'm falling for her. Hard. Maybe, I shouldn't trust my own judgment right now."

The tension eased as Jackson sat back down, the weight of his admission hanging in the air. Miles gave him a reassuring pat. "We get it, Jax. We don't want to see you get hurt again. It's been a long time, but we all remember the last time you fell this fast was with Amanda, and you lost your bloody mind after that. Just…keep your eyes open, all right? We've got your back, no matter what."

Jackson nodded, grateful for his friends' support, even if their concerns stung. He remembered everything as if it had happened a week ago and not a decade. It was Amanda, his previous co-star whose career had been miles ahead of his own at the time, and the fallout that came after she left him for someone else. The resulting behaviors left Jackson close to losing everything after being deemed too high risk for studios to hire. At the time, Jackson had cut everyone out of his life. Anyone who tried to rein him in, that was.

***

Miles had tried for weeks to get Jackson to respond to him. Calls, texts, emails, nothing worked. Day after day, another article, another headline showed his best friend on the verge of catastrophe.

"Donovan's Done: Studio in Talks to Replace Leading Man Due to Continued Trouble on Set." Miles shook his head as he read. Jackson was about to be fired from another film because he was continuously showing up to set late, if at all, and he would be drunk or high when he did show up.

Miles had headed to Jackson's penthouse flat, intent on refusing to leave until the door attendant let him in.

"I'm getting into that room one way or another," Miles had demanded.

"He doesn't want to see anyone."

"He doesn't know what he wants," Miles replied, softening his tone. "Come on, you've seen him, you've seen the stories. You know me."

The door attendant shifted uncomfortably, his eyes darting between Miles and the elevator.

"Mr. Donovan was very clear about not wanting any visitors."

Miles stepped closer, his voice low and urgent. "Listen, mate, I get it. You're just doing your job. But this isn't about following orders anymore. It's about saving a life."

He pulled out his phone, the harsh glow of the screen illuminating the worry etched on his face.

"Look at this," he said, showing the door attendant the headline. "If we don't do something now, it might be too late."

The door attendant's expression softened as he read the article, realization dawning in his eyes. "I had no idea it had become this bad," he murmured.

"That's why I need to get up there," Miles pressed. "Jackson's not thinking straight right now. He's pushing away the people who care about him most. But I know him better than anyone, and I'm not giving up on him."

He leaned in, his gaze intense. "Please, let me help him. I promise, I won't leave until I know he's safe."

The door attendant hesitated for a moment, torn between his duty and the weight of Miles's words. Finally, he nodded, stepping aside to let Miles pass.

"Thank you," Miles said, clapping the man on the shoulder as he hurried toward the elevator.

As the doors slid closed, Miles leaned against the wall, his heart racing. He knew the road ahead wouldn't be easy, but he was determined to stand by Jackson's side, no matter how long it took.

The elevator dinged, signaling his arrival at the penthouse. Miles took a deep breath, steeling himself for the battle ahead. He knew Jackson would resist, would try to push him away like he had everyone else. But Miles wasn't going to let that happen.

He stepped out into the darkened foyer, the silence broken only by the distant sound of the city below as he made his way toward the living room. A sense of unease crept over him, the air heavy with the weight of Jackson's despair.

"Jax?" he called out, his voice echoing in the emptiness. "It's Miles. I'm here, mate."

No response came, but Miles pressed on, his determination never wavering. He knew that somewhere in this sprawling penthouse, his best friend was lost and hurting, and he wouldn't rest until he brought him back into the light.

Miles found Jackson collapsed on the floor in the hallway. He was barely breathing.

"Jax! Mate! What did you take!?"

Miles rolled Jackson over onto his back. A strained gurgling noise sounded in Jackson's throat.

"How much did you take?!" Miles screamed, slapping his best friend across the face, hoping to rouse him. Seconds passed, Miles pulled back Jackson's eyelids, revealing pinpoint black pupils.

"No! Not like this, mate! Not like this!"

They've been here before. Miles was no stranger to a "bit too much." But it always had been Jackson to the rescue.

Miles tried to calm his panic as he pulled the Narcan from his pocket. "Don't you dare leave me, wanker," he screamed while shooting his only hope up his friend's nose.

With a blood-curdling screech, Jackson woke in a blind rage from the brink of death, violently fighting off Miles with the strength of a man twice his size.

"Do it! Beat the shit out of me, Jax!"

Confused, Jackson settled. "What the fuck...Miles?"

"You're done, mate." Tears streamed down Miles's face. "I don't care how much you did; I don't care why... You're done."

***

For the next three days, Miles remained by Jackson's side, a steadfast presence in the face of his friend's darkest moments. The bathroom floor became a sanctuary, cold tiles pressing against their skin as Jackson's body fought against the grip of withdrawal. Sweat beaded on Jackson's brow, his muscles tensing and trembling as waves of nausea and pain crashed over him.

Miles sat beside him, his back pressed against the wall, watching helplessly as Jackson curled in on himself, groaning in agony. The air was thick with the scent of sickness and desperation, but Miles never flinched, never turned away. Instead, he reached out, placing a gentle hand on Jackson's shoulder, a silent reminder that he wasn't alone.

"It's going to be okay, Jax," Miles murmured, his voice soft and soothing. He reached for a washcloth, running it under cool water before pressing it against Jackson's fevered skin. The cloth felt like a balm against Jackson's neck, a momentary reprieve from the fire that raged within him.

Jackson's eyes fluttered open, bloodshot and haunted. "I can't do this," he rasped, his voice raw and broken. "It hurts...everything hurts."

"I know, mate. I know." Miles tightened his grip on Jackson's shoulder, his heart aching for his friend. "But you're stronger than this. You can beat it."

Jackson shook his head, tears streaming down his face. "I'm not...I'm weak. I let everything fall apart."

"No, Jax. You're not weak. You're human." Miles shifted closer, his presence an anchor in the storm of Jackson's emotions. "We all make mistakes. But you have the strength to overcome this. How many times have you done this for me? I believe in you."

Jackson's body shuddered, another wave of pain crashing over him. He gritted his teeth, his fingers scrabbling against the tiles as he fought to breathe through the agony. Miles held him steady, whispering words of encouragement and comfort.

As the hours ticked by, the two friends remained huddled on the bathroom floor, battling Jackson's demons together.

Jackson's breath continued to come in ragged gasps as he clung to Miles, his body racked with tremors. The cold, unforgiving tile pressed against his bare skin, a stark contrast to the searing heat that seemed to consume him from within. He squeezed his eyes shut, trying to block out the harsh fluorescent light that filled the bathroom, its unnatural glow casting distorted shadows on the walls.

"I can't...I can't do this," he whispered, his voice hoarse and broken. "It's too much."

Miles brushed a strand of sweat-soaked hair from Jackson's forehead, his touch gentle and reassuring. "Yes, you can, Jax. You're not alone in this. I'm here, I won't let you fail, and I'm not going anywhere."

Jackson's mind reeled, fragmented memories and emotions swirling in a dizzying kaleidoscope. The faces of those he had hurt, the bridges he had burned, the opportunities he had squandered—they all flashed before his eyes, a relentless reminder of his mistakes. He felt the weight of his choices pressing down on him, suffocating him, dragging him deeper into the abyss of self-loathing and despair.

"I've ruined everything," he choked out, his voice barely above a whisper. "My career, my life...I've lost it all."

"Breathe, Jax. Just breathe." Miles's voice was calm and protective, nearly paternal. "You're going to get through this."

As the door opened, a quiet click caused Jackson to jump slightly, his heart racing with sudden panic. The movement sent a fresh wave of nausea surging through him, and he swallowed hard, fighting back the bile that rose in his throat.

"Who is that?" Jackson's voice was a hoarse whisper, barely audible over the pounding of his pulse in his ears. He struggled to sit up, his limbs trembling with the effort. "I can't be seen like this."

Miles placed a gentle hand on Jackson's shoulder, steadying him. "It's all right, mate. It's just—"

But Jackson wasn't listening. His mind was reeling, his thoughts spiraling into a vortex of anxiety and shame. He couldn't bear the thought of anyone else witnessing his downfall, seeing him reduced to this pitiful, broken shell of a man.

He had wanted too badly to rebuild his image, to shed the bad-boy persona that had nearly destroyed his career. And now, here he was, huddled on the bathroom floor, a sweating, shivering mess. The irony was not lost on him.

"Please, Miles." Jackson's voice was a desperate plea, his dark eyes wide and haunted. "I don't want anyone to see me like this. I can't...I can't face them."

Miles hesitated for a moment, his brow furrowed with concern. He knew that Jackson needed support and to see that he wasn't alone in this fight. But he also understood the depth of his friend's pride, the fear of being vulnerable in front of others.

"All right, Jax." Miles's voice was soft, reassuring. "I'll handle it. You just focus on breathing, yeah? I'll be right back."

With a final squeeze of Jackson's shoulder, Miles rose to his feet and crossed the room, his footsteps echoing on the marble tiles. He paused at the door, glancing back at Jackson with a look of fierce determination.

"We're going to get through this, mate. Together. I promise you that."

And with those words, he slipped out of the room, leaving Jackson alone with his thoughts and the relentless grip of withdrawal.

Jackson leaned his head back against the cool porcelain of the bathtub, closing his eyes against the harsh glare of the overhead lights. He focused on his breathing, on the steady rise and fall of his chest, trying to find a measure of calm amid the chaos.

But even as he fought to center himself, his mind drifted to the past, to the choices and mistakes that had led him to this moment. The all-consuming regret was a bitter taste on his tongue, a leaden weight in his chest.

Miles's voice, soft but firm, cut through the haze of Jackson's anxiety. "It's just D, Ty, and your sis. We all want to be here for you, because fuck, Jax, we love you. They are sneaking a doc in through the basement. Please do whatever he asks. We want you back."

Jackson's heart clenched at the words, at the depth of emotion in his friend's voice. He could feel the tears burning behind his eyes, the lump forming in his throat. He knew that he had pushed them all away, that he had hurt them with his actions and his addiction. But even now, even at his lowest point, they were still here, still fighting for him.

He swallowed hard, forcing himself to meet Miles's gaze. In those familiar eyes, he saw a reflection of his own pain, his own fear. But he also saw love as unwavering and unconditional. At that moment, he knew that he couldn't let them down again.

"I promise." He nodded, his voice rough with emotion. "I'll do whatever it takes."

Miles's hand tightened on his shoulder, a silent acknowledgment of the weight of those words. Jackson leaned into the touch, drawing strength from the connection, from the knowledge that he wasn't alone.

And for the first time in a long time, Jackson believed that maybe, just maybe, he could find his way back to the light.

***

"Why so serious over there? You boys get over here!" Sydney yelled in their direction.

"Brilliant idea, Syd!" Miles, the instigator, chimed, giving a quick wink at Jackson before flinging himself into the rooftop infinity pool fully dressed, causing a rousing level of laughter and cheering from the group and onlookers. Dean and Tyler joined Miles while wearing far more appropriate swim attire.

Walking over to the pool Jackson's gaze returned to the striking brunette, her deep eyes staring at him while floating, her presence commanding his attention even from a distance. He felt her allure pulling at him, a gravitational force he found himself helpless to resist. He didn't understand why but he instinctively knew he needed to keep her in his life.

***

Lilly wandered off from the group as if to express her boredom in having not been the center of attention for a while, exploring the roof, checking to see if any other celebrities or notable people she could latch on to were present.

Perhaps she would run into someone more famous than Willa's little boy toy. Her eyes, sharp and calculating, flicked toward something—or someone—beyond the group's line of sight.

Cassy followed Lilly's gaze, only to find nothing amiss in the crowd. The sense of unease lingered, however, like a note held too long in a song.

"Everything okay, Lilly?" Cassy asked, concern threading through her words.

"Perfectly fine," Lilly responded, her tone light, almost too light. There was a glint in her eye that Cassy couldn't quite read, a silent thrill that didn't match the serene setting of their gathering.

CHAPTER THIRTEEN

The Paparazzi

Sunlight filtered through the sheer curtains of Jackson's upscale hotel room, casting a warm glow on the two intertwined figures lying in bed. Willa's dark wavy hair spilled across the pillow like tendrils of night amid the sea of white linen. Her deep, expressive eyes were locked with Jackson's intense brown ones, mirroring the calm that had enveloped them.

"Jax," Willa whispered, her voice soft yet laden with emotion, "I never thought..."

"Shh," Jackson soothed, his accent wrapping around her like a comforting blanket. His thumb gently stroked the back of her hand. "You don't need to think about anything right now, Love. Just be here with me."

The serene bubble that surrounded them popped as the shrill chime of Jackson's phone sliced through the tranquility of the morning. The screen lit up with an onslaught of urgent text messages, each one cascading over the last like a relentless wave.

"Damn," Jackson muttered under his breath, his brow furrowing as he reluctantly untangled himself from Willa's embrace. He reached for his phone, his muscles tensing as he scanned the contents of the messages. With a sense of urgency, he swung his legs off the bed and stood, his tall, athletic frame casting a shadow across the room.

"Is everything okay?" Willa asked, propping herself up on one elbow, concern etching her features as she watched him pull on a pair of pants with haste.

"I need to make a call," he replied, his voice tight and worried. Without another word, he grabbed a shirt from the back of a chair and stepped out onto the balcony, leaving Willa alone with her thoughts.

The door clicked shut behind him, and Willa drew her knees up to her chest, wrapping her arms around them. She rested her chin on her knees, her eyes fixed on the balcony door where Jackson's silhouette moved with tense energy.

Willa's heart raced, anxiety gnawing at her insides. She knew their relationship was still in a delicate bloom, yet the sudden shift in Jackson's demeanor unsettled her. What could have possibly come through on that phone to cause such immediate concern?

From beyond the glass, Jackson's profile was laced with lines of concentration as he spoke into the phone. The morning breeze tousled his black hair, but he seemed oblivious to the balmy air, or the picturesque view of the Miami skyline displayed in front of him. All his focus was directed at the conversation unfolding, one that Willa could not hear but felt intrinsically connected to by the tightening knot in her stomach.

She longed to press her ear against the glass, to bridge the distance between them and understand the source of his distress. But she remained motionless, her fingers absently tracing the spot on the bed where Jackson's warmth still lingered, waiting for him to return and dispel the growing storm of questions swirling inside her.

The balcony door clicked shut behind Jackson, a reverberation that seemed to echo in the silence of the room. Willa watched him as he turned to face her, the crease between his brows deepening with every step he took toward the bed. His intense eyes, usually so full of warmth, now held a seriousness that made her own heart skip uncomfortably.

"Is everything all right?" she asked, her voice barely above a whisper, the words catching slightly in her throat.

Jackson sat on the edge of the bed, the mattress dipping with his weight. He reached for her hand, his grip firm yet reassuring. "It was my publicist," he began, his accent doing little to soften the blow of his next words. "There's going to be a story, Willa."

Her pulse quickened, and she could feel the cool cotton of the sheets beneath her fingertips as she clutched them instinctively.

"She said they received word last night...there are photos of us." Jackson's voice faltered for just a moment before he composed himself again. "It doesn't sound like anything disastrous but suggestive," he said, his thumb gently stroking the back of her hand. "Kissing, going up the room, by the pool. And there are others from earlier in the week, the alley, the hotel."

"Photos?" The single word twisted in Willa's gut; the images it conjured sent a shiver down her spine despite the warmth of Jackson's touch.

"Yes, and some tabloids have got hold of them. They're planning to run a story about it—" He hesitated, his gaze never wavering from hers, "—something about me with an 'unknown woman' in Miami, a fling or something more, etcetera. The PR team wants to get ahead of it. They're pressing for a statement, whether to confirm or deny..."

Willa felt the room spin ever so slightly, her mind racing as she considered the implications. The exposure, the scrutiny—it was all too much, too soon. She swallowed hard, trying to steady her breath as she withdrew her hand from his grasp and wrapped her arms around herself protectively. It hadn't even been a week from outside the safe cocoon of Magnolia, and her worst fears were starting to come to fruition.

"Jackson, I—" Her throat tightened, the rest of her sentence lost in the sudden rush of fear that threatened to overwhelm her.

"Hey, hey," Jackson's voice softened after seeing the panic in her eyes, "it's all right, these things happen from time to time. Just as quickly as they pop up, they fade. I don't have to say much or anything at all, really, but not addressing it can look like there is something to hide. And I'm sure you will look lovely." He smiled.

His assurance was meant to comfort, but Willa knew the situation was far more complex than mere vanity or an invasion of privacy. With each passing second, she became acutely aware of how the simple act of falling for this man had irreversibly intertwined their lives, binding her future to the unforeseen consequences of his fame. Had she known who he was, surely, she would never have gone to bed with him that first night. She remembered the elevator, the camera, there was no way her face wasn't captured.

Willa's gaze darted to the window, her eyes reflecting the turmoil churning inside her. She could almost see the headlines splashed across every screen, every paper, invading the quiet life she'd so carefully pieced back together.

"Jax," she said, her voice barely above a whisper, "I'm sorry. It's not that simple, it's not just about if I look all right or if it's too soon or…" A tear trickled down her cheek, unbidden but honest in its descent. "It's more complicated than that."

He frowned, confusion and concern etching his handsome features as he tentatively moved closer to her.

"Complicated how?" Jackson murmured.

"The photos," Willa began, her hands trembling as she wiped away the tears. "It's not just some annoyance or occupational hazard for me. They're like a beacon, a spotlight shining on me. It's attention I can't afford." Her breath stumbled as the image of Killian's cold, calculating stare flashed in her mind, the way shadows seemed to cling to him, a darkness that once threatened to swallow her whole.

"Killian," she forced out the name like it was poison on her tongue. "My ex, the reason I fled, if he sees those pictures, if he knows where I am… The danger—I can't even begin to explain." She looked away, unable to bear the weight of Jackson's gaze as she laid bare her deepest fear.

Jackson's expression softened, the creases of worry giving way to a protective resolve. He wanted to reach out, to pull her into his arms and shield her from the ghosts of her past, but he remained still, sensing her need for space to breathe, to gather the scattered pieces of her courage.

"Your ex," he repeated quietly, turning the idea over in his mind as though it were a puzzle to solve, an enemy to vanquish. "I had no idea —"

"Please," Willa cut in, her plea wrapped in the vulnerability that danced in the depths of her expressive eyes. "I never wanted any of this. How stupid I was. You'll be exposed because of me, too; it's not fair. I should have run the moment you let me know who you were. This is my fault."

Her shoulders slumped, defeat whispering its cold touch along her spine.

"Slow down," Jackson replied with a steady voice, "you are not at fault for this. How could you be? It was me. I should have been more careful, less affectionate in public."

Looking back, it was his passion for her that made him, in his mind, act so recklessly, exposing her so quickly to his world. When they were together, the pressure he felt to be "on" constantly in public had all but disappeared. He knew it was selfish, but he was desperate to keep that feeling.

"This is not something you have to face alone." Thoughts of seeking revenge on this unknown villain filled his mind, as did what he could do to protect her, and how far he was willing to go to keep her. "That's not how this works..."

The words surprised him as they came out of his mouth. Flashes in his mind of walking away from show business calmed him. It was then he realized...while he knew he had started to genuinely care about Willa—he was drunk on his physical attraction to her and the inescapable desire to be with her—he realized that over the past few days, he may have actually fallen in love with her.

But as much as he wanted to fight for her, to stand by her side against whatever shadows lurked in her past, he recognized the absolute terror that lived in Willa's heart; a terror that had little to do with tabloids and everything to do with survival.

Jackson's hand brushed the air before settling gently on her cheek, the warmth of his palm a stark contrast to the chill of dread that had settled over Willa. His thumb caressed her skin, tracing the line of her jaw with a tenderness that made her heart constrict.

"You don't have to do this alone," he murmured, his dark eyes searching hers, imploring her to believe not just in him but in them. "I knew there was something from your past. You had alluded to that, but I didn't realize this man was a real threat and you were in danger."

The hotel room felt too small, too exposed, as if walls made of mere glass and steel could do nothing to keep out the specter of her past. Jackson's touch was comforting, yet it couldn't quell the rising tide of panic at the thought of Killian's dark shadow reaching out for her once more.

"Jax," she began, her voice trembling despite her attempt to steady it, "you don't understand. Those photos have locations. He'll come looking for me, and I can't..."

She swallowed hard, the words catching like thorns in her throat.

"What are you saying?" Jackson insisted, his voice firm, but Willa shook her head, a tear breaking free to trail down her cheek.

"I have to go back to Georgia tonight. Go back into hiding. To be where he wouldn't think to look for me."

Her gaze held his, pleading for him to see the impossible situation they were in. She could feel herself quickly building back the walls Jackson had started to break.

Distance yourself from him, a voice in her head screamed. *It's too risky.*

Her voice strengthened.

"I like being with you, Jackson, a lot. But realistically, how? You didn't actually think this was turning into something, did you? How can we possibly make this work with me there and you constantly traveling everywhere else? This was just fun, never something real." She forced a condescending laugh.

But her eyes spoke the truth; she was dying inside. She knew she wanted him, wanted whatever this was between them. She was lying to him just as she was lying to herself. This meant something to her.

And he, well, he wasn't one to just *fall in love after a good fuck*, he thought. To make him feel this way so quickly...this was different; this was real... He started to speak, to argue, but the panic in her eyes told him that her decision was made. It wasn't just about safety or distance; it was about the reality of their lives intersecting at the most dangerous crossroads.

Jackson's career, life in the public eye, it was all a game of exposure—exactly what she needed to avoid.

Willa's hand found its way to his, their fingers intertwining for a fleeting moment—an acknowledgment of the bond they shared, even as it slipped through their grasp like grains of sand. The message between them was clear: whatever was developing between them as intensely as it was, was no match for the relentless pursuit of a haunted past.

"Don't do this," Jackson pleaded, hoping to make sense to her. His voice intensified. "Don't act like you don't feel this, that you can so easily walk away. Like this means nothing."

He was angry, and his expression was dark. He grasped to find meaning in a situation that was quickly devolving. Jackson's expression crumpled like paper in the rain, the lines of his face showing the conflict raging within him. In the dim morning light filtering through the curtains of the upscale hotel room, his dark eyes, usually pools of strength, were now reservoirs of sorrow and understanding. He watched Willa, the woman who had become an unexpected compass in his world of fame and chaos, her every word tugging at the moorings of his heart.

"Jax," Willa whispered, her voice fragile as the silence enveloping them. She looked at their intertwined hands, the contrast of his sun-kissed skin against her own seeming to reflect the divide that was growing between them. "You can't be involved in this..."

There was a crack in her voice as she spoke, a tremor that traveled through the air and settled heavily in the space around them. Her words were laden with love, each syllable drenched in the agony of impending separation. Willa's eyes, deep and expressive, met Jackson's with a piercing intensity. They told stories of shared moments, whispered promises, and dreams that now seemed as distant as the stars above Miami's infamous streets.

"Being together, especially publicly, it's just going to bring more attention and risk," she continued, her breath hitching as she fought back tears. "It's better if we just...if we end this now, before it goes any further. Before my past destroys everything you've worked for."

Willa felt the weight of her own words crushing her from the inside out, each one a heavy stone added to the wall she was hastily erecting between them, a barrier to protect them both but also a prison keeping her locked in her fears.

Jackson's hand tightened around hers, a silent plea, a last grasp for connection. But even as he held on, there was a resignation in his eyes, a recognition of the tumultuous reality they found themselves in.

"What are you talking about?" he said simply. "I'm not afraid of some ghost from your past."

His voice, barely more than a whisper, was still the most powerful sound in the room. It echoed off the walls, reverberated through Willa's soul, and settled as a somber note in the symphony of memories they had created.

"Celebrity arrogance," she replied, her voice cracking under the strain of her emotions.

The tears she had been holding back now broke free, spilling over in silent streams down her cheeks as she hastily rushed around the room collecting her things. With each teardrop, she felt a piece of her resolve weaken, yet her determination to keep Jackson safe from the shadows of her past remained unyielding.

"Jax," Willa said, her lips trembling as she uttered his name, "you have to let this go. For your sake...for mine."

Her words were a heavy shroud, wrapping around them both, signaling the end of a chapter that had only just begun.

Jackson's shoulders slumped, the line of his body a testament to defeat. He looked up at Willa with eyes that held a sea of questions, each one crashing against the possibility of a different ending.

"Is there...any chance?" His voice was a whisper, a thread of sound barely tethering him to the hope he clung to. Vulnerability bared itself in the simple furrow of his brow, the slight quiver of his lips.

Willa stood before him, her own silhouette, a contrast of strength and fragility. She shook her head, the movement slow and deliberate, as if it took all her strength to make even that small gesture. Tears choked her words, lending them a tremulous quality that pierced the quiet of the room.

"I can't risk it, Jackson," she said, each syllable heavy with the gravity of unspoken fears. "Killian...if he finds out about us, I don't know what he'd do, I only know what he has done. And your career, your...life—it's too much to gamble."

"Tell me," he demanded. "Tell me what he's done before you walk out on this. Tell me why you're so afraid. Give me that much."

Willa took a deep breath in while closing her eyes, forcing herself to remember.

"My name isn't Sullivan. Sullivan is my grandmother's maiden name. I changed my name to help protect me."

The gravity of what she was about to disclose...

"We met years ago; the hospital I was working at the time. High stress, always together... In the beginning, things were great, of course, but after a while, things got really bad, and it took me about a year to escape him. After I first decided to leave, I went back to Maryland, foolishly thinking my family would provide support, but no... Killian started stalking me, I went to the police. They told me there was nothing they could do. It was my word against his."

Willa could see the weight of her history in Jackson's eyes. It was a mixture of concern, compassion, and silent rage.

"I was feeling helpless and didn't know where else to turn...so..."

She paused, trying to regain a sense of control over her voice.

"I went back to him. At first...it seemed like maybe it would be ok; he was remorseful, and," she slowly shook her head, "nothing had changed. My being back made *his* life easier, and I was suffocating. Things got worse, worse than before and..."

Jackson softly wiped a tear from Willa's cheek. She instinctively pressed her face toward his hand. Even in such a dire situation, his touch had a way of completely disarming her.

"I left again, moved in with Lilly, the one with short black hair. I stayed there for a while, but he was relentless. Showing up at all hours, trying to get me to come back. His threats got worse. I went back to the police, again, useless. They told me a protection order was only as strong as the paper it was written on, and he would know it would be filed, and they are not instantly enforced... There was a whole hearing, and the officer told me that Killian would likely get to me before they could, and um...their advice was to quit working in medicine and move...a lot. To try to create a paper trail of addresses to make it more difficult for him to find me...that eventually he would...get bored..."

"And that's how you ended up in Georgia?" Jackson said softly.

"I could take it anymore. I jumped on the first plane leaving DC and just decided I'd figure out the rest later." She took a deep breath. "I know he harassed Lilly for a while. I never told her where I went because..."

"You were trying to protect her."

"This way she could tell him she didn't know, and even if he tracked her, she still didn't know. I assumed he would eventually leave her alone."

"Damn...I'm sorry...I had no idea...the night we met..."

"How could you have known? The night we met, I just didn't want to feel any of this anymore. For the first time in years, I forgot. I didn't think about it, or him... You made me forget...even if it was just for a few moments."

"You don't have to run."

"You're the first taste of freedom I've had in..."

"Stay."

She drew a breath, trying to steady the storm within her chest.

"It's not just about me. Killian has a history of trying to intimidate anyone he believes may be interested in me. Even if it is clear that I don't want them... I can't imagine what he would do if he found out about you... How I feel about you. I can't let you get hurt because of me, Jax. It's not just the embarrassment I feel for my past, how... With the things I've done, the secrets Killian knows that he would use against me to hurt me, to hurt you. He's unstable; it's the danger he could now bring to you that terrifies me."

She watched Jackson, her deep, expressive eyes a mirror to the turmoil that shook her core, reflecting back the depth of emotion that this moment carved into their story.

"Willa, I think I'm falling in love—"

"Don't...don't finish that sentence. Don't make this any harder than it already is," she said, tears streaming down her cheeks.

Jackson reached out, his fingers intertwining with Willa's in a grip that conveyed all the words his throat struggled to form. His dark brown eyes, usually so intense and commanding, now shimmered with a vulnerability that tugged at her heartstrings.

"Willa," he began, the timbre of his voice a blend of melancholy and resolve, "I'll respect whatever you decide. Your safety is what matters most, but—is there any chance...any chance at all...you might be overreacting?"

His question hung in the air, it stung... *Of course, another man who thinks I'm crazy*, she thought to herself, but there was a fragile hope wrapped in the warmth of his touch. Willa felt the weight of his gaze; he wasn't judging her. The thought that she could be misjudging the situation, letting fear cloud her judgment...she wanted Jackson to be correct. She wanted to be overreacting; she wanted this to be nothing more than a post-traumatic delusional level of paranoia...but deep down, she knew the truth.

For a moment, she allowed herself the luxury of sinking into the comfort of Jackson's presence, the security his mere closeness brought. She leaned toward him, her lips meeting his in a kiss that was both a goodbye and a silent prayer for a different ending. It was a gentle, fleeting connection that carried the depth of their brief but intense bond.

"I hope I am," Willa murmured against his mouth, her voice barely audible over the quiet hum of the world outside the hotel room. Her heart clenched within her chest, the pain of parting laced with the faintest glimmer of hope that maybe, just maybe, her fears were unfounded.

Reluctantly, she withdrew from his embrace.

"If I don't leave now, I'm afraid I won't be able to," she whispered. "Why couldn't you have just stayed some random stranger in an alley and not be someone...I...already miss?"

The small distance between them felt like miles as she began to gather her belongings scattered across the room, each item a reminder of the moments they had shared, now tainted with the bittersweet sting of farewell. Her silhouette traced a haunting outline against the muted morning light that seeped in through the sheer curtains. The soft rustle of fabric against fabric punctuated the silence as she slipped into her jacket, each movement deliberate, echoing the finality of her decision.

Jackson watched, an ache spreading through his chest, tendrils of longing wrapping tight around his heart. He stood motionless, knowing any attempt to bridge the gap between them would only serve to deepen the wound already forming. His voice was barely a whisper, strained with the effort to mask the turmoil beneath.

"Will..."

The word, filled with love and pain, hung in the air, a fragile echo that seemed too small for the enormity of what it signified.

In response, Willa paused at the threshold, her hand resting on the door handle. She turned, her gaze piercing through the distance that had crept between them, locking onto Jackson with an intensity that contradicted the serenity of her outward appearance. His eyes, those deep pools of dark resolve, conveyed more than words could ever hope to: the love that bound them, the understanding of their situation, and the sorrow of parting—all silently spoken in the briefest of glances.

And then she was gone, the click of the door closing behind her like a thunderclap in the stillness of the room.

Jackson remained frozen, the imprint of her gaze etched into his memory, an exchange that would haunt him long after her departure.

CHAPTER FOURTEEN

The Fundraiser

ACT 3

Willa's fingers traced the rim of her coffee mug, the ceramic cool against her skin despite the steam rising from within. She looked exhausted, a combination of poor sleep and the heavy weight of knowing she may have walked away from the best thing that could have ever happened to her. The morning light filtered through the curtains, casting a soft glow over Cassy's kitchen, where they sat opposite each other at the worn wooden table.

"Everything just snapped back to normal for everyone so quickly," Willa murmured, breaking the silence between them. She looked up, meeting Cassy's hazel eyes. "It's like...nothing ever happened, but I feel this gaping hole of loss."

"But, it did," Cassy replied gently, her voice grounding Willa back to reality. "And Killian can't take that memory from you. You can't let Killian keep holding you hostage, Willa. Not emotionally, not anymore."

A sigh escaped Willa's lips as she nodded, her dark wavy hair brushing her shoulders.

"But it doesn't help. The memories are all I have, and I know, I just...I can't help but think about Jackson and how things ended." Regret laced her tone, the weight of her choices pressing down on her. "God, I miss him, Cassy. It scares me how much. I know...logically, I know...it was the best decision I could make at the time. But now, Cass, the dust has settled. The story came out and faded just like he said it would." Willa traced the edge of a worn magazine.

"Look at him," Cassy said, tapping her finger over a photo of Jackson and Willa in Miami. Willa's face wasn't visible in the photo, but it was no doubt her—her hair, her dress, the corner of her smile. Across the table from her was Jackson.

"Look at how he was looking at you, Willa," Cassy encouraged. "Call him. What would be the harm? Just see how it feels. What do you think?"

Before Willa could answer, her phone buzzed with a reminder of her scheduled call with Lilly.

Excusing herself, she stepped onto the porch, the humidity wrapping around her like a familiar blanket as she dialed Lilly's number.

"Hey, Lil," Willa greeted, her voice laden with the turmoil inside her.

"Why do you sound like that? Willa...please tell me you haven't done anything rash," came Lilly's immediate response, her concern palpable even through the phone line.

"I'm just thinking about Jax," Willa confessed, leaning against a pillar, the rough texture pressing into her back.

"Please, don't," Lilly pleaded. "Girl, you've come so far. Thinking about Jackson leads to wanting to call him, which leads to wanting to see him and trying to start something up again—it'll just complicate everything for you. And honey, I mean this with love, but do you think he's just been sitting around pining for you the past month or whatever? I mean...you remember what he looks like."

The conversation continued, both women entrenched in their positions until Willa finally acquiesced. "I lost my chance. You're right. Okay, I won't call him. For now."

"Promise?" Lilly urged.

"Promise. Call me tomorrow? Let me know how the opening went?"

"Of course, Will! I'll be sure to take plenty of pictures."

Disconnecting the call, Willa remained on the porch, the vibrant greenery of Magnolia Shores surrounding her. She felt torn, the past and future pulling her in opposite directions.

***

In DC, Lilly stood before the full-length mirror in her bedroom, the soft glow of the vanity lights casting a warm hue over her skin. She slid her hands down the sides of her gown, a deep emerald green that flowed like liquid silk, caressing her curves with an almost sentient touch. The dress was both daring and refined, its plunging neckline and backless design striking a perfect balance with the floor-length hem. Her short black hair, usually tousled in a carefree manner, had been sculpted into an elegant shape, each strand in its rightful place.

As she applied a final touch of crimson to her lips, Lilly's thoughts wandered to the Gala and the monumental effort it had taken to bring it together. She remembered the countless late nights and frazzled mornings, the endless calls and emails. But more than anything, she remembered Willow, now Willa—her best friend, her confidante. Willa had poured her heart and soul into creating the women's center, working tirelessly even as her own life unraveled. The memory of Willa's passion and dedication was a knife twist in Lilly's chest.

Until a short time ago, Lilly believed she would never see her friend again. She reflected on that random night in Savannah when her Willow appeared like a ghost, surrounded by others who seemed to know her all too well. A stabbing pain clutched Lilly's heart. Willow had been alive all this time, three years, and never reached out. Had it not been for that night in Savannah, Lilly knew she still would not know her friend was alive. She felt betrayed. How could Willow leave her in the dark after all they had been through? She pushed the thoughts aside. She knew Willow had her reasons, and Lilly hoped she could one day forgive her, and they would be able to truly rebuild their friendship.

The car arrived at the steps of the event, a grand edifice of marble and glass that stood like a god over the city. The driver opened Lilly's door, and she stepped out onto the walkway, adjusting the train of her gown to avoid stepping on it. The night air was crisp, biting at the exposed skin of her back and arms, but she welcomed it; waking her senses and making her feel alive.

She walked through the lobby, her stiletto heels clicking against the polished marble floor. Signs and banners lined the halls, their colors and designs conspicuously tasteful. One caught her eye, and she paused for a moment to take it in: "Willowbrook Women's Mental Health Residential Center Fundraiser." The words were emblazoned over a stylized image of a willow tree, its branches heavy with leaves. Lilly's gaze lingered on the banner, her mind flashing back to the day the hospital had chosen the name. "Willow Burke, Willowbrook," Lilly said to herself with a saddened smile.

A knot of people had formed near the stage, where an extensive digital check stood on a display. Lilly's heart skipped a beat as she read the most recent donation amount: $250,000. An anonymous donor had put them above their five-million-dollar goal. Relief washed over her, followed quickly by a wave of emotion so intense it nearly buckled her knees. The Center would be funded for at least the next three years. Willa's dream would become a reality.

"Lillian Harrington," a deep voice intoned from behind her. She turned to see Dr. Abraham Randanowitz, the hospital's Chief of Staff. He was tall and silver-haired, with the rugged good looks of a former athlete. His tuxedo fit him like a second skin.

"Abe," Lilly said, offering her hand. He took it, then pulled her into a gentle, not-quite-familial hug.

"You look stunning," he said, releasing her. "Absolutely stunning."

"Thank you," she said, her voice soft. "You clean up well yourself."

Randanowitz gestured toward the stage with his glass. "Can you believe it? We broke the goal. We're set."

Lilly nodded, unable to find words. The two stood in a comfortable silence, watching the crowd.

"We all miss her, you know," Randanowitz said after a moment. "Willow. She was one of the best."

Lilly's throat tightened. "Still is," she whispered quietly to herself.

Randanowitz gave her a long, measured look. "Have you heard anything?"

"No," Lilly lied, shaking her head. "Nothing."

He placed a hand on her shoulder, squeezing gently. "I'm sure she's okay. I have faith. It would be very hard to come back here. She just needs some time. She'll come back to us."

Lilly looked away, blinking back the sting in her eyes. "I hope you're right."

Randanowitz let his hand linger for a moment, then withdrew. "I should circulate. We'll talk later?"

"Of course," Lilly said, turning back to him with a forced, brittle smile.

As Randanowitz disappeared into the throng, Lilly finished her champagne in a single, unladylike gulp. The liquid bubbles burned a trail down her throat, and she welcomed the brief, numbing warmth that spread through her chest. She made her way to the edge of the room, where tall windows overlooked the city. Washington glittered below, a jeweled spiderweb of streets and buildings.

Lilly touched a finger to the glass, tracing an imaginary line through the cold surface. *Come back, Willa.* The silent request echoed in her mind, unanswered and unanswerable.

The sound of a spoon tapping against a glass filled the room, and Lilly turned to see Randanowitz on the stage with a microphone. The crowd began to quiet, and Lilly started to walk toward the center of the room, her movements slow and deliberate.

"Ladies and gentlemen," he said, his voice crackling through the speakers. "Thank you all for coming tonight. Your generosity and support mean the world to us. We are thrilled to announce that about fifteen minutes ago, we exceeded our fundraising goal for the Willowbrook Women's Mental Health Residential Center."

A murmur of approval swept through the crowd, followed by a smattering of applause. Lilly's hands came together, the sound of her own clapping distant and hollow in her ears.

"For those who may not know, the Center is named in honor of Dr. Willow Burke," Randanowitz continued, "whose vision and dedication have been the driving force behind this project. Though she is not with us tonight, we know she is here in spirit."

Lilly's chest constricted, and she struggled to draw a full breath. She made her way to a side corridor and leaned against the wall, closing her eyes. The tension in her shoulders, her neck, her jaw was unbearable. She thought about Willow's disappearance, about the lack of note or message, about the police and their useless questions. Most of all, she thought about Killian and the fear in Willa's eyes the last time they had spoken.

Lilly opened her eyes and stood straight, composing herself. She walked back to the nearest elevator, pressing the button with a decisive jab of her finger. The doors opened, and she stepped inside, the plush carpet swallowing the sound of her heels. She pressed the button for the terrace floor and watched the doors slide shut, sealing her in the protection of velvet and brass.

The ride was swift and silent. When the doors opened, Lilly stepped into a small foyer and walked to a set of glass doors that led to the outdoor terrace. A burst of cold air greeted her as she opened the doors. She shivered, hugging herself against the chill.

The terrace was empty in contrast to the crowded ballroom below. Lilly walked to the edge and looked out over the city. The wind tugged at her hair, her dress, and she let it have its way with her. She felt a tear escape the corner of her eye, carried off by the wind before it could trace a path down her cheek.

"Lilly." Her heart raced as she heard the smooth, familiar voice of Killian Helmar. She turned to face him, her breath catching in her throat at the sight of his imposing figure and piercing blue-grey eyes.

"What are you doing here?" she asked, trying to keep her voice steady despite the rush of fear and anger coursing through her veins.

"I couldn't resist the chance to see you," he purred, taking a step closer. His tailored suit hugged his toned body, oozing confidence and arrogance.

"You're not welcome here," Lilly spat, her words laced with venom. "She hated you."

Killian's lips curled into a smirk as he closed the distance between them. The scent of his cologne filled Lilly's senses, stirring up memories of their past together.

"That's never stopped us before," he murmured, voice low and dangerous. He let his hand drift to her hip and squeeze, fingernails pressing through the silk of her dress. "Admit it, you miss me."

Lilly turned away her gaze as she tried to anchor her racing heart—until Killian's mouth ghosted across her throat like ice. Rational thought shattered.

"Stop," she gasped, twisting away.

"Why should I?" he whispered. His hands slid around her waist, trapping her. "You love this little game of cat and mouse...the chase...the capture...me fucking you...hard." His words were velvet-coated steel.

Lilly struggled to breathe as Killian's words sent shivers down her spine. But before things could escalate further, she mustered all her strength and pushed him away.

"I mean it, Killian," she said firmly.

His fingers tightened into a claw-like grip as she tried to back away, a smirk twisting his lips.

"Fine," he said with an unsettling grin. "But do you think your precious donors would be interested in learning the true reason behind your 'oh so charitable' involvement in this project?" He raised an eyebrow. "Your guilt for fucking me. Your best friend despised me, ran from me, and yet while everyone searched for her, you crawled right into my bed."

Memories crashed into Lilly: nights of desperate fury and passion after Willow vanished. Nights when she'd clung to Killian's depraved comfort just to feel something.

"I missed her, and I was angry at her for leaving. Being with you…makes…made…me feel closer to her somehow, but you…you are a mistake."

"One, you seem eager to repeat," Killian taunted while tracing a finger down the exposed part of her chest.

Lilly shook her head forcefully.

"No," she said firmly, finding strength, "not anymore."

"Why?" he breathed as he pulled her closer and slowly dragged his tongue from her collarbone to just below her ear.

Lilly let out a soft moan as Killian's fingers tangled in the slit of her gown, gathered the long fabric from the side of her dress above her thigh, exposing her leg to the chilled air before sliding his hand between her legs.

"We can't." Lilly's pulse climbed.

"Why?" His lips brushed her ear, voice a rasp, sliding her thong to the side and letting two fingers enter her. "You're fucking soaked."

"We can't…" Lilly moaned as Killian continued to stroke her from the inside while grinding his palm into her clit; she was so close.

"Because…because I…I finally have a chance…to make things right with her…can't let this ruin it."

"Make things right?" Killian repeated mockingly. "Lilly?" Then after a pause, he said, "Did you find her? Do you know where she is?"

Lilly's eyes widened in fear, and she involuntarily took in a sharp breath. She had just exposed Willa's alive.

"No, of course not. I have no idea where she is," Lilly lied, trying to regain control of the situation.

"You're lying." He pulled out and slammed his fingers through her hair, yanking her face up. "Tell me!"

Before she could answer, his palm cracked across her cheek. Pain flared, and she tasted blood. Lilly cried out in pain and shock, cupping the side of her face that now throbbed from the impact.

"I can't," Lilly pleaded, tears welling up in her eyes.

"How long have you known where she is!?"

"About a month," she cried when Killian asked again about Willa's whereabouts. "I found her a few weeks ago."

"Where?" Killian demanded sternly.

"I can't, please," Lilly begged, "I promised her."

"You, precious little fool." Killian sneered. "As if I don't know your schedule."

Lilly's heart raced as she remembered the twisted, toxic relationship she had with Killian. After Willow's disappearance, they had become even more enmeshed in each other's lives.

"She's in Georgia," he said triumphantly. "You were in Savannah before Miami, which you just got back from. I can't say I've ever been to Savannah...but there's no time like the present."

"Killian, no," Lilly pleaded, panic rising in her chest. This was not how the evening was supposed to go. "Please, she's moved on, please let her be."

"Moved on? What do you mean she's moved on, Lilly?" A dark and desperate flame was evident in his eyes.

"I can't, Killian, please!" Lilly's voice cracked, terror straining her words as Killian's hand snaked around her throat, tightening like a vise.

"Tell me, Lilly, or I swear I'll throw you right over the side of this balcony."

"They broke up...but he loves her." Lilly gasped, choking on her words.

Killian's grip slackened, releasing her with deliberate slowness.

"Who is he?"

"I don't know," Lilly lied, her pulse pounding in her ears. "Just some guy."

"What kind of guy, Lilly?" he demanded, his voice a low, menacing growl.

"What do you want to hear, Killian, that he's rich, important, famous? That he's better than you? Well, he is...but it's not hard to be a better man than *you*..."

"Who is he, Lilly?" he roared, flinging her to the floor with brutal force.

"Killian, please...let it go..." Lilly sobbed, collapsing to her knees, tears streaming down her face. "You have me..."

But Killian dismissed her cries, turning toward the elevator with a chilling resolve. Casting a final, derisive glance over his shoulder, he sneered at Lilly, a sinister gleam in his eyes.

"You'll never be her, Lilly. And you wonder why she didn't tell you where she was going." His laughter was a harsh, mocking sound. "Only three weeks of knowing where she is…and the first time we see each other…I finger-fuck it out of you."

As the elevator doors closed behind him, Lilly was left in the oppressive silence. She knew it wouldn't be long before Killian was on Willa's trail, relentless and unyielding. Lilly would have to confess everything to her friend—that Killian knew where she was, that it was her fault he found out, that she had never severed ties with him after Willa left, and that she had been sleeping with the enemy for the past three years. Lilly knew this betrayal meant losing Willa forever, but her friend's safety was her only priority now.

Chapter Fifteen

The Betrayal

Down the coast, back in Magnolia Shores, Willa paced her apartment, the wooden floorboards creaking softly underfoot. The room was bathed in the muted hues of dusk, shadows stretching and contorting with each hesitant step she took.

Her thoughts drifted to Jackson, his kind eyes that always seemed to understand her unspoken fears, his gentle strength that made her feel safe and cherished. The memory of his arms around her, his heartbeat a steady rhythm against her own, haunted her. She ached for that security.

With a deep, shaky breath, Willa picked up her phone. Her fingers trembled as she typed a message, each letter a battle against the uncertainty gnawing at her. Her heart pounded against her ribs, each beat echoing the fear and hope intertwined within her.

"I miss you. I'm so sorry." She sent the words, a tangible echo of her longing, a fragile bridge stretched across the chasm of their separation. It had only been a few weeks, but maybe he *had* moved on, and if so, it would at least be closure.

Time seemed to slow, each second stretching into an eternity. The silence was oppressive, filling the room with a weight she could barely bear. Her mind raced with doubts, each one louder than the last, until the phone vibrated in her hand, pulling her from her spiral.

"I can't stop thinking about you, about those nights. Willa, please, let me back in." Jackson's reply appeared on the screen, simple yet potent enough to bring tears to her eyes.

A sob caught in her throat, raw and sudden, the emotional dam within her breaking. Willa clutched the phone close to her chest, her fingers digging into the smooth surface as if it could somehow draw Jackson closer to her. His confession lit up the darkening room, casting away the shadows of doubt and fear.

The phone rang in her hand, startling her, but it wasn't Jackson; it was Lilly...

"I'm so sorry, Willa," Lilly stammered over the line, her words tumbling out in a hurried mess. "At the fundraiser, Killian was there. He knows."

"Go on," Willa urged, an icy calm settling over her tone, belying the fury that churned in her gut.

Lilly took a shaky breath, her voice barely above a whisper.

"We were fighting about you, and I don't remember what I said, but he knows you're alive and in Georgia and that you're involved with someone. I thought if he knew there was someone else, maybe he'd stay in DC."

The revelation was a punch to Willa's chest, her heart pounding like a drum in her ears. Betrayal snaked its way through her veins, a venomous thread that threatened to unravel her composure.

"What!? How could you do this...how could you do this to me? Why would you even speak to him?!" Willa's voice erupted, louder than she intended, a scream that echoed off the high ceilings, reverberating back to her as if the very walls were accusing Lilly alongside her.

There was a pause, a choked sob, and then Lilly's confession poured forth like a dam breaking.

"Because, when you disappeared...Killian was all I had left of you." Lilly continued, "I thought you'd died, and to find out you just left me there... Like I meant nothing to you. All those years of friendship, sisterhood, and you left me to go start a new life without me."

Her cry was raw, a wound exposed to the air.

"How could you do that to ME? Some of us can't just pick up and leave when things get difficult, Willow!"

The accusation hung between them, a heavy fog that settled over Willa's thoughts. She sank onto the edge of her bed, the familiar creak of the mattress offering no comfort. Jealousy? It had always been the hidden thorn on the rose of their friendship, but...was it now?

Willa's dark eyes stared at nothing as she absorbed the weight of Lilly's words, feeling the last threads of their bond fray and snap.

Willa's fingers clenched the phone tighter, her knuckles blanching. Lilly's voice, once a melody of their shared laughter and secrets, now carried a discordant truth that made Willa's pulse race with a mixture of anger and sorrow.

"Ever since college," Lilly's voice trembled through the line, "I've been jealous of you, Will. You don't understand. You were always...the smart one, the strong one, the one who had it all together."

The quiet hum of the air conditioner was the only sound in the room as Willa struggled to process Lilly's words. She could almost see Lilly pacing in her own room, wringing her hands—a nervous habit from their study sessions during psych exams.

"When you vanished, when you ran from Killian, it was like I was losing everything all over again."

The confession came out in a rush, laced with bitterness.

"You didn't just leave him, Willa; you left me too. Just like after Mom had died, there I was, trying to fill the void with whatever would numb the pain."

Willa's gaze drifted to the window where streetlight filtered through, casting shadows across the hardwood floors. She remembered those days vividly, how Lilly's vibrant spirit seemed to dim with each passing week, and there was nothing Willa could do to stop it.

"I didn't mean for it to happen...at first we were both just so angry at you for leaving, and the longer you were gone, between the grief and loneliness and the drugs he always had on hand...the easier it got," Lilly confessed.

"Oh my God…Lilly…you are fucking Killian?" Willa asked with shock in her voice, already knowing the answer.

"I'm so sorry, Will, it never meant anything, just being able to escape for a while… He'd make me forget." Lilly's heart broke as she revealed the truth. "But then I found you again, and I will do anything to make this right. He knew I had been in Savannah, and when he said he would find you there…"

Willa gasped as the realization set in.

"I begged him not to find you, to just let you be. I told him you were finally happy and had a new life, that you would never take him back, that you…were in love with someone else, someone who's better than him, rich, famous, powerful, everything he's not."

"LILLY!" Willa screamed.

"I just wanted to hurt him for being the reason you left…"

"Is that the truth, Lilly…or are you actually more afraid you'd lose *him*…if he came looking for me?"

"Willa, I'm sorry." Lilly sobbed on the other end of the line.

Willa sat frozen, the phone pressed to her ear, the betrayal seeping into her bones.

She realized the depth of Lilly's despair, mirroring the desperation she herself had felt in Killian's relentless grip. The mind games, the gaslighting; Killian was so skilled. Of course, he would pick her. Lilly was the closest thing to real family Willa had. Maybe, Lilly never stood a chance… But this—the reason didn't matter anymore. Killian was on his way.

Chapter Sixteen

The Arrival

"I'm still in shock, Cassy. Just like that? She handed me right back to him on a silver platter."

Cassy, leaning against her desk, offered a soft, reassuring smile.

"Do you think he will really try to find you?" Cassy asked with a gentle concern.

"From what Lilly said…he could already be on his way," Willa said.

"Well, maybe he will make a few laps around downtown Savannah, not find you, and go home," Cassy offered, already knowing how unrealistic it would be.

Magnolia Shores was about twenty minutes from Savannah's historic district. If Killian did arrive, he would, of course, check the surrounding towns in the Greater Savannah area.

"But you're not alone, Willa. Not this time. We've got your back, the whole town does, sweetie. If he shows, which we all hope he doesn't, it will never be like what you went through before. This time, you have people who care, who will protect you," Cassy continued.

"You know that actually kind of does make me feel better," Willa said with a sigh of relief and a genuine smile. "I actually do have people now, don't I?"

"Yes, and we love you," she said, giving Willa a hug. "Let me go grab us some lunch across the street." Cassy checked her watch. "When I get back, we'll sit down and come up with a game plan, okay?"

"Thank you, Cass," Willa said as her friend slipped out the door, leaving her in the quiet office. The sounds of the little town filtered in through the half-open window.

A few seconds later, the bell above the door jingled.

"You forget something, Cass?" Willa called with a slight laugh, expecting Cassy's return. But the reply that came was not from Cassy.

"Just you," a low, paralyzing voice said, sending a visceral chill down Willa's spine.

It took her a moment to summon the courage to turn around. There, in the doorway, stood Killian. His blond hair was as immaculately styled as ever, those piercing light steel-colored eyes, cold and calculating beneath the façade of casual attire; a well-fitted shirt that hinted at the physique he maintained with rigorous self-control, jeans that were clearly designer despite their attempt at nonchalance.

"Killian," she whispered, her voice barely audible. The hatred that surged within her was potent, yet there was an undeniable undercurrent of longing for a past that could never be reclaimed, a past before the hurt, the betrayal.

Her eyes rose up his six-foot-four-inch frame to meet his. Their eyes locked, and in that gaze, a tumultuous history played out; a battlefield of emotions where fear clashed with misplaced desire, and loathing warred with memories best left buried. Willa stood frozen, a statue in the sanctuary she had built far from the reach of this man.

"Look, I didn't come here to cause a scene." Killian's smooth voice broke the silence that had settled like frost. "Lilly let it slip you were in this area, and I figured I would look you up."

"You did, huh? Just thought 'hey, after three years I'll look up that woman who disappeared in the middle of the night because she hates me'?" Willa's voice was laced with a power she had long forgotten, anger simmering beneath each syllable.

"I'm sorry for the surprise, Willow. Truly." Killian's words were coated in an earnest tone that collided with the icy detachment in his eyes. He stepped closer, and she could see the practiced concern carved into his features. "I shouldn't have come without warning. But...I've missed you."

Missed her? The apology sounded genuine, but Willa's mind recoiled, memories assaulting her, a past where his words were weapons and every touch a trap. As he reached out and gently grasped her shoulders, a tremor of panic rippled through her. His grip anchored her not to safety, but to the nights stained by fear and pain, to the moment when he had torn her world apart.

"Don't..." Her voice was lost amid the echoes of screams from years ago, her breaths coming in shallow gasps as if the air in the room had thinned. "Just leave." She tried to regain control over the trembling in her voice.

"Come on. Can you honestly tell me *this* is the life you really want? Look at this place," he said, motioning his arms around the office. "You're better than this. Baby, come home. Things are different now... I'm different now. It won't be like it was before—"

She cut him off. "What was it like before? Huh? I would love to know how much your memory has twisted reality."

Since Willow had left DC, things for Killian had started to unravel. He knew this. Killian had been able to hold things together for about six months after Willow had left, but slowly, his temper worsened. He had considered switching hospitals and attempting to start over, but word had already gotten out that Killian was an unreliable loose cannon. No one was willing to take a chance on him. The only reason St. Al's had kept him on staff was to minimize the negative attention the hospital would receive if Killian was fired and acted out.

It didn't take very long before people started putting the pieces together to realize that Willow had kept Killian in check. As much as he had tried to manipulate the narrative that Willow was the unstable one, people could see through it. Killian knew the only way to restore his reputation was to convince Willow to return to DC so things would return to "normal." He thought it would be simple. Find her, show up, fake an apology, play up their romantic past, remind Willow of the original plan for fortune and fame, and then bring her back.

It was utterly implausible to think that Willa may have actually come to like her slower-paced life on Magnolia Shores. Or that she had built a chosen family that had been instrumental in her healing. She had no intention of walking away. Yes, her identity was no longer hidden. Killian had found her. Willa had played all types of scenarios in her mind if this were to actually happen. Previously, her plan had been that if Killian ever found her, she would simply board the next plane and disappear again. But now, she thought of Cassy, Sydney, Emma, and how much more she would actually lose if she let Killian's intimidation efforts work.

"I'm not going back with you. That's not the life I want anymore. I'm different now," she said with firm confidence.

"People don't change like that, Will. You know that. Don't lie and pretend you don't miss it. I can see it in your eyes: that longing. You want to be back on top, Will. Being recognized, people being in awe of your abilities. Punishing those who did you wrong." He flashed a devious, knowing grin.

For a brief second Willa thought about it. What would happen if she did go back? What *would* people say? Would they throw themselves at her feet and apologize, would they tell her how wrong they had been and how their lives over the past three years had been torture without her there to save the day. A touch of darkness flashed in her eyes and Killian jumped on it.

"I'm nothing without you, Will, I know that now," Killian continued. "We used to be so good together, unstoppable, but I fucked it all up. It's my fault." He slowly backed Willa up against the office wall, lifted her chin up and gently kissed her.

"Losing you changed me. Let me prove it to you." Killian's voice whispered in her ear. His voice was desperate and pleading, each word carrying the weight of regret. He pinned Willa against the wall of the office, his hands on either side of her head as he leaned in to kiss her again. She tried to resist at first, but his touch was too familiar, too intoxicating. Against her better judgment, she gave in to the heat of his lips on hers.

"You ruined us," she whispered back, but her body betrayed her resolve even as she said it. "It could never be the way it was or the way it was supposed to be."

All the years of hurt and torment seemed to melt away as he trailed kisses down her neck, sending shivers down her spine. His hands began roaming over her body, igniting long-buried desires that she thought she had extinguished long ago.

"I know," he responded between kisses, "and I'll spend the rest of my life making it up to you, just please...give me another chance."

Willa's mind screamed at her to stop, to push him away and run as far as she could from his suffocating grasp. But her heart, damaged as it was, ached for the man he once had been—the man who had swept her off her feet and promised her the world. The same man who had shattered her trust and broken her spirit. But still, that glimmer of hope refused to die.

Hesitantly, Willa's arms slid around his neck, deepening the kiss. Killian growled with approval, taking it as a sign of submission. He pressed his hips against her, letting her feel his arousal, and she couldn't help but respond; their passion reignited like dry kindling waiting for a spark.

In that moment, they were transported back to a simpler time before the darkness had consumed them both. But Willa knew this was only temporary, an illusion. Once their lust was sated, the harsh reality of their dangerous relationship would rear its ugly head once more.

Killian mistook the passionate response as a sign of forgiveness, a green light to continue. His hands ventured down her curves, seeking to touch her in a way he remembered all too well.

Willa purred, the heat rising in her displaced, as her thoughts trailed back to a man who had started to change her, strengthen her.

"Jackson," Willa whispered, her eyes snapped open, the haze of desire lifting as the reality of her current situation reawakened her.

"What did you just say?" Killian seethed, his eyes engulfed in rage. While he was trying to seduce Willow, she was thinking about another man.

"I...was...thinking..." Willa sputtered, stunned by her own admission. There was no denying it; she wanted Jackson. Jackson had awakened places in Willa's psyche that she hadn't known existed or at least was too afraid to explore alone.

"So, there is someone else? I thought Lilly was just trying to piss me off when she let that little bit out. Who the fuck is Jackson?"

"Everything okay in here?" Cassy's voice thundered into the room like the cavalry arriving just as the fortress was about to fall. Hearing Cassy's voice snapped Willa out of her near trance-like state.

Killian turned his head slightly toward Cassy, his hands tightening on Willa's shoulders. Cassy's gaze flicked between Killian's hands and Willa's terrified expression, understanding the unspoken message... it was *him*. Her protective instincts flared, and she stepped forward with fierce determination.

"Let her go, Killian," Cassy commanded, her voice cutting through his façade of calmness.

"This is between me and Will," Killian growled, his composure slipping away.

Cassy refused to back down. "Like hell it is." She moved closer, ready to defend her friend at any cost.

Willa whimpered as Killian abruptly released her.

"This isn't over, Will." His frustration radiated from him as he stormed out of the room, leaving behind an unsettling sense of unfinished business.

Cassy rushed to Willa's side, wrapping her arms around her trembling friend.

"Are you okay? What did he do to you?"

Willa shook her head, tears streaming down her face.

"Nothing... He just kissed me and...I let him." She felt ashamed and weak for giving in to him so easily.

"God, Cassy, what's wrong with me? I don't want him, I don't want him back in my life...but whenever he touches me. If you hadn't come back when you did...I...I may have given in."

Cassy held onto Willa tightly, understanding her struggle all too well.

"It's okay," Cassy reassured her. "You two have a very complicated history, and it wasn't always bad."

Willa nodded, feeling comforted by Cassy's words. Part of her still loved Killian, or at least the idea of who she thought he could be. She couldn't deny that a small part of her still wanted him, despite everything he had put her through.

"I know," Willa choked out between sobs.

Cassy held onto her friend for a few more moments before gently pulling away.

"Oh my God..." Willa tensed again, remembering. "Cassy, just before you came in...I said Jackson's name."

***

The bell above Lavonte's door chimed as Cassy and Willa exited, their stomachs full but their minds unsettled.

"Everything will be all right," Cassy reassured her, squeezing Willa's hand as they walked down the historic tree-lined street toward Willa's apartment.

Willa managed a nod while she clutched her phone like a lifeline, her eyes scanning the streets and alleyways.

"He's not finished with this yet," Willa said.

As they approached the apartment, Willa spotted a solitary figure perched on the first-floor porch steps. Her heart lurched into her throat, hammering against her rib cage. She stopped dead in her tracks, her hand trembling as she reached for Cassy, her other fumbling with the phone.

"Hey, it's okay," Cassy said, her grip tightening around Willa's arm. "Remember, you're not alone."

The figure rose, his movements deliberate and unhurried. Willa's mind was racing with scenarios of confrontation and escape. If this was round two with Killian, she wanted to be ready.

"There she is," came a voice, warm and comforting as the Georgia sun after a summer rain.

Chapter Seventeen

The Switch

Relief crashed into Willa like a wave as Jackson stepped forward, illuminated by the streetlight, his dark brown eyes locking onto hers. The fear melted away, replaced by an unexpected surge of excitement.

"Jackson!" The name escaped her lips in a half-sob. She sprang toward him, her body colliding with his. His arms enveloped her in a fortress of muscle and warmth, lifting her from the ground, a sanctuary she had missed terribly.

"It's only for tonight," he murmured, breathing deep into her hair, his voice tinged with regret. "I must be in New York tomorrow, but I needed to see you."

"Follow me," Willa whispered, her voice raw with emotion. There was no hesitation as she led him to her apartment.

Once inside her room, the space where vulnerability and strength now coexisted, Willa closed the door behind them. She reached for Jackson instinctively, with urgency conjured from weeks of yearning. His lips pressed against hers, his hands on her hips. Everything from earlier in the day was erased by his touch. This is where she wanted to be. Fear be damned. She surrendered into his arms. The faint lights were still on in her apartment, their shadows peeking through the window curtains as the chilled Georgia evening air filled the room.

As the door closed behind them, Jackson's warm brown eyes found Willa's and held them in a stare that spoke volumes. He leaned forward, his hands cupping her cheeks gently as he pulled her toward him for a tender kiss. His lips brushed against hers, soft and hesitant at first, then with a more urgent, claiming hunger. Willa melted into him, sinking into his embrace like a drowning woman finding air.

She traced his jawline with her fingers, feeling the rough stubble underneath her fingertips. He groaned low in his throat as she ran her fingers through his hair, tangling them in the strands. The sound sent shivers down her spine.

"I thought you'd never come back," she whispered.

"I couldn't stay away," he admitted quietly, hands wrapped around her hips, guiding her to the bed.

"You've underestimated how much I need to see you, hold you, taste you," he continued with a gravelly voice.

The backs of Willa's legs grazed the side of the mattress.

"Now...get on the bed." His voice was low with deep intensity.

She obeyed, lying down on her back.

Jackson climbed over her; a leg on either side of her, he sat back on his heels, staring down at her.

Willa noticed a mischievous flicker in his eyes. It was Jackson, but darker. There was a raw, primal energy emanating from his entire being.

Willa slowly bit her lower lip, looking up at him.

She pulled him closer still, arching her back to push herself into him harder.

"Willa..." His voice was rough with desire now.

He started to trail wet kisses down her neck, which rapidly turned into gentle nips and bites, sending chills racing across her skin.

"Oh God..." Willa moaned softly at the touch of his warm mouth on her sensitive skin as he pressed her deeper against the mattress.

Willa took in a sharp breath as Jackson's mouth closed around her hardened nipple poking through her thin shirt, her bra doing nothing to conceal her arousal. He nipped at her peak over her shirt, his teeth making her squirm in anticipation. His hands slipped under her shirt, sliding it over her head, fingers tracing the lace of her bra before he removed it as well.

He unbuttoned her jeans, his fingers shaking slightly from longing and need. She helped him, raising her hips so he could slide them off and reveal lacy panties already damp with her arousal.

Jackson moaned at the sight, his cock straining against his own jeans. "You're so fucking perfect," he murmured, leaning back to run his eyes appreciatively over every inch of exposed skin.

He returned his attention to the apex of her thighs, running a finger lightly over the fabric covering her center. His touch ignited sparks beneath her skin; she squirmed at the sheer thrill of it all. He peeled away the last barrier between them, sending shudders coursing through both their bodies.

"Spread your legs for me," he commanded gently, and she obeyed without hesitation. His gaze roamed over her glistening and ready body before settling on her flushed face.

"Good girl," he breathed before descending upon her.

He traced light circles with his tongue teasing her swollen clit, causing Willa to writhe beneath him in ecstasy.

"More...more..." Willa pleaded.

"Not yet..." Jackson said with a low guttural laugh. "Patience...Love," he added, giving her inner thigh a gentle corrective bite.

The pressure built within her. Willa tried to push herself against him, desperately seeking more friction, but his grip on her hips made it impossible.

Willa let out a tortured sigh, "Jax..."

Jackson looked up at Willa from his task, meeting her gaze with half-lidded eyes as he slid two fingers inside her.

"Fuck, I love how you taste," he murmured huskily between licks.

She met his words with a low whimper as she felt him quicken the pace of his fingers within her, matching the rhythm of his tongue on her throbbing clit.

"Cum for me, Love. Cum for me."

The pressure built in waves until finally cresting into an orgasm with a wave of aftershocks more intense than Willa had experienced before.

"Good girl."

Jackson moved to hold her close again as he lay beside her, watching her come down, eyes half-closed and cheeks flushed with a continued desire.

"Are you all right, Love?"

"Yes...that was...what was that?" Willa slowly said.

Willa had never been edged, never craved that torturous delay woven with exquisite torment. She'd always been the one in control with partners, dominant. But tonight, through Jackson's touch, words, and voice, she was powerless in a sensually spiritual way.

Willa, wrapped in Jackson's arms, savored this intimate moment under the soft glow of the dimly lit room, the cool breeze wafting in through the open window.

She shifted, pinning Jackson beneath her, his hips firmly between her thighs.

With a wicked grin, Willa started grinding her hips against him, reveling in the feeling of him hard beneath her, but loathing that he was still clothed. She leaned forward and began to slowly unbutton his shirt, taking her time to kiss and lick every inch of exposed skin as she made her way down, as he simultaneously unbuttoned his jeans.

Jackson groaned in ecstasy as Willa's lips trailed down his sculpted abs. Unable to wait any longer, he gripped her hips fiercely, forcefully pulling her onto him. The sensation of her, hot and wet, pushed him to the brink.

***

Killian stood rooted to the ground, trembling with fury as he watched the silhouettes dancing behind the flimsy curtains. His blood boiled as he saw the shadow of a woman, her body etched into his memory, moving rhythmically atop a figure that wasn't him. When the shadows shifted, showing the man dominating Willow, Killian's vision turned red.

He hurriedly made his way to the apartment door, ready to break it down, to kill the man who dared touch his property, but he needed more proof. He listened closely to hear the voices on the other side. He pressed his ear to the door, his heart pounding in his chest, nearly loud enough to drown out the sounds from within.

"God, don't stop," Willow begged, her voice a raw, desperate plea that Killian recognized all too well.

A deep, accented voice joined hers.

"Willa," he growled, *"Fucking...perfect...pussy..."* he continued thrusting deep within her, *"fuuuuck...say my name, Willa...say it."*

"God. Yes. J-jack...son..." she gasped.

Killian's rage spiraled, his body shaking with its force. It was him...Jackson.

Another voice boomed from the bottom of the porch stairs. Lavonte emerged, his stance mirroring Killian's aggression.

"You lost, buddy?" Lavonte challenged, his voice a low growl. He saw the inferno in Killian's eyes and stood his ground.

With a condescending chuckle, Lavonte spoke again. "No need for violence, my friend. We all just love Willa and we ain't gonna let anyone...especially not you, hurt her. So, suggest you move along now and save yourself some trouble."

Chapter Eighteen

The Morning After

Willa awoke to the harsh light streaming in through the windows as the sun broke through the horizon. She groaned and pulled the covers over her head, trying to block out the unwanted intrusion. Jackson was already up, his strong figure silhouetted against the window as he packed his belongings into a small carry-on bag.

"Noooo," Willa begged, her voice muffled by the blankets. "Don't go."

A devilish smile played on Jackson's lips as he turned to face her, his eyes sparkling mischievously. "Have to, Love. Gotta be in New York by 2:00. Taping is at 4:00, and it will air tonight at 11:30."

"And then where will you be?" Willa asked, her voice filled with longing and sadness.

"On a plane back to London," Jackson replied, his tone tinged with regret.

"Fucking London," Willa scoffed, her frustration evident.

"But," Jackson sat down on the edge of the bed next to her, his eyes shining with excitement, "I never got a chance to tell you last night because...well." He smirked, glancing around at the disheveled sheets and scattered clothing still covering the floor.

"But we got the official word a few weeks ago. They've green-lighted season two and..." Jackson intentionally paused, enjoying the suspense as Willa's eyes widened in anticipation. "We're filming in Savannah."

"What?! Are you serious?" Willa exclaimed in disbelief.

"Yes, ma'am. You'll be stuck with me for twelve weeks, and if it's anything like the first season, it will be closer to sixteen weeks."

Willa's heart swelled with joy. She couldn't believe that she would have more time with Jackson. Months with him. She grabbed him by the shirt, pulling him down onto the bed. Wrapping her arms around him, she kissed him passionately.

"When does it start?" she asked eagerly.

"A week from Thursday," Jackson replied, a hint of excitement and nervousness in his voice.

Willa looked at him, stunned. "Why didn't you tell me?"

"You told me to stay away. I didn't want to hurt you," Jackson explained, his eyes softening as he met her gaze.

He continued, "I'm so glad you reached out. I don't know how I could have been this close and not contacted you."

She touched his face gently, her fingers tracing the line of his jaw.

"I missed you," she whispered, her voice trembling with emotion. "I missed you so much."

Jackson leaned in, pressing his forehead against hers.

"I missed you, too, Willa. Every single day."

They lay there for a moment, wrapped in each other's arms, savoring the warmth and comfort of being together. The future seemed uncertain, but for now, they had this moment. And that was enough to fill their hearts with hope and love.

***

"Okay, let me get this straight," Sydney said. "Lilly, Willa's supposed best friend hosts a benefit in her missing friend's honor to fulfill said best friend's dream, and at said benefit she tells her best friend's terrible ex, who she's been sleeping with since best friend disappeared exactly where to find this missing friend. Terrible ex immediately gets on a plane and shows up in best friend's town, confronts her at work, begs her to take him back, she says no...he gets mad and storms off?"

"That's not all. He came back," Cassy murmured, her voice barely rising above the blues crooning from the speakers.

"Fuck, what?" Sydney questioned. "When? Where?"

"Last night," Lavonte said. "Confronted him outside Willa's place."

"He was on her porch," Cassy continued.

"Wasn't she with...last night?" Sydney inquired.

"Yeah and...um. There is a pretty good chance Killian may have...heard them," Lavonte murmured uneasily.

"Wait, slow down, who heard what with who?" Emma's bright green eyes clouded with concern and confusion, and Sydney's jaw set in quiet defiance.

"Oh my God, Emma, Killian heard Jackson fucking Willa last night. Keep up!" Sydney explained with concern for Willa, covered by annoyance at Emma.

Lavonte continued, his expression serious.

"I've spoken to the cops already," he said quietly, ensuring only they could hear. "And I've given the neighboring towns a heads-up about Killian. I don't know what his plan is, but the look in his eyes last night...that man ain't right."

"Thank you, Baby," Cassy replied, her voice carrying warmth despite the circumstances.

"Does Willa know?" Emma asked. "I mean, has anyone checked on her today?"

"I don't think so, but she's with Jackson," Cassy said.

"Oh...do we really need to ruin their reunion with this?" asked Sydney.

"Ya gonna have to tell her," Lavonte said.

"Why can't we just have Killian arrested?" Sydney blurted out, her voice a mix of frustration and hope for an easy resolution. "He shouldn't be allowed to just waltz into town after everything he's done to her. He's only here to make her miserable."

As if summoned by the urgency of their conversation, the door to the bar opened with a definitive creak, allowing the warm Savannah breeze to seep into the room. The Magnolia Shores sheriff, a broad-shouldered silhouette against the doorway, stepped inside.

"Mornin' ladies, Lavonte," he greeted, tipping his hat slightly. The sheriff's arrival punctured the bubble of their private worries, and they straightened in their seats, each wearing a different shade of apprehension on their faces.

"Sydney was just askin' about Killian Helmar," Cassy said, gesturing to the sheriff with a nod. "Wonderin' why we can't get him locked up before he causes any real trouble."

"Understandable," the sheriff replied, resting a hand on the back of an empty chair. His gaze met Sydney's, steady and solemn. "We can't arrest a man for what he might do, only for what he's done. And right now, Killian hasn't done anything concrete to warrant being put behind bars. He's just *potentially* a threat. We've got to abide by the law here, even when our gut tells us something else."

The words hung heavy in the air, a stark reminder of the limitations they faced. Sydney exhaled sharply, her fingers tightening around her glass. They were stuck in a waiting game with Killian, and the rules were not in their favor.

The sheriff's boots scraped the worn floorboards as he circled the chair, opting to lean against the table instead.

"Look," he began, his voice a low rumble that seemed too large for the small bar, "we all know Killian and Willa have history. We all believe Willa's side—hell, who wouldn't? But officially, we can't pin anything on him without solid proof."

"Officially?" Cassy echoed, her tone laced with skepticism. Her hazel eyes darted to the gleaming bottles lined against the mirror behind the bar as if seeking a reflection of some answer they hadn't yet considered.

"Whatever happened between them was in another state and years ago. And well, we don't have that jurisdiction," the sheriff continued, his hat held loosely in one hand while the other gestured vaguely toward the door, as though pointing to a distant past. "Aside from being seen around town lately, Lavonte seein' him 'round Willa's apartment last night... Just ain't enough to bring him in."

At the mention of Willa's vulnerability, Emma shifted in her seat, her fingers nervously entwining. The dim light of the bar seemed to deepen the lines of concern etched into her face. Sydney placed her glass down with a muted thud, her jaw set in frustration.

"Being seen isn't a crime," Sydney muttered, her words tinged with the bitterness of helplessness. She turned to Cassy, and their eyes met in silent communication—a language of fear and resolve.

Cassy's posture stiffened, the protective streak within her awakening like a coiled spring. "Then we need to be ready," she stated firmly, her gaze sweeping to include both Emma and Sydney.

"Ready for what?" the sheriff's brow furrowed, the creases mirroring his concern.

"Ready for anything Killian might do, for what he will inevitably do. Ready to protect our own," Sydney replied, her voice carrying a steely edge that challenged her soft exterior. "We'll do what we have to."

"Let's hope it doesn't come to that. I'd hate for you ladies to get yourselves involved in something you shouldn't," the sheriff said, placing his hat back on his head and giving them a nod of respect mixed with caution. He knew these women were not to be underestimated.

As the sheriff's footsteps faded away, the group remained seated, their shared silence speaking volumes. They were bound by more than friendship; they were united in a cause that was suddenly much larger than themselves.

"Oh, here she comes." Sydney nodded toward the door as Willa walked over to their table, distracted by her phone.

"How'd the goodbye go?" Cassy said sweetly in Willa's direction.

"Uhhh...I miss him so much already and it's only been an hour," Willa whined, her fingers hovering over her phone screen where she was able to watch the little dot of Jackson's flight as it moved up the coast toward New York.

"Will…" Sydney started, "we need to tell you something."

"Will, last night," Lavonte took over. "Killian was here."

"In the bar?" Willa questioned.

"No, I ran into him on the porch outside your door."

"WHAT? WHEN?"

"Sweetie," Cassy grabbed Willa's hand as she lowered herself into one of the empty chairs, "we think he knows Jackson was here. We think he may have heard you two last night."

The color drained from Willa's face. "No, no, that can't be possible."

"Old doors…windows…walls," Lavonte said. "Not very insulated."

"Oh my God…you mean he may have HEARD me and Jax last night?!" Willa exclaimed, cradling her head in her hands with a mixture of fear of Killian and embarrassment that others in town may have also been able to hear.

"You need to hear the plan. We worked it out," Cassy continued.

"Plan?" Willa echoed, hope threading through the worry lines on her forehead.

"Yep. Safe houses, lookouts, the whole nine yards. Even some creative ideas for neighborhood watch," Sydney chimed in.

"Ghost tours!" Emma suggested cheerfully. "We can use those ghost tour crowds as cover. We can do them here in Magnolia and over in Savannah. Our own little secret patrols."

"Ghost tours?" Willa couldn't help but let out a faint laugh, a momentary respite from the tension. Leave it to Emma, the textbook southern belle, to blend strategy with historic charm.

"Trust me," Cassy continued, her tone shifting to that assertive timbre that demanded attention, "if Killian so much as jaywalks, he'll have the sheriff slapping cuffs on him before he can blink."

"Thank you," Willa breathed out, allowing herself to sink into the solid reality of the plan. Her friends were her fortress, and with them, maybe she could weather the storm that was Killian.

CHAPTER NINETEEN

The Interview

"This is so exciting!" Emma squealed as she watched Willa scurry around the apartment.

"Girls, let's go!" Sydney yelled from the bottom of the stairs.

The word spread fast that Jackson was going to be on the country's most popular late-night talk show and the town was buzzing, wondering if Magnolia would be mentioned during the interview.

Willa and Emma joined Sydney at the bottom of the stairs as they hurried over to *Luis's*, where Lavonte was preparing for a little watch party.

The trio walked in, spotting Cassy at their usual table.

"I can't believe how many people are here." Willa laughed. "It's just a silly interview."

"This is a big deal for us. We don't have celebrities staying overnight in our little town." Cassy gently elbowed Willa in the shoulder.

"He was only here for like eight hours and how did anyone even know?" Willa asked.

"Probably the 'JACKSON' the whole town heard you scream running across the square to him last night. People tend to notice things like that." Lavonte threw his hands up near his face, pretending to squeal like a little schoolgirl.

Sydney joined in immediately.

"Eeeeeeeeee...he's so dreamy," Sydney said with an overly emphasized southern belle accent.

"Knock it off, you two. You're embarrassing me." Willa blushed. "Besides, he's not going to say anything. He's going to talk about the show and nothing more. It's still all way too new."

Lavonte turned up the sound on the bar TV just as the host finished up his comedic opening monologue: "And up next, Jackson Donovan."

"Shush, y'all." Cassy announced, "He's up next."

***

The next town over, Killian Helmar sat alone at the end of a dimly lit bar in Savannah's east end near the river, a half-empty glass of bourbon casting an amber glow beneath his steady gaze. The heavy air was fragrant with the musk of spilled drinks and the sharp tang of disinfectant. He swirled the liquid slowly, the single ice cube repetitively clinking against the glass.

"Somthin' on your mind there, Honey?" The husky voice of the bartender said as she wiped down the bar.

"I came here for love, you know," he said, his voice smooth like the aged bourbon before him. "To win her back." Killian's polished charm seemed to falter slightly under the weight of his true intentions.

The bartender, a woman in her early 50s with a classic rough-edged tone and skeptical eyes, offered a noncommittal grunt while she continued wiping down the counter with a ragged cloth.

"That so, huh?" she replied, sounding unimpressed.

"Her friends..." Killian continued, his tone a careful mix of regret and frustration. "They've poisoned her against me. Can't even get close without them interfering."

"Sounds rough," the bartender murmured, though her attention had already drifted to the array of bottles behind her.

Not receiving the undivided attention he was seeking, Killian glanced around the bar, noting the pockets of people absorbed in their own worlds, when a sudden shout cut through the hum of conversation.

"Hey, Doll, switch the channel, will ya? This game's a blowout!" A patron called out from across the room, gesturing at the television mounted on the wall.

Without missing a beat, the bartender grabbed the remote and flicked through the stations. The screen jumped from the sports game to a commercial, the vibrant colors of a late-night talk show intro filling the room.

"Isn't that—" the bartender began, only for her words to fade into the background as Killian fixated on the TV.

"Tonight, we're excited to welcome back to the show one of America's favorite imports, who's rapidly becoming a household name stateside, gearing up to shoot the second season of his hit show, a psychological and paranormal thriller, Mr. Jackson Cole Donovan, everyone," the host's voice boomed from the speakers.

A man, dressed in an impeccably tailored black suit, smiled warmly from the TV, his dark brown eyes alight with the charisma that had made him a fast-rising star. The crowd roared as he settled into a plush seat opposite the show's host, the backdrop glittering with the skyline of a city far from here.

"Thank you, thank you. You're all too kind. It's a pleasure to be back." The hair on the back of Killian's neck stood at attention. That accent was unmistakable—the same one that had whispered sweet nothings into Willa's ear, the same one Killian had heard through the thin walls just last night. "*Willa, say it*"—"*J-jack...son*"—the memory taunted Killian from the screen.

"I've heard season two will be filming in Savannah, Georgia," the host continued.

"Yes, there's a very haunted history in that city. It's going to be brilliant," Jackson continued, his eyes slowly gazing toward the camera.

"And I apologize, Jackson, but these women in the audience will have my head if I don't ask...what about your love life?" The host pressed on, leaning forward with a humorous, predatory eagerness. "Any special someone waiting back home 'across the pond'?" The host joked using a fake British accent.

Jackson's smile didn't falter, but his eyes darted away for a fraction of a second, betraying a hint of nervousness.

"No, no, there's no one back home. I'm focusing on my work at the moment," he deflected, eliciting laughter and applause from the unseen audience.

"But, I will say I'm greatly looking forward to spending as much time as possible in the Savannah area this year." His trademark brooding grin bewitched the audience.

"Leave it to a Brit to be so intentionally cryptic," the host chimed in. "Time for a quick break, and we'll be back with more of Jackson Donovan."

Killian's jaw clenched as he observed the exchange. Here was the mysterious stranger who had effortlessly slipped into Willa's life and now sat on national television, charming the masses while secretly acknowledging Willow. And as the crowd cheered on, oblivious to the tension playing out across Killian's features, a cold plan began to crystallize in his mind.

Lilly's words echoed in his mind, "Rich, powerful, famous, in love with her, huh?" Killian muttered under his breath. His piercing gaze fixated on the screen as the wheels turned within him. If this really was the new man in Willow's life, it would be increasingly difficult for Killian to get Willow back to DC and reclaim his old life.

CHAPTER TWENTY

The Flight

B ^{ing}

"Ladies and gentlemen, we have begun our descent into London. Please turn off all..." the flight attendant's voice faded into the background as Jackson tried to rouse himself after the seven-hour flight from New York to London. Despite years of traveling, he still hadn't gotten used to jet lag.

The plane landed with a gentle bump, and Jackson flipped on his phone. He had a car waiting to take him back to his posh Primrose Hill penthouse. Navigating the airport labyrinth, casually dressed, a baseball cap and dark glasses sufficiently camouflaged his identity successfully at 2 a.m.

Once settled into the car, his phone rang.

"What the hell are you doing awake now?" he asked, laughing lovingly into the phone.

"The twins have been doing a synchronized swimming routine on my bladder for the past two hours. That's why I'm awake," came the sweet voice of an Englishwoman. "I saw you. You looked amazing," she continued. "But...I have to know...Jackie, where were you?"

"New York?" he replied, confusion creeping into his voice.

"No...before that," the voice demanded, sterner now.

"Ames, I'm not doing this right now."

"Your flight was supposed to land and have you settled into the hotel by 6 p.m. the day before the show. Alex said you didn't show up at the hotel until two hours before the taping… Where were you?"

"I'm exhausted. Can't this wait?" Jackson hissed, annoyed at being interrogated so early.

"Was it her? Did you see her again?"

"Ames…"

"Jackie, don't you dare lie to me."

"Fuck, yes, okay. I was with her… Are you happy now? Is that what you wanted to hear?"

Amelia Donovan, "Ames" since childhood, let out a deep sigh. Jackson's sister had been playing manager, agent, assistant, and basically every other role to help her baby brother succeed from a very early age in his career. Ames was the only person allowed to call Jackson "Jackie," a nickname he actually hated but Ames continued to use as she insisted it kept him "grounded."

"I knew it! I knew you couldn't be trusted on your own," she joked, her tone much lighter.

"You're like eighteen months pregnant, Ames…and can't fly. How were you going to stop me?" The smile in his voice was contagious.

"So, how was it? How is she? What did she say? Tell me everything!"

"Really, everything? You sure?" he playfully teased.

"Ugh, Jackie, yes, you can leave out the parts where you sleep with her." He laughed.

"It was…wonderful. She's as beautiful as ever. But…"

Ames cut him off. "Don't overthink this."

"She's still hiding something."

"You said she has been through a lot, right?"

"Yeah."

"You have to be patient with her."

"I know…I—"

"No, Jackie, you don't," she interrupted him with genuine concern. "I know you mean well, but you will never know what she went through. You can't; you weren't there, you're not her."

"I want her to trust me."

"She will, in time. Right now? I wouldn't expect her to," Ames continued compassionately.

Neither of them spoke for what seemed like forever.

"Remember my time at Uni?" Ames said gently, vulnerably. "Remember what happened…"

"Ames, I know," Jackson responded, heartbreak in his tone.

"Remember how scared I was, always looking over my shoulder? You don't know what that's like…not for a woman." She took a deep breath in. "Look at your life. It's the exact opposite of something someone who has gone through what she did would want. Your life is constant attention and rightfully so. If people stop caring about you, stop watching you…you don't work…your career is over. Her life is hidden. If people are watching her, it could be her life. Be patient with her."

"This is crazy. A few days in Miami, one night in Georgia. How can I feel like this?"

"You're in love, baby bro. Trust me…the fact that she is taking this risk with you at all means she feels it too, even if she doesn't fully know it yet…but Jackie," Ames let out a concerned sigh, "he stalked her, hurt her in ways we can only imagine…if you push too hard…too fast…you'll scare her. Be patient…she'll see the man you are, who you really are."

Jackson stared out the window, the London streets a blur as they sped by. "I hope you're right, Ames. I really do."

"I always am. Now get some rest, Jackie. You're going to need it." Ames's voice was filled with warmth and confidence, soothing his anxious heart.

"Thanks, Ames. I love you."

"Love you too, baby bro."

He hung up the phone, leaning back into the seat, a mix of exhaustion and hope swirling within him. As the car navigated through the quiet streets of London, Jackson allowed himself to dream of a future where

Willa trusted him completely, where they could build something beautiful together despite the chaos of their lives.

Chapter Twenty-One
The Confrontation

It had been about a week since Killian had shown back up in Willa's life. Over the past few days, he had been a continuous looming presence, not interacting with Willa directly, but instead working his way into the hearts of the locals.

"I think he's here to win Willa back," one elderly woman whispered, tucking a silver strand behind her ear, eyes twinkling with mischief.

"They were engaged, I heard," someone said.

"Ooh, how romantic," cooed the other, clasping her hands together as if witnessing the climax of a love story.

"Romantic?" A third voice cut through the air, laced with skepticism. "Lavonte says to be wary of him. Says he could be dangerous."

"I don't see that, though. He's just lovely."

"A doctor, too."

"And that Willa is just looking to break his heart by getting on with that actor boy."

"They say she just ran right off with him one day to Miami, breaking that sweet boy's heart."

"Can't trust those Hollywood types."

Willa felt her cheeks burn; the weight of their words settled on her shoulders like the thick Georgia air. She quickened her pace, desperate to distance herself from their prying eyes and well-intentioned gossip.

At the homemade baked goods booth, Sydney and Emma stood nibbling on free samples. Willa approached them, her frustration clearly visible across her face.

"I can't believe this," she murmured, leaning in close to the girls. "Killian wasted no time, everyone's falling in love with him and I'm the cruel heartless bitch who ruined his life."

Sydney reached out, placing a reassuring hand on Willa's arm. "We are not letting down our guard," she affirmed with conviction. "We know what he is capable of. He won't win us over."

"Ugh...it's maddening," Willa said, laying her head in her palms.

The sound of footsteps on cobblestone heralded Lavonte's approach. His presence was always a comfort. "I just saw him carrying groceries for old Mr. Miller," he announced, joining the trio at the booth. "You're right, Willa, Killian's not dumb," Lavonte added, his voice low but firm. "I'm sure he is thinking he can win you back by getting this town to love him."

"He just wants to make me look like a fool. How could such a 'nice boy' do all the horrible things I claimed... Ugh...I'm going home, I'll catch up with you all later," Willa said as she turned away.

Willa's heels clicked against the cobblestone as she made her way across Johnson Square, the verdant canopy of oaks draped with Spanish moss swaying almost violently above. As if almost on cue, Killian stepped out from around one of the giant trees.

"Will...don't you see? Even this whole town of yours wants to see us together." Killian's voice was smooth like honey but laced with a deadly poison that sent an icy jolt down Willa's spine.

Killian stepped closer, his smirk never wavering as the setting sun cast an ominous glow on his sharp features.

"It's a new me," he laughed smugly, his eyes glinting with a cold and calculating malice.

"You've said that countless times before." Willa rolled her eyes. "Besides, new or old, it doesn't matter," Willa retorted, her voice trembling in frustration not fear. "I want nothing to do with you. I've moved on. Why don't you scamper off and go do the same?" She flicked her wrists in an exaggerated attempt to shoo him away.

"And what about your little London boy toy?" Killian prowled closer, his tone laced with mockery. "You actually think you've got something real with him?"

"Maybe I do," Willa said through gritted teeth, standing a little straighter, being fueled by more and more irritation with every word Killian uttered.

"Really? Because when he was asked on TV about being in a relationship, he clearly said he wasn't... Interested in the town, I think he said." Killian's laugh was like a knife twisting in her gut.

"Wonder if he's ashamed to be with you," he mercilessly continued. "You *are* a great dirty little secret, or maybe he sees you as nothing more than an easy fuck when he comes through town."

She swallowed hard, tears brewing in her eyes. She tried to muster the strength to force them away and not let Killian see her break. But his words were like arrows piercing her heart, announcing every deep-seated fear she had about her fragile relationship with Jackson.

"Stop it, Killian," she whispered, her voice barely audible over the rustling leaves.

"Oh, Will, poor baby. Face it, he can have anyone... And...he probably does. Hell...I bet right now he's got some starlet choking on his cock," Killian jeered playfully, but a cruel smile rested on his lips.

Willa felt her resolve start to crumble, a single tear escaping down her cheek. She opened her mouth to defend her relationship with Jackson but stopped short, realizing the futility of engaging in Killian's twisted game.

"I know what you're trying to do," she managed through gritted teeth, wiping away the traitorous tear with a delicate finger. "Trying to make me question everything, make me believe I'm unlovable, that YOU are the only one that could love me. It won't work this time."

"Time will tell, Willow," Killian said, his voice dropping to a sinister whisper as he leaned in close, his hot breath on her face sending chills down her spine. "You've got no one else. I AM the only one who understands you, and you know it. The only one who still wants you after all you've done. Does this town know? Does your precious Jackson know who you really are?"

With a final look of defiance, Willa turned and stepped past him, her steps quickening as she fled from Killian's presence.

"It's ok, sweetheart! I forgive you!" Killian announced across the square, loud enough to be heard by the many onlookers but not so loud to appear intentional. "We can work this out, Willa, I still love you!" he continued, slowly following her; the echoes of his voice haunted her to the sanctuary of her apartment.

Willa raced up the steps of her apartment, her heart pounding against her rib cage. She fumbled with the keys at the door, her hands trembling as she tried to shake off Killian's lingering shadow. Once inside, she leaned against the door, gasping for air and trying to calm her racing thoughts.

"Pathetic," she muttered to herself, berating her own weakness. She thought back on all the times she had stood up to him, confronted him on his bullshit, before she had ever feared him. She desperately wanted that part of her back instead of the frail little girl she viewed herself as now.

But it wasn't over. The sound of footsteps ascending the staircase outside sent a fresh wave of dread through her.

"Open up, Willow," Killian called from the other side of the door, his voice carrying a dangerous edge. "We're not done here."

She remained silent, hoping he would leave, but the persistent, slight knocking continued.

"Fine," he said after a moment, his words slicing through the door. "You don't want to talk to me? How about I go talk to the press instead? I'm sure they would love to learn all about Mr. Donovan's whore."

Willa's breath choked in her throat. She couldn't let him do that.

"Go...away...Killian," she said, her voice stronger now, though her insides were still quaking with fear.

"End it, Willow." Killian's voice, cold as ice, floated through the door. "End it now. You already know what I'm capable of, Willow... Does he?"

"Leave him alone," Willa cried. "Killian, please. He's innocent in this. He doesn't know. Please...don't hurt him."

"End it. And he and I will never even meet."

Willa could hear the smile of victory in his voice.

"Fine...you win, Killian," she sobbed, "you win."

CHAPTER TWENTY-TWO

The Wife

It had been days since Killian Helmar's silhouette last loomed in Willa's doorway, but his threats hung heavily in the humid air. Since then, he had seemingly retreated into the background. Willa had caught glimpses of him in the square, laughing with other women, his blond hair shining under the sunlight, his intense eyes not looking for hers. She wanted to believe it was all empty threats, and he was moving on, but the knot in her stomach tightened at the thought. It felt like the calm before a storm, and she couldn't shake off the dread that it was all just an act. What man would have moved to the city of his ex if he had moved on?

Lost in her thoughts, Willa barely noticed she had arrived at her destination, Sydney's quaint little bookshop and café. She pushed open the door, the familiar scent of old books and the sound of the bell announcing her arrival, offering a brief reprieve from her worries.

"Jackson can't stay in the dark about this, Will," Sydney cut the silence. "Killian's a ticking time bomb."

Willa's fingers twisted a strand of her long, wavy hair; an old nervous tic. She knew Sydney was right but admitting it out loud felt like another victory for Killian.

"I know," she whispered, her voice barely carrying over the bustle of the store's customers. "But what if telling Jackson just paints a bigger target on his back?" she said, trying to talk herself out of the inevitable.

"Better he knows what he's walking into than be blindsided. Will, he has no idea Killian is here let alone knowing Killian is pissed that you're involved with someone else…and *he's* that someone," Sydney continued, her usual buoyancy dampened by the gravity of their conversation.

"Killian thinks I ended it."

"But, Willa…you didn't. Right now, Killian's been minding his own business, thinking you're newly single and heartbroken." Sydney continued, "But you can't actually believe he has any other reason for staying around *that doesn't involve you.*"

"Right but…" Willa tried to make an excuse.

"Jackson starts filming here in a few days. What is your plan for that? Just tell Jackson to never come to Magnolia? You'll just meet him places? Yeah…that doesn't seem suspicious at all, Will…"

"But, Syd—"

Sydney cut her off. "When Killian sees Jax in town, which he will…he'll know you have been lying about it being over."

A shiver ran down Willa's spine at the thought. She pulled her cardigan tighter around her shoulders, though the evening air was still comfortably warm. The last thing she wanted was for Jackson to become collateral damage in Killian's vendetta.

"All right," she conceded with a heavy heart. "I'll tell him everything tonight."

***

Willa gripped the steering wheel until her knuckles whitened, her mind a whirlwind of excitement and trepidation. The car's headlights cut through the encroaching dusk as she navigated over the bridge toward the refurbished mansion, now a luxury hotel in the heart of Savannah's historic district where the studio had set up residence.

With each mile that brought her closer to Jackson, her heartbeat quickened. Memories of their last embrace, passionate and full of promises, played on repeat in her head. But now there was a secret wedged between them, a secret that threatened to unravel the delicate tapestry of trust they'd woven together.

Pulling into the hotel parking lot, Willa parked her car and exhaled a shaky breath. She paused momentarily, gathering the shards of her courage before stepping out into the cooling evening air. Her heels clicked against the pavement as she approached the hotel entrance, echoing her racing heart.

Willa scrolled through text messages between her and Jackson, searching for the room number he had sent her.

"Here," she texted with trepidation.

The walk from the lobby to the elevator to Jackson's suite felt like an eternity to Willa. Every step echoed in her mind, amplifying the fear and guilt gnawing at her insides. She stood outside his door, hand poised to knock, but for a moment, she thought about fleeing. The reality of what she had to confess hit her hard. How would she explain to Jackson that Killian had returned to her life?

She and Jackson had been talking daily since his surprise visit to Magnolia. Their connection remained strong despite the complications of work schedules and time zones. But she never mentioned Killian. Not once. She had carried this giant lie of omission, letting it fester and grow between them.

"Jackson!" His name escaped her lips as a sigh when she finally caught sight of him in the doorway. The warmth of his smile instantly melted away some of her anxiety. They embraced, and for a fleeting second, everything else fell away. His arms around her felt like coming home.

"There she is. I've missed you, Love," Jackson said, his accent wrapping around each syllable she desperately craved. His eyes searched hers, and in them, she saw the reflection of her own love, tinged with concern and longing.

"I've missed you, too." Willa's response was muffled against his chest. As they parted, the weight of her secret pressed down on her, heavier than ever. She could feel the words stuck in her throat, a painful lump she couldn't swallow.

Jackson's suite was as elegant as it was intimidating, much larger than Willa's apartment in Magnolia.

What am I doing here, she thought to herself.

The hotel suite was a reminder of the entirely different worlds that she and Jackson lived in. He was proud, confident, rich, and famous, yet grounded, and she was an unlovable train-wreck from DC with a dark past she had been running from for years. She didn't belong in this world...his world.

Tonight, it felt like a stage set for a drama she wasn't prepared to act in. He led her to the couch, his touch gentle but firm, sensing her unease. They sat close, and he leaned in, knees touching, the silence between them thick with unspoken words. Jackson leaned in to kiss Willa when she suddenly pulled back.

"What's wrong, Love?" Jackson asked, his voice soft but insistent. He took her hands in his, his thumb tracing soothing circles on her skin.

Willa's heart pounded. The moment of truth had arrived.

"Jackson, there's something I need to tell you," she began, her voice trembling. She took a deep breath, trying to steady herself. "Killian...he's back."

Jackson's expression shifted from concern to confusion, then to a hardened determination.

"What do you mean, he's back?"

"For about a week now, he's been...around. Lilly slipped up at the fundraiser... He found out where I was...and came here," Willa confessed, her voice barely a whisper initially, but then she found a tone of strength.

"He showed up in Magnolia, the same day you did. He had apparently been staying in Savannah, trying to locate me. We got into a heated discussion, he made some threats... I didn't know how to tell you. I didn't want to bring you into the middle of all this... We barely know each other... I didn't want to worry you."

Jackson's grip on her hands tightened, his eyes blazing with protective anger.

"The person you fear most has been just wandering around your town, and you didn't think that was something worth me knowing?"

"Honestly, I didn't want to think it was actually happening. I was scared," she admitted, tears welling up in her eyes. "Scared of what he'd do. At first, it didn't matter; you and I weren't even speaking, and then you showed up, and I was just too worried about losing you. The longer I waited to tell you... I just...I thought I could handle it, I thought I could convince him to leave, and it would just go away...but he hasn't and..."

Jackson leaned into the back of the couch, rubbing his forehead with his hands. "What threats?"

"It's not important..."

"What...threats, Willa?"

"He said to end it with you. If I didn't, he would make sure you...didn't want me anymore. He would expose things to the media...about everything about our past, mine and his...anything that would make you...leave."

"So what? Let them know."

"You don't understand. There is so much more than what you know." Tears started rolling down Willa cheeks. "But it's ok. I told him I ended it. Since then, he's been around but...basically ignoring me..."

"Wait, what do you mean there is more? You found out he was still married, you tried to leave, he threatened you with harm if you left, you stayed thinking you had no other choice...and you finally were able to run. You did, you moved to a small town, you started over, and he FOLLOWED you here. He sounds mad, crazy. Willa, people may be more compassionate than you give them credit—"

"There is more," Willa cut Jackson off.

"Okay and?"

"You don't understand...we can't be together."

"No, Willa...no, you're not doing this again, not because of him."

"It's the only way."

"Dammit, Willa! I won't let this man interfere with OUR life."

"She died..." Willa choked on the words. "She died, Jackson, and it was my fault."

The color faded from Jackson's generally warm complexion.

"What are you talking about? Who...died...Willa?"

"His wife..."

Chapter Twenty-Three
The Unconditional

Jackson paced around the living room in the massive hotel suite all night. The soft glow of the city lights filtered through the windows, casting a dim, restless ambiance over the space. Willa was asleep, curled in the fetal position on the couch, her face softened by the vulnerability of sleep. Jackson adjusted the throw over her on his next lap around the room, his heart aching for the peace she seemed to find only in slumber. Willa was physically and emotionally exhausted, years of secret regret and silent guilt released in a torrent the night before.

Jackson's thoughts swirled with Willa's confession, the words replaying in his mind like a haunting echo.

"She died, Jackson, and it was my fault."

"Who...died...Willa?"

"His wife..."

He looked down at Willa, passed out on the couch, this fragile, vulnerable creature before him. *This wasn't her fault,* he thought, *it couldn't be.* Not all of it anyway, but how could he prove it?

His memories continued to unravel, repeatedly replaying the secret she had kept hidden so long.

***

"I don't believe you," Jackson said in disbelief.

"I killed her…" Willa sobbed uncontrollably.

After a long pause, Jackson continued.

"Walk me through…everything, Willa," he said cautiously, once he knew what had happened, there would be no going back.

"I've already said too much… This would end your career," Willa said, grabbing her bag to leave.

Jackson grabbed Willa by the arm, pulling her back to him, facing each other.

"Why aren't you in prison? Willa, if you killed someone, why aren't you in prison?"

"It's not like that… It's just… It doesn't matter, it's my fault, Jackson."

***

Killian's wife, Melanie, had tracked Willa down in DC. The two of them had gotten into a heated confrontation inside of a restaurant bar.

"She had been drinking, a lot. We both had…but…I didn't know she had been watching me all night…with him… I didn't know…and he and I were…and I…I…"

Jackson tried to keep his expression neutral, but Willa could see the bead of anxious sweat forming on his brow.

Willa started hyperventilating, no longer able to get the words out.

Jackson wrapped her in his arms, resting his cheek atop her head as she cried into his chest.

"She just kept shouting about how I ruined her family. I was the reason he was acting the way he did, how we had made such a fool out of her…him leading a double life with me while still playing Mr. Perfect at home. She blamed me for him becoming distant to his family, no longer being involved in his kids' lives because of me and this fucked-up thing we had built..."

"Breathe, Willa...I've got you, breathe," he said.

"I should have called someone... She shouldn't have been driving... She shouldn't have been alone, but I didn't care, Jackson, I didn't care... I just wanted her...gone."

Willa learned from Killian that when Melanie had gotten back home that night, she had taken her own life, naming Willa in a suicide note as the reason for her actions.

***

"She isn't responsible for this... That poor woman, but this isn't Willa's fault," Jackson mumbled under his breath, the words a desperate plea to make sense of the chaos.

Willa stirred on the couch. She slowly opened her eyes, glancing around the room with a touch of confusion. It took a moment, but Willa realized where she was and the confession she had exposed hours before.

Her eyes caught Jackson's. He had settled into one of the oversized chairs across from the couch, his elbow on the armrest, resting his head on his fist.

He looked terrible, Willa thought. *Had he been up all night?* Jackson's eyes were bloodshot and glossy, his hair tousled but not in the ever-so-intentionally messy way that was his trademark. Willa was too afraid to speak. What was he thinking about her? Was this it? Was this the last straw? Would Jackson end things for real?

Jackson broke the silence.

"It's not your fault. I don't know how, but it's not. Any number of reasons could have pushed her to end her life." Jackson began carefully, "He tortured you for years, but what about her... Fifteen years? Twenty years?"

He let out an exasperated sigh.

"Numerous women would have come in and out of his life. It wasn't your fault. She just couldn't take any more...because of him...and...and...that's what we'll say."

Willa sat upright on the couch, Jackson's words not yet sinking in.

"And that's what we'll say?" she repeated in a whisper, reality setting in.

Choking back tears, she rushed over to the chair where he was sitting. She dropped to the ground, placing her head on his lap, wrapping her arms around his legs. Jackson pulled her up to sit on his lap; her head pressed into his shoulder, his arms tight around her.

"Why?" Her voice cracked, a raw edge slicing through the quiet of the room. "Why...why would you do that? Why do you want to be with someone like me? Why...why are you fighting so hard for this?"

Her tears soaked into Jackson's shoulder, the weight of her insecurities spilling out.

"I'm not worth this."

Jackson gently lifted her chin, his touch tender yet firm, guiding her eyes to meet his. "Never say that."

"I just don't..." Willa's words faltered, her voice a trembling whisper.

"I see you, Willa," Jackson interrupted, his voice steady and filled with conviction. "It took me years to climb out of my own darkness. But I did. Willa, I see it...that fire that carried me through...I see it in you. From the moment I first kissed you...I felt it. 'She'll be unstoppable one day,' I thought, and I knew I needed to be a witness... I'm...I'm in love with you."

His words penetrated the layers of doubt and fear that had wrapped around her heart for years. No one had ever said anything like that to Willa before. It was as if Jackson had seen the essence of who she was, the strength she herself had forgotten existed. She realized in that moment how she had been keeping Jackson at arm's length, unconsciously terrified that he would be no different from any other man who had played a pivotal role in her life.

"How did I miss this?" Willa thought to herself, her mind racing with realizations, each one hitting her like a tidal wave. Killian was the culmination of every man in her life she had ever attempted to trust. She had been desperately seeking security, understanding, and the type of love that could only come from someone who had survived hell just like she had. She realized she had not actually trusted Jackson until this very moment.

"And that's what we'll say," she repeated, her voice more decisive, more resolute, as she stared into Jackson's eyes.

Willa adjusted herself on Jackson's lap, wrapping her arms around his neck. She kissed him with a passionate vulnerability that now, for the first time, she recognized as love—not just lust or desperation, but genuine love. Jackson truly saw her, and she finally saw him.

Their lips met, and the kiss ignited something deep within them both. Jackson's exhaustion melted away in the heat of their connection. He had been craving Willa since the day they met, and every day apart, he had a dull ache in his heart, but now, in this moment, he felt her vulnerability and knew he had to tread carefully.

"Are you okay?" he whispered into her ear, his breath warm against her skin.

"I am now," she whispered back, her voice carrying a new-found strength. She could feel him stiffen beneath her, and she shifted her hips, drawing a gasp from him.

"Sorry," Jackson muttered, a touch of embarrassment in his voice at his own arousal.

"Show me you love me," Willa breathed into his neck, her words a plea wrapped in desire.

"Are you sure?" Jackson asked, his voice tinged with concern and longing.

"Yes," she replied, her tone leaving no room for doubt.

Jackson wrapped Willa up in his arms and carried her to the bed. Intense, passionate sex had never been an issue, but this time was different. Willa had no more secrets from him. She was exposed, completely vulnerable, and he stayed. Not just stayed but still desired her, perhaps even more fiercely than before. As he moved over her, she felt herself surrender completely. She was safe with him. Every touch, every kiss, the weight of him on top of her, the pressure she felt...this was different. This was love.

Jackson's movements were slow and deliberate, each touch an affirmation of his devotion. He kissed her deeply, holding her body with reverence that made her heart ache with joy. Willa clung to him, her fingers digging into his back as if she were afraid he might disappear. But he didn't. He was there, solid and real, grounding her in the present moment.

In the aftermath, as they lay tangled in each other's arms, Willa looked up at Jackson, her eyes brimming with tears of gratitude and love.

"Thank you," she whispered, her voice filled with emotion. "Thank you, for loving me."

Jackson brushed a strand of hair from her face and kissed her forehead.

"Always," he replied softly. "I will always love you, Willa. No matter what."

Chapter Twenty-Four

The Wedding

The day had arrived. Beneath a canopy of ancient trees draped in Spanish moss, the ceremony space lay in wait, a living painting crafted by nature and adorned by man.

Sydney, poised at the threshold, graced the aisle with elegance, every step a silent promise of unwavering support for her soon-to-be sister-in-law. All eyes then turned to Emma, resplendent in white, the gown hugging her figure like it was spun from dreams and woven by fairy hands.

Amid the assembled, Willa sat next to Cassy, her posture a study in grace under pressure. Beside them, Lavonte offered a comforting presence, his attention switching between the ceremony and the two women he knew so well.

Across the aisle sat Killian, superficially engaged in conversation with some poor, naïve local girl who'd fallen for his charm and, unbeknownst to Emma or the others, secured Killian's presence as her date.

Killian observed the scene through calculating eyes, noting Willa's solo attendance. A smug satisfaction crept over his features.

She's alone, he thought triumphantly, *and before this night ends, she'll be mine again.*

Amid the genteel chatter and laughter that followed the ceremony, Cassy, Lavonte, and Willa mingled with the locals under the dappled shade of ancient oaks.

"Darling, I must say," an elderly woman with silver hair approached Willa, her voice a tender murmur amid the hum of conversations. "I am a bit saddened to see Killian with someone else." She clasped Willa's hand, her touch as delicate as the petals of the magnolias blooming nearby. "The town's been all abuzz, you know. Some folks really hoped y'all would patch things up."

Willa offered a smile, gentle and serene, the practiced calmness of one who has weathered many storms.

"Thank you for your kindness," she replied, ensuring her voice was steady and imbued with an assurance she didn't quite feel. "But please don't worry about that. It would have never worked out," she said with an attempt at a nonchalant shrug. Willa actually felt a sense of relief seeing Killian with someone else.

As the group transitioned to the reception area, the air was filled with the subtle fragrance of gardenias and the distant sound of a jazz band tuning their instruments. Willa found herself at a table adorned with crystal and fine China, surrounded by Emma's extended family, and of course, Cassy and Lavonte.

Across the lawn, however, Killian stood like a guard, his piercing gaze fixed on Willa. The way the black sequins of her gown captured the waning light, casting prisms on the linen tablecloth, seemed to ensnare him. He noted the empty chair beside her, its vacancy a silent taunt; the muscles in his jaw tightened imperceptibly. His mind raced with the possibilities, with schemes and scenarios, each fueled by a potent blend of desire and indignation.

Yet, the world around continued undisturbed. Servers weaved through the guests, offering delicacies on silver platters, while the setting sun painted the sky in hues of peach and lavender, over Emma and Eric, lost in each other's gaze as they floated across the dance floor.

It was then that a subtle shift occurred—a hush in the rhythm of the atmosphere, as Jackson Cole Donovan slipped through the back entrance, his presence nearly undetectable amongst the merriment.

"My apologies for my late arrival, Love," he murmured, arriving beside Willa. His dark eyes found hers, the warmth in them melting away the hours they'd spent apart. "Shooting ran over, but there was no way I would miss this with you."

In the midst of the festivities, a tiny gasp drew their attention. A flower girl, with little curls bouncing in her hair like tiny springs, had spotted Jackson and darted toward the bride, her little hands gesturing animatedly. "How do you know him!?" she chirped, her innocent query piercing the veil of adult complexities.

Emma, aglow with nuptial bliss, crouched to the child's level, her voice a soothing melody. "Jackson? Well, he's dating my dear friend Willa." She pointed over in Willa's direction.

"She's so lucky," the young girl said before bouncing away.

As these words floated across the tables, they landed upon the ears of one who wished not to hear them. Killian's face hardened, his chiseled features casting shadows that reflected the turmoil within. His blue-grey eyes, once cold and calculating, now flickered with the flames of betrayal. Willa, his Willa, had lied. She hadn't severed ties; she had entwined herself with another.

The realization struck Killian like a viper's bite. Anger coiled tightly within him, seeking an outlet, a target—and it found one in the unsuspecting Jackson. This was his moment, and Killian decided to reclaim the narrative and expose the secrets he believed would unravel Willa's world. If he could not possess her, he would ensure no one else could stand the sight of her.

His mind spun wicked webs of confrontation as he watched the couple on the dance floor twirl amid a sea of applause. Soon, very soon, he would unleash his venom, and Willa's haven in Magnolia would become her cage of shame.

Killian's approach was silent, predatory, as he navigated the throng of wedding guests and made his way toward the bar where Jackson stood. The clink of glasses and murmurs of conversation became a muted backdrop to the tension that curled around him.

"Jackson Donovan," Killian said with a tone of feigned cordiality, extending a hand not in friendship but as a prelude to battle. "We haven't had the pleasure."

Jackson turned, his dark eyes meeting Killian's gaze with an unnerving steadiness. "I know who you are," he replied, his voice tinged with a note of both warmth and warning. His hand met Killian's, the handshake brief and unyielding.

A waiter passed by, offering hors d'oeuvres adorned with truffle and lemon zest, but Killian merely sneered, waving his hand over his face as if shooing a fly away, his gaze still pinned onto Jackson. Cassy watched the exchange from afar, her heart racing as she saw the tension escalate between the two men. Cassy looked at Lavonte, her eyes begging him to intervene. Lavonte shifted in his seat, sensing the coming storm.

"Let him handle this, Cass." Lavonte's eyes shifted toward Jackson. "He's got this." One thing about Lavonte was that he was an excellent judge of character. He instinctively knew that Jackson was no one to attempt to intimidate. Jackson would do anything for Willa, the same way he would do anything for Cassy. They were kindred spirits in that respect.

"Let Willa see her knight in shining armor at work. Killian won't get him riled," Lavonte said cupping Cassy's hands.

Undeterred by Jackson's composure, Killian launched into a lurid recount of his past entanglements with Willa. He painted their intimacy with a vulgarity designed to shock; his words laced with venom.

"I remember this one time I had her bent over a desk... Well, I'm sure you know how rough she likes it, begging to be punished, or maybe that was just with me." He continued, "She was never shy, our little Willa." Killian sneered, hoping to see a crack in Jackson's armor. "A real firecracker—any place, any room, any surface, any...well." Killian grinned. "Yep, always panting for more, that one, but I'm sure you already know that."

Jackson's jaw tightened, that was his Willa Killian was so blatantly attempting to disparage to anyone in earshot, and his composure wavered for but a moment before snapping back into place.

"Why are you here, Killian?" Jackson's smirk was cool as ice, challenging Killian to push further. "She's moved on. Go find someone else to torment." He laughed, speaking to Killian as if he were a child.

"She's mine," Killian growled, the possessiveness in his voice unmistakable.

"Clearly not," Jackson said distractedly, uninterested in Killian's justification, while glancing over at Willa, who was dancing with Emma.

"She's a homewrecker, did she tell you that?"

"Yep," Jackson said, his back to the bar, looking out into the crowd, and sipping his drink.

"And you're okay with that?"

"Takes two to wreck a home, Killian," he said smugly. "Everyone has a past."

"So, she told you she is responsible for my wife's death then?" Killian probed further, certain this would be the blow to bring Jackson to his knees.

"Wow, you're really desperate, aren't ya, mate," Jackson replied, his voice like silk, which only irked Killian more. Jackson turned to look Killian in the eyes. "If she's so awful, why are you trying so hard to get her back?"

Killian's face flushed red with anger, the color rising from his neck over his face.

"These attempts are so transparent, Killian," Jackson spoke coolly, leaning in so only Killian could hear. "Has this worked in the past?" Jackson continued, leaving no time for Killian to respond. "I'm well aware of Willa's history, the pain she's endured, especially at your hands, and the strength she's shown surviving in spite of you. There's nothing you can say to change my opinion of her."

The ease with which Jackson dismissed his provocations struck Killian's nerves. There was no satisfaction here, no triumph in seeing another man crumble under the weight of his words. Jackson wasn't intimidated by him, and this was something Killian wasn't used to.

Across the yard, Willa felt her stomach drop; she had just laid eyes on Jackson and Killian talking. Panic gripped her, her breath catching in her throat. Jackson already knew everything about her. He had pledged to stand by her. But what if, what if it wasn't true? Whenever Willa saw Killian, she immediately felt small, unworthy, and unlovable. The sight of the two men together filled her with dread. She took a hesitant step toward them when Jackson glanced at her with a subtle shake of his head, silently telling her to stay back.

Willa forced herself to walk over to Lavonte and Cassy, trying to mask her nerves. She didn't want this meeting between Killian and Jackson to overshadow such a wonderfully romantic evening.

Cassy noticed the tension in Willa's posture and leaned in. "Hey, everything okay?"

Willa forced a smile, her voice trembling slightly. "Yeah, just…worried about Jackson. Killian can be so…manipulative."

Lavonte, always the calm observer, nodded. "Jackson's got this, Will. Even if he is seething inside, it's not showing, which must be driving Killian crazy. He's one hell of an actor, Will," Lavonte joked, trying to lighten the mood.

"Thank you," Willa quietly laughed, her eyes darting back to where Jackson and Killian stood, a silent prayer on her lips. "Trust," she whispered to herself. Jackson had promised to protect her, to stand by her no matter what.

Meanwhile, Jackson's gaze never wavered from Killian's, his calm demeanor unshaken. "You see, Killian, your tactics might have worked on others, but they won't work on me."

Killian's lips curled into a sneer. "You think you know her? You think you know everything she's done?"

Jackson's expression remained serene. "I know men like you, Killian. You are so out of control in your own life that you can't help but try to control others. Desperately needing attention to fill the gaping sense of emptiness you feel."

"Desperately needing attention? That's funny coming from someone like you," Killian barked, implying Jackson, being an actor, was no better than himself for craving attention.

"You really don't see it, do you?" Jackson looked at Killian with a mixture of pity and disdain. "You, Killian, are the reason you are so miserable. There is nothing Willa or any woman can do to change that. Unless you come to terms with your role in all of this, you're in for a life of struggle and longing."

"Who the fuck do you think you're talking to?" Killian's eyes blazed with fury, his hands clenching into fists at his sides.

"Struck a nerve, did I?" Jackson chuckled, leaning in closer. "Tell me I'm wrong. But you wouldn't want to cause a scene now, would you? Let all these fine people see the real you?"

"Fuck you, Jackson," Killian hissed under his breath. "This isn't over."

Jackson leaned in even closer, his voice barely above a whisper. "It is for you. Walk away, Killian."

Killian glared at Jackson for a long moment before turning his back and walking away, his retreat signaling the end of the confrontation. Jackson watched him go, a sense of relief washing over him.

As Jackson turned back toward the crowd, his eyes found Willa's. She was standing with Lavonte and Cassy, her face a mix of worry and hope. He smiled at her, a reassuring smile that told her everything was going to be okay.

Willa felt her heart swell with love and gratitude. She had finally found someone who believed in her, who stood by her no matter what. As Jackson made his way back to her, she knew that no matter what challenges lay ahead, he would be there, just like he promised.

Jackson reached her, wrapping his arms around her in a comforting embrace. "Love you," he whispered in her ear. "He's gone."

Willa nodded, tears of relief streaming down her face. "For how long?" she whispered back.

"Doesn't matter." Jackson smiled, pulling her in tighter. "He's powerless right now."

Willa released a deep sigh of relief, positioning herself with Jackson's arms around her, her back to his chest. She looked around the grounds, seeing her best friends, her chosen family, people she never expected to love in a place she never expected to be, with a man she never expected to meet, let alone fall in love with. She felt loved, safe, and wanted, but above all, she felt accepted.

"Willa," Jackson paused, a curious look coming to his face. "Remind me, Love, who told you Melanie killed herself?"

Willa looked up at Jackson, confused. "What do you mean? Killian told me right after he found out."

"That's what I thought..." Jackson continued. He raised an eyebrow while looking down into Willa's eyes.

"And do you have any reason to believe he may have lied about the details of her death?"

CHAPTER TWENTY-FIVE

The Designer

ACT 4

*T*hree Months Later

The studio was a whirlwind of activity, a symphony of silk and lace. As Willa stepped inside, her eyes widened at the sight of the exquisite creations that surrounded her. Bolts of fabric in every hue imaginable lined the walls, while mannequins donned half-finished gowns, their ethereal beauty hinting at the masterpieces they would soon become.

"Welcome," a warm voice called out, and Willa turned to see a stunning older woman with piercing blue eyes and an air of refined elegance approach. "I'm Eliza Montague. It's such a pleasure to meet you, Willa."

Willa felt a flutter of nerves as she extended her hand, but Eliza's firm grasp and genuine smile put her instantly at ease.

"Thank you so much for agreeing to work with us," Eliza said, her Spanish accent tinged with gratitude. "I can't tell you how stunning you will look in one of our original designs."

Willa's eyes sparkled with excitement.

"I've been following your love's career for quite a few years now. Dressing him for an event is always a pleasure. But this...to dress his lady friend to accompany him is quite the honor. He's only ever walked a red carpet alone. You surely are very special. Let me show you some of the ideas we've sketched for the Gala's theme."

Eliza quickly guided Willa to a drawing table surrounded by multiple assistants and associate designers.

"We'll want something that showcases your natural beauty while also making a bold statement," Eliza continued. "This is your introduction to the world...it *must* be memorable. We want people to be talking about you for weeks."

Eliza nodded, a thoughtful expression on her face as she deeply studied Willa's face and frame. "Yes, I can see this working beautifully for you. We do a modern twist on a classic silhouette, perhaps with a daring neckline and unexpected pop of color.

"Why are you standing there like statues? Go, Go." Elize barked orders to the assistants around her. A flurry of fabrics, tape measures, and crystal embellishments filled the room.

Willa took a step back, overwhelmed by all the movement and excitement. It was surreal. In less than a year, she went from Georgian recluse to being on the arm of one of the most famous men in the world.

The exposure still terrified her. Despite Killian having gone quiet after the confrontation he had with Jackson at Emma's wedding, Willa still could not shake the feeling of dread. The more comfortable Willa became with Jackson and her ever-changing life, the louder the little voice in her head would scream, *He hasn't forgotten about you.* And for a moment in this luxury high-end designer's Barcelona loft, Willa thought of calling the whole thing off and returning to Magnolia.

Willa shook the thought from her head.

CHAPTER TWENTY-SIX

The Costume Institute Benefit

The final preparations for the annual New York CIB Gala were completed. Eliza and her team worked tirelessly to ensure that every detail was perfect, from the intricate beading on Willa's gown to the crisp lines of Jackson's tuxedo.

Willa stood before the full-length hotel mirror, her heart racing as she took in the sight of herself in the finished gown. The Grecian-inspired gown, deep champagne-colored silk, clung to her curves, the fitted bodice giving way to a flowing skirt that pooled at her feet. Intricate gold embroidery adorned the plunging, draped neckline, catching the light with every movement.

"You look stunning," Jackson murmured, coming up behind her and placing a gentle hand on her waist. "Like a goddess."

Willa felt a flush of warmth spread through her at his words. The intensity of his gaze through the mirror sending a shiver down her spine. "I feel like one," she admitted, her voice soft and full of wonder. "I never thought I could feel this way again."

Jackson turned her to face him, his eyes searching hers. "You're a survivor, my Love. A fighter. And tonight, the world will see that. They'll meet the incredibly beautiful, strong, confident woman I see every day."

Tears pricked at the corners of Willa's eyes, and she blinked them away, not wanting to ruin her carefully applied makeup.

"Don't you dare make me cry. This look two hours." She softly laughed. "But thank you and not just for tonight," she whispered, reaching up to cup his cheek. "For everything. For believing in me, even when I didn't believe in myself."

Jackson leaned in, pressing a soft kiss to her forehead. "Always," he promised, his voice raw with emotion.

Eliza appeared then, a knowing smile on her face as she took in the tender moment. "I hate to interrupt," she said gently, "but it's time. Your chariot awaits."

The sleek black limousine glided through the bustling streets of Manhattan, its tinted windows offering Willa a brief respite from the chaotic world outside. In addition to Willa and Jackson, inside the limo sat Eliza, two of her assistants, the ones responsible for making sure Willa and Jackson looked impeccable all night long, and Jackson's two personal assistants, Alex and Sonia.

Sonia was a newer addition to Jackson's entourage. His longtime manager and sister, Ames, was still pregnant with twins, so Sonia was hired, after glowing recommendations, to assume responsibility for all the important details of Jackson's day-to-day life.

The door opened, and the crowd's roar intensified, washing over Willa in a dizzying wave.

Steeling herself, Willa stepped out onto the red carpet, her hand clasped tightly in Jackson's. Immediately, the cameras turned toward them, a barrage of flashes and shouts assaulting her senses.

The dazzling camera flashes illuminated the red carpet in a frenetic strobe, the din of voices rising to a fever pitch as celebrities glided by in an elegant parade. Willa stood at the edge of the crimson sea, her heart pounding against the confines of her chest, threatening to break free. She glanced over at Jackson, his chiseled features calm and composed as if he'd done this thousands of times before. And he had—the CIB Gala was just another night for him, another chance to dazzle the world with his magnetic presence.

"When Alex waves you forward, I'll tap you on the shoulder," Sonia began, her voice calm and organized, cutting through the chaos. "Then go, stop on the first mark, count, turn, pose. Up the steps to the next mark, stop, pose. Up the final set of steps, walk, next mark, walk, hit the final mark, and then you're done." She grinned. "Then it's time for some long overdue drinks!"

Willa nodded, trying to absorb Sonia's rapid-fire instructions.

"Damn, I didn't realize walking had so many rules." Her mind felt like it was short-circuiting, the weight of the moment pressing down on her like a physical force. She wasn't used to this—the glamour, the attention, the sheer magnitude of it all. In this world, every little thing was important, with hundreds of ways to fail. It was a world away from the quiet streets of Magnolia Shores or even the relentless goals she pursued during her medical career. Of course, there had been hospital benefits to build new wings or start a new program, but nothing like this. In her previous life with Killian, Willa had been a big fish in a small pond, but Jackson...Jackson was a whale, his world the ocean, and Willa was microscopic in comparison.

"If you get confused, just look at Jackson," Sonia continued, her words barely registering through the haze of Willa's thoughts. "He's done this a million times. He's a pro."

Willa glanced over at Jackson again, feeling a flicker of something deep in her chest. He was a force of nature, the man who could command a room with a single look. And yet, there was a gentleness to him, the vulnerability that he kept hidden from the world. But now, standing on the precipice of the red carpet, Willa felt like she was seeing him for the first time. The way the lights played off the angles of his face, the confident set of his shoulders, the easy, assured grace with which he carried himself. He was a man who belonged in this world, a man who had earned his place in the spotlight. For the first time, Willa realized she didn't need to be the "powerful" one in the relationship. She didn't need to carry the weight of everything… Jackson, unlike any before him, was self-sufficient. Willa didn't need to change him or mold him into the type of person she wanted by her side, as she had failed for years to do with Killian. It was a slightly uncomfortable realization, but a surprisingly pleasant change.

"Okay," Willa told Sonia, clutching Jackson's hand tightly. His palm was warm and firm against hers, a steadying presence in the midst of the chaos.

"Oh, and smiles!" Sonia said, giving Willa's shoulder a gentle tap.

As Jackson led Willa forward, flashes of light exploded around them, the paparazzi clamoring for their attention. Willa blinked against the onslaught, her grip on Jackson's arm tightening instinctively. She could feel the warmth of his body through the fabric of his tuxedo, a reassuring presence keeping her grounded.

"Jackson! Jackson, over here!" one of the photographers shouted, the rapidly flashing cameras making the direction unknown.

"This way!" a photographer shouted, gesturing wildly to the left. Jackson turned smoothly, guiding Willa with him as they angled their bodies toward the clamoring press. The flashes intensified, a dizzying strobe of light that threatened to blind her. Willa blinked rapidly, trying to clear the spots from her vision.

"Give us that sexy brooding stare!" another called out, his voice cutting through the din.

Jackson turned toward every voice, his smile easy and confident. But Willa could see the slightest tension in his jaw, the way his eyes narrowed almost imperceptibly.

Jackson loved acting. He loved escaping reality to live life as another, and he enjoyed the opportunity to experience life in different eras, countries, and lifetimes. However, Jackson wasn't in love with the attention. He hated these types of events, but his professional mask hid his discomfort. This was all part of his job, a different form of playing make-believe.

While Jackson's presence was very much a comfort, Willa could feel the sudden weight of expectation pressing down on her, the pressure to make a good impression, but it was short-lived.

As they neared the entrance to the museum, Willa caught a glimpse of herself in one of the many mirrors lining the red carpet. For a moment, she hardly recognized the woman staring back at her. Gone was the timid, broken girl she'd once been. In her place stood a strong, confident woman, her head held high and her eyes shining with determination. No games, no secrets, no manipulations, Willa was just...Willa, seeing her true self for the first time.

And as she looked up at Jackson, Willa knew he saw it too. The change in her, the strength that had always been there, just waiting to be unleashed in a safe environment. With a smile, she squeezed his arm gently, a silent thank you for everything he'd done to help her get to this moment.

"Gorgeous, darling!" the shouting continued.

"Who's the girl?"

"Jackson! Who is with you?"

"Are you dating? Is it serious??"

Willa felt her heart skip a beat, a flicker of uncertainty dancing through her. But before she could even begin to formulate a response, Sonia's voice rang out loud and clear.

"Willa Sullivan!" she proclaimed, enunciating each syllable with precision. "S.U.L.L.I.V.A.N."

The crowd erupted into a frenzy of whispers and speculation, the reporters clamoring for more information about the stunning mystery woman on Jackson Donovan's arm. Willa could feel their eyes boring into her, dissecting every inch of her appearance, trying to unravel the secrets of her past. Panic washed over her.

She tightened her grip on Jackson's arm, drawing strength from his presence. He leaned in close, his breath soft against her ear.

"You're doing wonderful, darling," he murmured, his voice low and reassuring. "Just keep smiling and let them wonder."

Willa nodded, a rush of gratitude flooding through her. She knew that Jackson understood the demons she battled, the scars she carried beneath her polished exterior. And yet here he was, standing beside her, his unwavering support being broadcast live to millions.

As they continued their ascent up the stairs, Willa could feel the weight of countless gazes upon her, the murmurs of the crowd swirling around them like a gathering storm. But she refused to let it shake her and allow the ghosts of her past to dim the brilliance of this moment. Tonight, she was reborn.

Behind her, Sonia moved with practiced grace, her nimble fingers adjusting the delicate train of Willa's gown with each step. The whisper of silk against the red carpet was lost amid the clamor of the crowd.

Willa could feel the gentle tug of the fabric holding her back and started to panic. She glanced behind her to see Sonia gently dislodging Willa's train from a rogue nail from one of the red carpet's stays.

"That could have been so embarrassing," Willa whispered to Sonia, gratefully.

"I've got you." Sonia smiled, looking up at Willa.

As Willa took her next steps ascending the marble staircase beside Jackson, a deafening noise split the air, followed by a chorus of terrified screams. Willa felt a heavy weight slam into her chest, knocking the breath from her lungs as she stumbled backwards. Her heel caught on the edge of a step, and she fell hard, her head cracking against the sharp edge of the marble.

Pain exploded behind her eyes. She could feel the warm trickle of blood down her temple, the metallic taste of it on her tongue. She struggled to catch her breath as her mind raced with a single, terrifying thought: *What just happened?*

Around her, the world had erupted into chaos. People were running in every direction, their faces contorted with fear and panic. Willa could hear the distant wail of sirens and the shouts of security personnel trying to restore order. But all she could focus on was the pressure on her chest and the sickening realization that something was very, very wrong.

Did I just trip? she wondered, her thoughts sluggish and disjointed. *Is this all just a horrible dream?*

She tried to sit up but couldn't. Willa felt a searing pain shoot through her head, and she knew with sudden, terrifying clarity that this was no dream. This was real, and she was in trouble.

She tried to turn her head, searching desperately for Jackson, but her eyes refused to focus; all she could see was a blur of unidentifiable faces, and hear screams twisted with horror and disbelief.

Hands were all over her, pressing against her head, checking for a pulse. Willa wanted to scream, to beg them to stop, but her voice seemed to have deserted her, lost in the maelstrom of terror that gripped her.

Please, she thought, as the edges of her vision began to darken. *Please, let this be a mistake. This is just a nightmare.*

After a moment, the pressure on Willa's chest was gone, and she gasped for air, her lungs burning as she gulped in desperate breaths. The world spun around her, a dizzying kaleidoscope of flashing lights and muffled screams. She blinked, trying to clear the haze from her vision, but everything remained blurred as if she were looking through a fog.

"He's been hit," a voice shouted, cutting through the chaos like a knife.

Willa's heart seized in her chest, her breath catching in her throat.

No, she thought desperately. *Please, no.*

"Twice," another voice confirmed, the word falling like a death knell.

The world seemed to tilt on its axis, and Willa felt a wave of dizziness wash over her. She struggled to sit up, ignoring the pain that lanced through her skull, the sticky warmth of blood trickling down her face. All that mattered was getting to Jackson, making sure he was okay.

As she pushed herself up on shaking arms, Willa caught a glimpse of his face, and the sight stole the remaining breath from her lungs. His eyes were closed, his features slack and pale beneath the bright lights of the red carpet. Blood blossomed across the front of his tuxedo, a vivid crimson stain marring the crisp white shirt that seemed to grow with every passing second.

"Jackson," she whispered, her voice breaking on his name. "Please, stay with me. You can't leave me, not now."

She reached for him, but strong hands gripped her shoulders, pulling her back. She fought against them, desperate to get to Jackson, to hold him, to will him to live. But her strength was fading fast, the edges of her vision blurring as the pain in her head intensified.

This can't be happening, she thought, tears streaming down her face. *It's all just a horrible dream. I'll wake up any second now. Wake up, wake up.*

The man she loved was slipping away from her, his life bleeding out onto the cold, hard ground. She closed her eyes, letting the darkness take her.

***

"Is she hit?" someone called out, their voice distant and distorted.

"No, I don't think so," a familiar voice responded, closer this time. It was Sonia, her tone now stern and commanding.

"What about the blood on her chest?" a voice called out, the words cutting through the haze of Willa's thoughts.

Willa blinked, trying to focus on the source of the voice, but her vision was blurred, the edges of her sight tinged with black. She could feel the sticky warmth of blood all over her skin, the coppery scent filling her nostrils, but she couldn't tell if it was her own or someone else's.

"It's his!" Sonia exclaimed, her voice rising with panic. "Dammit, there's so much of it."

Willa's heart seized in her chest, a cold numbness spreading through her veins.

The noises were gunshots.

The weight was Jackson.

The blood was Jackson's.

Willa could feel everything closing in around her, the air thick, the edges of her consciousness fraying like a worn tapestry. If Jackson died, a part of her would die with him, the light in her world extinguished forever.

Strong arms lifted Willa from the cold, hard ground, cradling her against a broad chest. The scent of gunpowder and sweat mingled with the coppery tang of blood, assaulting her senses. Sirens wailed in the distance, growing louder with each passing second, their urgent cries piercing the night air.

The man holding Willa shifted his grip, cradling her head against his chest as he responded to a voice on his radio.

"Affirmative," he responded. "Donovan?"

"En route to Cornell. Traffic locked down. Requesting Medivac to East Meadow Central Park," came the clipped radio response, the voice on the other end tight with tension.

Willa's mind raced, trying to piece together the fragments of information. *They're taking Jackson to the hospital. He's not dead yet.*

"Please," she whispered, her voice barely audible above the chaos. "Please, you have to save him."

The man holding her tightened his grip, his voice low and soothing.

"We're doing everything we can, ma'am. Just hold on a little longer."

***

"Willa? Can you hear me?" Sonia's voice echoed off the walls of the limo. "We're almost at the hospital. Just hang on, okay?"

Hospital. The word jolted through Willa like an electric shock, and suddenly, everything came rushing back in a dizzying, sickening flood. The Gala. The red carpet. The gunshots. Jackson.

"Oh God, Jackson."

She tried to sit up, panic clawing at her throat, but a firm hand on her shoulder held her down.

"Easy, Willa," Alex murmured, his voice low and soothing. "You hit your head pretty hard. Try not to move too much."

But Willa barely heard him, her mind consumed by a single, terrifying thought.

"Jackson was shot. He's hurt. He could be... No. No, he can't be. He can't."

Tears stung her eyes as she reached for Sonia's hand, gripping it like a lifeline.

"Jackson," she whispered, her voice hoarse and trembling. "Is he...alive?"

Sonia exchanged a glance with Alex, her expression unreadable in the dim light of the limo.

"He's in surgery," she said carefully, her tone measured and even. "The doctors are doing everything they can."

The limo lurched to a stop, and suddenly, there were hands everywhere, pulling her out of the vehicle and onto a gurney.

The harsh fluorescent lights of the emergency room assaulted Willa's senses as she was wheeled through the automatic doors, her head throbbing in time with the rapid beat of her heart. Sonia's voice, usually so confident and self-assured, wavered with barely concealed panic as she relayed information to the medical staff.

"She's bleeding from her head," Sonia said, as the emergency staff rolled Willa into the ER. "She hit her head on the edge of the marble step when he fell on her.

"She's been going in and out of consciousness for the past fifteen minutes," Sonia explained, her words punctuated by the sharp click of her heels against the linoleum floor.

"Was she shot?" one of the staff asked while removing Willa's blood-soaked gown.

"No, that blood's the boyfriend's," Sonia said, nodding at the gown.

Willa struggled to sit up, fighting against the gentle but firm hands that sought to keep her still.

"Jackson," she croaked, her voice hoarse and barely recognizable to her own ears. "Where's Jackson?"

But no one seemed to hear her, or if they did, they chose to ignore her desperate plea. Instead, they swarmed around her like bees, poking and prodding, shining lights in her eyes and asking questions that she couldn't quite seem to grasp.

This isn't right, she thought, her mind foggy and disoriented. *I need to find Jackson. I need to make sure he's okay.*

With a burst of strength she didn't know she possessed, Willa pushed herself up off the gurney, ignoring the startled cries of the medical staff as she staggered to her feet. The room spun sickeningly around her, and she had to grab onto the edge of a nearby chair to keep from falling.

"Ms. Sullivan, please," a nurse pleaded, her voice gentle but insistent. "You need to lie back down. You may have a skull fracture."

But Willa shook her head stubbornly, instantly regretting the motion as a fresh wave of pain lanced through her skull.

Dr. Stanfield placed a firm hand on her shoulder, his touch abrasive and restraining.

"Willa, I need you to lie still," he said. "Jackson is being taken care of, but right now, we need to focus on you. You've suffered a serious head injury, and we need to make sure there's no internal bleeding."

"No," she insisted, her words slurring slightly. "I need to see Jackson... He can't die," she said while trying to fight off the two men attempting to hold her down.

"Get 2mg of Lorazepam into her now, settle her down before she hurts someone," someone shouted.

Sonia appeared at her side, her face etched with worry and concern.

"Willa, honey, you need to let the doctors take care of you," she said softly, reaching out to guide her back toward the gurney. "Jackson is in surgery. There's nothing you can do for him right now."

"No!" Willa screamed, defeated.

As the medication kicked in, the staff's voices and faces blurred together in a haze of pain and confusion. Willa desperately tried to fight the sleep. But her efforts were futile. She regretfully started to close her eyes, but just before she let the void take her, her eyes focused briefly on the whiteboard behind the nurse's station.

"J. Donovan -Trauma – GSW x 2 - ESI Level Resuscitation - XFER - OR4 - Critical"

Jackson was at the brink of death in surgery, and she was powerless to stop it.

CHAPTER TWENTY-SEVEN

The Man Hunt

Willa woke up in a quiet room. The lights were low. In the corner of the room, a duffle bag lay on the chair. It had been in the limo. Alex had packed a change of clothes and other basic essentials for both Willa and Jackson for after the event.

Willa disconnected the IV in her arm, opened the bag, took off the hospital gown, put on her trusty old leggings and an oversized hoodie she found. She knew it wasn't hers, but it was still very familiar, she just couldn't quite place it. She held the soft fabric to her face, the scent was an intoxicating mix of sandalwood, vanilla and leather, warm and comforting. She slipped it over her aching head before sitting back down on the edge of the bed.

She was trying to piece together what had happened. She knew she was in the hospital but couldn't remember why...

Where was I before this? How did I get here?

Slowly, it started coming back. Willa remembered being in her hotel room, all glammed up; she remembered looking at herself in the mirror. But who was in the background of the mirror? She knew she was with someone. The blurred image made her feel warm and safe. Then another flash, and she was standing on a red carpet. Some woman was with her yammering instructions about something. Willa looked over to her side as if expecting to see someone standing next to her, but she was alone.

The door to Willa's room opened, and a striking Black woman with the kindest eyes walked in.

"Cassy?" Willa said, immediately recognizing her dear friend.

"Yeah, baby, I'm here."

Willa burst into tears.

Cassy was followed by Lavonte.

"We saw it on the TV. They were broadcasting live. We jumped on a flight as soon as we could," Cassy said, sitting on the bed next to Willa. It was only a two-hour flight from Savannah to JFK.

The sight of Cassy made it all come back.

"He's dead, isn't he?" Willa asked, wrapping her fingers tightly inside the sleeves of Jackson's hoodie.

"No, no, he's not," Lavonte's deep, comforting voice announced. "But he is still in surgery. Do you remember what happened?"

"We were at the CIB Gala…and then there was screaming…and I fell," Willa's voice broke as she remembered the weight she felt on her when she couldn't breathe.

"He fell on me, didn't he? That was the weight, wasn't it?" she asked, her voice becoming void of emotion.

"Yes, baby, it was," Cassy said with tears in her eyes.

"He shot him…didn't he? He…shot Jackson," Willa said as a coldness enveloped her entire being.

"They think the shooter was Killian," Lavonte said compassionately. "Between the security camera footage and all the witnesses' descriptions, it sounds like him. They'll get him, Willa."

"Get him?" Willa asked monotone.

"In all the chaos he was able to slip away, Will," Cassy said softly. "Everyone is looking for him. There are cops everywhere, all over this hospital, roadblocks in case he tries to leave the city. His face is all over the news. The police will find him."

"This is my fault," Willa said. "I knew it. I did this to him. I told him it wasn't safe. I was a liability."

Cassy put her arm around Willa who immediately pushed her off. The look in Willa's eyes terrified Cassy. Her eyes were dead inside. Cassy had never seen this side of Willa. Cassy had been there to comfort her, wipe away her tears, hold her as she cried.

"He loves you. It doesn't matter how many times you would have warned him, Jackson loves you, Willa. This was a risk he was willing to take," Lavonte said.

"It should have been me," Willa stated.

The door opened again to a man in his mid-50s in a long white lab coat.

"Update, doc?" Lavonte asked.

"Well, the good news, Willa, is that outside of the laceration to your scalp, a couple of stitches and pretty bad concussion you're ok. There is no skull fracture and no intracranial hemorrhage— internal bleeding. We would still like to keep you overnight to keep an eye on you."

"What about?" Lavonte glanced up at the ceiling, indicating Jackson was on a higher floor. "She doesn't know."

The doctor let out a large sigh.

"Willa, Jackson was shot twice. Once in the chest and once in the back. The wound to his chest..."

Willa stiffened her posture and raised her hand, motioning for silence to the doctor.

"Don't talk down to me, I'm a physician," Willa stated frankly with a sneer.

It was the first time she had referred to herself as a doctor in nearly four years. Willa never wanted to draw attention to her previous life. But nothing mattered anymore. Killian had found her; her cover was blown. Playing it safe got Jackson hurt. Playing nice was no longer a necessity. Dr. Willow "The Bitch" Burke was coming out of retirement.

"Ok, Doctor...Mr. Donovan sustained two gunshot wounds. One to the left lateral chest resulting in a tension hemopneumothorax, and one to the right lower back with the bullet lodged in the L2 vertebra with fracture. Immediately following the gunshots, he fell down a partial flight of marble stairs, resulting in multiple rib fractures, pulmonary contusion, and possible additional spinal trauma. He was in respiratory distress on the scene. He was intubated and bagged en route to the hospital. Upon arrival, Mr. Donovan underwent an emergent left thoracotomy for control of intrathoracic hemorrhage. A torn segment of the left inferior pulmonary vein was identified and repaired with 5-0 Prolene suture. Additional bleeding from the intercostal artery at rib six was ligated. Approximately 1.2 liters of blood was evacuated from the left chest cavity. Lung laceration was debrided and closed with absorbable suture. Chest tube was placed. Then he transferred to ICU intubated and sedated. He'll spend the next three days on ventilation and then we'll work to wean him. Once he's more stabilized, he will need spinal fusion of L2-L3. Surgeon should be in the next day or so to go over that plan in more detail with you, Dr. Sullivan."

"Uh-huh," was the only sound Willa could make, her rage barely contained below the surface. She knew exactly what the doctor was telling her. Jackson was not out of the woods. It was a miracle he was alive at all.

Killian tried to take the only thing she ever truly loved away from her... And no one knew where he was.

CHAPTER TWENTY-EIGHT
The ICU

Manhunt Day: 2

Willa stepped out of the shower, wrapped herself in a bathrobe, and sat at the edge of the hotel bed. The remote control to the TV was lying on the bed next to her. She was still numb. Nothing felt real.

The television flickered to life, casting a blue hue over the living room. A woman with perfectly coiffed hair and a polished demeanor spoke in a traditional news anchor's tone.

"We have an update on the shooting at last night's CIB Gala," she announced, her voice tinged with sympathy. "It has been confirmed that A-list actor Jackson Donovan remains in critical condition at one of the area's top trauma centers, according to a press release from his team."

The screen switched to a typed statement, presumably written by Sonia.

"Regarding last night's tragic events, we want to extend our gratitude to all those involved in Mr. Donovan and Ms. Sullivan's care—including event security staff, police officers, first responders, doctors, and nurses. At this time, Mr. Donovan remains in critical condition at a level 1 trauma center. We pray for his quick and full recovery. Ms. Sullivan was discharged home after receiving treatment for a blunt head trauma. More details will be released as they become available. The families of both individuals request privacy during this difficult time."

"What a sad story," remarked the anchor before Willa changed the channel.

"The alleged shooter has been identified as Killian Helmar, a psychiatrist from Washington, DC," reported the male journalist, turning to his co-host. "Sources say Helmar, ex-marine and widowed father of three, had been having an affair with Willa Sullivan-Burke for years prior to his wife's death…which begs the question, are we dealing with a dangerous love triangle here?" The reporter smirked while raising an eyebrow.

Willa flipped to another channel.

"Body cam footage from last night's CIB Gala shooting has just been released," announced the news reporter. "We want to warn viewers that the unedited video may be disturbing for some and is not recommended for younger audiences.

"We'll give parents a moment to remove children from the room," added the anchor.

Willa walked over to the TV. The screen then displayed a side-angle view of the chaos. The sound of the gunshots, then Jackson's motionless body crashing, rolling down a few steps before taking Willa to the ground as well, his body resting on top of hers.

The footage cut to another angle, showing an officer attending to Willa while others lifted Jackson off of her. In this view, Willa's shimmering champagne gown was covered in blood, and Sonia's commanding voice could be heard on the recording. The camera switched once more, this time focused on Jackson as the first responders rushed to stabilize him a mere feet away from where Willa lay. The feed ended.

Willa's jaw clenched. Now she had seen it. She watched her love collapse to the ground in an instant. A burning sensation radiated from her chest slowly consuming her entire body. There was no turning back. No hiding. No feeling sorry for herself. Killian would pay for this. And if Jackson died, Willa decided Killian would too…by her own hands.

"That was difficult to watch," remarked one of the news anchors.

"Definitely," agreed the other. "But we must commend New York's finest for their quick and heroic actions."

Cassy returned to the living room and saw Willa watching the news coverage.

"Honey, turn that off," she said gently.

"No...I want to see it," replied Willa with quiet rage in her voice. Cassy had never heard her speak like this before and it sent a shiver down her spine.

"Willa—" began Cassy, trying to calm her down.

"He tried to take him from me, Cassy," interrupted Willa, her eyes almost black with anger. "I never thought he had the guts..."

"Willa, honey," Cassy said again, trying to connect with her.

"He's gone too far, Cassy... When it was just me, that was one thing," Willa continued, the cryptic ice in her voice never wavering.

"Willa?"

"I let him, Cass. I let him break me. I was weak. I was tired. In the end, I let him torture me for years because I thought that was all I deserved... But he has no idea...no idea what he's done, Cassy."

Willa looked into Cassy's eyes. The depths of their darkness sent a chill down Cassy's spine.

"Willa...you're scaring me."

"He hurt the only one I actually care about..." Willa started to pace.

"But in the beginning, Cass, Killian was intimidated by me. Did you know that? Did you ever *really* understand our dynamic?" Willa started to laugh to herself, the sounds slowly getting louder and louder.

"It was all me, Cass," Willa continued with a near diabolical tone. "I wanted him. I wanted money. I wanted power, and there was no one on this earth that was going to stand in my way... I feel it. I feel it, Cass... She's back... The bitch is back...and Killian has no idea what I am capable of."

"I don't think any of us do, Willa," said Cassy with a worried tone in her voice.

***

Manhunt Day: 6

Back at the hospital a few days had passed when a doctor approached Willa, Cassy and Lavonte in the private surgical ICU waiting room.

"The back fusion went well. Took out the bone fragments and actually grabbed the bullet too. Normally, we would leave it, but it was right there."

"Do you still have it?" Willa asked.

"Why, you want it?"

"Yes."

"I'll see what I can do," he said with a smile.

"Can I see him?"

"Sure."

The doctor turned to Cassy and Lavonte. "If you two could stay here for now, he needs a lot of rest."

"Of course," Lavonte said holding Cassy's hand, "we'll grab some coffee or something, maybe head back to the hotel for a bit. Let you two have some time."

***

The doctor slowly opened the door to Jackson's room. "He's pretty out of it."

"That's ok," Willa whispered.

"Take your time," the doctor whispered, giving Willa's shoulder a squeeze.

Willa pulled up a chair next to his bed. She could hear the faint beeping in the background from the numerous machines.

Jackson was lying still on the hospital bed; he was still unconscious. He looked so small, so fragile. Yet, a few days ago, he was larger than life.

Willa breathed in deep; her resolve crumbled at the sight of him. Collapsing beside him she finally allowed the tears to fall. She placed one of her hands on his, while laying her other arm on the bed rail and placing her head on her arm to rest. She slowly traced the outline of his fingers. "I love you. I'm so sorry," she whispered falling asleep on her own arm.

CHAPTER TWENTY-NINE
The Agent Sonia

Manhunt Day: 8

Willa walked the corridor from the hospital hotel, where she had been since Jackson's back surgery, to the hospital. She navigated the cold halls, making her way back to the elevator that led to the private ICU room that housed Jackson. All the while, she was being followed by Sonia and a very large man in an all-black suit. After giving her statement to the police and recounting her entire relationship with Killian, Willa now had a bodyguard. Yuli, went everywhere she went, which did very little to make her feel more secure. The safest she felt was when she was in Jackson's room. He was still heavily sedated. Willa didn't even know if he knew she was there, but she would sit next to him all day anyway.

Sonia and Willa walked toward the service elevators on the opposite side of the unit.

"I saw the footage," Willa said. "You were amazing, Sonia. How were you so calm?"

Sonia stared at the elevator numbers as the two ascended. "It's not the first time."

"What? Jackson's been shot at before?!" Willa said in surprise.

"No, first for him. Not for me," Sonia said calmly. "I only started working for Jackson about four months ago."

"I didn't even know. Where were you before?" Willa said, realizing she had been too preoccupied all this time to really notice Jackson's team.

"Ten years in the FBI," Sonia said casually.

"What? The FBI? To be an assistant manager to Ames and a publicist? Isn't that a bit of an extreme career change?" Willa said.

"Willa, I'm not just one of Jackson's assistants. I'm the head of his security detail. About four months ago, he brought up concerns related to your safety, which, of course, included his." Sonia turned toward Willa.

"Willa, we have been tracking Killian for the past four months. We have monitored his every move. We learned he had purchased a one-way ticket from Savannah to JFK set to land two days before the Gala. We didn't know for sure what he was up to, but both Jackson's personal security and the security at the Gala were increased.

"Why didn't I know this? Why was this kept from me?" Willa said with anger in her voice.

"Jackson didn't want to take any chances and didn't want you to have another reason to worry if he let you know he was concerned. You were already so on guard as it was; there didn't seem to be a reason to put more of a burden on you."

***

"Oh you're terrible, young man, behave yourself," a sweet elderly voice chuckled. "Now you better eat something," she said as she placed a tray of food on the table in front of him.

"Yes, mum," a hoarse voice said in his faint accent.

Willa gasped from the hallway and ran into the hospital room.

"There she is," his weak voice said.

"Jackson, you're actually awake!" she said, tears falling from her eyes as she ran to his side.

"Be careful with him now," the sweet nurse said as she gently pushed Jackson's hair back off his face. "He's still pretty delicate."

"I promise I'll be careful." Willa leaned over Jackson's hospital bed, lightly cupping his cheeks in her hands as she leaned down and kissed him. Jackson slid his hand across her cheek, up through her hair, and pulled her closer.

"Ahem," the nurse noised. "What did I just say?" huffed the sweet nurse with an almost grandmotherly touch, looking at Willa.

"Don't go getting him all excited. I told him the same thing this morning." She shook her head with an almost comical sense of disapproval. "Once he's cleared, you two can molest the heck out of each other, but for now, no. I'm counting on you, young lady, because I don't trust this one." The nurse smiled, wagging a pointed finger at Jackson.

"Yes, ma'am," Willa laughed.

Willa sat down at the side of his bed. "I can't..." She lowered her face and started to cry. "I'm so sorry."

"Hey, look at me, Love," Jackson said softly, his voice cracking from the inflammation the intubation tube had caused. Willa's eyes met his. "This isn't your fault."

"But if I..."

"What? Left me?" He tried to force a smile through his pain and continued exhaustion.

The nurse finished hanging a bag of IV medication.

"This is going to make him pretty tired again. Then he starts physical therapy at 2 p.m."

The nurse looked lovingly at them both. She had seen the news, she knew who they were and what they had just been through. Seeing them still so loving to each other made her hopeful for their future.

CHAPTER THIRTY

The Plan

Manhunt Day: 10

Over a week had passed since the shooting, and Jackson was still essentially confined to his hospital bed. His body was weak and vulnerable. The hospital was on high alert with increased security due to the media frenzy now surrounding the hospital after Jackson's location leaked. In his room, Sonia, Willa, two police officers, and the lead detective were deep in conversation, trying to come up with a plan to lure Killian out of hiding.

Jackson's sharp voice cut through the tense atmosphere. "You want to use her as bait?! Absolutely not," he said, shaking his head. "Find another way."

The detective chimed in with a somber tone. "At this point, it seems like our best option. We've exhausted all other leads and interventions. There's a nationwide manhunt, but nothing has led us to Killian yet."

One of the officers added, "We believe he's still in the city, waiting for an opportunity to finish what he started."

His partner continued, "And unfortunately, our security footage isn't conclusive enough. We can't definitively prove that Killian was the one who fired the shots. He matches the descriptions, and you have the history, of course, but we need something more concrete to pin him down."

"You think he doesn't know he's a 'person of interest'?" Willa said annoyed. "His face is plastered all over TV. There is only one reason he isn't coming forward to clear his name... motherfucker did it. What's more concrete than that?"

Sonia interjected with a possible solution.

"We could use a decoy," she suggested. "Someone who looks like Willa. We can release photos of her coming and going from the hotel to the hospital. Maybe that will draw Killian out long enough to be taken in for questioning."

The detective saw potential in this idea. "We can set up a faux sting operation at the hotel," he said excitedly. "Make security look lax so that Killian sees an opportunity to slip in undetected. When he shows up at the room, we'll be ready to take him down."

"What if he doesn't fall for it?" Willa asked. "What if he's expecting this?"

"We'll deal with that when the time comes," the detective replied, his voice full of determination. "For now, let's find our decoy Willa and keep you out of harm's way."

The detective and Sonia left to finalize their plan while the officers remained outside Jackson's hospital room door. Willa's bodyguard, Yuli, stood vigilantly by the elevator, ready to protect her at all costs.

***

Manhunt Day: 14

Willa sat on the edge of Jackson's hospital bed, flipping through TV channels, watching images and videos of Kristen, her doppelgänger, wearing a hat and large sunglasses, traveling around the city, going from hotel to hospital to a café, picking up flowers. The waiting was unbearable.

"This isn't working... He hasn't made a move," Willa said.

"He will," the detective said, slowly pacing around the room.

Willa noticed Jackson was becoming more and more restless. He was severely limited in his ability to move. He was bound in a stiff brace that wrapped his chest and back completely to allow his spine to heal, but it placed pressure on the ribs that were broken from his fall and the thoracotomy, making breathing even more painful. His right leg was clearly weaker since the shooting. He had a limp and was using a cane to help steady himself. The doctors and physical therapists reported being impressed by his progress, but made it clear he would likely never be back to 100 percent.

***

Manhunt Day: 32

"These things take time. We need to be patient. That's when he'll start to get sloppy," the detective said.

"No, this has to stop, it's been over a *fucking month*. And you have no leads." Willa's eyes lit with fire. "Just fucking use me already!"

"No," Jackson said, "that's exactly what we are trying to avoid."

"Do you want to live in this hospital forever?" Willa snapped at Jackson. "I'm tired of fucking hiding. He's not fooled by her. He knows it's not me." Willa defended her decision. "She is always covered up, Killian needs to see my face. He needs to know he can get to the real me."

"We could try alternating," the detective said. "Having Willa out and around while still having Kristen at the hotel swapping them out."

Jackson slowly walked over to Willa, gently wrapping his arm around her.

"He's winning, Jax. He wanted to punish me, and he's doing it."

"I know, Love," Jackson said, slightly defeated. "And I need to get out of this bloody room." Confinement in the ICU, away from windows, never knowing for sure if it was night or day, was starting to wreak havoc on Jackson's psyche.

The decision was made to move the operation to the hotel.

Willa and Jackson would be secured on a separate floor from the sting, but Willa would be seen out and about town with security following her.

Sonia released a statement to the press saying that Jackson had a slight medical setback and that his recovery was taking longer than expected.

They decided to continue pretending that Jackson was in the hospital by using one of his stunt doubles. The hope was that if Killian wasn't going to show up at the hotel, he might try the hospital.

CHAPTER THIRTY-ONE

The Hotel

*M*anhunt Day: 35

Sneaking Willa and Jackson out of the hospital and replacing them with the doubles was easier than expected. Security was heavy on their floor. The floor had been bought out; they were the only ones staying on that level. Officers were by every elevator, stairwell, and outside of their suite's door.

Alex and additional staff were assisting in setting up the hotel room. Jackson would still need physical therapy and follow-ups, but everything had been arranged for him to get care right at the hotel to minimize the chance of him being seen out of the hospital.

"Okay," Alex started." Physical therapy is set up for three times a week; they said you no longer need the brace. Other than that, they just said you should be able to do whatever is comfortable, but to avoid lifting anything super heavy or bending, twisting. All the same stuff they have been saying for weeks until after you see the doctor on Friday."

Jackson nodded, and Alex and the team left the room.

Jackson and Willa were finally alone.

It had been five weeks since the shooting, and they had not had a second to themselves. The need between them was palpable.

Jackson sat down on the edge of the bed. Willa walked over and sat next to him. Her fingers traced the outline of bruising on his hand from where one of the many IVs had been.

"Why don't we get you in the shower?" she whispered with a gentle smile. "It will be a nice change from the hospital one."

She took his hand and led him over to the bathroom. She helped him to remove his shirt. Tears filled Willa's eyes as she saw the healing scars on his chest, one from the first bullet, one slightly lower from where the chest tube had been, and the most prominent scar, the thoracotomy scar, wrapped from his back under his shoulder blade across the rib line to the front of his chest. She delicately traced her fingers over them, a rogue tear falling down her cheek.

Jackson lifted her chin so their eyes met.

"I'm fine," he said sweetly. "I heard women like scars; they make a man look dangerous," he added with a wink.

"Ha! I think another dangerous man is the last thing I need right now." Willa smiled, gently shaking her head.

Willa started the water to let it warm up. She turned around and placed her hands on either side of his hips.

"Remember, you can't bend," Willa murmured, her fingers trembling as they eased his sweatpants down past the tender incision on his lower spine.

Jackson breathed heavily. He tried to fight his arousal seeing Willa on her knees before him, but his body craved her.

He's still fragile, Willa said to herself.

His body, however, was screaming for her. The pulsing erection drew her in. They were alone, no hospital staff, no security detail.

"No bending, heavily lifting, twisting... Other than that...anything that's comfortable," Jackson said, taking Willa's hand and pulling her into the shower fully clothed.

Willa tore at her clothes, slipping them off until she was naked, her slick skin sliding against his. She sank to her knees, Jackson's back pressed firmly against the cold marble, eyes locked onto hers.

"No bending," she purred, her breath hot on his skin.

Her lips grazed his lower abdomen, the shower's steady stream cascading over them. Jackson's fingers dug into Willa's hair, guiding her, desperate for release. Willa instinctively opened her mouth and took him in fully.

Jackson let out a desperate moan at the feeling of the warmth of her mouth engulfing him in contrast to the cold marble against his back.

Willa continued working him with her mouth, sliding him in and out while simultaneously using her hands on him. It had been too long.

Jackson tried to deny himself, not wanting the moment to end, but couldn't resist. He wrapped her long, wet hair around his wrist and pulled her head back as he came, marking her with the streams of cum dripping down her breasts.

"Do you think you're able to..." Willa started to say while standing under the shower spray, letting the evidence of his pleasure slip down the drain.

"Bed, now," Jackson commanded, cutting her off.

They moved over to the bed.

Willa's legs draped over his shoulders.

Jackson, driven by desperation and pain, feasted on her. He needed her to forget, to think only of him, not the perilous situation they found themselves in, not the trauma of the past weeks, only his mouth, his breath, his tongue ravishing her.

Willa's body trembled as his fingers slid inside, his thumb circling her clit, lips worshipping her inner thighs.

She was close, her body tensing, overwhelmed by his touch.

Willa's thighs quivered, her back arching off the mattress as pleasure coiled tight in her belly. Jackson slipped his fingers out, gripped her, tipping her hips lightly up, and pulled her closer to the edge of the bed again. His mouth descended again, fast and hungry, but lower than before. Willa gasped as his tongue repeatedly landed on the secret spot just below her entrance. His lips and tongue worked her ass in tandem, fingers still pumping deep inside her while his thumb continued to firmly massage her clit, igniting a fire that spread through her core.

Willa, completely overcome, gasping for air, begged Jackson not to stop, finally screaming his name with a piercing tone during her release that the officers standing guard at the door could hear.

CHAPTER THIRTY-TWO

The Bait

Manhunt Day: 36

The first tendrils of dawn's light crept through the curtains, bathing the hotel room in a soft glow. For the first time in over a month, Willa lay wrapped in Jackson's arms, her dark wavy hair fanned out on the pillow, her deep eyes closed in a fitful sleep. The calm before the storm, she thought, feeling the weight of the day ahead pressing down upon her even in slumber.

Her phone's shrill ring shattered the tranquility.

Sonia's voice filtered through. "Willa, open up, it's time," she said, a statement laced with unspoken urgency.

Willa's heart skipped a beat. Today was no ordinary day; it was the day she took control of her narrative and would step into the public eye to lure Killian from the shadows where she knew he lurked. There was no possibility in Willa's mind that Killian had left town, not after all this, not after what he'd done. He would want to explain to her why, in his delusional mind, this was the way to win her back.

She slipped from the warmth of the bed, casting a glance at Jackson. It still felt so surreal that he was a man whose entire life had been horrifically altered because of her and yet, he remained by her side.

She wrapped herself in a robe, its fabric whispering against her skin as she crossed the room. Her petite figure, often mistaken for fragility, moved with a purpose that spoke volumes of her inner fortitude. At the door, an officer nodded curtly, stepping aside to allow Sonia entry.

Sonia stepped in, clutching two garment bags. Her eyes held a spark of determination, mirroring Willa's own. Without wasting a moment, she hung the bags on the bathroom door, the thud of the hangers a reminder of the heavy reality they faced.

Willa exhaled slowly, steeling herself for what was to come. Every step forward was a step away from the past that haunted her, a past that had brought her here, to this pivotal moment when she would face her fears head-on.

Sonia's subtle nod toward Jackson was fleeting, a mere acknowledgment of his brooding presence on the edge of the bed before her attention pivoted back to Willa. She unzipped the first garment bag with practiced efficiency, laying out its contents on the chair beside them: an oversized black T-shirt and dark jeans that would allow Willa to blend into the crowds, a University of DC School of Medicine baseball cap, a subtle indication that this would really be Willa, and oversized sunglasses for a touch of anonymity, and black heeled boots to give her height and confidence.

Willa's gaze, however, lingered not on the casual disguise but on the other bag as Sonia revealed its contents. A bullet-proof vest, tailored to fit Willa's slight frame—a shield against the unthinkable. Beside it, a small array of radio and recording equipment lay silent, waiting to be activated.

The sight triggered a visceral reaction in Willa; a tremor rippled through her body, and the reality of what she was about to do hit her with full force. This was no rehearsal, no hypothetical scenario—it was the tangible embodiment of danger, a reminder that Killian was more unpredictable than ever.

Killian had killed before, in combat, and he struggled deeply with the trauma from his military career. Willa had helped him through multiple flashbacks and nightmares over the years when they loved each other. He was, of course, still effectively violent with only his hands, but never since she had known him had he even owned a gun, let alone used one on a civilian. Willa didn't know this version of Killian at all, heightening her anxiety.

Jackson shifted on the bed, his dark eyes shadowed with worry.

"I don't like this," he murmured, the frustration evident in the tense set of his jaw. The fact that he couldn't be there to protect her, to stand by her side, gnawed at him. Jackson felt the weight of their situation, the gravity of using Willa as bait. He knew the team had run through every possible outcome and every contingency plan, but Killian's volatile nature made each moment uncertain.

"Are you sure about this?" Jackson asked, his brown eyes searching hers for any sign of doubt as he stood up, wincing with pain.

"I have to be," she whispered, the words more for herself than anyone else. She could hype herself up all she wanted with the belief that when pressed, she could take Killian down, but she knew she was lying to herself. If Killian had wanted to really hurt her, to even kill her, he could, and she would be powerless to stop him. But she had to try.

"Jax, he may not even show today," she said. "We all assume the second I step out of here, he will instantly appear out of nowhere." She forced a laugh.

"It's true," Sonia chimed in. "We have no idea where he is... He could be in another state for all we know. He will likely need to see some kind of media coverage to even know where Willa is in the city. It will likely be days before we get word he's been spotted," Sonia reassured them both. "Don't use up all your energy today worrying. We have a ways yet to go."

Sonia watched the exchange, a silent sentinel preparing to guide Willa through the gauntlet. Sonia had organized operations like this numerous times, she understood the stakes, the necessity of composure in the face of fear.

The tremor in Willa's hands betrayed her calm composed exterior as she reached for the vest, its weight cold and unyielding. She drew in a shaky breath, attempting to still the quake that had taken residence in her bones.

Sonia's voice sliced through the tense silence of the hotel room, soft yet insistent.

"Try not to panic," Sonia said to Willa, her eyes sympathetic but resolute.

The bitter irony wasn't lost on her. It took the involvement of a famous *man*, his unintended entanglement in her violent past, and his near-death injuries, for the authorities to finally take action. She was no longer invisible. Her name and face were all over the media coverage. She had the full attention of the police, the FBI, the very institutions that had once failed her. The weight of this injustice sat heavy on her chest, a fire kindling within, but Willa knew this was not the day to dwell on battles of the past.

Jackson watched her, his concern etched deep in the furrows of his brow. He wanted to envelop her in safety, to shield her from the world's cruelties, but he knew that Willa's spirit could never be caged. She had faced demons before, both within and without, and emerged stronger each time, after this Willa would be an unstoppable force.

Sonia's practical voice, void of unnecessary warmth, sliced through the charged atmosphere of the hotel room. She extended a hand to Willa, gesturing toward the protective gear with calculated efficiency.

"Here is what's going to happen," Sonia began, meticulously unfolding the plan. "First, we are going to get you suited up."

Willa felt the vest's weight settle over her chest, the fabric of her shirt pulling taut against the padding. The radio's presence was a cold touch against her side, while the earpiece nestled into the curve of her ear whispered promises of constant vigilance.

"You're going to walk in with me just like Kristen has been," Sonia continued, precisely outlining each step. They would pause outside the hospital; a momentary stage for a performance designed to lure out a ghost from Willa's past.

"Adjust your hat, flip your hair around, clean your sunglasses on your shirt—so your face is exposed long enough for pictures to be taken to prove that it's you. The pictures will hit the media in minutes. If...when Killian sees them, he'll show himself."

The simplicity of the actions did little to steady Willa's heart, which drummed a staccato rhythm against the vest. As Sonia spoke, Jackson sat motionless, his dark eyes tracing every contour of Willa's face as if committing it to memory, engraving it onto his soul.

"Then we are going to go in, take the elevators up to the ICU where Kristen is waiting." Sonia's plan unfurled further, each word painting a path that led Willa away from safety and into the lion's den. Yet, uncertainty gnawed at Willa's resolve.

"What if something goes wrong?" Her voice was a quiet tremor, betraying the fear she fought to subdue.

"There are police and agents all over the hospital," Sonia responded, her tone adopting an edge of firmness as she pointed to the panic button nestled among the array of gadgets. It was a small beacon of security, a lifeline amid the chaos that could ensue.

"This little button—it's also like a GPS. We will always know where you are, and if you get in trouble, just push it."

The assurance brought little comfort to Willa.

"But sometimes technology fails," she said. "Don't I get some kind of weapon?"

Sonia's face went rigid as she let out a slow sigh.

"It's too risky, Willa. We don't know if Killan will be armed. We have every reason to believe he will be, but we don't know. What we do know is he is ex-military special ops, and any weapon we send you in with could easily be taken from you...and used against you."

"Right," Willa mainly said to herself as her fingers brushed over the button, feeling its deceptive smoothness.

Sonia's eyes held hers, imparting a silent message that they were doing everything within their power to keep her safe.

"You'll only be alone for about three minutes at the most," Sonia finished, her gaze unwavering.

"ALONE?!" Jackson's voice echoed off the hotel room's walls, his disbelief palpable in the charged air, the protest a guttural force that shook him to his core. "Why the fuck will she be alone?"

Willa felt the tremor of his words as if they were her own pulse, quick and hard. Jackson's eyes, the look in them—a blurred composition of fear, anger, and an insurmountable desire to protect. Willa couldn't look at him; it was almost enough to unravel her carefully composed demeanor. She had never seen him scared. Despite years of experience and professional training, Jackson was doing a terrible job of hiding his fear and feelings of powerlessness. Willa had never felt more cherished.

Sonia shook her head, addressing Jackson with a calmness that seemed alien under the circumstances.

"We can't have a bunch of new people showing up today, that would be a huge red flag. We need to work with the same crew, the same faces that have been here all month. Between the crossing of Kristen, Yuli, myself, the officers stationed on watch outside the unit, there is a brief point where she will be in the service elevator alone," Sonia explained methodically, her hands gesturing to the sequence of events as if she were conducting an invisible orchestra. "In an elevator. Alone," she repeated.

Jackson's jaw tightened, every line of his body rigid with the unspoken plea to take Willa's place. But the plan was unyielding, and so was the reality of his injuries, invisible as he sat, the only indication of his vulnerability, the cane at his side.

"Willa and I will walk into the hospital together. We'll go up the elevator to the ICU and make the switch with Kristen. I'll be sure Willa gets into the staff elevator to go back, and Kristen and I will continue our usual walks around the hospital," Sonia explained. "Yuli will meet her at the bottom service elevator and escort her to the SUV in the secured lower-level parking garage." Sonia continued, "Once the media releases the true photos of Willa and Killian goes looking for her, he will only find Kristen and me."

Sonia's gaze flickered to Willa's for just a moment, an unspoken reassurance amid the strategy. It was a short window of time Willa would be unescorted, but in the world of risks and shadows, even a heartbeat alone felt like a lifetime.

Willa watched the exchange, feeling the weight of Jackson's concern and Sonia's professional detachment press upon her from opposite sides. She was a solitary figure caught between the man who wanted nothing more than to shield her from harm and the calculated risk that promised a chance at ending this nightmarish game of cat and mouse.

The room held its breath, waiting for Willa to speak, to break the spell of tension that wound around them. Yet, in the silence, it was Willa's resolve that spoke volumes, her quiet courage resonating louder than any words could. It was her battle to face, and though the thought of those three minutes gnawed at her, she understood the necessity of the darkness before the dawn.

He could see the subtle tremble in her shoulders. He wanted to believe that she would be all right, that the plan would unfold without incident, but the protective instinct that raged within him wouldn't be silenced.

He watched her, his heart torn between admiration and dread. She was the embodiment of courage, standing tall in the face of danger that sought to drag her back into darkness. And though his body was marred by wounds that bound him to nothing more than a bystander, his spirit stood unyieldingly beside her.

"I need to do this. I need to do something. I don't want to hide anymore," Willa declared, her voice steady despite the conflict brewing within her. It was a statement of intent, a warrior's cry against the invisible chains that had bound her for far too long.

The shooting, the moment that had nearly taken Jackson's life, had been the catalyst that fused the Old Willow with the new. She had faced her fears, had stood at death's door beside him, and now she emerged, tempered like the finest blade. Killian would be caught, maybe not today, but justice would be delivered, on her terms, by her hand.

Jackson's hand, a gentle force, lifted her chin. His gaze locked onto hers, and the world, with all its threats and shadows, melted into the peripheries of their shared moment. In that tender yet desperate embrace, their lips met. It was a kiss laden with unspoken promises and the taste of bittersweet goodbyes.

"Come back to me," he whispered against her lips, his voice low. Despite his commanding screen presence, this man, who had navigated the revolution of fame and emerged as a beacon of integrity in the quiet morning light of a New York hotel room, was just a victim of circumstance, a man in love.

As they pulled apart, the silent strength in Willa's eyes was a mosaic of vulnerability and fortitude, power and doubt, guilt and revenge pieced together by experiences that would have shattered a lesser spirit. And though she quaked at the precipice of confrontation, her resolve remained unshaken.

***

Willa and Sonia approached the hospital's entrance. The morning fog clung to Willa's skin, but a coolness in the air hinted at the gravity of the day ahead. They moved purposefully, their shadows stretching long behind them on the skyscraper-lined sidewalk.

Like vultures drawn to the scent of a story, Paparazzi clustered near the entrance, cameras poised to capture the moment. Willa, aware of every heartbeat thrumming against the vest beneath her shirt, paused. With practiced ease, she lifted her hand to adjust the brim of a baseball cap emblazed with her alma mater's seal, brushed her hair behind her ears, then, as if on impulse, removed her oversized sunglasses. She polished them against her shirt, a deliberate action that unveiled her face just long enough for the flashbulbs to immortalize her feigned tranquility.

"Remember, it's just another walk in the park," Sonia whispered, pitching her voice low for Willa's ears alone.

Willa turned toward her companion, the corners of her mouth curving into a smile that didn't quite reach her eyes. She tossed a mock-serious glance at Sonia, quipping softly about the absurdity of smiling through a storm. The photographers lapped it up, their shutters clattering like applause as the two women shared a laugh that was more performance than genuine mirth.

"Let's get this over with," Willa murmured, the smile slipping from her lips as they crossed the threshold into the relative sanctuary of the hospital's corridor.

Sonia nodded, her expression settling into a mask of casual indifference that contradicted the tension simmering beneath.

"You're doing great, Will," she reassured, her voice a gentle undercurrent to the chaos around them. Her words were for Willa alone, a lifeline thrown amid the tempest of flashing lights and prying eyes.

As they navigated through the lobby, Sonia's smile remained fixed, a masterclass in composure. "Remember, you're happy, relaxed. You're going to visit the love of your life who is healing wonderfully, and everything is great," Sonia murmured, reminding Willa of the script of their two-person performance.

"Everything is great," Willa repeated her cynical tone muffled by the fake, forced smile on her face as Sonia guided them toward the elevator with a touch that was both comforting and conspiratorial.

As the elevator doors slid closed, enclosing them in a temporary refuge from prying eyes, the hospital, an edifice of healing and hope, was now a stage. Every step was choreographed, every breath measured, as she prepared to hunt the demon she had helped to create.

Willa maintained her facsimile of calm as the elevator ascended, the hum of its machinery a low soundtrack to the quickening pulse that thrummed in her ears. She pressed her lips into a line, summoning the image of a serene smile, one she had practiced countless times before in the mirror of her own self-restraint.

"Halfway there, Willa. It's almost over," Sonia whispered, her voice a velvet lullaby meant to ease the edges of Willa's fraying resolve. There was an undercurrent of steel in her tone, a testament to the gravity of their mission.

"Yeah, for today," Willa murmured, the words barely escaping her lips as she took in the suffocating world around her. It was a temporary performance that held permanent consequences. There was no guarantee that Killian would show up on this day. *This could go on for weeks,* Willa thought. Each step felt like navigating a minefield dressed as a hospital corridor.

"A day at a time, Willa. It will get easier," Sonia responded, her voice steady and reassuring. It was a mantra for survival in this high-stakes game.

As the numbers on the elevator panel illuminated one by one, marking their journey toward the ICU, Willa felt the weight of every choice that had led her to this moment. Each digit was a step closer not just to confronting Killian but to reclaiming her life, which had been so cruelly rewritten by his malice.

The elevator dinged softly, and the doors glided open with a hush that seemed to echo through the sterile hallways of the nearly vacant ICU. Willa stepped out, her fingers reflexively smoothing the fabric of her oversized shirt. The vest underneath was a hidden protector against unseen but deeply felt threats.

As Willa walked, her mind traced the steps that had led here, the path winding back through memories shaded by the DC skyline, the Spanish moss which held whispers of Savannah's historic streets, the tropical heat of those Miami nights, the Gala heartbreak, and now the sterile, cold New York hospital halls.

The changeover was seamless, a practiced dance between doubles where every step had been meticulously choreographed. Kristen slipped on the oversized sunglasses and adjusted the baseball cap on her head, effectively taking on Willa's silhouette. With a nod that barely disturbed the still air of the hospital room, they acknowledged the swap was complete.

Willa stared at Kristen for a moment. Here was a woman whose job was to pretend to be Willa, take, and overcome whatever abuse would come "Willa's" way as a result. The whole concept seemed alien. There were people in this world who genuinely felt a calling to help others, and it made Willa smile to herself.

"Are you serious?" Sonia barked into her earpiece. "Of all fucking days. Make sure the team is aware. I don't want this messing anything up."

"What's wrong?" Willa said, clenching her jaw.

"It's nothing, really." Sonia continued, "They're doing some kind of emergency maintenance on the south staff elevator, so you are going to go down the north elevator instead. It's on the other side of the unit. It's not a big deal. Instead of turning right out of the elevator, you and Yuli will go left instead. Slightly longer walk, but you'll still end up in the garage, and the SUV will be there."

"Oh, okay." Willa turned away, her focus narrowing to the path ahead—a short walk down the sterile corridor that smelled faintly of floor wax. A ride in the elevator which would hum quietly as it descended. She would meet Yuli, then two *left* turns to freedom.

"Short walk, down the elevator, Yuli, LEFT, LEFT, and free," she murmured under her breath, the mantra threading through her consciousness, wrapping around her resolve. Each repetition was a balm to the adrenaline coursing through her veins, a mental talisman against the cloak of dread attempting to settle upon her shoulders.

The distance to the elevator shrank with each measured stride, the heels of her boots clicking silently against the polished floor, reminding her of the sound her stilettos made in the marble lobby of Jackson's Miami hotel the night they met. Soon, soon, this horrible nightmare would be over.

There was a mechanical beep as she pressed the elevator button, a sound that reverberated too loudly in the hush of the hallway. The doors slid open with a whisper, an invitation to enter the temporary sanctuary of its confines.

"Walk, elevator, Yuli, left, left, and free." The words were a cadence now, keeping time with the beat of her heart. She stepped inside the elevator, aware of the camera tucked in the corner, a silent witness to her journey. Her finger hovered over the button for the basement, and with a press, the doors sealed shut, encapsulating her in the transitional space between what had been and what was to come.

"Elevator, Yuli, left, left, free." The litany continued, a soft incantation that wrapped around the steady thrum of the machinery as the elevator began its descent. She could feel the pull of gravity, a tangible reminder of the earth below and the weight of the day's significance.

"Three minutes. Just breathe," Willa whispered, her voice a silken thread in the quiet of the elevator as it descended toward the basement level. The rhythm of her breathing became the metronome by which she measured the time slipping away, each exhalation a reminder of the danger that lay close at hand yet outwardly unseen.

The elevator dinged softly, announcing its arrival with a sound that seemed too gentle for the gravity of what awaited her. Doors slid open with a hush to reveal the cold, stark basement. Seafoam-green subway tiles lined the walls, their glossy surfaces reflecting the dim fluorescent lights overhead, casting an eerie glow on the concrete floor.

"Yuli, left, left, free," the mantra continued. But now, the chant faltered in her throat.

"Yuli?" Willa's voice was a feather on the heavy air, her call more a whisper than a shout. The sound seemed to be absorbed by the basement's dense silence, as though even the walls were conspiring to keep her isolated. She scanned the stark expanse for any sign of the bodyguard, but the void where he should have been remained unbroken.

Straight ahead, a long hallway stretched into the shadows, silent and foreboding. To the right, another corridor mirrored the first, equally deserted and unwelcoming. But it was to the left that Willa's gaze instinctively traveled, seeking the familiar bulk of Yuli, the mammoth bodyguard whose presence was meant to signal safety and the near end of this perilous act.

A giant bulletin board loomed about twenty feet away, plastered with notices and memos—a mundane island in a sea of tension. Beyond it, another hallway veered left, but the space where Yuli should have been standing guard was conspicuously, alarmingly empty.

Willa's heart hammered against her ribs, the pulse throbbing in her ears louder than the silence of the place. Her mind raced, thoughts cascading over one another as she grappled with the absence of her expected escort. The lack of Yuli's towering figure sent a ripple through the calm façade she had maintained thus far, a crack in the armor she wore over her deep-seated fears. Something was terribly wrong.

"Yuli?" she tried again, a hint firmer this time, yet cautious not to raise an alarm. Her eyes darted across the clinical sterility of the basement, searching for shadows that might conceal him, a flicker of movement, anything that indicated his presence. But the only response was her own breath, returning to her in puffs of anxiety.

Willa's fingers trembled as they reached for the radio on her encased torso; the vest felt suffocatingly tight now, its weight a reminder of the gravity of her situation.

"Hello? Sonia? Anybody?" Her voice crackled through the static of the communication line, a beacon of hope rapidly diminishing as no reply came. Only static answered back, a harsh and unfriendly hiss against the backdrop of her escalating fear.

"Shit...now what," she muttered to herself, the veneer of control starting to slip. Willa's hand clung to the elevator door, propping it open, as if it were a lifeline anchoring her to safety. With a shaky exhale, she brought out her phone, swiping it alive with a desperate thumb.

The screen lit up, a mockery of connectivity—no service. Yet there, tauntingly, the hospital guest Wi-Fi network signal glared at full strength, a cruel reminder of a world buzzing just beyond her reach. Her heart pounded, a drumbeat of dread echoing through her ribs. Out there, somewhere beyond these sterile walls, life went on. People were laughing, arguing, falling in love, oblivious to the dangerous game being played in the bowels of this Manhattan hospital.

"Great," Willa breathed, the word laced with sarcasm, her mind racing as fast as her pulse. The cold tiles beneath her feet seemed to leech warmth from her body, her once-steady resolve cooling with each passing second. But panic was a luxury she couldn't afford—not when every instinct told her that time was slipping away, and with it, her chance to end this nightmare once and for all.

She had to move, to act, despite the fear that clawed at her throat.

"Come on, Willa," she whispered to herself. "Simple, go back up. Wait...if Yuli isn't down here where he is supposed to be? Something must have gone wrong. What if upstairs is no longer safe? Ok…left, left, free," she continued to herself, a private pep talk meant to infuse courage into her faltering spirit.

The absence of Yuli, the static of the radio, the lack of cell service. She didn't have a choice, she needed to move. She was resilient and intelligent, a woman who had faced far worse than an empty hallway, a broken radio, and a useless cell.

With a deep breath that did little to steady her nerves, Willa stepped fully into the basement corridor, letting the elevator doors close behind her with a resolute thud. Ahead lay a path fraught with uncertainty, each step a test of the strength she knew she possessed. Alone she might be but defeated she was not.

Willa's dark eyes glinted with the reflection of her phone's screen, a beacon of irony in the dimly lit basement. With no signal to call for help, she found herself in an absurd predicament that would have been comical if not for the danger it spelled out.

She bit her lip with frustration as she muttered bitterly about the twisted fate that allowed for online shopping but not emergency calls.

"Seriously! I could buy fucking shoes online right now but can't call the goddamn police. Fabulous! Fuck!" The words spilled out, raw and edged with panic and rage, echoing off the cold, rigid walls.

"Okay, Will, focus… You can kill the team later…right now…two lefts and free, just go Will," she coached herself, attempting to plant her feet firmly on the path of resolve. Phone still clutched in her trembling hand, she sprinted forward, her boots pounding against the concrete with a rhythm that matched her racing heart.

"Left," she whispered as she passed the first corridor, a blur to her peripheral vision. Just one more turn stood between her and the promise of safety, one more barrier to freedom.

Her mind raced with thoughts of Jackson, his concern, his love—a lifeline she clung to as she neared the second left. But before she could make the turn, reality shifted, bringing with it a chill that seeped into her bones. It happened so suddenly, so unexpectedly, that for a moment, the world seemed to pause, waiting for her next move.

CHAPTER THIRTY-THREE

The Basement

Willa choked on the air, her steps faltering as the figure before her materialized like a specter from her nightmares. The cerulean blue of the scrubs seemed to mock her with its calmness, a stark contrast to the maelstrom of panic rising within. The man's blond hair peeked from beneath the surgical cap, a loosened surgical mask dangling precariously from one of his ears as if taunting her with the half-hidden sneer she knew all too well, and clipped to the waistband of the scrubs, hanging, was a stolen ID badge with a picture that looked nothing like the current possessor.

"You," she breathed out, the word a shard of ice that cut through the haze of fear.

Desperation clawed at her fingertips as they fumbled for the panic button nestled against her rib cage—a lifeline that refused to answer her call. Each press yielded nothing but the cold silence of betrayal. Yuli's towering form, which had multiple concealed weapons, absent, and the static of the radio offered no comfort and no promise of rescue.

Her heart beat franticly against her chest, each pulse a reminder of the danger Killian posed—a danger that had once whispered sweet nothings in her ear and now stood unmasked, his predatory gaze locking onto hers with an intensity that spoke volumes of his intent.

Willa's gaze locked with Killian's, the air between them thick with a history of pain and fear. Her hand trembled slightly as she clutched her phone, the device a useless weight in the face of such a palpable menace. She could feel the sting of unshed tears threatening to break through her composure, but she forced them back. She would not crumble—not here, not in front of *him*.

"Wh-why?" The word emerged barely above a whisper, laced with a mixture of incredulity and despair. Years of looking over her shoulder, of jumping at shadows—Killian had ingrained himself into the darkest recesses of her psyche, an omnipresent ghost that haunted her every step.

Her mind raced, memories flashing like lightning: the subtle, unnoticed beginnings of control disguised as love, the sharp escalation into violence, the terror that had gripped her so completely it became a constant companion. He had been a chameleon, seamlessly blending love with malice until she could no longer tell where one ended and the other began.

As she steadied her voice, reclaiming a sliver of the resolve that had carried her this far, Willa sought answers, though she doubted any explanation could mitigate the damage wrought.

"Why did you do all this?" Her fingers unwittingly danced across the phone's screen, hoping against hope for a signal, a lifeline, anything.

In his silence, in the coldness of his stare, lay the weight of their shared past, a past that Willa had struggled to shed like a second skin, only for it to find her again in this sterile, subterranean corridor. Despite the fear, despite the uncertainty, she stood her ground, facing the man who had once claimed to love her, now her most dangerous adversary.

Killian's voice sliced through the dim basement with the precision of a scalpel, his words devoid of warmth.

"You won't get a signal down here," he said coldly, observing her with an unsettling interest.

Willa's hand, which had been tapping and swiping at the useless phone screen, stilled. She registered the undeniable truth in his statement; this far beneath the hospital's bustle, they were ensconced in a cocoon of concrete and steel. She felt the futility of her actions, the isolation of their surroundings closing in like a vise. With a frustrated sigh, she relinquished her futile attempt at communication and slid the device back into the pocket of her dark jeans.

Her heartbeat pounded in her ears, a relentless drum heralding a primal response to danger. Yet as the cold reality settled over her, Willa straightened her spine, refusing to cower before him. Every fiber of her being hummed with the desire to survive, to overcome the man who had once made her feel so small, so powerless. Her eyes, those windows to a soul forged in adversity, met his gaze unflinchingly, the air between them charged with the electricity of unspoken history and unresolved conflict.

"Why?" she finally asked again, her voice steady despite the tremor of fear dancing along her spine. "What were you doing there? I have so many questions." There was an edge to her words, a blade sharpened on the whetstone of betrayal and pain.

Killian tilted his head, the motion almost birdlike, predatory. He stepped closer, reducing the physical distance as if trying to erode the barriers she had painstakingly erected against him.

"Why did you leave DC?" His question hung in the air, tinged with a deep, seething possessiveness. He sought not just her presence but ownership of her reasons, her soul.

"Because I had to..."

Willa's fingers curled into fists at her sides, the cool air of the basement a stark contrast to the heat that flushed her cheeks. She felt the weight of Killian's gaze upon her, oppressive and unwelcome, like the humid Savannah summer she'd learned to endure as a refuge.

"Because I didn't love you anymore, Killian. You made it impossible to!" The words erupted from her, raw and laced with years of pent-up anger and fear.

"I was terrified of you, and clearly, I had good reason... I—"

"Everything fell apart!" Killian's interruption sliced through her declaration, sharp and sudden. He stood motionless except for his chest, which rose and fell with an erratic rhythm, betraying the calculated calm he presented.

Willa's heart hammered, each beat echoing the truth of his words. Yes, things had fallen apart, but the chaos left in the wake of their relationship's collapse was Killian's doing. His innate talent for twisting reality gnawed at her insides, a reminder of the manipulation she'd once mistaken for care.

"And whose fault is that?" Her narrowed gaze locked with his, a challenge etched into the defiant tilt of her chin.

Killian took a step forward, the destructive grace of his movements at odds with the sterile surroundings. His eyes, those steely blue-grey orbs, held a glint of something unspoken, a dark whisper from their shared past.

"Stay away from me," Willa commanded, her voice ringing with authority, disguising the shudder she felt in her knees. She could sense the shift in the air, as if the very walls were leaning in to witness what unfolded between them.

"There are agents all over this hospital looking for you."

The warning hung heavily, a specter of consequences that loomed just beyond the reach of Killian's hubris. He paused, the distance between them charged with an electric current of unyielding wills. In that standoff, the world seemed to hold its breath, awaiting the next move in a deadly game of chess.

Killian's laughter was a cold echo in the cavernous basement, bouncing off the seafoam-green tiles with a mocking air.

"Well, they aren't very bright then," he said, his voice laced with derision as he surveyed Willa's rigid stance. "I knew this is where they would bring him...and you."

He slowly licked his lips while gently shaking his head. "I've been here ever since."

Willa heard her pulse thundering in her ears. The revelation hung between them like a guillotine blade, sharp and waiting. Her mind raced, trying to reconcile the man she once craved so desperately with this monster before her.

"You've been here the whole time," she whispered, the words barely escaping her lips.

The fluorescent lights above flickered momentarily, casting Killian's features into a familiar play of light and shadow. He stood still, his blond hair, the piercing eyes, hospital-issued scrubs marking him as much a part of the hospital as he was an intruder within it.

In that moment, the omniscient gaze of the universe seemed to close in around them, observing the unfolding drama with detached curiosity. It witnessed the jagged edges of a fractured relationship, the remnants of a connection severed by fear and betrayal. It saw the trembling defiance in Willa's posture, the iron will that kept her standing even as everything inside her screamed to flee.

And somewhere beyond the confines of that basement, across the tangled threads of destiny and consequence, agents moved in the shadows, their presence once a silent promise of safety felt miles away from the cold, hard reality confronting Willa now.

Killian's laughter echoed hollowly down the empty corridor, bouncing off the seafoam-green tiles in an epic display of mockery. He shrugged nonchalantly, his posture relaxed despite the tension spiking the air between them.

"It's very easy to hide in plain sight, Will," he said with a casual arrogance that twisted the gravity of his stalking. "You know that."

Willa clenched her fists at her sides, fighting the tremor that threatened to convey her fear. She stood rooted to the spot, her eyes locked on Killian's as if by sheer force of will she could hold him at bay. The vest beneath her clothes felt like an armor of false confidence against the piercing gaze of the man who seemed to see right through it.

"Hide in plain sight"—the words resonated with the cold truth. In this labyrinth of clinical hallways and impersonal rooms, Dr. Killian Helmar had been a ghost, unseen yet ever-present, watching her every move from the shadows.

"Why?" Willa's voice cut through the silence, sharp and desperate. "Just answer me, why won't you just leave me alone?"

Her question hung suspended in the artificially chilled air of the basement, and for a moment, the omnipresent hum of hospital life above them seemed to pause, acknowledging the weight of her plea. Willa's heart pounded against her ribs, each beat a drum of defiance. Her dark eyes, usually so expressive, narrowed into slits that concealed the turmoil within.

Killian tilted his head, considering her, the corners of his mouth twitching with the semblance of a smile that didn't reach his steely eyes. In that sterile corridor, stripped of all pretense, the dynamic between them was laid bare—a twisted dance of predator and prey, where one sought freedom and the other domination. But even as Willa's voice quivered with the strain of confrontation, there was a strength in her stance, a silent declaration that she would not be hunted any longer.

"Because I love you, Willa, and I know you still love me... You just got...confused," Killian said, his voice threading through the silence of the corridor with an eerie calmness in contrast to the madness behind his words.

Confused? The word was a knife, twisting with every syllable, attempting to carve out the truth she clung to. But no, she knew love—real love—was not suffocating or cruel; it didn't stalk its prey with relentless obsession. Love was not Killian.

She steadied her breath, gathering the fragments of courage that lay scattered within her. She thought of Jackson, his embrace a fortress, the way his hypnotic eyes held storms yet offered shelter. His love was a cure, healing the wounds Killian had left, a testament to the strength she'd rebuilt, piece by painstakingly earned piece.

"Confused?" Willa managed, her voice a mix of resolve and fear. "There is nothing 'confusing' about the hatred I feel for you. I deserved better. I found better. I am better without you."

Killian's façade faltered, a crack forming in the mask he wore. There was desperation there, the kind that came from knowing control was slipping through his fingers like sand. He took a step closer, trying to reclaim the ground between them, but Willa held firm. She could almost see their past—those early days when they met, two ambitious souls en route for greatness, before the darkness seeped in, staining everything.

"Love doesn't torment, Killian," she continued, her voice gaining strength. "It doesn't hide in shadows, waiting to pounce. It doesn't nearly kill the people I care about." Her clear reference to Jackson, though unspoken, hung between them—a reminder of what Killian had done, the line he'd crossed.

Killian's lips again twisted into a semblance of a smile, but it was devoid of any genuine warmth.

"You think you're so strong now, don't you, Willa? Why, because you're some celebrity's fuck-toy, playing hero with the authorities?"

Willa's gaze never wavered from Killian's, her dark eyes reflecting a history of pain transformed into power.

"I am strong," she affirmed. "Not because of who I'm with or who's watching, but because I've seen the depths of my own hell and climbed out. I've faced my demons, and I'm standing here, in front of you, battered but unbroken."

Her hand moved instinctively to the panic button concealed beneath her clothing, pressing again in vain. Silence answered, a reminder of her solitary standoff. Yet she drew from an inner wellspring of resilience, a force that had propelled her through years of doubt and struggle, through the hallowed halls of medicine, and into the lives of those she now helped heal.

"Your idea of love is distorted, Killian. A reflection in a broken mirror," Willa said, the echoes of her defiance wrapping around the cold, seafoam-green tiles. "But I see things soooo clearly now. And I am done being your obsession."

Killian didn't respond, he only stepped closer, stared down at her with hooded eyes and that same chilling slight smirk.

*Shit...*she thought, *I've done it now.*

Willa was filled with instant regret, like so many times before... she had challenged him. She had seen this look before... She knew what it meant; what he was planning to do next...to her.

Willa's expressive eyes darted from shadow to shadow, her mind racing for a plan, a prayer, an exit strategy, anything that would lead her out of this dungeon and back into the warm embrace of Jackson and her freedom.

CHAPTER THIRTY-FOUR

The Liability

In the confines of a hotel room where lavish opulence met crippling anxiety, Jackson paced, limping, with restless energy. His muscular build, typically an embodiment of strength and stability, now betrayed by his inner turmoil. Unable to sit still, he moved across the room, his boots thudding softly against the plush carpet, mirroring the erratic beat of his heart. Light streamed through the windows, casting long shadows that played over his tan skin and intensified the tortured look in his deep brown eyes.

Despite the officers' presence, a barrier of isolation enveloped Jackson, their voices reduced to a low hum as his thoughts spiraled around Willa. He had only recently entered her life, yet the connection between them pulsed with an urgency that defied explanation. He knew she was confronting demons from her past, and every second away from her side amplified his concern.

As he turned on his heel to pace the length of the room once more, the sharp "ping" of his phone sliced through the tension. Instantly, he lunged for the device, thumb swiping over the screen with practiced urgency. An alert—unassuming yet laden with potential implications—beckoned him to a reality that awaited beyond the digital glow.

Jackson's hand was a blur as he snatched the phone from the nightstand, releasing a deep gasp, a live alert from Willa. Why? His mind raced, grappling with the possibilities, as his thumb tapped the screen with an almost reckless force.

"Come on, come on," he muttered, the officers around him casting curious glances in his direction. The app loaded, and there it was—Willa was live. Despite the disruption in cellular phone connectivity, she was fully connected to the hospital's Wi-Fi.

Willa's phone, though tucked away, was broadcasting something far more severely ominous. As Jackson held his phone, the black screen on the feed held steady, and the reality of her situation filled the room with a chilling clarity through the audio feed.

A voice sliced through the silence of the live stream—a voice that curdled Jackson's blood.

Killian.

His words were a twisted serenade of possession and malice, a disturbing symphony that played on every nerve in Jackson's body.

"Fuck," he breathed out, his voice barely audible.

The officers, now rigid with attention, craned toward the sound emanating from Jackson's clenched grip. Their faces, usually stoic and unreadable, betrayed a flicker of horror as the confrontation unfolded in real time, reaching them from the depths of Willa's pocket universe.

"That's her?" one officer whispered. They all knew they were mere spectators to a scene playing out far away from their reach, witnesses to an intimacy borne of terror and desperation.

Jackson's eyes never left the screen, even as he felt the officers mobilize around him, the tension in the air reaching a crescendo. He didn't need to see Willa's face to know her terror; he heard it in the tremble of her voice, felt it in the rapid cadence of her breathing. It was as if the darkness that enveloped her had taken a solid form, pressing against him through the miles that separated them.

Run, Willa, he willed silently, his entire being focused on the unseen struggle that played out in the palm of his hand.

"Get her out of there!" Jackson's voice tore through the room. The officers around him were a blur of motion and urgency, fingers pressing against earpieces, voices crackling commands into radios. They were orchestrating an extraction that seemed to move at the pace of molasses compared to the galloping of Jackson's heart.

"Command, this is Unit Two, we need immediate entry to the basement level," one officer barked into his phone, his words slicing through the charged air.

"Copy that, coordinating with SWAT now. Stand by," came the disembodied reply, clinical and detached.

"We know—" Sonia's voice broke through on the radio, cutting off the officer mid-sentence. She was the voice of reason amid the chaos, like a seasoned professional with nerves of steel.

"We are holding back," she continued, her tone steady yet laced with an undercurrent of tension that matched the situation's gravity.

The room fell silent, every officer pausing, their eyes flicking between Jackson and the handheld device that held them all hostage to Willa's fate. The decision to wait was a gambit that placed Willa's life on the razor's edge between rescue and ruin.

Jackson's fists clenched and unclenched at his sides. The weight of inaction bore down on him; every second ticking by was another where Willa remained in danger.

"Fuck holding back? Get her!" he demanded, his voice climbing to a crescendo of desperation. The words carried his accent, a sharp edge slicing through his usually calm demeanor.

There was a crackle over the radio before a voice cut through the static.

"Jackson—Detective Davis here. We can't pull her out yet," he said, his tone firm yet not without empathy. He understood the stakes as well as anyone. "This is our only chance; there was an unexpected tech failure—if she can get him to admit he is responsible live, we have him… She's brilliant."

Jackson's breath hitched as the truth of the detective's words settled upon him. Willa, with her unyielding spirit and sharp mind, was indeed brilliant. She was playing a dangerous game, one that required finesse and courage in equal measure. She was out there alone, facing a monster with nothing but her wits and the hope that her plan would work.

As the realization dawned on him, Jackson's posture shifted, she was on her own. A part of him—a part that had played heroes and villains alike on screen—wanted to wrench control from fate itself, to storm into that basement and shield her with his own body.

"Take me to her now," he demanded, his words leaving no room for argument.

The officers exchanged uncertain glances, well aware of protocol yet equally cognizant of the desperation swirling in Jackson's gaze.

"Mr. Donovan—Look," began one officer, but Jackson was already moving.

"Now!" His command of desperation ricocheted off the walls.

The officers, trained to deal with crises, found themselves momentarily at a loss. Jackson Cole Donovan, the star, the icon, was rapidly crumbling before their eyes.

"Sir, we understand, but you can't—"

Jackson dropped to his knees. "You don't understand. She's down there, alone, with a madman because of me. Because I couldn't protect her."

He looked up at one of the officers, desperately fighting back tears. "He's going to kill her."

The officers' resistance waned under the weight of Jackson's despair. They understood duty, sacrifice, and, perhaps in some distant corner of their hearts, love. With a curt nod, the lead officer turned to his team, issuing orders through the crackle of a radio.

"We're moving Donovan," the officer said tersely.

"Are you fucking crazy? He's a liability!" a stern voice from the radio replied.

"Look, he's halfway out the door already," the officer lied, looking down at Jackson. "Either we catch up with him now, or you'll have to deal with him when he gets there."

"Fine! His irrational ass is your personal responsibility now. If he compromises this scene, it's your ass."

In the charged silence that followed, Jackson, with the assistance of the officer, rose to his feet.

"Remember, you're about as powerful as a kitten right now, so let's avoid any heroics that might get you killed and me fired, k?" the officer said, trying to loosen the palpable tension.

Jackson nodded with silent gratitude to the officer.

Chapter Thirty-Five

The Showdown

Willa's back pressed against the cold concrete wall, the damp air of the hospital basement clinging to her skin like a sinister reminder of the darkness around her.

"Confused," Killian's words echoed in Willa's head. Willa's voice cut through the stale silence, each syllable measured, a veil of calm barely concealing the storm of emotions brewing within her. Willa's deep, expressive eyes, usually a well of compassion, now bore into Killian with an intensity Killian had not seen from her before.

"You lied to me, you raped me, you stalked me, and you almost killed the only man I have ever actually allowed myself to fully love."

He loomed over her, his eyes reflecting a flicker of satisfaction at her acknowledgment of what he perceived as love, content even in her accusations.

"Don't say that, Will," he cooed, the smooth confidence in his tone juxtaposing the sharpness of his gaze. "You know I hate when you try to make me jealous."

His words hung in the air, a twisted declaration from a mind unraveled by obsession, unable to accept the severance of a bond he believed unbreakable. Willa, however, stood resolute, a striking figure of defiance against the man who sought to claim her soul as his possession.

Killian stepped forward and reached for her.

"Let go of me!" she screamed, her voice echoing off the damp concrete walls. Willa's long, dark hair fell in disarray around her face as she struggled against Killian's hold, her deep eyes ablaze with a fire fueled by fear and indignation.

Killian's hands, like vises on her shoulders, tightened their grip as he pushed her against the wall, the pressure mounting against Willa's slender frame. The sterile chill of the basement wall seeped through the fabric of her T-shirt, but it was the heat of his touch that sent shivers cascading down her spine.

Killian, unmoved by her plea, leaned in closer, his breath hot upon her ear.

"He almost died because of *you!*" Willa's accusation sliced through the air, sharp and unwavering. Her words were more than an expression of anger; they were a testament to her resolve, a challenge to the man who dared claim ownership over her every breath.

"That was an accident..." he said, the casual dismissal of his tone at odds with the severity of his actions.

Willa's heart pounded fiercely against her chest, each beat a drum of survival. Confusion laced with fear tightened around her throat, yet she managed to muster the strength to question him, her voice struggling for clarity.

"What do you mean that was an accident?" The words tumbled out, a cascade of disbelief and desperate need for understanding.

The basement, with its stark fluorescent lighting and the scent of various chemicals mixed with dampness, seemed to shrink around them, as if the walls themselves were pressing in on Willa, compounding the intensity of the moment. Killian's physical dominance was palpable, yet it was the psychological hold he believed he had over her that Willa knew she had to break.

Killian's expression shifted subtly, a flicker of something dark and unreadable passing through his piercing eyes. It was a look that spoke volumes of his fractured psyche to the twisted reality he existed in—one where Willa was not her own person but an extension of his will.

His breath was hot and ragged. The emptiness of the hospital basement seemed to amplify the sound of his voice, a tremor of possessiveness lacing each word as he loomed over Willa.

"Do you have any idea what it's like for me to see you with him? The photos, online, TV, magazines, everywhere." His eyes, those celestial blue-grey pools that once promised safety but now only reflected terror, bore into her.

Willa, though dwarfed by his physical presence, held her ground. Her heart raced, yet her voice remained steady, a testament to her unyielding spirit, even in the face of her fears.

"What do you mean it was an accident, Killian? Why did you shoot him?" she pressed, her dark eyes searching his for a shred of truth amid the chaos he sowed.

The air hung thick between them, charged with the weight of Willa's question.

Killian's grip on her shoulders tightened, his fingers digging in with a possessive fury worse than Willa had experienced with him before. His eyes drilled into her as if he could somehow imprint his will onto her soul.

"People seeing you. Knowing who you are, knowing you're mine, but with HIM. So blatantly cheating on me? They see him touching you, kissing you, knowing he's fucking you!? It's very disrespectful, Willow, when you belong to me!" The words tumbled from Killian's lips, each one laced with venom as he tightened his hold on her.

Fear-laced confusion, swelled within her chest like a riptide threatening to pull her under. Her deep, expressive eyes widened in shock at the delusion spilling from Killian, his conviction as unsettling as it was unfounded.

"Cheating on you!? You thought I was cheating on you!? After three years apart!?" Willa's mind was spinning.

"Oh my God, Killian, you are truly delusional," she uttered, her voice trembling but the underlying strength of her character piercing through the terror.

Killian's face contorted with a mixture of pain and anger, his chiseled features twisting into a mask of near psychotic fixation. His body loomed over her, casting a shadow that felt colder than the chill of the basement air. Willa, caught in his iron grasp, realized that the only thing more dangerous than Killian's physical strength was the distorted reality he clung to.

His voice, however, took on an eerie calm.

"No, I'm seeing things more clearly now than ever, baby," he murmured, the softness of his tone a stark contrast to the pressure he placed on her shoulders that threatened to bruise.

Pain lanced through Willa's body, but her mind raced with purpose. She knew this might be her only chance. There had to be someone watching, someone who saw the live feed, someone who knew she was ensnared in this chilling dance with danger. Jackson, with his protective nature and intense eyes that missed nothing, or Cassy, her saving grace whose loyalty was as unwavering as the Georgia oaks, or Sydney, whose quick thinking led to strong actions, or even Lilly... Someone must have picked up on the distress threading through every word she spoke, hidden beneath the fear.

With each throb of pain from Killian's grasp, Willa clung to a single thread of hope: the knowledge that somewhere beyond these suffocating walls, Sonia and her team knew Willa never made it out of the hospital, and help was on its way.

"What do you mean shooting Jackson was an accident, Killian?" she repeated, the question slicing the dank air of the hospital basement with a precision that belied the tremor in her heart.

Killian's eyes, mirrors of madness, flickered with something dark and unreadable. His breath, hot and heavy, brushed against Willa's face as he leaned in closer. The scent of his cologne, once familiar, now mingled with the musty odor of neglect that pervaded the space around them. It was a sinister perfume, one that spoke of desperation and decayed dreams.

"An accident...the timing," he whispered, his voice a serpent's hiss that seemed to slither through the shadows. His fingers tightened further, nails digging into her skin, punishingly so, yet Willa stood resolute, her own fear honed into a weapon sharper than any blade. She was not the same woman who had once wilted under his touch; she was the embodiment of every challenge she had ever faced, every scar that marked her journey.

"Tell me, Killian!" The demand surged from deep within her, fueled by the agony of uncertainty and the fury of betrayal.

He hovered over her, the oppressiveness of his presence threatening to crush her will. But even as darkness encroached upon her senses, Willa's resolve remained unbroken. She thought of Jackson, of his unwavering support, of a love that had bloomed in spite of the scars they both carried. She would not let Killian's twisted vision of reality win.

"Jackson...was never supposed to be part of this," Killian said, almost contemplatively, as if discussing a change in weather rather than an act of violence. His grip shifted, not relenting, but in a perverse caress, his thumb brushing the line of her jaw with a false tenderness that made her skin crawl.

"Answer me, Killian," she quietly pressed. She needed to keep him talking, to pull the confession from the depths of his fractured psyche.

"It's a curious thing, unconditional love," he mused, his gaze never leaving hers. "It can make you see enemies where there are none, create battles that don't need to be fought."

"Who...Killian?" Willa asked again, choking over her words while a single tear betrayed her composure, trailing down her cheek, as a terrifying realization began to set in.

"Who were you aiming for?"

CHAPTER THIRTY-SIX

The Realization

In the dim glow of the parking lot outside of the basement-level parking garage, the SWAT team crouched low, a living shadow against the concrete. Their breaths hung heavy in the air, eyes trained on the hospital's multiple exits. The static crackle of the radio broke the silence.

"Hold position, she's almost got him," Detective Davis's voice was firm yet tinged with anticipation.

Through the tension, across the lot, Jackson Donovan was a storm of desperation and fury. Willa's phone still transmitting moment by moment their reality. His tan skin glistened with sweat as he wrestled against the restraint of multiple officers, his muscular yet weakened frame straining for release. The determination etched onto his chiseled features spoke volumes of his resolve to reach Willa.

"Let me go!" His English accent seared through the night, a stark contrast to the usual calmness that graced his tone. The officers, aware of his public persona, now witness to the raw, unfiltered passion of a man frantic to save the one he loved.

"Jackson, you have to trust us," an officer pleaded, trying to meet his frenzied gaze.

But Jackson's dark eyes were locked onto the hospital doors as if he could will them open with sheer force. The officers' grip tightened in response to another surge of his athletic frame, their own bodies bracing against his vigor.

"Listen to me!!" Jackson barked, the veins in his neck standing out like cords as the crippling realization set in.

"He wasn't aiming for me!" Jackson screamed, "HE WAS AIMING FOR HER!"

"Jackson, stand down!" The command came sharply from a seasoned officer, his voice laced with authority yet not devoid of empathy. He understood the gravity of love and sacrifice.

The SWAT team remained statuesque, a testament to discipline, while mere yards away, Jackson fought with a desperation only love could evoke. The officers holding him glanced at each other, silently acknowledging the shared burden of containing a man whose only thought was the safety of his beloved. They were the barrier between him and chaos.

"Willa," Jackson whispered under his breath, a prayer into the restless night. It was a plea for her survival and a vow that he would never cease to fight for her. Even as the officers pinned him back, Jackson's spirit reached out, intertwining with Willa's in the unseen battle that raged beneath the surface.

Chapter Thirty-Seven

The Confession

Willa's skin, chilled and clammy with sweat, now revealed small drips of blood slowly dropping down her arms, Killian's grip finally piercing her skin, his towering presence remained a cage she could not escape.

"If it wasn't him," Killian's voice sliced through the stillness, smooth yet laced with an edge of madness, "it would be someone else, Will. Someone else would come and try to take you away again. I couldn't let that happen."

His words sent a wave of realization crashing over her. The danger was not just to Jackson; it was a threat that loomed over anyone who dared to draw close to her. Anyone who might offer her a semblance of the normalcy she craved.

Willa's mind raced, even as she anchored herself in the moment, her resolve hardening like steel. She could feel the weight of every choice that had led her here, each step echoing through the hollow space. She knew she needed to keep him talking, to peel back the layers of his delusion until the truth was laid bare.

"Killian," she pressed, her voice firmer now, cutting through his distorted reality with the precision of a scalpel, "who were you aiming for?"

The air between them was charged, electric with the tension of unspoken truths and the gravity of what was about to be revealed. Willa knew, in that moment, that the answers she sought were within reach, if only she could maintain the delicate balance between fear and determination that kept Killian engaged, kept him on the precipice of confession.

Killian leaned closer, brushing his cheek against hers. She could feel his breath, warm and unsettling on her cheek, as he pulled her closer still, his face descending toward hers with the inevitability of nightfall.

"It was the only option," he murmured, his voice a low rumble that reverberated through the hushed space between them, "but he...stepped...backwards."

The words hung heavy in the air, laden with implications that snaked their way into Willa's consciousness, cold and insidious.

Willa's heart pounded, she was hyperventilating, starting to feel faint, but a defiance raged through her veins. She knew she had to keep him talking, he needed to say it. Willa needed to hear him say it.

"Say it... Say it, you bastard, you coward... Who were you aiming for?! Say it!"

"It was going to be so quick, baby...right here." He slowly slid a hand up from her shoulder to tap her left temple. "You wouldn't have even felt it. I didn't want you to suffer." His grip was unyielding, as if he were the arbiter of life and death, bestowing upon her a twisted form of mercy.

Before she could recoil from the chilling confession, his lips crashed against hers with an ownership that stole her breath away. It was a forceful, desperate kiss, laden with the madness of possession. Willa's mind recoiled in horror, her stomach churning with revulsion at the contact. Yet, beneath the layers of fear and disgust, her pride took hold.

Her lips, no longer passive, pushed back against Killian's with a vehemence that startled and excited him. She engaged him, passionately kissing him, biting his lower lip as she had done so many times before, causing him to moan with pleasure, but this wasn't a return of affection; it was a declaration of war.

With a sharp turn of her head, she broke the kiss, tearing his lip, her breath ragged with exertion and adrenaline.

"Never again," she whispered, the taste of his blood lingering like poison on her tongue. She spat the words out with the blood, each syllable a nail in the coffin of his delusions.

CHAPTER THIRTY-EIGHT

The Rescue

"GO! GO! GO!" The commander's voice cut through the crisp morning like a blade, shattering the silence into a thousand fragments.

In an instant, the SWAT team sprang to life, their movements a choreographed dance of precision and urgency. They approached the hospital's side entrance—a heavy metal door that looked inconsequential compared to the gravitas of the moment.

The lead officer's boot collided with the door, and it gave way with a jarring crash. The sound echoed down the sterile corridors, heralding the arrival of justice.

As they approached, Killian towered over Willa, his eyes enraged, blood dripping from his chin.

A sharp crack split the air as the electrodes from a taser found their mark on Killian's broad back. His body convulsed, once, twice, thrice—a grotesque puppet with its strings viciously pulled by invisible hands of law enforcement. He crumbled to the ground like a tree being struck by lightning, his fall echoing the demise of his delusions of control.

Willa stood frozen, barely registering the chaos, until strong arms lifted her up. It was Yuli, whose grip was both gentle and firm. He had the eyes of someone who had seen too much yet still managed to find compassion in the storm.

"It's over," Yuli murmured, less to reassure her and more as a solemn vow.

As Killian lay incapacitated, twitching with the aftershocks of high voltage, Willa collapsed in Yuli's arms allowing herself to be led away from the darkness of the basement, away from the man who believed the ultimate act of love was causing her death and toward the light of a new day where the shadows no longer held sway.

Yuli's strides were quick and purposeful as he navigated the hall, through the garage to the parking lot. Each step was a defiance of the ordeal she had endured, a silent promise to carry her out of that place of shadows and into safety. Willa, her mind still reeling from the encounter, felt the cool air of the outside world wash over her.

At the sight of Yuli with Willa limp from exhaustion in his arms, the officers who had been restraining Jackson released their grip. With a mixture of physical pain and desperation, Jackson surged forward through the sea of bodies, his gaze locked onto Willa.

"Put me down, Yuli," Willa's voice, though laced with fatigue, did not waver. It was the assertive command of a woman who had survived the unimaginable, reclaiming her autonomy. Yuli obliged without hesitation, setting her gently on her feet, inspired by strength emanating from her slender frame.

Willa wasted no time; her legs, though shaky, propelled her toward Jackson. Their reunion was imminent, the culmination of fear and hope crashing into a single moment. As she stepped into his embrace, the lingering echoes of terror dissolved completely. She was enfolded by his warmth, his presence; an anchor in the turmoil of her storm-ravaged heart.

"It's finally over," she tearfully whispered against Jackson's chest, her words a soft declaration of an ending and a beginning. The trials that once seemed insurmountable were now behind them, and in their place, the possibility of healing loomed, vast and infinite.

CHAPTER THIRTY-NINE

The Trial

The courtroom, with its towering ceilings and the echoes of resolute footsteps, held a solemn air as Killian was escorted in. Impeccably dressed in a bespoke suit that distracted from the shackles binding his wrists with a chain to his ankles. His face exuded confidence. For the briefest moment Willa saw him, not the delusional menace he'd become, but the man who cherished the most intimate sins of her past, her ally, her partner in crime, her sole future; the man she would have killed for, died for... A part of her longed to reach out to him, desperate to find the phantom of a man she had always believed him to be though he never really was, longing to make this all just a bad dream.

Killian glanced over at Willa; she fought back a tear.

"Always love you," he mouthed in her direction.

Willa looked away as Jackson placed his hand gently on her thigh. She saw the concerned look of confusion in Jackson's eyes as he watched the interaction. Willa placed her face in her hands and quietly sobbed.

Jackson glared into Killian's eyes as Jackson wrapped his arm around Willa and pulled her into his chest, partly to comfort her, but also as a point to Killian that regardless of what conflicted feelings of affection she may still hold for Killian, she was Jackson's now.

"Dr. Killian Helmar," the judge began interrupting the silent standoff, her voice resonating through the chamber, "you stand before this court today facing serious charges including:

Attempted Murder in the Second Degree,

Assault in the First Degree,

Criminal Possession of a Weapon in the First Degree,

Menacing in the First Degree,

Reckless Endangerment in the First Degree, and

Stalking in the Second Degree.

How do you plead?"

Killian's lawyer leaned in, whispering last-minute counsel before turning back to the judge.

"Your Honor, my client enters a plea of not guilty to all charges."

A murmur rippled through the gathered crowd, a mixture of shock and disbelief given the amount of evidence stacked against him.

Killian remained motionless, save for the clench of his jaw, as the gravity of a plea without contest settled like dust after a storm.

The days that followed would be a carousel of emotion for all involved. Day after day Willa relived her life since meeting Killian. On day four of the trial the witnesses started filing in.

***

Dr. Abraham Randanowitz approached the witness stand. Willa tried to breathe away the sick feeling that had settled in her gut. It was a mixture of contempt and forgiveness. Anger and understanding. Years of misery could have been spared had Radz helped Willa that first fateful day.

He was sworn in, his hands shaking slightly as he recited the familiar words. The prosecutor wasted no time, beginning with the hardest question first. "Dr. Randanowitz, please tell us about your interactions with Dr. Willow Sullivan, or Burke as you would have known her, before she changed her name and went into hiding."

Radz's gaze swept over the courtroom, a fleeting look of shame passing across his features as he glanced toward Willa. His voice was softer than she remembered, but no less pained.

"She was a promising resident at St. Asclepius, where I was one of the attending psychiatrists. Talented, bright..." He paused, swallowing visibly. "But in the spring of her fourth year, she came to my office in obvious distress."

His words hung heavily in the air, and Willa fought the impulse to look down, to avert her eyes from the collective focus of the room. She could feel everyone waiting, breaths suspended like a fine mist of judgment.

"Please describe what you observed at that time." The prosecutor's tone was gentle but insistent, guiding Radz toward the memories he seemed so desperate to avoid.

"Her face was bruised," Radz continued, his eyes locking onto some distant point above the jury. "There were marks around her neck that she had been covering with a scarf." He hesitated again, and Willa's skin prickled with the same sensation of being cornered, trapped, as she had felt that day so many years ago.

The prosecutor leaned in. "Did she tell you what had happened?"

"She started to. She said...the bruises were from Killian...Dr. Helmar." Radz's voice broke slightly over the name, and Willa watched as he grappled with the weight of his admission. "She was frightened. Frightened and ashamed. She...she asked for help."

The silence in the courtroom was oppressive, like the charged air before a storm. Willa closed her eyes for a moment, and the memories flooded back, unbidden and fierce. She had been so certain that Radz would protect her, would offer the sanctuary she so desperately needed. But his reluctance and dismissal left her exposed and vulnerable in the very place she had sought safety.

"And did you provide that help?" The prosecutor's question was as direct as an arrow, aimed precisely at the target of Radz's failure.

"No." The single word came out cracked and small, and it seemed to shrink him before their eyes. "No, I didn't."

Willa saw the courtroom dissolve into whispers, heads leaning together like conspirators, the sound merging into a steady drone. It was happening again, this unbearable feeling of being abandoned, of having nowhere to turn. She was there, on the bench in his office, hearing him say he didn't want to get involved, and knowing she had to go back to the apartment she shared with Killian, back to the twisted semblance of a life she couldn't escape. She opened her eyes and focused on Radz's lined face, on the sad truth etched into his features.

Radz took a deep breath, like a diver preparing for one last plunge into the dark. "I turned her away. Told her I couldn't be involved in domestic issues between colleagues." The words were edged with regret, each one a small blade. "I was a coward."

The prosecutor stepped back, allowing the admission to settle, allowing Radz to steep in his own guilt. Willa felt her pulse throb in her temples, the sound a frantic reminder of the panic that had gripped her after Radz had refused to help. She recalled the dizziness, the hopelessness, the way the floor seemed to tip and sway as she left his office and walked out into the sterile, impersonal corridors of the hospital, so small and alone.

"No further questions at this time, Your Honor."

The defense attorney rose slowly from his seat, his movements imbued with a theatrical flair that demanded attention.

"Dr. Randanowitz," he began in a smooth, measured tone, "isn't it true that many physicians, when specializing in a field such as psychiatry, tend to further subspecialize in even more niche areas?"

"Yes, that is correct. It happens often," replied Dr. Randanowitz, his voice steady yet tinged with the weight of experience.

The attorney leaned forward, his eyes gleaming with a mix of curiosity and calculated intent.

"And isn't it also true that you, personally, have dedicated decades to a subspecialty within psychiatric medicine through extensive work, practice, and clinical research?"

"Yes," came the quiet affirmation.

"Please, Doctor, could you enlighten this court on the particulars of your subspecialty?"

With a heavy sigh, as though resigned to the inevitable scrutiny, Dr. Randanowitz responded, "Women's Mental Health and Trauma Recovery."

"And just to clarify for everyone present, when you say 'trauma,' you mean it encompasses domestic violence, physical abuse, emotional abuse, rape...correct?"

The defense's words hung in the charged silence of the courtroom before the attorney continued with deliberate precision.

"Yes," the doctor confirmed in an almost imperceptible nod.

"Exactly," the defense attorney said, striding purposefully toward the jury with a self-assured air. "Dr. Randanowitz is an expert in the care of women who have suffered violence at the hands of those they loved."

Willa, a silent observer, felt a grim confirmation settle in her gut. It was all too predictable. Radz had earned his repute in this field, which was precisely why she collaborated with him on her ambitious Recovery Center project.

With a tone laced with scorn, the attorney pressed further.

"With all due respect, Dr. Randanowitz, do you honestly expect this court to accept that a woman in genuine distress, reported that she was attacked by her lover, and you inexplicably sent her away even after she showed evidence of her bruises? It is almost inconceivable, given your extensive knowledge of intimate partner violence, that you would fail to recognize such blatant signs when they entered your office."

Dr. Randanowitz opened his mouth to respond, his words faltering on the brink of escape, only to be abruptly cut off.

"Tell me, did you know Dr. Helmar to be particularly violent?" the attorney demanded, his voice coldly accusatory.

"There were rumors," Radz admitted in a voice scarcely louder than a whisper, laden with regret. "I should have done something. I should have intervened. But I didn't."

"Rumors...from what I understand, there were plenty of 'rumors' surrounding Drs. Helmar and Burke. But as we all know, rumors are not facts," the attorney retorted sharply.

Fueled by a sudden surge of anger, Randanowitz's voice rang out, "I was mad at them!" His exclamation reverberated through the courtroom, drawing gasps and murmurs alike.

The defense attorney pounced on the moment, his tone dripping with accusation.

"Excuse me, Dr. Randanowitz, are you suggesting that your presence here today is motivated by your personal animosity toward Dr. Helmar?"

"No, that's not what I meant..." the doctor stammered, his protest drowned out by the rising tension.

"That's exactly what you just said," the attorney insisted, his words slicing through the fragile atmosphere.

"I—" Randanowitz tried again, only to be met with the impatient interjection.

"I think we all heard you quite clearly."

"Counsel!" the judge intervened firmly. "Let the witness finish his answer. Please go ahead, Dr. Randanowitz, and explain."

Taking a deep, trembling breath, Dr. Randanowitz began.

"There were numerous rumors circulating about Willow and Killian. Willow was exceptionally bright, full of promise, but their relationship was fraught with volatility. Their constant altercations on the unit, the inappropriate...intimate contact so blatantly on display, it all began to overshadow the Center project. Regardless of the legitimacy of the rumors, and, sadly, most of them were true, sponsors started withdrawing their support. We were on the brink of having to shut down the program because of the turmoil that Willow's relationship with Killian had sown. When she came to me that day, I...I didn't want it to be true. Had I known that Killian's actions had escalated to the point of beating her and raping her, I would have been forced to take decisive action. It would have undoubtedly cast a harsher spotlight on the project...we couldn't afford to lose any more investors."

As he spoke, fresh tears began to trace sorrowful paths down his weathered cheeks, each drop a testament to his inner torment.

"Willow, I'm so sorry," he whispered softly, the admission finally breaking down his guarded façade as the courtroom fell into a heavy, pained silence.

***

"The state calls State Witness #2, Cassandra Mitchell to the stand."

The chair wobbled slightly as Cassy pulled herself into it. Her eyes locked on Willa's, a lifeline tossed across the courtroom. They were darker than usual, heavy with anger and resolve. Willa wanted to grab on to that lifeline, but her grip was too weak, her heart too unsure.

"Please state your name," the clerk instructed.

"Cassandra Mitchell," Cassy declared, her voice unfaltering as she focused on Willa. The connection between them was a taut line, stretched tight with memories and shared struggles. Willa felt it pull against her, grounding her in a moment where everything else seemed fluid and unreliable.

The prosecutor approached the stand. "Can you tell us about the incident you witnessed shortly after Dr. Helmar arrived in Magnolia Shores, Mrs. Mitchell?"

Cassy shifted slightly, never breaking her gaze.

"I came back to our office building after picking up lunch for Willa and me," she began, her words colored with the heat of the memory of that Georgia afternoon. "I saw him there. Killian. He was in our office, uninvited."

"Describe what you saw." The prosecutor's tone was firm, coaxing more from Cassy, drawing out the details as the courtroom listened intently.

"He had Willa pinned against the wall." The words were crisp and direct, each one landing with precision. "He was kissing her...she was crying, struggling to get away from him."

"I told him to get his hands off her," Cassy continued, her voice shaking slightly with remembered rage. "He didn't let go right away. It wasn't until I threatened to call the police that he finally left."

The tension in the courtroom was electric, a charged hum that seemed to vibrate beneath the surface of every word. Cassy's testimony wove a tapestry of violence and terror, but also one of fierce loyalty. She had been Willa's anchor, a constant presence when the rest of the world seemed intent on drifting away.

"What was Willa's condition after Dr. Helmar left?" The prosecutor pressed, aware of the impression Cassy's testimony was making.

"She was scared. Shaking." Cassy's eyes finally broke away from Willa, scanning the faces in the courtroom. Her own expression was a mixture of fury and sadness. "It was the first time I'd ever seen her that afraid."

"Thank you, Mrs. Mitchell. The court appreciates your testimony."

The defense attorney rose from his seat with a commanding presence, drawing attention like a magnet with his movements, which were as rehearsed and fluid as a seasoned performer.

"Mrs. Mitchell," he began, his voice dripping with condescension and his tone dipping like a hawk preparing to swoop. "You're close friends with Dr. Burke, correct?"

"Sullivan and yes." Cassy's response was sharp and defiant, a verbal jab that cut through the tension in the room.

"Close enough to want to protect her, even if it means exaggerating the facts?" He let the question linger in the air, a dark cloud casting a shadow over the carefully constructed landscape of truth that Cassy had painstakingly laid out.

"I'm not exaggerating," she countered, her voice filled with strength and conviction that turned heads in the courtroom. "That's what happened."

The attorney feigned a look of sympathy, nodding slowly as if addressing a particularly young child who just couldn't grasp the lesson.

"Isn't it true, Mrs. Mitchell, that when you arrived Dr. Suuulivan ...was engaged in a mutual display of affection with Dr. Helmar? In fact, didn't Dr. Sullivan thank you for walking in when you did, as Dr. Sullivan told you that, had she and Dr. Helmar not been interrupted, they would have engaged in consensual sexual contact?"

Willa bristled inwardly, a storm of emotions swirling within her. How did he know that? Killian must have overheard them.

"No, that is inaccurate," Cassy lied calmly, casting a glance toward Killian. "Willa was terrified."

"Did Dr. Sullivan file a police report after this reported 'terrifying' interaction?"

The attorney's questions came rapid-fire, each one an accusation in disguise, like arrows aimed to pierce through her defense.

"No." Cassy's words were solid and unwavering, a pillar of resolve in the face of scrutiny. "She didn't have any faith in the legal system at that point."

"Convenient, Mrs. Mitchell, don't you agree?"

The attorney's smile was that of a snake, slippery and cold, a predatory grin that left a chill in its wake.

"Thank you. No further questions."

Cassy stepped down, the connection between her and Willa a thread pulled taut, vibrating with the intensity of all that had passed between them.

As Cassy reached her seat and offered a small, resolute nod, Willa knew that the lifeline was still there, waiting for her to grasp it, to hold on until everything else faded away. She inhaled deeply and felt her spirit rise with the oxygen, a slow ascent toward hope.

"The court will take a short recess to allow preparation of the next witness, Ms. Lillian Harrington."

***

Lilly's heels clicked a hesitant rhythm on the courtroom floor, a sharp staccato against the hushed expectations that crowded the room. As she settled into the witness chair, Willa saw their years together distilled into one breathless moment, heavy with betrayal and possibility. She met Lilly's eyes, searching for some acknowledgment of the past they shared, but Lilly looked away.

Willa's breath was shallow; each inhalation tinged with uncertainty. Lilly had been a constant in her life until she wasn't. Lilly was the reason Willa's cover was blown. She was the reason Killian arrived in Georgia.

Which version of Lilly was currently on the stand? Willa's oldest friend, her sister? Or one of Killan's other victims? One who hated Willa for leaving? One who would lie, cheat, steal? One who would do anything to protect Killian?

"Please state your name for the record," the prosecutor prompted.

"Lillian Maire Harrington." The name fell between them, heavy with history. Lilly smoothed the fabric of her dress, her movements as precise and controlled as ever. But Willa could see the tension beneath the surface, a restlessness that couldn't quite be concealed.

The prosecutor wasted no time, diving straight into the heart of what they needed.

"Ms. Harrington, you and Dr. Burke have been friends for a very long time, correct?"

"Yes"

"Is it reasonable to assume that out of others in Dr. Burke's life YOU would be one who would know more of the personal aspects of the relationship between Dr. Helmar and Dr. Burke?"

Lilly hesitated, the pause stretching thin before she caught it with a deep breath.

"I guess that's true."

"Is it correct that you were the first to meet Dr. Helmar outside of a professional capacity regarding his relationship with Dr. Burke?"

"Yes"

"How would you describe the relationship you witnessed from your perspective?"

"They were..." She searched for the right words, for words that wouldn't tear at old wounds. "Complicated. Passionate. Toxic." She spoke like a connoisseur of tangled emotions, a curator of dysfunction.

Willa's stomach twisted as Lilly recounted the early days of what had seemed a perfect match, their ambition and brilliance blinding them to everything else. "They were unstoppable," Lilly continued, her tone tinged with admiration and envy. "At least that's how it looked from the outside."

From Lilly's perspective, their lives had seemed like an intricate dance of power and promise, a dance that Willa now knew was doomed from its first steps. The years folded in on themselves, the distance between them collapsing in the space of a single, unbearable memory.

"What happened when you began to see behind the façade?" the prosecutor pressed. "They tore each other apart." Lilly's words were bare, stripped of any pretense. "Willa was ambitious. Driven. She pushed Killian so hard. She...always said she saw this potential in him. She wanted him to be the best version of himself, but he..." Lilly paused trying to gather her thoughts.

"There was just something about him. I saw it too. Something about him makes you want to be with him, encourage him, support him...admire him...but the second that stops, or he thinks it stops, like he thinks you don't think he's as special anymore...he changes and gets dark...fast." Lilly looked over at Willa.

"That's what I saw between he and Will. Her star just kept rising and once the hospital agreed to the Center project that she dreamed up...she was miles ahead of him now... Before they had been this...cute package deal... Killian and Willow... They got away with everything. It was like impossible to hate them even when they were...well...fucking assholes." Lilly turned to the judge remorsefully. "Sorry, Your Honor, but it's true.

"What people didn't see was that, yeah, Will was the driving force, but he thrived on it. It was like he had this special little thing, Willa, that no one had, and he was destined for great things because she chose him."

"Interesting, Ms. Harrington, thank you. Could you please tell us when you first noticed a shift in their relationship?"

The courtroom air grew heavy as the attorney leaned forward.

"Once the hospital picked up the Center project. Willa didn't really have time to keep pushing Killian's career forward by making sure he got recognition for things she actually did. I remember when she told me about the Center. She was ecstatic but the next words out of her mouth were that she needed to make sure Killian became Chief Resident. Or when they finally secured the first Center sponsors, she had to make sure Killian was lead author on some journal article or something... Which he was completely aware of by the way. Every time something good happened to Willa he knew something good would come his way...like she would keep things even. "

"Did she ever tell you why she would do all that?"

Lilly's lips twitched into a resigned smile, her voice thick with frustration and tenderness.

"Yeah, I would give her such shi—a hard time for it. She worked so hard to get what she wanted and then would have to do it all over for him...but she said it was because she loved him, she didn't want to be without him...and he would get soooo jealous any time anything good happened to her. He would basically throw a tantrum that she owed him now because ..." Lilly shrugged. "It's like once he realized he could ride her coattails the idea of her leaving him behind was too much."

A brief silence befell the room before the attorney's tone turned somber.

"Ms. Harrington, I understand the difficulty of this next subject, but the defense will undoubtedly bring this up. With that in mind, may I ask: how long after Dr. Sullivan's disappearance did you begin an intimate relationship with Dr. Helmar?"

A hush fell over the courtroom, punctuated by an array of gasps, murmurs of shock, and whispered expressions of disbelief. The judge's sharp voice cut through the disturbance. "Order! Order! Any further outbursts, and this court will be closed to the public."

Lilly lowered her head, a rush of shame and humiliation washing over her. She drew a deep breath, raised her gaze with trembling determination, and quickly wiped away a solitary tear that glistened on her cheek.

"About a month or so," she confessed in a trembling tone. "I know it was wrong—"

"You are not on trial here, Ms. Harrington," the attorney interjected softly, his voice laced with compassion.

Lilly shifted uneasily in her chair, her slender legs crossing and uncrossing in a nervous rhythm. "If you would, could you please tell us about your interaction with Dr. Helmar on the night of the Willowbrook Center Fundraiser?" Lilly enjoyed the spotlight, but not like this, never like this.

"The night of the fundraiser, Killian showed up. I figured he would, but I didn't know for sure. I hadn't seen him in a month because I had been traveling around for work, which is when I found out Willa was alive. Umm...the night of the fundraiser I had stepped outside to get some air. It was an overwhelming night. I had only just learned she was alive... Killian found me out there... Sorry..." More tears dripped down her face.

Her voice faltered, and more tears rolled silently down her cheeks.

"It's all right, Ms. Harrington. Please, take your time," the attorney reassured her.

"He...wanted us to get a room in the hotel the benefit was being held in."

"Are you saying that Dr. Helmar showed up uninvited to a fundraiser you were having for your—at that time missing best friend, Dr. Helmar's ex-girlfriend—and he was asking you to engage in sexual relations with him?"

"Yes...but I told him no." Lilly sniffled, looking at the ground.

"And how did he take that, Ms. Harrington? How did Dr. Helmar handle that rejection?" the attorney inquired.

"He grabbed me, he started to kiss..." Lilly couldn't speak, she couldn't bring herself to disclose the rest of the night.

"Ms. Harrington, is it fair to say Dr. Helmar didn't take it very well and that he continued to pressure you into having sex with him against your will?"

Suddenly, an outraged cry erupted from the defense attorney. "OBJECTION! Leading," he bellowed.

The judge's hammer came down with a resounding tone.

"Sustained," the judge reluctantly responded. Looking over at the state attorney, she said, "Proceed cautiously."

"My apologies, Your Honor. I just hate to see a woman suffer," replied the DA. "Ms. Harrington, if you could please, in your own words, describe what happened after you refused Dr. Helmar's advances."

Gathering her resolve, Lilly straightened her posture. Her eyes briefly met a knowing gaze from Willa, a silent acknowledgment of shared history and regret, her sole hope of mending what was broken.

With a voice that trembled between defiance and despair, Lilly recounted.

"I told him no, that it was a mistake. Everything our twisted relationship was...was a mistake. I had only wanted him because he reminded me of Willa and I missed her so much but then things got out of control, and I wanted to be with him, but I wanted to leave too. I think he was surprised when I said no... I never...told him no...even if I wasn't in the mood I still always said yes... Which is my fault I know but...that night...I said no...and he pushed...and...I said I couldn't sleep with him anymore that this all had to end if..." she let out an exasperated sigh, "if I was ever going to make things right with Willa."

"Then what happened?" the attorney prompted softly.

"I panicked..." she admitted, her voice barely a whisper. "He didn't miss a beat...he started demanding I tell him where she was and how long I'd known, and I refused..."

"Go on," the attorney coaxed gently.

Lilly explained, her hands trembling as she recalled the details.

"He knew my schedule...he always knew my schedule. He knew I had been in Savannah for work."

"And did you tell him where she was?" the attorney asked, an edge of urgency threading his tone.

"No...no, I didn't. I swear, I didn't," she insisted, voice cracking under the weight of her memories. "But he...that's when hit me, threw me on the ground... I tried...I tried to convince him to stay..."

"What do you mean, you tried to convince him to stay?" he pressed further.

With a final, anguished sigh, Lilly confessed, "I told him he could have me... I would have done anything to prevent him from tracking down Willa."

"Did he accept your offer?" the attorney asked quietly.

"No, Willa was alive, and he knew where she was. I don't think anything in this world would have stopped him from going to her."

The defense attorney rose with a commanding presence, an unwelcome intrusion in the tense atmosphere of the courtroom.

"Ms. Harrington," he began, his voice slicing through the silence like a knife, "isn't it true that you feel betrayed by Dr. Sullivan? After finding out she fled and intentionally didn't tell you where she went?"

Lilly met his gaze, her eyes unwavering and resolute.

"I did," she admitted softly, each word carefully measured. "But I understand now. I understand why she didn't tell me."

The attorney pressed on, his tone sharp and probing.

"And isn't it true that when Dr. Helmar left you, it was also a betrayal? What was it that he said to you before he walked out on you? Remember, you're under oath, Ms. Harrington."

"He said...that I would never be her," Lilly replied, her voice tinged with a quiet strength.

"Ouch, that had to hurt," the attorney said with a feigned look of sympathy, his expression a mockery of genuine concern. "So is it reasonable to believe your testimony is an attempt to get back at him for leaving you? For choosing Dr. Sullivan over you...just as so many other people had in the past."

"Objection!" The DA's voice rang out, cutting through the charged air.

"I retract my last statement. No further questions," the defense attorney smirked. He'd already laid the groundwork for the jury to come to his conclusion.

Willa watched as Lilly left the stand, her footsteps resonating with a defiant yet fragile rhythm. There was an unfamiliar quality in Lilly's expression, a glimmer of something that looked remarkably like freedom. It was there, tentative but undeniable, in the firm set of her shoulders, in the way she held her head high even as the weight of the past threatened to pull her down.

The courtroom erupted into a flurry of movement and sound as the judge called a recess. Willa remained seated, the noise and activity swirling around her in a blurred haze. She felt a dizzying sweep of emotions, a tumultuous clash of old wounds and new possibilities colliding with enough force to leave her breathless.

Lilly's testimony had stripped them both bare, exposing their vulnerabilities to the harsh light of truth. Yet within that raw exposure, Willa saw the glimmer of something unexpected and rare. It was there in Lilly's eyes as they met hers, the distance between them shrinking until it was nonexistent.

It was redemption.

***

Closing Arguments

The state attorney began his address to the jury with a measured cadence that filled the hushed courtroom.

"Over the past week, you have been presented with a mountain of evidence and facts woven together into this case," he declared, his voice resonating with authority. "There can be no doubt that the defendant, Killian Helmar, discharged the gunshots that forever altered the life of Jackson Donovan—a harmless bystander whose everyday existence now bears the indelible mark of permanent injury, which will cast a long shadow over his professional future. We have irrefutable video evidence and numerous eyewitness testimonies confirming these grievous actions. Equally indisputable is the fact that the defendant's primary target was his ex-girlfriend, Dr. Willow Sullivan. We have all heard his live confession, a chilling admission that leaves no room for ambiguity."

Stepping forward with purposeful strides, his eyes swept across the room—the gathered spectators, the etched expressions of shock and sorrow—and finally, they locked onto Killian, who remained seated, still and implacable, his jaw clenched as though carved from stone.

"Let us not allow ourselves to be misled by attempts to sully the character of a woman who has borne nearly a decade of unspeakable trauma, inflicted by the hands of the defendant," he continued, his tone rising with righteous indignation. "As testified by previous character witnesses, Dr. Helmar harbors a long, damning history of abuse, manipulation, and callous mistreatment of women. The day the defendant orchestrated his murderous plot to end Dr. Sullivan's life was not a case of impulsive passion, but rather the final step in a meticulously planned series of actions driven by an obsessive desire. To grant Dr. Helmar any measure of leniency would be nothing short of a death knell for Dr. Sullivan, leaving her vulnerable to further harm upon his eventual release."

He paused, allowing the weight of his words to settle, before continuing with deliberate emphasis, "Furthermore, we must not overlook the physical scars now etched onto Jackson Donovan's very being—a grim testament to Dr. Helmar's violent outburst. These wounds, both visible and hidden within the psyche, cry out for justice—a justice that accurately reflects the magnitude of these crimes."

A subtle shift in his tone betrayed a hint of bitter irony as he added, "This is not a case of unrequited puppy love. What we are confronted with is either a man so intellectually inept as to be unaware of the consequences of his own actions—despite holding a doctorate and national board certification in psychiatry—or, as the required psychological evaluations have starkly noted, a man so emotionally fractured that he is incapable of experiencing empathy. Regardless of the once-intimate relationship between the defendant and Dr. Sullivan, the overwhelming evidence paints a portrait of premeditated, obsessive, and controlling behavior."

The jury, their eyes flitting back and forth between the impassioned attorney and the stoic figure of Killian, absorbed every word. Killian's calm was unnerving, as if he were an unyielding iceberg under the watchful scrutiny of a relentless sun. Yet, the attorney's resolve never wavered.

"Let it be clear," he asserted, "that it was his all-consuming obsession which drove him to commit these acts of violence—violence that was not a response to any alleged mistreatment or manipulation on Dr. Sullivan's part."

With each carefully chosen word, the state attorney dismantled the defense's narrative of Killian as a victim of unrequited love, replacing it with a chilling tableau of premeditation and relentless danger. The very air within the courtroom thickened with tension, as if charged with the weight of impending justice.

"The evidence, mounting and indisputable, demonstrates that Dr. Killian Helmar's fixation on Dr. Sullivan was not the product of mutual adoration—it was a possession, a delusion in which he believed she was his exclusive property, never meant to be shared."

He concluded with a somber finality, "Given the severity of the defendant's actions and the lifelong impact on the victims, the recommendation is clear: the verdict must reflect not only the gravity of these offenses but also the necessity for an environment where rehabilitation can be appropriately pursued."

As the state attorney concluded his stirring presentation, the courtroom transformed into a stage painted in somber hues, underscored by a steady hum of whispered anticipation and collective breaths held in suspense.

"The state rests."

Killian Helmar's defense attorney rose, his silhouette starkly outlined against the towering windows that loomed over the courtroom like silent, imposing sentinels. He cleared his throat, the sound resonating through the room and commanding everyone's attention with a practiced, authoritative ease.

"Ladies and gentlemen of the jury, Dr. Helmar is not the monster the state wants you to believe he is. He's a man who loved deeply and lost everything." His voice, rich and persuasive, reached out for sympathy, attempting to twist the cold, hard facts into a more palatable, sympathetic narrative.

Willa watched him work, the old, familiar fear bubbling to the surface. The fear that Killian, with his silver tongue, could talk his way out of anything, even something as grave as this.

"We are not here to dispute the tragedy of events that transpired. However, it is imperative that this court considers the full context surrounding Dr. Helmar's actions before laying down a verdict."

The attorney paced slowly and deliberately before the bench, his footsteps echoing in the hushed courtroom. Each word was chosen with meticulous care, as though he were crafting a work of art.

"Dr. Sullivan systematically destroyed my client's sense of reality. Driven by her cold, calculated behavior and abandonment, he acted in a moment of emotional crisis." His voice was laden with a pleading, almost tragic timbre, as if the weight of the world rested on his shoulders.

A murmur rippled through the observers, a mix of shock and skepticism at the audacious attempt to shift blame onto the victim. The atmosphere was thick with tension, a palpable mix of disbelief and intrigue.

The attorney continued, casting a glance toward Willa, whose composure remained unshaken, like a statue carved from marble.

"It is essential to recognize the complex relationship dynamics that led to this incident. Dr. Sullivan, while undoubtedly affected by these events, had engaged with Dr. Helmar in a manner that, intentionally or not, fueled his deep-seated emotional turmoil. Dr. Sullivan was the mastermind behind their devious behavior throughout their relationship. It was Dr. Sullivan's obsessive nature toward wealth and power that brainwashed Dr. Helmar into believing she was his only chance for success in his career and overall happiness."

The gallery, mesmerized, leaned forward in anticipation, waiting for the final spin of his narrative.

The attorney pressed on, his voice rising to a crescendo. "What occurred was not a cold, calculated act, but rather a spontaneous eruption of passion—a human heart pushed beyond its breaking point.

"Find him guilty," the attorney said, pausing dramatically, "of loving her too much but nothing more. The defense rests."

In the gallery, Willa's heart sank. Jackson and Cassy simultaneously wrapped a comforting arm around her. Willa almost laughed at the absurdity of the situation, but the sound lodged in her throat, leaving a metallic, bitter taste. She glanced at Jackson, whose eyes remained focused and steady, unwavering amid the turmoil.

The judge's voice sliced through the heavy air like a sharpened blade.

"Members of the jury, you have heard the closing arguments. You will now retire to deliberate," she intoned, her tone a mix of resolve and finality.

Willa's entire being pulsed with a feverish rhythm, her fingertips buzzing with an electric sensation that made every drawn-out second feel like a silent scream echoing in a vast, empty chamber. The clock in the corner of the dimly lit attorney's office ticked away with maddening precision, each tick-tock resonating like a hammer on an anvil, as if time itself were reluctant to move forward. The soft hum of the fluorescent lights above added to the tension, their flickering casting uneasy shadows across the room's maroon walls.

"How long?" Willa asked, her voice barely rising above a whisper, yet heavy with urgency.

"It could be minutes or weeks before they reach a verdict," the attorney replied solemnly to Willa and Jackson. His words hung in the air, a thin veil of uncertainty. "Nothing to do now but wait."

The moment seemed to stretch into an eternity, each heartbeat like a distant drum, and at once, it shattered into immediacy when the attorney's phone buzzed sharply, slicing through the heavy silence. He answered, his expression shifting with the news.

"They're done. They reached a verdict in fifteen minutes," he announced, his tone a mixture of surprise and inevitability.

"Is that good?" Jackson questioned, his voice tinged with a mix of hope and dread.

"It's quick, so we know it's going to be unanimous," the attorney continued, his words steady but with an undercurrent of gravity.

"Regardless, he will serve time for the shooting. There is no way around that. Everything else, we'll see." The weight of his statement settled over them like a heavy fog, leaving the room silent once more, save for the persistent ticking of the clock.

***

The jury filed back into the hushed courtroom, their footsteps echoing softly against the polished wooden floor. The tension was palpable, a heavy presence that seemed to hang in the air like an impending storm.

"Will the defendant please rise," the judge instructed, her words slicing through the silence like a knife.

Killian straightened his posture, his every movement exuding an aura of absolute control, or perhaps it was defiance, etched deeply into the lines of his face and the set of his jaw.

"Have you reached a verdict?" the judge inquired, her voice even and measured, resonating with the gravity of a sacred decree.

"Yes, Your Honor," came the firm response as the foreman, a stoic figure, handed the slip of paper to the waiting bailiff, who in turn delivered it to the judge with practiced formality.

"And is your decision unanimous?" the judge asked, her gaze unwavering.

"Yes, Your Honor," the foreman replied. The judge unfolded the paper, her eyes flickering over the words before she swiftly closed it, maintaining her composed demeanor.

"And how do you find the defendant?" she asked, her voice a calm anchor in the charged atmosphere.

The foreman remained standing, the room holding its collective breath as every eye turned to witness the pivotal moment. His voice rang out, clear and resolute.

"We the jury find the defendant, Killian Helmar, guilty on all counts."

In that instant, Willa's vision blurred, the meticulously structured world of the courtroom dissolving into a swirl of raw emotion—the charged air, the weighty verdict pressing down like a tangible force, and an overwhelming, impossible relief that swept through her. It was over, yet paradoxically, it felt as though the battle had only just begun.

"The court thanks the jury for its service. You are dismissed," the judge's firm, steady voice continued, cutting through the emotional haze. "Sentencing will take place six weeks from today. Court is adjourned."

With a sharp rap of the gavel, the proceedings concluded, leaving behind an echo that lingered in the hearts of all present.

CHAPTER FORTY

The Sentence

Six Weeks Later

The atmosphere in the courtroom was thick and oppressive, like the charged air before a violent summer storm, ready to burst. Along the back wall, reporters huddled together, their cameras clicking relentlessly as if weapons poised to capture every glistening bead of sweat and every shudder of anxiety on the faces before them. Killian's children, who had lived under the strict legal guardianship of his sister since the tragic passing of Melanie, sat quietly, their young eyes wide with a mix of fear and resignation. Family members gripped one another's hands tightly, their bodies taut with a palpable tension, as though each of them were waiting for a life-altering verdict that might redefine their very existence. Meanwhile, court officers stood immovable like silent statues, their presence a steadfast barrier against the surging tide of emotions.

Willa sat between her attorney and Jackson, a mask of poise barely concealing the fear beneath. All breath in the room paused when the defendant arrived. Killian Helmar, shackled and flanked by his counsel, wearing a state-issued jumpsuit with the letters D.O.C. imprinted on the back. The irony was not lost on Willa.

The bailiff's authoritative voice cut through the murmur of the room as she called the court to order. In the ensuing hush, the judge's resonant tones shattered the silence like a finely honed blade.

"This matter is before the court for sentencing, following the jury's unequivocal verdict of guilty on all counts:

Attempted Murder in the Second Degree,

Assault in the First Degree,

Criminal Possession of a Weapon in the First Degree,

Menacing in the First Degree,

Reckless Endangerment in the First Degree, and

Stalking in the Second Degree."

Each charge weighed heavily in the room, the announcement casting a somber pall over the gathered witnesses like a dense, unyielding fog. The only sound that accompanied this declaration was the scratch of a reporter's pen on paper as the judge proceeded to recount that fateful day in May when Dr. Helmar, in a moment of harrowing recklessness, discharged a military-grade automatic rifle at the Costume Institute Benefit Gala in Manhattan. Her words painted a vivid picture of chaos—a scene where, in a desperate bid, Killian had aimed for Dr. Willa Sullivan but instead gravely injured Jackson Donovan.

In that instant, the memory of mayhem, the piercing screams, the frantic rush of panicked bodies surging toward safety, washed over Willa, her grip on the cold, hard table tightening as if it might anchor her to sanity.

The detailed narrative continued, revealing the defendant's desperate thirty-two-day flight from justice, his obsessive and repeated surveillance of Dr. Sullivan, and his eventual capture through a meticulously coordinated law enforcement operation.

Willa's throat constricted as the weight of these revelations pressed down upon her, every word a reminder of the inescapable reality of the man before her.

The judge explained that the prosecution maintained Killian's actions were driven by an "extreme emotional disturbance" stemming from alleged long-term emotional abuse. To amplify the gravity of this claim, she delved into the expert testimony and highlighted a CPL 730 psychiatric report that diagnosed Killian with Narcissistic Personality Disorder intermixed with unmistakable antisocial traits. Despite the damning evidence, Killian sat detached, as though he were merely an observer of someone else's misfortune, a subtle smirk tugging at the corner of his lips while his eyes glinted with cool calculation.

The judge continued systematically confirming the trial's established facts, while also noting absence of prior criminal convictions in New York for Killian.

She then laid out the shadow of aggravating factors that cloaked his actions: the deliberate use of a highly lethal weapon in a densely packed public venue, his sinister intent to target an innocent, non-combatant individual, his prolonged evasion of justice, and his relentless campaign of stalking.

"Killian Helmar, you have been found guilty of a series of violent felonies and related offenses that strike at the very core of public safety and individual security. While I acknowledge the complex and deeply personal history you share with Dr. Sullivan, the court cannot excuse or mitigate the severity of your actions."

In that moment, as Killian's eyes briefly flickered toward Willa, she saw within them the chilling depths of darkness, a silent promise, a latent threat, and an unyielding refusal to relinquish his hold on the past.

Raising her voice to a resounding crescendo that reverberated through the now completely silent courtroom, the judge declared, "Accordingly, it is the judgment of this Court that you be sentenced as follows:

Count One—Attempted Murder in the Second Degree: Indeterminate term of five to twenty-five years in state prison.

Count Two—Assault in the First Degree: Indeterminate term of five to twenty-five years, to be served concurrently with Count One.

Count Three—Criminal Possession of a Weapon in the First Degree: Indeterminate term of five to twenty-five years, concurrent with previous counts.

Count Four—Menacing in the First Degree: Determinate term of four years, concurrent with the above.

Count Five—Reckless Endangerment in the First Degree: Determinate term of four years, concurrent.

Count Six—Stalking in the Second Degree: Determinate term of four years, concurrent."

Willa's breath hitched sharply as the finality of the sentence bore down upon her. The judge's clinical and meticulous recitation underscored the multifaceted nature of Killian's crimes, addressing every nuance with ruthless precision. Even the slightest movement—a subtle twitch of the jaw—betrayed the defendant's internal reaction as the impact of the verdict penetrated his ironclad façade.

"Your effective sentence is therefore five to twenty-five years in the custody of the Department of Corrections and Community Supervision," the judge intoned, her voice carrying the weight of irreversible consequence. "The actual length of the sentence you will serve in prison shall be no less than five years, after which you will be eligible for controlled release, contingent upon the parole board's discretion. Additionally, credit will be applied for the forty-five days you have already served."

With those final, devastating words, every listener in the courtroom was slammed with the harsh reality of Killian's judgment; the magnitude of the decision sent tremors of inevitability surging through the hushed assembly.

"You are remanded to the custody of the Department to begin serving your sentence immediately. This court stands adjourned."

Willa struggled to contain the torrent of tears threatening to burst forth, each blink a desperate battle against the overwhelming wave of raw emotion ready to flood over.

"Five years!? That's all. After everything he has done, he can walk free after only FIVE years?" Willa collapsed to her knees, clutching the wastebasket beside the state's table, her body racked with violent, heaving sobs.

Jackson dropped beside her, his hand moving in soothing circles on her back.

"How is this possible?" he demanded, his voice rising in anguish as he looked at the attorney. "He will hunt her down the moment he is free. And what about me? My life, my career?! This damn limp!" Jackson stood shakily, his cane a stark reminder of a shattered past. "I was an action star; I did my own stunts. That's over now, and he gets to..."

"Willa, Jackson, please. I know this is disappointing news. But you have to understand. He will not be paroled. The state will attend every hearing, making it crystal clear that Killian is now and will always be a danger to society. He's not getting out."

CHAPTER FORTY-ONE

The Book Promotion

Two Years Later

The studio lights cast a soft glow on the set as the host returned from the commercial break, her smile warm and welcoming.

"And welcome back," she announced with practiced ease. "We are joined here today by Dr. Willa Donovan, psychiatrist and best-selling author of the novel 'Live To Tell: A Journey from Obsession to Acceptance,' a psychological thriller based on her life, including the shooting of Hollywood heartthrob, her now husband, Jackson Cole Donovan, along with the subsequent trial of convicted felon Killian Helmar currently serving up to twenty-five years in a maximum-security prison."

Willa, poised and composed, gave the slightest nod acknowledging the gravity of the topics nestled within the pages of her book. Clad in a tasteful, fitted charcoal suit that complemented the depth of her eyes, she offered the audience a serene smile, one that had learned to mask the tumultuous storms of her past.

"Thank you for joining us today," the host said, turning her attention to Willa with an air of familiarity that belied the formality of their surroundings.

"Of course, it's my pleasure," Willa responded, her voice carrying the subtle timbre of resilience. The pleasantries exchanged between them were light, a delicate dance atop the surface of deeper, darker waters. Willa's fingers traced the spine of her book, lying on the table before her—a physical testament to a journey fraught with danger and emotional upheaval.

"This is an intense book," the host began, her expression contemplative as she turned another page, her finger pausing over a particularly harrowing passage. "Some of these scenes are like... Wow! How difficult was it to sit down and write about all of these traumatic events, especially given they are real?"

The question hung in the air, its weight settling around them like the humid embrace of a Savannah morning. The camera zoomed in slightly, capturing the slight shift in Willa's posture as she leaned forward, ready to dive into the heart of her experience.

"Difficult may be an understatement," Willa replied, her deep eyes holding the camera's gaze as if reaching out to every viewer who might be wrestling with their own shadows. "It required revisiting places in my mind that were steeped in such pain. But there's healing in reflection, in transforming those experiences into words that might, in turn, help someone else find their way out of the dark."

Willa's fingers brushed the cover of her book, a tactile connection to the story that had shaped her, broken her, and ultimately set her free. A testament to resilience, to the belief that even amid the most shattering of life's trials, there is hope for redemption.

"Tell us a little more about the journey you took writing this book."

"Before everything that unfolded with Jackson and the trial," Willa began, her voice carrying a resonance of vulnerability that commanded the room's attention, "my past was a private affair, a series of chapters I never intended to share. My entanglement with Killian—it reshaped me in ways that still resonate." She paused, a deliberate intake of air filling her lungs before she continued.

"Looking in from the outside, I struggled to recognize myself. The woman reflected back was steeped in shame, not for enduring an abusive relationship," Willa turned her gaze directly toward the camera, a silent plea for understanding shimmering behind her eyes, "because that is nothing anyone should ever feel ashamed about."

Her fingertips grazed the surface of the armchair, tracing patterns as she collected her thoughts.

"What truly haunted me was my own role in the anguish I faced. It was my low self-esteem, my diminished sense of worth, that guided me into Killian's orbit."

A flicker of pain crossed her features, raw and unguarded.

With a slight tilt of her head, Willa's expression darkened, reflecting a history of internal battles fought and slowly won.

"In Killian, I found a distorted reflection of my deepest insecurities. Our connection, it wasn't love; it was a trauma bond, a mutual dance of destruction. And when he shattered me" —her voice wavered, but she pressed on— "it dawned on me: I had allowed this devastation. My life's priorities were so misaligned, I was losing myself. If I stayed, I feared at best, I'd become indistinguishable from him, and at worst, I'd end up dead. That thought terrified me more than anything."

The host leaned in, mirroring Willa's intensity with a nod of gravitas.

"So you ran," the host prompted, giving voice to the decision that had propelled her toward an uncertain future far from the ghosts of her past.

"Yes," Willa affirmed, the word a quiet echo of the resolve that had once driven her footsteps away from the chaos. "I ran." Her eyes momentarily lost focus, as though she could see across the miles and years to the moment she'd fled to Magnolia Shores, a desperate escape not only from Killian but from the person she feared she might otherwise become.

Willa's fingers traced the cool surface of the ceramic mug cradled in her palms, a small comfort against the probing gaze of the host opposite her. She offered a wry smile, acknowledging the winds that had carried her to salvation.

"Georgia and Magnolia weren't intentional," she began, her voice steady despite the whirlwind of memories. "I stood at the airport, numb from revelations and fear, and I asked for the first flight 'out.' No plans, no expectations, just a flight away from the life I knew."

The studio lights cast a soft glow on Willa's wavy hair, and the dark strands were a stark contrast to the light vulnerability now visible in her eyes.

The host leaned forward, arms resting on the gleaming desk separating them.

"You say that town changed you. Can you tell us more about that?" Her tone was gentle but insistent, inviting Willa to unveil the transformative power of a place unknown to her.

Willa's gaze shifted to a distant point, as if the very walls of the studio had dissolved to reveal the verdant landscapes of Magnolia Shores.

"It wasn't so much the town itself," she mused aloud, her voice taking on a reflective quality. "There are countless charming towns across the country, each with their own allure."

The host nodded, her expression one of profound understanding.

"It's the people," Willa emphasized, a softness touching her features as she remembered. "You see, individuals who've endured what we term 'Adverse Childhood Experiences' often find trusting and forming healthy relationships challenging because they haven't known true safety or security. When I stepped into Magnolia, it was Cassandra and Lavonte Mitchell who extended their hands first."

Willa paused, a fond chuckle escaping her as she pictured the Mitchells in her mind. "They were almost too kind, so much so that my first instinct was to build walls. Their sweetness seemed surreal, impossible. My past had taught me that all love is conditional, no one does anything for the goodness of others, especially not strangers."

The studio lights glinted off the subtle moisture in Willa's eyes, betraying the emotion she felt recalling those days.

"But there I was, with nowhere to live, no job, and within a week, thanks to them, I had both an apartment and employment. They asked for nothing in return, and trust me, I have tried to repay their kindness over the years. They simply are two of the most genuinely good souls one could meet."

She leaned forward slightly, her voice dropping to a more confidential tone.

"Cassandra and Lavonte didn't just help me survive; they took me under their wing like surrogate parents. And through them, I witnessed what a healthy relationship truly looked like—for the first time. They argue, sure, they're human, but they always put each other first. It was incredibly comforting to see...but also incredibly frightening."

The host nodded, leaning in to mirror Willa's earnest energy, her voice warm yet probing. "Frightening? Could you explain what was scary about witnessing their healthy relationship?"

"Of course," Willa replied, her gaze turning introspective. "Seeing Cassy and Lavonte together was like holding up a mirror to my own life and realizing just how distorted my view of love and relationships had been. It grounded me in a way that was deeply unsettling. Recognizing that their kind of love, their mutual respect and care was possible. It made me see just how far I'd strayed from what was healthy. It was terrifying to acknowledge that I had so much work to do on myself if I ever hoped to find something even remotely similar."

"And then there's Jackson," the host said, a knowing smile playing at the corners of her mouth. "Tell us about when you knew he was the one for you."

"It wasn't one single moment but a collection of them," Willa explained, her gaze turning inward as she sifted through memories. "Jackson had this innate ability to see beyond what I presented to the world. He recognized the potential within me, a potential for change, for growth, that I was blind to.

"Jackson was the first person to truly make me feel safe...that nothing would ever happen to me again because he was this brilliantly powerful protective influence. I was so inspired by him, by who he was as a person. How he had climbed out of the depths of his own despair, how he, like me back then felt he knew it all, didn't need anyone else, was selfish and arrogant. But once he hit his rock bottom, everything changed for him. There were so many people around him who loved him and he had just been pushing them all away. Which was exactly what I had been doing since being in Magnolia. Here I had this wonderful group of people who cared about me and loved me, and I never let them know who I really was until Lilly showed up."

"What was your 'rock bottom'?" the host asked, her voice gentle yet insistent.

Willa's eyes darkened with memories as she replied, "The night I told Jackson about Melanie, Killian's wife. I was absolutely certain that was the moment our world crumbled." She shifted in her seat, the sound of the fabric mingling with the weight of her words.

Her tone softened as she continued, "I was out of options. Would I have come clean if Killian hadn't shown up and started making threats. No, I don't think I would have. I would have just kept living the lie."

Willa's gaze held steady, unwavering and resolute, yet touched by a quiet, almost inexplicable gratitude.

"It's odd but I'm actually grateful for that. Not what he put me through obviously and not what he did to Jackson and Lilly and God knows how many others, but I was forced at that point to make a choice. Run, start over...again, lose Jackson, Cassy, Lavonte, Syd, Emma, the only real family I had ever known...or stand and fight. And fighting meant coming clean, being honest about everything to everyone for the first time... Honestly for the first time that I can even remember, even to myself. I had myself so convinced that I didn't need anyone and to have people, to care about people was a liability."

The studio, brimming with the invisible energy of countless viewers tuning in, seemed to hold its breath. Willa, however, remained composed, her demeanor reflecting a woman who had learned to swim in the depths of her own soul.

"When Jackson was shot, I felt violated. I had been doing things 'right' and I was happier than I'd ever been, than I ever thought I could be...and then I was punished for it. That's how it felt. I had learned to trust, to be comfortable in trusting and then all of a sudden, I wasn't worthy of those things. When Jackson...when I saw him that first night in the hospital unconscious...ugh...I was so mad at him. He should have run when I first told him everything. He never should have loved me; he never should have allowed me to love him. And the darkness came back...worse. Nothing mattered to me anymore. Being bad didn't work...being good didn't work... I was destined to suffer. So I claimed it. It was like two versions of myself melding together. "Old Will and New, the unyielding bitch and the sacrificial martyr."

Her voice grew softer as she delved deeper. "After the trial, I went deep into therapy for myself. I didn't know how to have these two opposing versions of myself exist at the same time. I wanted Old Willow's strength, cunning nature, take-no-prisoners' attitude, but I didn't want to lose the New Willa's compassionate, caring, empathetic side. The latter is where I found my true happiness."

"You've been very open about your therapy. Tell us more about that," she urged, the sound of her voice suggesting an eagerness to peel back another layer of Willa's transformative narrative.

A hush had fallen over the studio, the audience leaned forward, collectively holding their breath as Willa navigated through the depths of her story—a tale interwoven with the threads of vulnerability and courage.

She sighed, choosing her words with care as if balancing fragile stones. "A therapist needing therapy is not something many people think about. There is such a stigma around mental health in our society, even among mental health professionals. We believe we are expected to be flawless, that somehow having human weakness no longer makes us 'experts' in our field. Which isn't true. Many times, that vulnerability makes us better."

The host nodded, her expression a mix of professional curiosity and genuine respect for the journey Willa had undertaken—a journey that had led her from the shadows cast by towering Live Oaks in Savannah to the bright lights of the television studio.

"And the diagnosis?" the host prompted gently. "Not an easy thing to admit, I'm sure."

"It wasn't. It isn't." Willa paused, gathering her thoughts like scattered pieces of a shattered mirror. "Moderate Narcissistic Personality Disorder was definitely not a diagnosis I saw coming. Post-traumatic Stress Disorder, of course but NPD..." she said, feeling the weight of each syllable. "I was instantly ashamed. Not just for having the diagnosis but also for not seeing it myself... This is what I do for a living... How could I not see it in myself?"

The host, sensing the gravity of the moment, offered a respectful nod, acknowledging not only Willa's personal victory but also the universal truth that every journey was paved with the stones of hardship, courage, and ultimately, acceptance.

"Initially I resisted the diagnosis of NPD. Clearly this professional was not competent enough to understand what I was going through..." Willa tossed her hands up in the air. "And there it was... I was too special: others were too incompetent..." She laughed. "But she was 100 percent correct, obviously."

The conversation took a new turn when the host interjected, "But didn't the court psychiatry reports also indicate that Killian has Narcissistic Personality Disorder? That is rather alarming, isn't it?"

"All personality is on a spectrum. From what we consider 'normal' to 'disordered.' The real difference is how much those personality characteristics negatively impact the person's life."

"I see," the host said after a moment of reflection.

"A short look at my own past, the trauma bond with Killian, the things we did, the people we hurt... We were the same...almost."

"What do you think makes you different from Killian?" the host continued.

"That's simple...insight." Willa acknowledged, "My saving grace was knowing on some level I was responsible for my misery. I didn't know how exactly but I knew I had to have some kind of power over what was happening to me."

"And you're saying that someone with a more severe case, like Killian, doesn't have any?"

"More severe cases, those that would fall into a severe or even extreme category, don't have the insight needed to make a conscious change in behavior. They don't have the capacity for empathy. They are so self-focused it's impossible to tap into the idea that other people are actual individuals, that they continue to exist even when not in front of us."

"Sounds like you are saying there are different levels of the disorder and that impacts whether a person can recover from Narcissistic Personality Disorder."

"Exactly," Willa replied. "Those with severe or even extreme forms of this disorder cannot muster the insight necessary to consciously change their behavior. They are so self-focused that the very idea of acknowledging another's individuality becomes an impossibility. People are perceived as background characters or unnamed extras in the movie of their lives."

The host's curiosity deepened. "It's fascinating, but how is it that Killian, who seemingly doesn't acknowledge others as separate beings, became so obsessed with you that he would go to extraordinary lengths to reclaim you?"

"I don't believe Killian saw me as a real person. Because of our deep trauma bond, I think he viewed me as an extension of himself. So, when I left, he no longer had control over that part of himself and that, I believe, led to the obsession and stalking behaviors he showed."

"He was trying to be whole again?" the host ventured softly.

"Possibly," Willa conceded.

Finally, the host asked, "Do you think he will ever get paroled?"

"He's brilliant. He knows how to work a system, manipulate people... I think, unless he is monitored by officers that really understand the depths of his NPD, he could convince them to set him free...and that idea haunts me every day."

CHAPTER FORTY-TWO

Epilogue

Three Years Later

The glamour of the red carpet stretched before them like a gleaming artery, pulsing with camera flashes and the feverish energy of celebrity. Willa Donovan stepped into the chaos with Jackson Donovan beside her, five years and a world away from Killian's trial. The nominations hadn't been a surprise, they were the toast of award season, but their impact hit Willa hard.

Willa still struggled with every red-carpet event, instantly being transported to that fateful night at the CIB. The deep red of the carpet an instant reminder of the red of Jackson's blood. She and Jackson had been invited back to the CIB yearly until Ames, who now represented both Jackson and Willa, finally contacted the organization requesting they remove Willa and Jackson from the list. Neither Willa nor Jackson had any intent to return to *that* red carpet.

"Live To Tell" had transformed from scandalous headlines to best-selling novel to an Oscar-nominated film, and Willa's sleek designer gown was another skin she wore with practiced grace. Jackson, up for Best Actor for his own portrayal, kept a protective hand on the small of her back. Cassy, Lavonte, Sydney, Emma, and Eric—who trailed behind, more tourist than entourage. Surrounded by press and publicists, Willa navigated the chaos with a new-found poise, sharing knowing glances with Jackson that said more than words could convey.

Cameras clicked and reporters shouted over the velvet ropes, each cry a testament to Willa's transformation. Draped in midnight blue, the gown clung to her like a secret, the low-cut back an elegant echo of vulnerability turned strength. Her long dark hair cascaded in soft waves, framing a face that had learned to meet the world without flinching. By her side, Jackson's tall frame cut a striking silhouette in classic black, his hand a steady promise on her back.

"Are they all like this?" Lavonte asked, catching up to Jackson with Cassy in tow. The sea of voices surrounded them, but it was no match for Lavonte's natural resonance.

Willa gave a knowing smile. "This one's particularly...lively," she replied, her voice steady, tinged with humor.

"This is insane," Sydney interjected, the edge of sarcasm cutting through. She lifted her hand to shield her eyes from the flashes. "I feel like I'm in a zoo. Jackson, how do you do this all the time?"

"I'd like to say you get used to it, but I never have." Jackson laughed warmly.

Willa exchanged another look with Jackson, warmth passing between them as they held hands like a lifeline amid the pandemonium. She marveled at her own ease, a stark contrast to years of hiding. With Jackson, she'd learned to navigate both spotlight and shadows. He turned, dark eyes meeting hers with the same understanding. Five years.

Inside the cavernous expanse of the Theatre, anticipation crackled like electricity in a storm, igniting the room's lavish velvet and gold. Willa sat beside Jackson, her hand entwined with his, a touchstone of calm amid the spectacle of the Academy Awards.

The audience murmured as "Live To Tell" picked up award after award, the film adaptation of Willa's life transforming into an unstoppable force. Jackson's dark eyes met hers, both alight with disbelief and hope as his category drew near.

The presenter's, a former co-star of Jackson's, voice hung in the air like a question, "And the award goes to..." The presenter opened the envelope. "Ha...a surprise to absolutely no one...Jackson Donovan!"

"Jackson Donovan!" The words echoed through the hall, enveloped in a storm of applause. Jackson rose, his smile wide and incredulous, a portrait of shock and joy.

Willa's eyes glistened as she watched Jackson approach the stage. His poise was tempered by genuine emotion, a crack in his polished exterior that only she could fully appreciate. Beside her, Sydney and Cassy exchanged excited glances, their amazement written in bold across their faces.

Jackson took the podium, the ovation a wall of sound that enveloped him. He paused, the weight of the moment visible in the rise and fall of his chest.

"I have to admit," he began, a hint of laughter threading through his voice, "portraying Jackson was more challenging than I ever imagined... a very deep character." Laughter rippled through the crowd, a release of shared tension and delight.

He continued, his tone growing more solemn.

"This film...is a testament to resilience, not mine, but Willa's." His eyes found her, anchoring him as he spoke. "You are without a doubt the most amazing human I've ever known. Thank you for having the courage to tell this story and for trusting me to be a part of it, my Love."

Willa felt the warmth of the spotlight and the love of the friends beside her. Jackson's words were more than an acceptance; they were an acknowledgment of everything they'd survived. Her heart swelled, and her face flushed with gratitude and disbelief.

Willa's hand squeezed Jackson's again, a grounding connection in the whirlwind of accolades. Then came the announcement she knew would pierce the veil between past and present.

Best Picture. "And the award goes to..."

The room spun in slow motion as the words sank in, the applause swelling like a tidal wave. Willa rose, a gasp escaping her, the full gravity of the moment pulling at her heart.

"You deserve this, Willa," Cassy whispered, tears in her eyes.

"Go get 'em, Princess!" Lavonte cheered, his voice carrying through the tumult.

Willa, followed by the other producers, cast, and various crew members, moved to the stage, each step a stitch in the tapestry of her rebirth. When she reached the podium, the applause thundered, yet the world around her grew still, focused. Her eyes scanned the audience, finding the small cluster of friends who had become family.

She took a breath, steadying herself. She glanced at Jackson standing to her right.

"I never imagined I'd be standing here tonight," she began, her voice soft yet resonant, emotion wrapping around each word. "Years ago, I had nothing. No home. No hope. And then this little Georgia town, Magnolia Shores, changed that. It gave me family, Cassandra and Lavonte Mitchell, Sydney Harper, Emma Wilkes-Harper, and it led me to Jackson...and Lilly...I..." Willa's voice cracked.

"I'm sorry...I'm just...They really should not let me be the one who speaks...Terry?" She chuckled, wiping a tear of joy from her face.

An older gentleman stepped up the podium and hugged Willa. "Not a problem. I want to thank the Academy for this incredible recognition. To my fellow producers, Willa Donovan and Julianna Giordano—this award belongs to all of us. Your vision, your tireless work, and your unwavering belief in this story made every late night and every creative risk worthwhile.

"To the leading man and making his directorial debut, Jackson Donovan, your raw honesty was nothing short of extraordinary. You carried the heart of this novel into every frame, and I'm so proud to stand with you here tonight.

"To our screenwriters, thank you for transforming my words into dialogue that sings and scenes that resonate. To our cast, crew, department heads—production design, costume, music, camera, editing—every one of you poured your talent into this film. You brought Willa's journey ..."

As the speeches from various team members continued, Willa and Jackson slipped behind the others onstage to steal a quiet moment together before being ushered off stage.

***

The couple were escorted back to the media room for the obligatory post-win interview. Trophies in hand they were seated across from a bouncy young entertainment reporter.

"Congratulations! Best Actor, Best Direction, Best Adapted Screenplay, Best Picture and a bunch more! Were you surprised or, given that Live to Tell has been sweeping the top honors at every award show this season, did you expect this?" she said looking at Jackson.

"Never expect it, hope for it yes, but never expect it," Jackson said with a laugh.

"Would you say this is the highlight of your career so far?"

"Absolutely, to be a part of a project so raw, with such deep themes, to be recognized for that work, and to share it," he looked at Willa "...it doesn't get better than that."

"You've mention in the past that because of your back issues you can't accept the action-packed roles you became famous for anymore. Is your plan to move completely into directing?"

"I'd love to continue acting as well as directing. I just need to make sure the role is a good fit for me now physically so I can make the studio proud."

"Live To Tell certainly touches on some very serious subjects and to remember that actually happened is amazing!" the reporter continued, now turning to Willa.

"How difficult was it to relive your past on screen? Were there scenes that were too difficult for you to watch?"

"There is a scene that is very hard for me..."

"The rape?" the reporter asked.

"Umm...no...it's actually when we see Jackson in the hospital, but out of the bed. There is a scene where you see his injuries for the first time...and he's healed now. Well, they are scarred over now but...we have an amazing special effects team..."

"Yes, they won too!"

"Right...that's exactly how he looked...exactly." Willa began to tear up. "It breaks my heart every time."

Jackson wrapped his arm around Willa and pulled her in a little closer.

"Well, I know there are a ton of people wanting to get a piece of you two tonight so just one more question and then I'll let you go."

"Sure."

"How are feeling about Killian?"

"Oh, umm...great actually, his parole was denied so we get another five years to not think about him," Willa said with a smile.

"No, I mean the news from today..."

Willa's heart sank.

"Killian escaped prison. The news broke about an hour ago."

"What..."

THE END

Playlist

MUSIC CURATION BY RICK!

ALL I WANTED WAS U (Ex Habit, Omido) – *ALL I WANTED WAS U*

All I Need (Radiohead) – *In Rainbows*

Alarms (Mellina Tey) – *After All*

Are You Alright? (Lucinda Williams) – *West*

As Sharp As Knives (The Modern Electric) – *The Modern Electric*

A Fond Farewell (Elliott Smith) – *From A Basement On The Hill*

Bad Girl (Jake Daniels) – *Bad Girl*

Baby Came Home (The Neighbourhood) – *I'm Sorry...*

Baby Don't Go (Dum Dum Girls) – *I Will Be*

Baby's Arms (Kurt Vile, The Sadies) – *Baby's Arms*

Beating Heart (La Sera) – *La Sera*

Benediction (Thurston Moore) – *Demolished Thoughts*

Can't Think (Those Darlins) – *Blur the Line*

Common Burn (Mazzy Star) – *Seasons of Your Day*

Cool Morning Sun (Viva Voce) – *The Future Will Destroy You*

Cranekiss (Tamaryn) – *Cranekiss*

Crush (Cigarettes After Sex) – *Crush*

Don't Know How To Keep Loving You (Julia Jacklin) – *Crushing*

Don't Want to Know If You Are Lonely (Hüsker Dü) – *Candy Apple Grey*

Ever Fallen in Love (With Someone You Shouldn't've) (Tashaki Miyaki) – *Under Cover, Vol. 2*

Everything Is Free (Gillian Welch) – *Time (The Revelator)*

Eyes On You (SWIM) – *Eyes On You*

Fade Into You (J Mascis) – *Fade Into You*

Falling In Love (Cigarettes After Sex) – *Cry*

Fatal Attraction (Reed Wonder, Aurora Olivas) – *Fatal Attraction*

Favorite (Isabel LaRosa) – *Favorite*

Fear of God (Limi) – *The Best I Ever Had*

Flawless (The Neighbourhood) – *I Love You.*

Gypsy Death & You (The Kills) – *Keep On Your Mean Side*

HAUNTED (Isabel LaRosa) – *HAUNTED*

Happy Together (Filter) – *The Stepfather (Original Motion Picture Soundtrack)*

Heart Paper Lover (Marissa Nadler) – *Little Hells*

HEAVEN AND BACK (Chase Atlantic) – *PHASES*

Here Comes Your Man (Pixies) – *Death to the Pixies*

I Follow You (Melody's Echo Chamber) – *Melody's Echo Chamber*

I Need You (Nick Cave & The Bad Seeds) – *Skeleton Tree*

I Only Think of You (The Horrors) – *Primary Colours*

I'm In Love With A Girl (Big Star) – *Radio City*

I don't forgive you (Isabel LaRosa) – *YOU FEAR THE GOD THAT LOVES YOU*

Jigsaw Falling Into Place (Radiohead) – *In Rainbows*

LET THE WORLD BURN (with G-Eazy & Ari Abdul) – Remix (Chris Grey, G-Eazy, Ari Abdul) – *LET THE WORLD BURN (*

Lips Of Ashes – 2017 Remaster (Porcupine Tree) – *In Absentia (Remastered)*

Love Bomb (Grinderman) – *Grinderman*

Love me (Ex Habit) – *love me*

Love Will Tear Us Apart – 2020 Remaster (Joy Division) – *Love Will*

Tear Us Apart

Lust (Nyxara) – *Lust*

Mandy Love Theme (Jóhann Jóhannsson) – *Mandy (Original Motion Picture Soundtrack)*

Miami Showdown (Digitalism) – *I Love You, Dude*

My Kind of Woman (Mac DeMarco) – *2*

My Name (Reed Wonder, Aurora Olivas) – *My Name*

Never My Love (Isobel Campbell) – *Voices In The Sky*

Nothin' In The World Can Stop Me Worryin' 'Bout That Girl (The Kinks) – *Rushmore*

Okay (Chase Atlantic) – *Chase Atlantic*

Older (Isabel LaRosa) – *older*

Only For You (Heartless Bastards) – *Arrow*

Outta my head (Omido, Rick Jansen, Ordell) – *Outta my head*

Pink Steam (Sonic Youth) – *Rather Ripped*

Please Don't Leave (The Drums) – *Portamento*

Please Forgive Me (Molly Burch) – *Please Be Mine*

Saddest Sunset (Lili Haydn) – *Place Between Places*

Satellite (Guster) – *Ganging up on the Sun*

Secrets (Omido, Ordell, Rick Jansen) – *Secrets*

Shadow of Your Love (La Sera) – *Music For Listening To Music To*

SMUT (Jutes) – *SMUT*

Song To The Siren – Remastered (This Mortal Coil) – *It'll End In Tears (Remastered)*

Southbound (Artemas) – *southbound / test drive*

Stay (Ari Abdul) – *Stay*

Stockholm Syndrome (ARCANA) – *Stockholm Syndrome*

Take All My Love (Reed Wonder, Aurora Olivas) – *Take All My Love*

Taste (Jake Daniels) – *Taste*

The Killing Moon (Echo & the Bunnymen) – *Ocean Rain*

The Last Goodbye (The Kills) – *Blood Pressures*

Theme Number Sixty Eight (Pye Corner Audio) – *Black Mill Tapes (10th Anniversary Box)*

This Is Love (PJ Harvey) – *Stories From The City, Stories From The Sea*

This Mess We're In (PJ Harvey, Thom Yorke) – *Stories From The City, Stories From The Sea*

Tick Of The Clock (Single) (Chromatics) –*Tick Of The Clock*

Tom The Model (Beth Gibbons, Rustin Man) – *Out Of Season*

Two of the Lucky Ones (The Droge and Summers Blend) – *Volume One*

Wait (The Kills) – *Children Of Men Original Motion Picture Soundtrack*

Werewolf (Cat Power) – *You Are Free*

Wicked Game (Widowspeak) – *Gun Shy*

Wisdom (The Brian Jonestown Massacre) – *Methodrone*

You Know What I Mean (Cults) – *Cults*

You're Beautiful (Mojave 3) – *Ask Me Tomorrow*

About The Author

She writes about the lies we live for and the truths we run from.

Little is known about the author behind the name—by design. Rowan Noir tells stories of beautiful lies, dangerous men, and the women who overcome them. Her work walks the line between passion and peril, truth and manipulation exploring the darker sides of ambition, obsession, and redemption. She lives in a world where love is never simple, and survival is never clean. Some say she's lived every story she writes. Others say she's a muse with a wild imagination. Regardless, Rowan Noir always leaves a trail of smoke, secrets, and shattered hearts in her wake.